HOW TO KISS A ROYAL SPY

"I don't have the right to do this, but I'm going to do it anyway," he whispered.

He moved one hand to her jaw, cupping it while tilting her head back. Her mouth opened; whether in protest or shock, he couldn't tell. But it didn't matter, because he finally gave into the desire he'd been battling from that first moment he'd seen her on the lawn behind Maywood Manor.

As her arms stole up around his neck and she trembled within his embrace, the echo of their sweet, youthful kisses faded in the clamor of blood pounding through his veins and his heart hammering against his ribcage. Because it wasn't a girl he pulled close—it was a woman. And it wasn't just the lust-inducing feel of her pressing against him that inflamed his senses, it was the way she opened up to him, responding to his invasion with an enthusiasm that both startled and thrilled him.

If he'd ever needed confirmation that Evie was not the young girl he'd once known and that she was all grown up, this was it. Anything that had ever happened between them in the past couldn't begin to compare with this moment. . . .

Books by Vanessa Kelly

MASTERING THE MARQUESS

SEX AND THE SINGLE EARL

MY FAVORITE COUNTESS

HIS MISTLETOE BRIDE

SECRETS FOR SEDUCING A ROYAL BODYGUARD

CONFESSIONS OF A ROYAL BRIDEGROOM

HOW TO PLAN A WEDDING FOR A ROYAL SPY

AN INVITATION TO SIN
(with Jo Beverley, Sally MacKenzie, and Kaitlin O'Riley)

Published by Kensington Publishing Corporation

How to PLAN a WEDDING for a ROYAL SPY

VANESSA KELLY

ZEBRA BOOKS
KENSINGTON PUBLISHING CORP.
http://www.kensingtonbooks.com

ACKNOWLEDGMENTS

My love and thanks to my writing partner and husband, Randy, and to my critique partner, Debbie Mason. They have pulled me from many a plot bear pit and also fixed my grammar. I'd also like to extend my gratitude to the publicity and marketing team and the art department at Kensington, who give me great covers and who are unfailingly supportive of The Renegade Royals.

I also owe many expressions of gratitude to my agent, Evan Marshall, and to my editor, John Scognamiglio. They do everything they can to make my writing life easier, and I so appreciate it!

I dedicate this book to my ninety-one-year-old father, Phil Kelly—a classic example of The Greatest Generation. He was the first person to encourage me to follow my dreams and resist limiting myself. My dad is the best and kindest of men, and I am truly blessed to be his daughter.

Prologue

Death clawed at his boot.

Swiping away grit and sweat from his eyes, Captain William Endicott peered at the man crumpled at his feet. It was a French cuirassier, one of Bonaparte's elite cavalry officers. A dead officer, Will had assumed when he'd swung down from his horse a few moments ago, doing his best to avoid the tangle of broken bodies on the uneven ground. The battle had piled them up like a wave, one that had pounded relentlessly against the break wall of a British infantry square.

But this cavalryman, face down in the sodden earth, was alive. His gloved hand scrabbled desperately at Will's foot.

Breathing out a weary curse, Will pulled his sword from its scabbard and gingerly nudged the officer over with his foot. The Frenchman jerked as if he'd been kicked, then his entire body convulsed as he struggled to cough out clots of mud from his mouth.

Christ.

The poor bastard, obviously too wounded to move, had been drowning in the mud that washed ankle deep all around them from last night's torrential rains. His throat must be clogged with blood, dirt, and God only knew what else that had been trampled into a fetid stew over the course of the day.

Hours of untold violence had bludgeoned Will into a state of insensibility. He'd seen hundreds of men and horses blown apart, trampled, or hacked to bits on the battlefield. But this new horror blasted through his emotional fog. He knelt beside the wounded cuirassier, acting on instinct as he pushed the man onto his side and thumped his back, supporting him as he spat out the foul black sludge. Once the man was able to draw breath Will carefully rolled him onto his back.

The officer stared blearily up at him, his eyes clouded with pain and the approach of death. Blood seeped from a hole in his chest, darkening the wine-red fabric of the distinctive uniform of the French 13th Regiment, now barely distinguishable under its coating of mud.

The officer's cracked lips parted, his voice whispering out a single phrase: *"Merci, monsieur."*

Will had thought himself beyond feeling—outrage, regret, and even sorrow buried under the broken bodies of countless friends and men he'd known for years. Only survival mattered, and doing what needed to be done to carry out his commanders' orders. But now emotion battered its way up from somewhere deep inside him, surging in a black tide that threatened to close his throat. The target of his rage wasn't the officer lying before him, or even the enemy he'd fought so desperately all day. No, it was the tortured slide into death for this lone man, a soldier who had only been doing his duty, just like all the other unlucky souls this day—English, Scots, French, Prussians. They'd all simply followed orders to pound the other side into annihilation.

At what cost, Will couldn't begin to even fathom.

A moment later, the Frenchman coughed again and blood gushed from his mouth. He struggled once more for breath and then finally stilled, his gaze going fixed and glassy. Will closed the man's eyes then wearily hauled himself to his feet as he tried to hold back the disturbing emotions caused by this enemy soldier's death.

But he couldn't. The tide had been breached and everything he'd been holding at bay for hours came roiling up, making him light-headed. He tried to tell himself it was simply exhaustion, lack of water and food, and days of unrelenting tension and punishing physical and mental demands. It was more than that, though. He'd survived battles before and weathered the dangerous life of a spy in the Peninsula. And he'd done it with little fear and almost no doubt about his mission. But something had shifted today in a monumental upheaval that threatened to reorder his world. He imagined a pit opening under his feet, one that was dark and filled with too many unknowns.

Unconsciously, his hand reached out to grasp the mane of his charger. He leaned against the huge animal, taking comfort in its stolid strength and even in the acrid scent of its sweat. It felt like a miracle that something close to him was still alive.

You fool, get a bloody grip on yourself.

Now was not the time to fall apart like some untried lad. The battle was won, but the day wasn't over. Napoleon's retreat had turned into a rout, with the Allied cavalry regrouping and heading out in pursuit. Will needed to find and rejoin what was left of his regiment as soon as possible.

He'd spent hours riding the line, relaying Wellington's orders to various commanders. He'd had two horses shot out from under him and his right arm ached like the devil from cavalry charges earlier in the day when he'd relentlessly hacked his saber through milling ranks of French infantrymen. Will had been one of the lucky ones, surviving with only a few cuts, a minor slash across his back, and a knock to the head when he'd been thrown from his horse by an exploding shell.

And since he *had* survived, it was time to find what was left of the 1st Royal Dragoons and get on with his duties. The Union Brigade—three cavalry regiments including the 1st Royals—had suffered devastating losses in the first charge of the day, with the officer ranks decimated in the carnage. Major Dorville, Will's regimental commander, would be looking for him to help remuster the unit and harry the enemy on its retreat.

For a few moments, he stood quietly with his horse by the side of the road as a regiment of Rifles—or what was left of it—trudged by. Once they passed, he was about to swing up into the saddle when a familiar voice called his name. Relief washed through him as he turned and raised his hand to the officer cantering up to him on a gargantuan black charger.

The rider was a brawny young Scotsman, clad in the mud-smeared dress uniform of the Black Watch. Clearly, Captain Alasdair Gilbride had gone directly from the Duchess of Richmond's ball to join his regiment at Quatre Bras. The 42nd Highlanders had taken a fierce pounding in that battle but had still managed a quick march to Waterloo where they had acquitted themselves with great distinction. But their ranks had been decimated, and Will had lost sight of Alec earlier in the day. He breathed a silent prayer of thanks that his best friend had been spared.

The Scotsman swung down from his horse and pulled Will into a hearty embrace, thumping him on the back in what was, for Alec, an extravagant display of emotion. Will was not a small man by any means, but his friend was built like a brawler. Few could best the broad-shouldered warrior in a fight. But oddly enough for a man his size, Alec was self-contained and graceful, able to move with a lethal stealth that had been the downfall of many a Frenchman. He was also one of Wellington's most effective spies, and had been Will's partner in a number of missions in the Peninsular War.

Like Will, Alec was one of the illegitimate sons of England's royal princes. They were cousins, drawn together by inclination and duty, and by the fact that their status as royal bastards sometimes set them apart from their fellow officers and other members of the *ton*. Will had learned long ago to ignore the whispers of gossip—even if the crude, callous jibes still sometimes stuck in his craw—but the same could not be said for Alec. He'd fought often to defend their reputations over the years, pushing back at the sneering comments that questioned their parentage. Will tried to tell him it didn't truly matter what others said about them, but he and Alec both knew that wasn't true.

After the horror of today's battle, who or what their fathers were barely seemed of any consequence.

"Jesus, I'm glad to see you're still on this side of the dirt, Wolf," Alec growled, using Will's nickname. Fatigue and worry sharpened his normally subtle brogue, making him sound every inch the Highlander. "I haven't seen you since you went ass over tea kettle off your horse in that last barrage. I tried to get to you, but Napoleon's blasted Guard regiment got in my way."

"I was lucky with that one. I just got a knock on the head. Took me a few minutes to get my bearings after that, but I ended up right next to the line. Two Welsh fusiliers pulled me out of harm's way." Will eyed his cousin's battered uniform with its missing epaulette and cuffs sliced to shreds. "Uniform aside, you don't look much worse for wear."

Alec's expressive mouth pressed into a hard line as he glanced down at the dead Frenchman at their feet, and then at the dozens of bodies scattered by the side of the road. "Aye, luck was with me as well. Hardly a mark on me, and that's something of a miracle after the last few days."

He didn't sound particularly grateful. That was understandable, given the grievous losses the Black Watch had suffered in not one but two battles. Will knew it wouldn't be long before guilt would begin to creep in for both of them. Guilt that they'd survived when so many others had not.

For a minute or so, they gazed silently over the battlefield, watching the chaotic retreat of French troops in the distance as they fled south toward Charleroi with the British cavalry hard on their heels. What had once been farmland, with gentle green valleys and fields full of ripening rye, had become a nightmare landscape of mangled bodies of horses and men, the once-beautiful countryside a charnel house of death. And God only knew how many soldiers were still breathing. Too wounded to move on their own, they could only wait helplessly for aid that might never arrive.

"Picton didn't make it," Will said, referring to the commander of the 5th Infantry Division and one of Wellington's top officers. "He caught it during the attack by d'Erlon's corps."

"I heard. Hamilton got it, too," Alec grimly replied, "as did Hay, Brudenell Forbes, and Gordon. I can't even begin to count all the rest."

"Christ, what a disaster," Will growled. Bitterness choked him at the thought of young Hay. The lad was only eighteen years old, barely out of leading strings.

"At least we won the bloody thing, although we'd best get

going if we're going to help finish the job." Alec peered at the chaotic movement of men and animals heading away from them. Dusk was coming on rapidly now, casting long shadows over the battlefield. "I don't fancy chasing down Boney's Imperial Guard in the middle of the night, Wolf. Not if I can help it."

Will nodded. Getting the job done was what they did— no matter how ugly or pointless it seemed.

As they prepared to mount up, Alec glanced over, his gray eyes shadowed and somber. He looked hesitant, as if afraid to voice his thoughts. Will cocked an enquiring brow.

"Do ye think it was worth it?" Alec finally asked, unconsciously slipping into a heavier brogue. "After today, do ye think there's anything left worth saving? A good life, I mean, for us. For any of us."

"There'd better be, mate," Will grimly replied. "After the hell we've been through these last six years, there'd bloody well better be."

Chapter One

London
August 1815

After paying off the hackney driver, Will glanced up at the elegant town house on Upper Wimpole Street. He'd been to Sir Dominic Hunter's home three times in the last four years, when he'd been in London on Wellington's orders to share intelligence with the powerful spymaster. Although Dominic had initially recruited Will into the ranks of the Intelligence Service, it hadn't been long before he'd facilitated Will's transfer to the duke's staff of exploring officers—military men with the skills to draw maps, gather intelligence, work with local guides, and avoid capture by the enemy.

Dominic had selected Alasdair, too, plucking him from the Black Watch and transferring him to Wellington's staff. Alec had been a perfect fit for the job as a military intelligence agent. He spoke fluent Spanish and Portuguese, could sketch like a bloody engineer, and was as crafty as the devil himself. The spymaster had also suggested to the duke that Will and Alec partner on the majority of their missions, even though the usual way of things was for exploring officers to work with Spanish guerrillas who knew the terrain and the local politics. But Dominic had been insistent that Will and Alec work together, and Wellington had eventually agreed.

Why Dominic had been so intent on the partnership was a bit of a mystery, but the spymaster was known for taking a close interest in the lives of the illegitimate children of the royal princes. Aden St. George, for one, a former captain in the Royal Dragoons and one of Dominic's best spies, was a by-blow of the Prince Regent. It hardly seemed coincidental that three royal bastards had been recruited into England's spy service. Will often thought that Dominic had a secret purpose in store for him, and for Alec and Aden, too.

Of course, the war was now over, so what Dominic wanted hardly mattered anymore. No more skulking behind enemy lines, wearing absurd, filthy disguises, and taking risks that could have landed Will in a French prison. No, that part of his life was finished. He had other ambitions now, ones that would not be served by continuing his work in espionage. While men from good families had served in the Intelligence Service during the war, it was hardly looked on as a respectable profession for an officer and gentleman.

Will *wanted* a respectable life and career, one that would allow him to overcome the stigma of his parentage *and* his modest financial situation. In order to do that, he had to leave his current life far behind.

He came out of his reverie when two middle-aged women, their parasols taking up most of the sidewalk, sailed by. One made a pointed reference about "ill-mannered soldiers." Will stepped hastily back, just missing a poke in the eye from one of the absurdly frilly parasols.

When the older of the women threw him a withering glance, he responded with his most charming smile and tipped his hat with a flourish. The woman sniffed and muttered "Jackanapes" loud enough for him to hear, and he was hard put not to laugh. God, it was good to be back in England. Here, the greatest danger he faced was getting poked in the eye by a parasol or receiving cutting looks from the doyennes of the *ton*.

Grinning to himself, he ran up the steps of Dominic's house and lifted the knocker. The door swung open to reveal a plainly garbed, older man, one of Dominic's former field agents who now worked in his household. He took Will's hat and gloves and then turned him over to the butler, who had appeared as if by magic from the back of the house.

"Ah, Smithwell, still sneaking up on everyone, I see," Will said, twitting the solemn fellow.

"I leave sneaking to the lower orders, Captain Endicott," Smithwell replied with magnificent disdain. Smithwell loved to play the role of starchy butler, even though he had once been one of Dominic's more ruthless operatives. "Sir Dominic asks that you wait in the morning room until he is ready to see you."

Will sighed, knowing he might be waiting for some time. Dominic was often called to deal with urgent matters on a moment's notice, and he was not someone to be rushed. This meeting seemed like a waste of time anyway, since Will had no intention of accepting any mission Dominic might try to thrust upon him. In fact, today would be the day that he tendered his resignation from the spy game, once and for all.

Smithwell led him to the morning room that faced onto a small garden behind the house.

Will paused on the threshold, momentarily taken aback. He'd waited in this room before, and he remembered elegant but austere appointments in muted shades of blue and gray, complemented by well-made but plain furniture. Now, though, the room dazzled with yellow walls and red and yellow striped curtains that framed the large bay window. The old furniture had been replaced by plump-cushioned couches and comfortable armchairs covered in riotously gay floral fabric. It was as if the windows had been flung open and a summer garden had been transported indoors. The effect was enhanced by large vases of yellow roses, two on the mantelpiece and another on a round table in the window.

The room was so unlike Dominic, a man who rarely looked anything less than grim, that Will let out a bemused laugh.

"It's like being in a damn lady's boudoir isn't it? If I didn't know better, I'd think poor old Dominic had lost his mind," said a familiar voice.

Will turned to see his cousin leisurely rise from a wing-back chair tucked into a corner alcove filled with bookcases. "Alec! I thought you were tied at the heels to your regiment in Paris."

Unlike Will, who'd spent the last several weeks mopping up the remnants of Napoleon's army, Alec had marched to Paris with the troops enforcing the occupation.

"Aye," Alec sighed. "I had a rough go of it while you were off adventuring on the frontier. I envied you, you lucky bastard."

Will snorted his disdain. "Yes, I'm sure Paris was torture for you."

Alec, no doubt, had taken the sojourn as an opportunity to drink and wench his way through the city. No matter where he went, women always threw themselves at his feet. Will had often been forced to save his cousin's hide, dragging Alec off before some irate father or husband came after him with a shotgun or old blunderbuss and even, on one memorable occasion, a machete.

Alec gave him an evil grin but didn't rise to the bait. "When did you arrive back in London?"

"Just yesterday, although I've been in England for a few weeks. I was visiting with Aunt Rebecca in Hampshire. I wanted to see how she was getting along after my uncle passed away." Will still had trouble believing that Uncle Philip was dead, and it had troubled him greatly that he'd been unable to return to England in time for the funeral.

Will, the grandchild of a baronet, had been sent to live as the ward of Philip Endicott shortly after his birth. Uncle Philip, a cousin of the family, had been a prosperous gentleman, living a comfortable existence with his wife, Rebecca, in the Hampshire countryside. Childless, they had generously taken Will in, treating him as their own son and helping to minimize the scandal of his birth. Since Will's mother had died when he was less than a year old, the Endicotts had been the only family he'd ever known. His father, the Duke of York, had begun to exert influence on Will's life once he turned sixteen, but no one could replace Uncle Philip.

"How is your aunt?" Alec asked in a sympathetic voice.

Will shrugged. "Well enough. Uncle Philip's nephew inherited the property and the manor house, but my aunt has been amply provided for. She's taken a house near Basingstoke, close to her sisters."

Alec scowled. "And what about you? Did your uncle make any settlements on you, or have you been left out in the bloody cold?"

Will glanced at the trolley next to the fireplace that held a number of decanters. "What are you drinking? Looks like we have a wait, so I might as well join you."

He poured a splash of what he knew would be the finest cognac into a cut crystal glass. Years fighting the enemy didn't stop Dominic from occasionally availing himself of a little French contraband.

"By the way," he asked, wanting to avoid a discussion of his financial affairs, "what the hell has come over Dominic?" He made a vague gesture at the plush, softly feminine furniture. "This is hardly his usual sort of thing."

Alec inspected him with a narrow-eyed gaze, obviously debating whether to pursue the conversation about Will's present situation. There was little point and little to report. Though Uncle Philip had left him a genteel competence that was more than kind, it would hardly allow him to live the life of a gentleman. At least a gentleman who lived in London or wished for advancement in his military career.

"Sir Dominic recently married. Hadn't you heard?" Alec's sardonic gaze indicated he wasn't fooled by Will's dodge.

"I'd always thought him wedded to his work," he replied, genuinely surprised. "Who was the lucky lady?"

Alec rolled his eyes. "I haven't a clue, and I must say I'm not interested in the subject. And your unsubtle evasion—which, really, is rather pathetic in an agent of your caliber suggests that your uncle did *not* make a provision for you. Did everything go to that bloody fool nephew of his?"

"He did what he could, but most of the estate was tied up either by the entail or my aunt's marriage settlements." When Alec began to curse, Will held up a hand. "Uncle Philip was more than generous, and what he left should keep me going until I can get a promotion or a position in one of the ministries."

Alec let out a sigh and dropped into an elegant but fragile-looking chair. It creaked alarmingly under the impact of his imposing frame. "I wish you would let me help you, laddie. You know I have more than enough."

More than enough was an understatement. Alec was heir

to a wealthy Scottish earldom, of which his grandfather was the current titleholder. Under Scottish law, titles could be passed down through the female line, and Alec's mother— now long dead—had been the only child of the Earl of Riddick, and dutifully married when she'd had her brief affair with a royal duke. Along with Alec's aristocratic lineage came a generous allowance, one that he'd always been willing to share. But Will refused to take charity from his cousin, loath to become his or any man's dependant.

"And you know I'm not going to do that." Will swirled the amber liquid around in his glass before taking a swallow. They'd been over this a hundred times, and the outcome was always the same.

Alec's frustration was evident. "Well, don't blame me if you end up in the poorhouse."

Will laughed. "I won't. Now, why don't we change the subject?"

"Suit yourself." Alec's amicable tone set Will instantly on guard. "While you were in Hampshire, did you happen to visit with any of the local gentry?"

Christ. His cousin was truly incorrigible. "I didn't have the time."

Alec raised his eyebrows in exaggerated surprise. "You couldn't find one wee minute to stop in and visit with old friends? I find that hard to believe."

"Believe it," he said with a clear warning note.

Naturally, Alec ignored it. "How sad that you didn't have time to drop in on your old friends, Viscount and Lady Reese. I believe they have daughters, do they not? Twins, I think you said."

After setting down his glass on a ridiculously pretty and fragile table, Will propped a shoulder against the mantelpiece. "You do realize I can still take you?"

Alec let out a guffaw. "Try it, and see how far you get.

Now, back to the lovely Reese daughters and when you plan to see them. One in particular, I should say."

"Christ, man. You saw the girls once at a review, hundreds of yards away. And that was three years ago. You have no bloody idea what they look like."

When Alec started to argue, Will seriously contemplated hauling his cousin into the garden and giving him a bit of home-brewed. After his financial situation, Will's least favorite topic was Miss Evelyn Whitney, his childhood sweetheart for lack of a better term. Not that *he* would ever use that word in describing her. In fact, he rarely talked about Evie at all. But he'd apparently said enough over the years to give Alec an indication of his feelings for her.

Or, more correctly, what his feelings for her *used* to be. Evie was part of the past—a fondly remembered past, but one that no longer had any bearing on his life.

The fortuitous entrance of Smithwell spared him from having to forcibly shut his cousin's mouth.

"Finally," Will muttered as the butler ushered them up-stairs to Dominic's study.

"Coward," Alec muttered back.

"Remind me how old you are again?" he retorted as they reached the top of the staircase.

Alec flashed him an evil grin but held his tongue since Smithwell was tapping on the door to Dominic's study.

"Captains Endicott and Gilbride, Sir Dominic."

The butler stepped aside to allow them to pass. Will went in first but came to a sudden halt when he saw who was waiting for them. Alec plowed into his back, almost knock-ing him off his feet. Good Lord, they *were* like a pair of idi-otic schoolboys, or so the long-suffering look on Dominic's face suggested.

"Please come in, gentlemen," he said in a disapproving voice. "You don't wish to keep his Highness waiting, do you?"

"No, Sir Dominic," Will replied, trying not to wince at the reprimand.

He strode into the room and bowed to the man sitting in one of the leather club chairs in front of Dominic's desk. "Forgive me, sir. I wasn't expecting to see you today."

Frederick, Duke of York and Albany, commander-in-chief of the king's army, and Will's father, pulled his formidable bulk up from the chair. The duke stretched out his hand, greeting Will with more warmth than was his usual wont. "I imagine not, my boy. I understand you were given leave from your regiment to visit your aunt in Hampshire. My condolences on the loss of your estimable uncle."

"Thank you, sir. He was the kindest of men, and my aunt keenly feels the loss."

"As do you, I imagine," the duke replied. "I am, however, pleased to see you looking so well after all that ugly business in Belgium." He then turned to Alec. "Welcome back to England, Gilbride. I understand you also acquitted yourself well at Waterloo. You and the 42nd have much to be proud of."

Alec responded to the tribute with a bow of his head. "Thank you, sir, but my contribution was modest compared to most of the men in the regiment." His voice was somber, and Will knew he was remembering the high death toll the Black Watch suffered that terrible day.

"There were many good men lost that day. It hardly bears thinking about, does it?" A flicker of sorrow crossed the duke's round, rather florid face. Then he collected himself. "Such reminiscences are not, however, why I asked Sir Dominic to summon you both to meet me."

"Indeed not," said Dominic. "If you would like to take your seat, your Highness, we can proceed."

Will and Alec exchanged curious glances as the duke

settled his bulk into the chair. They silently took their seats while Dominic moved to his desk.

From behind that massive oak desk, Dominic managed many of England's intelligence agents, skillfully and invisibly exercising his formidable power. Or at least he had in the past. Will had heard talk of the spymaster's impending retirement and couldn't help wondering if his marriage had anything to do with it. Stepping away at the height of his influence and prestige was not a choice Will could see making in a similar position, and he found it hard to imagine how someone like Dominic could exchange his place at the center of power for a life of quiet domesticity.

A rather meditative silence settled over the room. The duke, never one to waste time or mince words, stared absently at a painting of a hunting scene on the wall behind Dominic's desk, his thick brows pulled together in a slight frown. The spymaster remained silent, clearly waiting for his superior to begin.

"Well, sir, why did ye bring us here today?" Alec finally asked, impatience giving his voice a faint burr.

Will winced at the break in protocol. But Alec had always been impatient with social niceties and rarely met a rule he wasn't tempted to break.

Dominic muttered something disapproving under his breath but, fortunately, the duke chose not to bristle up. Instead, he ignored Alec and lifted an eyebrow at Will. "I suppose I was the last person you expected to see today," he commented.

"I must admit to some surprise, sir." It seemed odd that his father would choose to visit Dominic's town house when he could easily order them to appear at his office at the Horse Guards. His father was also not in uniform and his carriage had been nowhere in sight on the street, all of which was highly suggestive of a desire to avoid prying eyes. "Perhaps you wished for this meeting to be unobserved by your staff at the Horse Guards?"

"I wish for it to be a bloody secret," his father said bluntly. "We've got a damned awkward situation on our hands, and we need you and your cousin to handle it."

Will didn't like the sound of that. "Indeed, sir? How can we be of assistance?"

When the duke's gaze flickered to Dominic, the spymaster took up the conversation. "Gentlemen, I'm well aware that you both deserve a well-earned rest. Nevertheless, your services are required on an urgent mission."

"Christ," Alec groaned. "Not Napoleon again, for God's sake."

Dominic cracked a slight smile. "No, he's well contained, I assure you. This is a matter closer to home. In fact, most of the mission will likely take place here in London."

"And what is the nature of this mission?" Will had to rein in his frustration. Dominic was correct. He and Alec did deserve a rest, and the thought of yet another espionage mission made him want to curse long and loud.

"The nature of the mission is stopping an assassination," the duke answered sharply. "Possibly a royal assassination that could happen within the next few weeks."

Even Alec couldn't help looking stunned. "Ye're joking, aren't you?"

The duke's gaze narrowed. "I wish I was, Captain, and I'll thank you not to interrupt me again," he said irritably.

Properly reprimanded, Alec grimaced and murmured an apology.

"Forgive me, sir," Will said, hoping to draw the duke's ire away from Alec. "Is there any indication of the target of such an attempt? Is it the Prince Regent, or perhaps yourself?"

Will and the duke were not particularly close—after all,

he hadn't met the man in person until he was sixteen. Still, the idea of his father facing that kind of danger tensed every muscle in his body. The threat of assassination wasn't hard to imagine, since it had been only three years since Prime Minister Spencer Perceval had been the victim of just such a foul crime.

Dominic smoothly took back control of the discussion. "At this point, we're lacking that sort of precise information." He glanced at the duke. "With your permission, your Highness, I'll start at the beginning."

"That would be helpful," Alec muttered under his breath.

This time it was Will who shot him an irate gaze, but Alec simply rolled his eyes.

"You are well aware, I assume," Dominic started, "that prior to the Act of Union there was a great deal of trouble in Ireland."

Will frowned. Though he was only a lad at the time, he'd certainly been aware of the turmoil and bloodshed that had plagued Ireland for years, with factions of Catholics and Irish Protestants united against the English administration in Dublin. In 1798, a group of Catholic rebels had fomented the most serious uprising, this time in league with the French, who had attempted to support the rebels with an invasion force.

Unfortunately for the rebels, bad weather and bad luck led to the scattering or capture of the French ships, and the insurrection had been brutally but effectively put down. The Act of Union of 1801, uniting the kingdoms of England and Ireland, had signaled the end of that revolutionary period, and the last fourteen years had been relatively quiet regarding Irish republicanism and Catholic emancipation.

In Will's opinion, the disabilities enforced by law on the Catholic population, both in England and Ireland, were markedly unfair. After all, he had a fairly good idea of what it felt like to be an outsider. But he knew that his father and most of the royals were vehemently opposed to Catholic emancipation, so he kept his views to himself.

"Yes," he replied, "but I thought the situation in Ireland was under control, especially since the creation of the Irish Royal Constabulary last year."

Robert Peel, Chief Secretary for Ireland, had supervised the creation of that Irish police force, nicknamed the Peelers after their founder.

"That's mostly correct," Dominic agreed. "Peel's men have been effective in containing disorder. But there are still occasional disturbances, especially regarding disputes over tenancy and eviction issues in the countryside. Those disturbances are met with force which, as you can understand, is deeply resented by the local populations."

"Then they should obey the law and not cause so much bloody trouble," the duke snapped. "They bring it down upon themselves with their damned agrarian outrages. If a landlord wants to evict some bloody useless Catholic tenant from his land, he has every right to do so."

Dominic's green eyes went as cold as ice chips. Will had the distinct impression he was struggling not to verbally rip the duke's head off.

"The situation is indeed disturbing," Dominic finally answered in a carefully neutral voice. "In any event, although Ireland is peaceful for the most part, the administration in Dublin is forced to keep a very close watch on the situation."

"Which, I assume, means eyes and ears on the ground," Will said.

"Spies, you mean," Alec said more bluntly.

Dominic waggled his hand in a *not exactly* gesture. "Let's just say there are those who fear the bloodshed that would surely result from another uprising, even though they are generally sympathetic to the Catholic cause. But given the circumstances, these particular individuals believe it a sensible course of action to pass their concerns on to Peel."

"They're informants, in other words," Alec said in a dry voice.

Dominic shrugged but didn't answer.

The duke glanced impatiently at the bracket clock on the mantel. "Get on with it, Dominic, will you?"

Dominic nodded, even though his thinned lips revealed his irritation. "There have been rumblings that cells of radicals are forming in Limerick and Tipperary, and also up north near Ulster. Most of the rumors that have reached us are likely just that—rumors. But a highly reliable source in Ulster has come into possession of some disturbing and credible information. According to this source, a group of these radicals may already be in England with the express intention of plotting the assassination of a high-ranking member of government, or even a member of the royal family. The most obvious targets would be Peel or Liverpool, or possibly the Regent. Others could be under threat too."

Will shook his head. "That's not much to go on."

"As usual," Alec said sarcastically.

"The defense of one's country never comes easily, Gilbride," the duke huffed.

Will hastily intervened before Alec could step into it further. "No, sir, it doesn't. And Alasdair and I stand ready to do whatever is necessary. But surely there are agents with both a greater understanding of the Irish question and intimate knowledge of where in London such conspirators might be found."

"Generally I would agree with you," Dominic said. "And I will give you the support you need in those areas. But there is one particular reason why you, Will, are most suited for this mission."

Uncharacteristically, Dominic hesitated, and faint warning bells began to sound in Will's head. "And that reason is?"

Dominic tilted his head, and a calculating look Will had never seen before briefly crossed his face. The bells in his head clanged even louder.

"Because an old friend of yours could possibly be involved in this conspiracy," Dominic said. "Her involvement is not necessarily by intention, but more likely by her association with certain persons."

"And who is this old friend?" Will slowly asked with a sense of impending doom.

"Miss Evelyn Whitney, daughter of Lord and Lady Reese," Dominic replied. "I believe you know her quite well."

Chapter Two

Will wondered if someone had knocked him on the back of his head since Dominic's words resisted any attempt to make sense of them.

"Bloody hell," Alec exclaimed. "Wasn't expecting that, were you?"

"Evie? Are you sure?" Will forced out.

"Of course we're sure," barked his father. "Do you think we would make a joke about this?"

"No, sir, but since your Dublin source is so vague, how can we be sure this information is correct?" Will shook his head. "It completely beggars belief that Evie—Evelyn—would be involved in something like this."

It was absurd. Evie was the sweetest, most gentle person Will had ever known. She was also painfully shy and loathed any sort of conflict. No one who knew her could believe for a moment that she could be involved in any type of criminal activity, much less a murderous conspiracy.

"Unfortunately, the facts do point to Miss Whitney's involvement," Dominic said calmly.

Will shook his head. "I refuse to believe it."

"Are you accusing us of lying, William?" his father asked in a cold voice.

"Of course not, sir, but—"

The duke cut him off. "Then you must believe that I am somehow wanting in intellect. I suppose you know better than your commander-in-chief and Sir Dominic, do you?"

"Sir, that's hardly fair," Alec objected. "Wolf never suggested that."

Before Will's father could unleash his ire on Alec, Dominic interrupted. "May I suggest some refreshment before we continue? Your Highness, allow me to fetch you a drink."

"Now that you mention it, I'm fairly parched," grumbled the duke. "Why the devil didn't you offer me one before?"

Dominic simply smiled at the older man. Although of common origin, Dominic had been raised with the royal princes, and understood how to manage them better than anyone. He was particularly close to the Duke of York, sharing his commitment to England's military and the well-being of its men.

The spymaster splashed some brandy into two glasses, handing one to the duke and the other to Will. He pointedly ignored Alec, who muttered under his breath as he got up to fetch his own drink.

The interlude gave Will time to wrestle his temper under control. The duke might be his father, but he was also a prince and could make life difficult for both Will and Alec.

"Forgive my outburst, sir," he said to the duke. "But the idea that Miss Whitney might be involved in criminal activity caught me by surprise."

"When was the last time you spoke to Miss Whitney?" Dominic asked.

It had been in Hampshire in 1811, when he'd taken a brief furlough to visit his aunt and uncle. Uncle Philip's lands butted against the Reese estate. Will had known the family since he was a boy, spending many a long day roaming the fields, woods, and stables with the Reese progeny. Back then, it had seemed impossible that he would eventually lose touch with them, even Evie.

"It's been four years, Sir Dominic."

He remembered his remarkably uncomfortable conversation with Evie at a ball held at the local inn. She hadn't forgiven him for abandoning their youthfully naïve dreams of a life together—her stiff demeanor and the wounded expression in her cornflower-blue eyes had made that abundantly clear. Nor had it helped that Eden, Evie's twin sister, had planted herself barely two feet away, glaring at Will the entire time. After that disastrous evening, Will had decided that the best thing he could do for the Reese family was to steer well clear of them.

"Then you don't really know her anymore, do you?" his father said.

"Perhaps not, but Evie would never hurt anyone. Not deliberately. Of that I'm sure," Will said doggedly.

Dominic leaned forward, resting his forearms on his desk. "I believe I can shed some light on this discussion. Apparently, Miss Whitney is soon to be engaged to a man who we suspect is involved with the Irish radicals. It is possible that she is unaware of his activities in this regard."

"A fiancé? This just gets better and better," Alec commented sardonically.

Will's hand had involuntarily jerked, splashing brandy over the rim of his glass. "Evie, engaged? She was a confirmed wallflower, the last I heard."

"It would appear not," Dominic replied. "Her suitor, and the suspect in question, is Michael Beaumont, the youngest son of the Earl of Leger."

Will didn't bother to hide his skeptical frown. "Why

would an English aristocrat's son be involved with Irish rebels?"

"Because this particular aristocrat's son is a Catholic," the duke said with heavy disapproval. "As is the entire Beaumont family."

"I hasten to add that there's no evidence against the earl or the other members of his family," Dominic said with a faint note of reprimand. "Lord Leger is an exceedingly respectable man and a loyal Englishman well regarded at both Court and Whitehall."

The duke let out a vulgar snort.

"That being the case, why is his son under suspicion?" Alec asked.

"Because Michael Beaumont is a radical in favor of Catholic emancipation," the duke said. "And he's not shy about voicing his opinions either, I might add. He's in thick with every damned Whig politician who might support his cause, despite the fact that there isn't a bloody chance in hell he'll succeed."

"That hardly sounds like someone who'd be involved in a conspiracy," Will said. "Gadding about town trying to drum up votes might make him a damned boring person to spend time with, but it's hardly stealthy behavior. Quite the opposite."

"Perhaps," Dominic said. "Or else he may believe that his position in society, coupled with his quite obvious behavior, would deflect suspicion."

Frustrated, Will stood and paced to the fireplace, then turned back to face the others. "I find it difficult to believe that Evie truly intends to marry Beaumont. For one thing, he's Catholic, and I can't imagine her parents would approve. Not Lady Reese, anyway. She's a——"

"Very sensible woman," the duke cut in. "Always liked Lady Reese."

The woman was, in fact, a thorough bitch *and* a snob, but Will kept his opinion to himself.

"The Beaumonts are an extremely wealthy family," Dominic said, "and Michael will no doubt do quite well by his father, even as a younger son. Lord Reese's fortune is merely respectable, and neither of his daughters will bring a significant dowry into their marriages."

Will had always suspected as much and had no doubt that Dominic knew the state of the Reese finances down to the last farthing. "I'm assuming there's been no formal announcement of an engagement." Just saying the words made his gut churn for reasons he didn't want to think about.

"It's expected shortly," Dominic replied. "So your window of opportunity is small."

"What, exactly, do you expect me to do?" Will asked cautiously.

"You're to sidle up to the girl and find out what's going on, of course," his father said impatiently. "You were close to her once, from what Dominic tells me. Get close to her again."

Will gave Dominic a hard stare. How the *hell* had the spymaster acquired that information? Not that there was any point in asking, and Will probably didn't want to know, anyway.

"You mean spy on her," he said. Spying on Evie was the worst idea he'd ever heard.

"We mean spend some time with her," Dominic replied in a soothing voice. "By renewing your acquaintance with her, you will be able to get closer to Michael Beaumont. He's the real target here, not Miss Whitney."

Will propped an elbow on the cool marble of the mantelpiece as he struggled to quell his anger. "But you do want me to *use her* to get to Beaumont."

Dominic let out a small sigh and leaned back in his chair. "I understand that this mission is . . . unpleasant on a personal level. You have feelings of loyalty toward Miss Whitney, which is commendable."

Not quite. What Will really suffered were feelings of remorse for *abandoning* her, as Evie had put it. Will *had* walked away from her, although he still thought it had been too much to ask a callow youth to pledge his devotion to a naïve young girl two years his junior. But in joining the army and in making it his calling, he'd hurt Evie. To force his way back into her life—to spy on her, no less—would be yet another betrayal of the girl he'd once cared for deeply.

"There's another way to look at it," Dominic continued, his piercing green eyes compelling Will's attention. "In doing this, you will be protecting Miss Whitney. I hope for her sake that Mr. Beaumont is not involved in this plot. But if he is, the sooner we unearth the conspirators, the better off the young lady will be."

Will jerked upright. "Are you saying Evie could be in danger?"

Dominic's craggy features took on a thoughtful expression, as if puzzling over what seemed a straightforward question. Will had to repress the impulse to stalk over and shake the answer out of him.

"I think it's safe to say she's not in any immediate danger," the spymaster finally replied with infuriating ambiguity.

Alec finally came to his feet as well, shoving his hands back through his hair with exasperation. "Could you be more specific? What, exactly, are we to be doing other than *getting close* to Evelyn Whitney and Michael Beaumont? Is there something specific you want us to look for?"

The duke again glanced at the clock. "I need to be getting back to the Horse Guards. There's no reason to be so bloody cautious with these fellows, Dominic. They know how to take care of themselves."

"Perhaps," Dominic said. "But Captain Endicott's previous history with Miss Whitney is a complication as well as an advantage. His loyalties are clearly engaged."

The duke waved an airy hand. "William isn't interested in a girl like *that,* are you, my boy? No dowry or political connections to speak of, and no looks to recommend her, either."

Will briefly contemplated bashing both Dominic and his father over the head with a fireplace iron. Evie might not be the greatest prize on the marriage mart, but she didn't deserve to have her name bandied about so carelessly.

Alec hastily jumped into the discussion. "Will's no downy one, you can be sure. Now, getting back to the mission . . ."

"Indeed," Dominic said. "Mr. Beaumont is the leading patron of the Hibernian Benevolent Association, an organization assisting Irish immigrants. It's attached to a small church in St. Giles that sponsors a charity school for the children of its parishioners."

"That hardly sounds like a hotbed for sedition," Will said.

Dominic shook his head. "Our sources in Dublin suggest otherwise. The Hibernian Association has become something of a clearinghouse for new Irish immigrants in London, and we suspect the radicals might be using it as a contact point or even a safe meeting place. We have been watching St. Margaret's, but our efforts have yielded us precious little information so far. It's become clear that we need someone on the inside."

"What does Evie have to do with any of this, aside from her personal relationship with Beaumont?" Will asked.

"She's heavily involved in supporting the work of the

association," Dominic said. He cracked a reluctant smile. "I can assure you that any number of wealthy gentlemen panic when Miss Whitney approaches. She is quite resolute and persuasive when it comes to supporting her charitable endeavors."

That sure as hell didn't sound like Evie. She generally hated going into company or talking to strangers. "How long has she been working with Beaumont?"

"About three years," Dominic replied.

"And is there any hard proof connecting Beaumont with this alleged plot?"

The spymaster waggled a hand. "Let's say compelling indications, rather. He's been corresponding with Daniel O'Connell, although we've not been able to actually get our hands on any of their letters."

"Who's Daniel O'Connell?" Alec asked.

"He's a damned Irish radical up to no good," snapped the duke. "Too bad Peel never had the chance to put a bullet through the confounded scoundrel."

"O'Connell and Peel are engaged in a political feud over the issue of Catholic emancipation," Dominic added. "Peel recently challenged O'Connell to a duel on the Continent, but it never came off."

"Shame, that," the duke groused as he hauled his portly frame to his feet. "I must be off, Dominic. See to it that the lads get the rest of their marching orders." He gave Will a stern look. "I'm counting on you and your cousin, my boy. We must squash this quickly and quietly. If it gets out that a group of Catholic radicals are planning an assassination, there could be a bloody uprising. We don't need a repeat of the Gordon Riots."

"As you wish, sir." Now that his father had given him a direct order, there was nothing Will could do to escape the assignment.

After Dominic and the duke left the room, Will dropped into his chair, pressing his forehead against his fists. "What a bloody nightmare."

"Aye, it's an unholy mess," Alec said. He swiped Will's glass and went to refill it. "By the by, did you have any idea that Miss Whitney was about to get engaged?"

Will sat up straight. "Why the hell would I? I haven't seen her in years. She went her way, and I went mine."

"Clearly," Alec said in a dry tone as he strolled back and handed Will his glass. "Even so, I can't imagine she's changed all that much. Doesn't sound like the sort of girl to get involved with a cabal of assassins."

Will snorted. "The entire notion is ridiculous. She has the softest heart imaginable, and she was always a shy little thing. The poor girl was a wallflower in training before she even made it to her first Season."

"No longer, apparently. Miss Whitney sounds like she's developed into something of a firebrand."

"I don't believe it. I'm sure this Beaumont fellow has taken advantage of her pliable nature. Evie's always had a tendency to allow others to lead her around by the nose. Her sister has been doing it to her for years."

Alec grimaced and set his glass down. "I wouldn't let anyone hear you say that. It bolsters the case against the poor girl."

"Christ." Will took a healthy swallow of brandy, hoping the liquid burn would dispel the cold knot of worry in the pit of his stomach. He knew beyond doubt that Evie wasn't guilty of treason, but he also understood how easy someone might find it to manipulate her. And she had a fatal tendency toward hero worship, too, as he well knew. Evie would have done absolutely anything for him when they were young. She was the same way with her siblings, especially her twin. Eden had been able to coax or bully Evie into all sorts of mischief, even things contrary to her own shy nature.

Could this Beaumont fellow be doing the same thing? Preying on Evie's gentle temperament for his own dastardly purposes? He'd rip the bastard apart if that was true.

"You do realize we have to take this job on?" Alec said. "Your father was not giving you the option to say no."

Will rolled his eyes, not bothering to respond to so obvious a point.

"Of course," Alec mused, "if we pull this off, we'll be bloody heroes. Our various royal relations will be overjoyed, and you can be sure we'll be rewarded with some tidy promotions. Maybe a knighthood, or title or two."

"It's not like you need any of those," Will said dryly.

"No, but you do, especially since you seem bloody well set on a career in the military. Now that the war's over there aren't as many opportunities for promotion, as you well know. You'll need to stay on your dear Papa's good side to advance through the ranks."

"Yes, I have figured that out."

"And that means you'll have to spy on your old sweetheart. Are you comfortable with that?"

"Of course I'm not comfortable with it, you idiot, but what choice do I have?" Will surged to his feet and began pacing the room. "Besides, we were only *sweethearts*, as you mawkishly put it, when we were so young we didn't know any better."

A sly grin curved Alec's mouth. "Ah, now, did you ever kiss her, laddie?"

Will halted in his tracks and glared at him. He and Evie *had* kissed, the summer just before her first Season. He'd been home on a visit from military college, and those slow August days had been magical because of her. Back then, he'd almost been able to imagine they might marry one day, and Evie had certainly dreamed such would be the case. They'd never truly discussed it and her parents would never have approved, but it had been a sweet, lovely fantasy while it lasted.

But then war and the spy game had intervened, crushing Will's adolescent fantasies to dust.

Alec gave an insouciant shrug in response to Will's silence. "So, how do you feel about her and this Beaumont character?"

"If he's using her in any way, I'll kill him."

"Obviously, but what if he's innocent? Would it bother you if Miss Whitney marries him?"

Will wanted to deny that Evie's marriage would affect him, but Alec was watching with a sharp, knowing gaze. Will had never been able to hide anything from his cousin, and he supposed he'd have to tell the truth if he said anything at all.

Once he had the truth sorted out, that is.

Fortunately, Dominic's return to the room forestalled that discussion. "Let's finish this up, gentlemen." He resumed his seat behind his desk. "Our source tells us that this assassination plot could come to fruition within weeks. We have precious little on which to proceed, so you need to get on this."

"How do you suggest we get started?" Alec asked.

"Lord and Lady Reese are currently hosting a house party at their Hampshire estate. I would suggest you get yourselves invited."

Will blew out an exasperated breath. "How? I've been out of touch with them for years."

Dominic showed his teeth in a mocking smile. "You're a spy. You'll think of something."

"That's helpful," Alec commented.

"Get as close to Miss Whitney and Michael Beaumont as you can," Dominic elaborated. "You need to get into St. Margaret's Church and the Hibernian Association to gain access to Beaumont's office, his correspondence, and any financial records that might provide information. And also to see who, exactly, is using the premises for meetings." Dominic cocked an eyebrow at Alec. "You're heir to an earldom, Alasdair. Tell them you've become interested in philanthropy and you're considering a large donation."

Alec snorted with open disdain. "And why would a Protestant Scottish aristocrat wish to make a donation to a charity for Irish Catholics?"

"Again, you're a spy. Make something up."

Will's mind was already turning to the task. "I assume you'll want lists of all those who attend St. Margaret's, and those who receive help from the charity on a regular basis, especially the men. Anything else?"

"Get your hands on any correspondence you can between O'Connell and Beaumont," Dominic said. "That could be decisive in proving his innocence."

"That'll be a neat trick," Alec muttered.

Will shrugged. "We've handled worse."

Alec cracked him a grin. "That we have." He looked at Dominic. "Who are we reporting to, you or the duke?"

"To the duke and to Aden St. George. Aden is taking over my position."

Will nodded. "So the rumors are true. Does your retirement have anything to do with your change in marital status?"

Dominic's grin erased ten years from his face. "It does. From now on, I'll be spending most of my time in the country at my wife's manor house. It's time to pass on my small portion of England's business to someone else."

Will was about to make a polite statement of congratulations when a soft knock sounded on the door.

"Enter," Dominic called.

The door partially opened and a woman peeked around it. "Is the duke gone?" she asked.

Dominic strode across the room to take her hand. "You're safe, my love. But York specifically asked me to convey his regrets that he missed you. He quite likes you, as you know."

The tall, slender woman who looked to be in her mid-thirties wrinkled her nose in a comical fashion. "I find that hard to believe, but I'll take your word for it."

Dominic led her into the room. "Chloe, I'd like you to meet Captain William Endicott and Captain Alasdair Gilbride. Gentlemen, this is Lady Hunter, my wife. She is also Griffin Steele's mother, which makes her your aunt."

Will and Alec had been in the process of making their bows, but that little tidbit stunned them into immobility.

Griffin Steele, the Duke of Cumberland's son and one of the richest men in London, had owned a number of gambling establishments and at least one brothel until he recently sold them. Will had met him once when he'd pulled Alec out of one of Steele's more notorious hells after Alec had fought with a man who'd tried to cheat him. Steele had summarily broken up the fight and cast the sharp out into the street. He'd then tendered his most humble apologies, and sardonically offered Will and Alec a *family discount*. Alec had been more than game, but Will had hustled him out the door as quickly as possible.

The idea that this lovely, elegant woman could be Griffin's mother was astounding.

Alec recovered first. "Aunt Chloe, it's a pleasure to meet you," he said with a flourishing bow. "Although I find it hard to believe that so beautiful a lady could be mother to our scoundrel of a cousin."

Will elbowed him in the ribs. "Please ignore Captain Gilbride, ma'am. He's an ignorant Highlander sorely lacking in manners."

Lady Hunter laughed. "Not at all. My son *is* a scoundrel. I'm delighted to make your acquaintance, gentlemen. Will you stay for tea?"

Dominic shook his head. "That will not be possible, my love. Gentlemen, I'm sure you have much to accomplish before your trip into Hampshire."

Will took the hint. "Perhaps another time, ma'am, when we return to London."

"I should like that very much." She cast a glance sparkling with mischief at her husband. "We should invite Griffin, too, and have a proper family reunion."

Dominic snorted. "I can scarcely imagine how delightful that would be. Now, be on your way, you two. My wife has been out shopping all morning and needs her rest."

Lady Hunter looked the picture of health to Will, but he noted her hand drifting to the gentle bump rounding out the front of her gown.

"Dominic, don't be a fussbudget. I'm perfectly well," she said.

Alec widened his eyes at Will, clearly reacting to the notion that Dominic, one of Europe's most lethal spymasters, was a fussbudget.

They quickly said their good-byes, collected their hats from Smithwell, and made their way to the street.

Alec shook his head in wonderment. "Never would have pegged Dominic for the domestic sort. And with a pregnant wife, no less." He cast Will a sly glance. "Well, if it can happen to him, I suppose it can happen to anyone. What say you, Wolf? Ready to give up the thrilling life of a spy for domesticated bliss?"

"Ask me again in a few weeks and I'll let you know," Will said.

After we stop an assassination attempt, prevent an outbreak of riots, and save Evie from marriage to a traitor.

Chapter Three

Evie Whitney watched in admiration as her sister's arrow flew straight and true, landing with a satisfying thud in the center of the target.

"Well done," she said to her twin. "It still amazes me how accurate you are, even though your eyesight is as bad as mine and you refuse to wear spectacles."

Eden flashed a satisfied smirk and handed her the bow. "That's because you think about it too much, Evie, just like you do about everything. All I do is aim for the big red circle and fire away."

It was more than that, of course, and they both knew it. Eden—or Edie, to friends and family—excelled at almost every activity she took up, despite the curse of dreadful eyesight. She had learned to compensate for her poor vision with an array of little tricks. It also helped that she was naturally graceful and confident, and adept at smoothing over awkward moments that might arise, say, from failing to recognize a friend from across the room.

Lacking her sister's talent and grace, Evie couldn't count the times she'd walked into potted plants or offended an acquaintance when she breezed right past them unawares.

Finally, when she turned twenty, she'd stood up to her mother and insisted on acquiring a pair of spectacles. Though they placed her even more firmly in the wallflower category, at least she was no longer in danger of falling down stairs or giving the impression that she was rude.

Evie notched her arrow in the bowstring. Taking a deep breath, she enjoyed the drift of the soft breeze across the back of her neck. It was a gorgeous September day, when summer slowly melted into fall and the sky seemed to shimmer with gold around the edges.

She glanced across the lawn to the back of Maywood Manor, her family's gracious old house. Lady Polk and her daughters, who'd been enjoying the late afternoon sun on the terrace, had gone indoors, no doubt in anticipation of the gong. Other guests, who had been strolling on the lawns or had joined Evie and Eden in the impromptu archery contest, had also drifted away to their rooms to change. Evie and her sister should be going up too, before their mother came out to scold them for being late.

Not that Mamma would dream of scolding *Eden*. She would just smile and chuck Eden under the chin, calling her a naughty puss before delivering a stern lecture to Evie. It was the natural state of affairs in their family, and had been for as long as Evie could remember.

"Are you going to shoot or just stand there all day like some kind of looby?" her sister said, stripping off her leather gloves. She dropped into one of the wrought-iron chairs under the canopy that sheltered the refreshments table. "Mamma will have our heads if we're late for dinner, so you'd better make this shot your last."

"You mean she'll have *my* head, don't you? You could set the house on fire and she'd find some way to excuse you."

Her sister's face twisted with sympathy. "It's beastly, isn't it?"

Evie stretched the bowstring and took aim. "It's not your fault, pet. It's just the way she is." She loosed the arrow and followed its flight.

Eden leaned forward, squinting. "You almost hit the bull's-eye that time."

"I've been practicing. Maybe one of these days I'll be as good as you."

"Dream on, Sister dear," Eden retorted as she came to her feet, lazily stretching her arms in front of her. "When it comes to—"

"When it comes to what?" Evie asked absently, retrieving her bonnet that had blown under the table. Her mother would scold if she saw her bareheaded outdoors, but the day was warm and fine and simply too lovely to wear one. Plopping the hat on her head, she turned to see her twin peering toward the house.

And felt as if the earth had just dropped away beneath her feet.

"Someone's coming," Eden said, "but I can't make out who it is, confound it."

Evie struggled to form the impossible words. "It's . . . it's Will. Endicott!"

Her twin's mouth dropped open. "Wolf? Are you sure?"

"Of course I'm sure." Evie blinked several times, as if that would somehow make Will disappear. "Do you think I could ever forget what he looks like?"

"Here, hand me your spectacles," Eden said. Before Evie could answer, she snatched them from her nose and held them before her eyes. Then she let out a low whistle. "Well, I'll be damned. It *is* Wolf Endicott. But who's that delicious-looking fellow he's got with him?"

Evie retrieved her spectacles. "I don't know and I don't care. What I *do* want to know is what that . . . that . . ."

Words often failed her, but never more so than today.

"Bounder? Poltroon?" Eden helpfully supplied.

Evie could only give her head a despairing shake in response.

At one time, Will Endicott had meant the world to her. She'd told him all the secrets of her soul and had adored him with the blind passion that only a young girl could feel for her first love. And she'd thought Will felt the same way, equally devoted to her and equally determined that they'd grow up and grow old together.

What a silly little fool she'd been. And what made it worse was that she really couldn't hold it against him. After all, they'd both been so young. Will had gone on to other things, of course, as had she—eventually. It was foolish to harbor resentment and anger, especially after so many years.

But as she watched him stride across the wide expanse of lush, green lawn, Evie realized how unprepared she was to see him again, as if she were still that wounded girl of sixteen.

"What in God's name can he be doing here?" she asked.

"I expect he's come to see you," her twin answered.

"But why now? He hasn't seen any of us in years."

Eden nodded grimly. "Let me handle it." She stepped forward to close the gap before Will and his companion reached them. "Is that truly you, Wolf Endicott? Goodness, what brings you to our quiet little corner of North Hampshire?"

While her sister greeted the new arrivals with her usual panache, Evie could only stand there, fighting the impulse to clench her fists into her skirts. She'd never been more grateful for her sister's skillful managing of an awkward situation.

Staring helplessly at Will as he responded to Eden's greeting, Evie took in his tall physique and handsome features. She'd seen him a few years ago at a military review in

London that her mother had insisted they attend, but he'd been several hundred feet away from where she stood, and was mounted on horseback. Now, at close quarters, she had no choice but to brace herself against the shock of his overwhelming physical presence.

He was no longer the lanky, eighteen-year-old boy of long-cherished memories. He was very much a man, with broad shoulders showcased by his close-fitting coat and long, muscular legs sheathed in breeches and riding boots. But his face had changed perhaps even more than his body. Those extraordinary pale blue eyes of his, so like a wolf's and startling against his tanned complexion, had naturally remained the same. But a hardened maturity had replaced their youthful gleam. His features were lean, the cheekbones and jaw hard-cut and formidably masculine. His expressive mouth was now bracketed with grooves, and faint lines extended from the corners of his eyes. Some would call them laugh lines, but she suspected he'd garnered them from squinting in the harsh sunlight of Spain. Besides, he didn't look like he laughed much these days, and after what he must have seen in war, she couldn't blame him. She could only stare at him and wonder at the changes to the boy she'd once loved.

Eden forestalled Will's somewhat labored greetings by throwing her arms around his neck and depositing a swift kiss on his cheek. "Oh, never mind that. It's splendid to see you, Wolf. We were all quite worried about you and our other friends after Waterloo, but you seem perfectly fit."

Will gave Eden a sheepish smile, obviously startled by her enthusiastic greeting. "Er, it's wonderful to see you too, Eden. And, yes, I'm fine."

Then he turned to Evie, his smile turning cautious, almost as if he expected that she too would throw herself into his arms. "Evie, it's splendid to see you again, too," he said rather formally. "You're looking well."

That was patently untrue. Evie knew her face must be flushed an unattractive red from a combination of heat and nerves, and her unruly hair was no doubt curling damply around her face. Never had she felt more awkward and graceless, and she wanted to bash Will over the head for putting her in this position.

"What are you doing here?" she blurted out. "Did my mother invite you?"

It would be just like Mamma to forget to tell her something so important.

Will snorted. "Not bloody likely. She looked like she'd swallowed a lemon when she caught sight of me in the entrance hall. Clearly, her feelings for me haven't changed."

Oddly enough, his blunt speech eased her anxiety. This was the Will she knew, not the formal, smoothly handsome stranger who'd greeted her. "And I'm being just as rude as Mamma, but you caught us by surprise."

He nodded. "I know, but I ran into your brother at White's. He invited us to come down with him and visit for a few days. It seemed a good opportunity to drop in on old friends and visit Aunt Rebecca."

"How is Mrs. Endicott?" she asked. "I hope you found her well."

Will hesitated for a second before responding. "Actually, she's gone to Bath with her sister. I missed her by a few days."

Evie frowned. Why hadn't he written to his aunt before coming down? The explanation for his arrival made little sense. He'd managed to ignore the Reese family for years, so why the sudden change?

With a little laugh, Eden stepped back into the conversation. "You have yet to introduce us to your companion,

Wolf." She gave the tall, brawny man standing slightly behind Will a decidedly interested perusal.

Evie repressed a sigh. She recognized that look on her twin's face and it usually signaled trouble.

"Don't mind me," the man replied. His mouth curved up in a rakish grin as he boldly stared back at Eden. "I'm just enjoying the view."

Evie didn't think she imagined Will's long-suffering glance at his companion.

"Forgive me, ladies. This is Captain Alasdair Gilbride of the 42nd Regiment of Foot, my good friend of many years' standing. Alec, may I introduce you to Miss Evelyn Whitney and Miss Eden Whitney."

"Ladies, it's a pleasure." Captain Gilbride swept them a flourishing bow. A bare hint of a Scottish accent colored his voice.

Eden dipped into an equally flourishing—and mocking—curtsey. "I'm sure the pleasure is ours," she said, batting her eyelashes in a ridiculously flirtatious manner.

Clearly, Evie's sister had just found a new source of interest. She could understand the reaction, since Captain Gilbride's imposing and almost intimidating physical presence was offset by a charming smile and spectacular gray eyes that gleamed with sardonic laughter. He appeared the sort of man who found a great deal of enjoyment in life. Evie could already envision her twin engaging the captain in a highly improper flirtation that would drive their mother demented.

"Hallo, what's everyone doing out here in the hot sun?" exclaimed a familiar voice.

Evie leaned around Will to see her brother hurrying across the lawn.

"Matt, you bounder," Eden cried, throwing herself in his arms. "We were beginning to wonder when you'd show up.

It was very naughty of you to leave us to entertain Lady Mary all by ourselves."

Matthew gave her a brusque but affectionate hug. "You'd think you hadn't seen me for a month. Besides, my fiancée is charming and you know it. I'm sure you've been having a monstrously pleasant time with her."

"That's one way of describing it," Eden said in a wry voice.

Lady Mary Park was almost as great a snob as Evie's mother, but she *was* the daughter of an earl, the grand-daughter of a duke, and was bringing quite a respectable dowry into her marriage to Matt. Mamma was in alt over the impending nuptials, and Matt—a kind brother and duti-ful son but not a person given to deep thinking—seemed more than pleased with his future bride.

Eden, however, couldn't stand her and Evie wasn't far behind in her low opinion of Lady Mary.

"Sis, how've you been keeping?" Matt asked, bestowing a brotherly kiss on Evie's cheek. "I see you've found Wolf and Captain Gilbride."

"It was kind of you to invite them down," Evie said po-litely. "What luck that you ran into them at your club."

A puzzled frown creased Matt's pleasant, round face. "Seemed more like Wolf hunting me down, actually. Oh, I say," he said with a laugh. "That's rather a fun joke, don't you think? Wolf hunting me down? Get it?"

Eden pinched the space between her eyebrows while Captain Gilbride peered at Matt with a bemused expression. Will, however, directed a rather baleful stare at her brother, which struck Evie as odd. He knew as well as anyone that Matt had a ponderous sense of humor, so why should it surprise him now?

"Yes, dear, I'm sure we all appreciated your little joke," Evie said. "But what do you mean Wolf *hunted* you—"

"Good Lord," Captain Gilbride said, whipping a pocket watch from his waistcoat. "Surely it must be past time to change for dinner."

Drat. Evie cast a nervous glance at the house. In the shock of seeing Will, she'd forgotten about dinner.

"Confound it," Matt exclaimed. "Mamma expressly sent me out to look for you. She wanted to see you before dinner, Evie. And she looked rather put out, if you want to know the truth. What have you done to rile the old girl up now?"

Her cheeks burning with embarrassment, Evie glanced at Will, but he simply regarded her with a quiet sympathy that looked too much like pity. "I haven't done anything, as far as I know, but one never knows."

"Don't worry about Mamma," Eden said. "I'll take care of her. But we'd better all get back to the house or there will surely be a scene."

"That sounds amusing," Captain Gilbride commented sardonically.

"Trust me, it wouldn't be," Will replied.

Evie was almost tempted to laugh. Much had changed in the last ten years, but one thing still had the power to unite them all—fear of Lady Reese.

Her impulse to laugh died when Will stepped forward, as if ready to take her arm and escort her back to the house. She had an alarming sense that if she touched him, she might just faint from sheer nerves.

Fortunately, her sister turned her back on Captain Gilbride, who was politely asking if he could escort her to the house. Instead, Eden slipped her hand in the crook of Will's arm. When he responded with a startled look, she flashed him a grin.

"Come along, Wolf," Eden said. "I'm dying to hear all about your adventures." She cast a saucy glance at Gilbride, who looked slightly taken aback by her rebuff. "I'm sure you and the captain got up to all kinds of trouble over there."

Chattering gaily, Eden pulled Will across the lawn. Captain Gilbride, looking peeved, trailed in their wake.

Taking Matt's arm, Evie started to follow at a slower pace.

"Looks like Edie's up to her old tricks." Matt's pleasant, rather stolid features registered his disapproval. "She'll have those two at sixes and sevens before nightfall."

Evie frowned. "She's just teasing Will, that's all."

"Hope so for your sake, Sis. We all know how you feel about Will. Wouldn't be very sporting of Edie to try and cut you out."

She went light-headed at the possibility of Eden falling in love with Will. What a dreadful development that would turn out to be.

Then she remembered it didn't matter, because she didn't love Will anymore. "Don't be silly. There hasn't been anything between us for a very long time."

"Well, that's good to hear. You know how Mamma feels about him."

Their mother had only tolerated Will's presence because his guardian, Mr. Philip Endicott, was a wealthy member of the local gentry from a distinguished family. Her father thought the world of Mr. Endicott and had always welcomed Will to Maywood Manor. Will's true parentage was never spoken of, but that didn't mean her mother wasn't fully aware of it. To Mamma, just as damning as Will's illegitimate status was his lack of financial prospects. According to Lady Reese's social barometer, for all the royal blood that ran through his veins Will had nothing to recommend him as a potential suitor.

Not that Evie had ever cared about his prospects. She would have happily left her quiet comfortable life in the country and followed Will behind the drum in order to be with him.

Unfortunately, Will had never called upon her to make that sacrifice. "You needn't worry. I'm sure Will's not here for any reason other than a simple visit to old friends."

Matt gave a noncommittal grunt. "If you say so, but he seemed fairly keen about wrangling an invitation from me."

They were about to mount the shallow marble steps that led up to the back terrace, but Evie held him back. "Then you weren't joking about Wolf hunting you down?"

"But it was . . . oh, I see what you mean," he said with a slow grin. "You mean I wasn't joking about the fact that he was insistent about coming down to the old pile."

"Yes, that's what I mean," she said, stifling a sigh. Matt was not the sharpest pin in the box, but he was a kind and affectionate brother.

"He was certainly keen on it, I'll say that. I was already out the door when he came dashing after me. Said he heard we were having a jolly house party and would like the chance to come visit with everyone."

"He actually said *jolly?*"

Matt pursed his lips, obviously thinking hard. "Yes, he did. In fact, Sis, he was so blasted adamant that I was convinced he wanted to come courting, if you see what I mean."

She pressed a hand to her bodice, hating the instinctive flutter of hope in her chest. "Yes, I do see what you mean."

But why would Will even consider trying to rekindle their old relationship? What could possibly have sparked an interest in something that had lain dormant—if not lifeless—for years?

"I don't suppose he's heard about you and Michael Beaumont has he?" Matt asked.

Michael.

Evie's silly flight of fancy crashed back to earth. She could almost imagine the stone of the terrace cracking under her feet with the force of the impact as she was brought down by the fell hand of guilt.

"No, I don't suppose he has heard," she said. "After all, why would he?"

Chapter Four

"There, miss, I think that's done it," murmured Cora around the hairpins still in her mouth. Evie waited patiently as the maid inspected her coiffure, resisting the impulse to fiddle with the pins and ribbons that held her thick ringlets in place.

Cora, lady's maid to both Evie and Edie, gave a final nod of approval. "Don't you be yanking away at those pins and ribbons, Miss Evie. That hair of yours is so heavy you'll bring the entire thing down."

Evie spun around on the low stool at her dressing table. "But I haven't even touched it!"

Cora snorted knowingly, as was to be expected from a servant who'd been looking after her charge for years. "You're thinking about it, though. But it looks perfectly lovely just the way it is, so don't you go messing about with it."

Evie eyed the arrangement of apricot-colored ribbons interwoven through her hair that made the locks fall in artful disarray around her temples and neck. Because the ribbons matched her gown, the effect was both tasteful and pretty, making the most of her thick, honey-colored hair. Unfortunately, Cora's efforts were wasted as soon as Evie donned her spectacles. Most men never looked beyond those, immediately classifying her as a wallflower.

Given her tendency to clam up around men the assumption was generally correct. Evie hadn't a clue how to flirt, giggle, or listen with rapt attention when a young man droned on about his horses, a bet he'd made, or the *capital* batch of snuff he'd just acquired. True, it sometimes chafed to spend social occasions sitting against the wall with the chaperones and old ladies, but most days she cared not a hoot about any of it, including whether or not her outfit was all the crack. After all, Michael liked her perfectly well as she was, so why should she worry about her looks tonight?

She knew the answer to that question, but Will Endicott had nothing to do with her life anymore. There was simply no reason to wish for his good opinion, especially since Michael had made it clear he intended to ask her father's permission to marry her. The only reason he hadn't done so already was in deference to the objections Mamma would surely make. Michael had suggested that a long, unofficial courtship would give Lady Reese time to know him and recognize how devoted he was to Evie.

Now that their unofficial courtship had been going on for over a year, Evie thought he'd waited quite long enough. The sooner she and Michael were married, the sooner she could escape from under her mother's thumb.

As Cora moved around the bedroom tidying up, Evie contemplated her future as Mrs. Michael Beaumont. They'd planned a quiet, comfortable life with an emphasis on their charitable work. Michael was no more interested in the social activities of the *ton* than she was, and the fact that he was a Catholic—albeit one from a wealthy aristocratic family—meant that he, too, was something of an outsider like Evie. Those similarities had drawn her to Michael from the first. She was convinced they would have a good life together, and she saw no reason why the fact that she wasn't wildly in love with him should be an impediment to the success of their marriage.

Just the opposite was true, as Will's sudden reappearance today had so amply demonstrated. After only a few minutes in his company, Evie had found herself grappling with a host of strong and decidedly disconcerting emotions. That was not what she wanted. Not anymore. She wanted Michael and the quiet life they would have together, not the fevered, almost desperate love she'd once felt for Will.

Squelching the sound of mocking laughter in her head, Evie picked up her evening gloves and went to fetch Eden. She'd almost reached the door connecting their rooms when she heard the familiar staccato click of heels in the hallway.

"Confound it," she muttered, and then pinned what she hoped was a pleasant smile on her face.

The door opened and her mother swept into the room. "You may go, Cora," Lady Reese said, barely acknowledging the maid's quick curtsey.

Cora slipped out the door but not before giving Evie an encouraging wink. Evie had to choke back a laugh.

"What are you snorting about in that unattractive way, Evelyn?" her mother asked. "Ladies do not snort."

"I just thought of something amusing, that's all."

"Please keep amusing thoughts to yourself. If there's one thing a man cannot abide, it's a woman who thinks herself clever. You already have too much of a reputation as a bluestocking as it is, and that is fatal, as you well know."

"Yes, Mamma," Evie said in a resigned voice.

She'd heard a variation on this lecture every day for the last ten years, and her resentment had gradually dimmed. Mamma believed such admonitions were part of her maternal duties, and Evie was convinced that she had no idea how wounding her sharp words could be. Her mother truly loved her, but that she found Evie a trial was abundantly clear.

"Let me have a look at you, my dear," her mother said, as she always did before a party. One would think she would acknowledge that her daughters were old enough to get dressed by themselves, but such was not the case.

Then again, their mother was still a great beauty. Unlike Evie and Eden, she was tall and slender with a perfectly proportioned figure and the finely turned ankle of a debutante. She had elegant features, brilliant green eyes, and luxuriant chestnut-brown hair. It had always been a source of grievance to her that her children—especially her daughters—took after Papa's side of the family, a line that harked back to hardy yeoman's stock.

"For once, you look rather elegant," her mother finally said. "That color suits you, and the cut of the gown is quite flattering. You don't look as top-heavy as you sometimes do." She shook her head. "But try not to eat so much tonight, my dear. You don't want to lose what little figure you have."

"Michael Beaumont doesn't seem to find me unattractive, Mamma," Evie said, unable to help herself. "In fact, he seems to quite like my, er, frame."

Her mother curled a lip. "How vulgar. But I suppose one cannot be surprised that Mr. Beaumont lacks a certain degree of elegance, given his background."

Evie barely managed not to roll her eyes. Though Michael's family sprang from ancient and distinguished roots, going back to the Norman Conquest, they were Catholic. To her mother, that constituted an unforgiveable sin.

Mamma glided over to the reading chaise in front of the fireplace, her burgundy and cream silk gown settling in graceful folds as she sat. "Evelyn, I realize that you are expecting Mr. Beaumont to make you an offer. And although your father and I have grave reservations about a union with his family, it would seem that you have few other prospects."

"What about *my* prospects, Mamma?" Eden asked, catching the last of their mother's comment as she entered the room. "I'm the same age as Evie, after all. Actually, I'm older, which makes me even more perilously on the shelf than she is."

Evie repressed a grin. Eden had preceded her into the world by a mere twenty minutes, a fact her twin took great delight in pointing out. But the odd thing was, Eden acted very much like a big sister and was protective of Evie in a way that sometimes seemed more consistent with a parent than a sibling.

Predictably, Mamma's face lit up when her favorite child walked into the room. "Don't be silly, Eden. You're exceedingly popular. Just the other day, Lord Barton complained to me that you barely notice him. And you could certainly do worse than him, my love. He is the heir apparent to a marquess, after all."

"He's boring and has the most appalling teeth," Eden said, ruthlessly disposing of one of her many suitors. "I refuse to have children with that man."

Her mother sighed. "Very well, but one of these days you must settle down. You can't go flitting about like a butterfly for the rest of your life."

"I don't know why not," Eden muttered, flopping down on Evie's bed.

"Eden, do not crush your dress," Mamma admonished. "Now, as I was saying to Evelyn—"

"Mamma, look at the time," Evie interrupted. "We're already late, and you know how much you hate that."

"It's unattractive to lecture your elders, my dear," her

mother said. "As I was saying, you have an expectation regarding Michael Beaumont. Despite your lack of other alternatives, you should not be making hasty decisions or settling too quickly on a match that may not be to your advantage."

Evie exchanged a startled glance with her sister. "I'm sorry, Mamma, but I don't understand. I thought we'd already ascertained that I *had* no other eligible suitors. How has that changed?"

When Mamma lifted one eyebrow, meeting her gaze with an arch, knowing look, a sense of foreboding crawled up Evie's spine. She had to struggle to find a coherent reply to her mother's unspoken challenge. "Do you mean Will? Mamma, surely you must be jesting."

"I never jest, Evelyn, at least not about something this important."

"Isn't that ever the truth," Eden muttered.

Evie ignored her twin. "You're wrong, Mamma. Will is at loose ends, that's all. He thought it might be nice to visit old friends." At least she hoped that's all it was.

Eden sat up, swinging her feet over the edge of Evie's high bed. "Do you really think Wolf's come down expressly to see Evie?"

"Don't call him by that vulgar nickname." Their mother smoothly came to her feet. "I cannot fathom why else he would visit. Goodness knows I never encouraged him to drop in like this."

Evie spread her hands wide. "Then why would you wish him to court me? You don't even like him."

"William has done very well for himself," Mamma said. "He is on the Duke of Wellington's staff and apparently enjoys the favor of the Duke of York. I imagine he'll have quite a good career in the military or the diplomatic corps."

"You certainly never saw an advantage in his association with his father before," Evie blurted out. "Quite the opposite."

Her mother quelled her with a haughty look. "That is simply not true. My reservations about William always concerned his lack of financial prospects."

That was a hum if Evie had ever heard one. Mamma had *always* objected to Will's scandalous parentage.

Eden snapped her fingers. "It's obviously because Michael's a Catholic," she said to Evie. "And because of his politics, too, I imagine. Mamma would rather you marry good old Will, even if he is the by-blow of a prince."

"That is enough from you, Eden," their mother said irritably. "Your father would be most displeased to hear you speaking in so crude a fashion." She turned her back on her favorite and glowered at Evie. "I want you to be pleasant to Will tonight. No ducking into the corner with Mr. Beaumont to discuss that dreary charity of yours. Try, for once, to be charming instead of acting like the bespectacled bluestocking you are so determined to be."

She didn't wait for an answer but swept to the door, her short train swishing softly behind her. "Gather your things and come down, girls. We don't want to be any later than we are."

"We'll be right there, Mamma," Eden said. "I just have to fetch my fan."

Evie groaned, wanting nothing more than to climb into bed and hide her head under the pillow. Thanks to Will's mystifying reappearance, the fragile truce between Michael and her mother would surely collapse. If Mamma had even a hint that someone else might be willing to marry Evie—short of the dustman or the butcher—she would leap on that chance.

"Lord, what a mess," Eden said.

"Thank you for stating the obvious. It's bad enough that I now have to manage Will, but I'll also have to keep Mamma away from Michael. The poor lamb was just beginning to think he was actually making headway with her, too."

"You'd better spend some time with Wolf if you have any hope of spiking Mamma's guns. I'll take care of your gentle-hearted swain if you like." Eden adopted a martyred expression. "I'll even ask him to drone on about Catholic emancipation. If *that* doesn't show you what a devoted sister I am, nothing will."

"That's not funny, Edie. Michael is the most honorable person I know, and the causes he supports cry out for justice. I'm very proud of him, even if no one else in this family seems to understand why."

Eden glided over to rest her hands on Evie's shoulders. "Darling, I do support him, and you." Her sister's cornflower-blue eyes, identical to her own, inspected her with a rare gravity. "But sometimes I wonder if his work is the only thing that's attracted you to Michael. It's admirable what he does, but it takes up most of his life and now it's doing the same with yours. Don't you want more than that from marriage? You've always wanted a comfortable home in the country and children to spoil."

A sudden lump formed in Evie's throat. She could never hide anything from her twin, nor could Eden hide anything from her. It was both the most wonderful and the most frustrating aspect of their relationship.

"Of course I do," she forced out, "and so does Michael. But his work is very important to him, and I understand that."

"Yes, but I'm worried that his work will always come before you."

Evie broke away from her sister and rummaged in her dressing-table drawer for a fan. "Would you rather Michael be a typical young buck, wasting his days gambling and racing his curricle and his nights drinking and whoring? That is how most of the men we know spend their time, isn't it?"

Eden scoffed. "Wolf's not like that at all. He's serious, and it's one of the reasons you got along so well with him. You were like two old scholars in an ivory tower, always reading and discussing things."

"And that's what Michael and I do as well, so I would think you would like that. Would like *him*."

"I do like him. It's just that I don't think you love him," Eden insisted. "Not truly. Not that way you want to love and be loved."

Evie sighed. She adored her twin, but she was like a mastiff with a bone once she got an idea in her head. "You mean like the way I *used* to love. No, thank you. I do not care to repeat that experience. Michael and I have a perfectly comfortable relationship based on mutual affection and interests. I wish for nothing more."

"Ugh. That sounds ghastly."

"It does not—"

"Yes it does, and you know it," Eden interrupted. "You'd never be happy in such a tepid relationship. You've always been passionate about things, about *people,* no matter how much you try to hide it. But you're not passionate about Michael Beaumont."

Eden took a deep breath, as if steeling herself for an unpleasant task. "Darling, don't bite off my head, but I think Mamma is partly right. I think you *are* settling for Michael, and that worries me."

The lump that had been forming in Evie's throat now felt like a rock. She sank back onto the padded silk stool of her dressing table. "But what else can I do? Spend the rest of my life here with Mamma ordering me about? As imperfect as life with Michael *might* be, I truly cannot envision spending the rest of my days with our mother." She peered up at her sister. "*You* don't want to spend the rest of your life with our parents, do you?"

Eden gave an insouciant toss of her head. "I can handle them, though I agree it's not an ideal situation. Then again, neither is marriage."

"That doesn't leave you with many options, now does it?"

Eden began wandering around the room, inspecting the Staffordshire figurines of Robin Hood and Shakespeare on the mantelpiece, and then the books on the small table next to the reading chaise.

"Well?" Evie finally prompted.

Her twin flashed her a dazzling smile, her eyes glowing with the vibrancy and zest for life that had attracted so many suitors over the years. "You know I've always wanted to travel, perhaps to Egypt or even India. I have to get married *someday,* but wouldn't it be wonderful if I could marry an explorer? I think it would be grand fun to see the pyramids and the temples of Luxor, don't you?"

"No," Evie said in a blighting tone. "It's so hot in those countries, and you hate the heat even more than I do."

"Now you're just being beastly."

Evie smiled at her sister's comical grimace. Her twin *did* hate the heat, and Evie couldn't imagine her dealing with the dust, disease, and other difficulties of foreign travel. But, selfishly, Evie couldn't bear the idea of Eden having grand adventures and leaving her behind. It would leave a tremendous hole in her life that Evie feared she'd never be able to fill.

She collected her fan and gloves and stood up. "We'd better go. I'm sure Mamma is breathing fire by now."

Eden glanced at the clock on the mantel. "Oh, confound it, you're right." She dashed through the connecting door to her room and returned a moment later with her fan.

They hurried down the hallway of the wing that housed the family apartments. When they reached the top of the broad staircase leading down to the front hall, Eden stopped her.

"Evie, what *are* you going to do about Wolf? You know Mamma's going to keep on about this. She'll do everything she can to throw you together. I wouldn't be surprised if she nipped in to change the place cards in the dining room so that you're sitting next to him."

"Drat. I hadn't thought of that, but I'm sure you're right. It would be just like Mamma to do something so annoying." She thought for a moment. "We need to find out why Will's here. I refuse to believe he has any interest in courting me, but something's definitely off. He was acting oddly out there on the lawn."

Eden started them both back down the stairs. "Leave it to me. I'll get the truth out of him, by hook or by crook."

Knowing Eden's methods, that sounded rather alarming. But Evie *did* need to know what Will was about. Even though she hadn't seen him in years, she still knew him well enough to form a clear sense he was hiding something. If she could find out what it was, then she would be in a much better position to manage both him and her mother.

"Well, all right," she replied. "But please refrain from anything too outrageous."

Eden winked at her. "You must be thinking of some other sister of yours."

When they reached the bottom of the staircase, Eden pushed her toward the drawing room. "Tell Mamma I'll be along in a minute."

Evie frowned at her. "Where are you going?"

"To the dining room. I need to check out the seating arrangements."

"Mamma won't like it if you reorder things."

"Pish," Eden scoffed. "Just leave everything to me."

Chapter Five

As Will bowed to the fourth matron Lady Reese had introduced him to, he realized it was another indication that Evie's mother had taken him on as her special project. For some inexplicable reason, she'd latched onto him as soon as he'd set foot in the drawing room, dragging him through the rapid round of introductions that focused on guests with the most distinguished titles. She avoided the younger people, particularly the unmarried girls. Will found that most interesting.

Unfortunately, Lady Reese's obsequious attentions had thus far prevented Will from getting close to his target, Evie, who didn't seem particularly interested in talking to him in the first place. Lady Reese had been gradually working him around the room in an obvious slow pursuit of her daughter, but Evie had adroitly avoided getting trapped. She'd learned long ago how to avoid her mother, and that particular skill was on full display tonight.

Actually Will had a feeling that Evie was doing her best to avoid *him*.

He could feel his pleasant expression slipping as he watched Evie take Michael Beaumont's arm, all but snuggling up to him. Beaumont seemed equally entranced with her, and Will had to give him credit for looking past the self-effacing exterior to the woman within. Evie had been deemed a wallflower years ago, her quiet manner and inability to engage in social inanities sealing her fate. Her insistence on wearing spectacles didn't help either, although he knew how much she hated having to squint at everything like a *dreary old mole,* as she'd once called herself.

Still, it had been something of a shock to see her this afternoon. The spectacles, combined with her drab gown and plain hairstyle, had made her look like a disapproving governess, not the sweet-natured, loving girl he'd grown up with It seemed as if all the joy of youth had been drained from her. Standing next to Eden—who was still larger than life and full of energy—had made the change all the more apparent.

But tonight, Evie was more the girl he remembered, younger and prettier in a gown of antique gold that burnished the highlights in her honey-colored hair and softly draped a surprisingly lush figure. Evie and Eden had always been sturdily framed girls, but they'd both grown into what could only be described as magnificent figures. But unlike her twin, whose bosom was on ample display, Evie made little effort to capitalize on her physical charms.

Not that Michael Beaumont apparently needed any additional encouragements. In fact, he gazed at Evie with a smile so fatuous it made Will clench his teeth.

The light tap of a fan on his arm recalled him to his surroundings. He blinked as he took in Lady Reese's arched, haughty eyebrows and the expectant expressions of Lord and Lady Portmire, an elderly couple he'd met only a few minutes ago.

"Well, William, what do you think of Lord Portmire's suggestion?" Lady Reese asked with a touch of asperity.

"Do you think his lordship, the Duke of Wellington, would agree?"

Good God. He'd completely lost the thread of the conversation. Will rarely had difficulty taking part in conversations while keeping his eye on a target—it was elementary spycraft—but Evie was throwing him off his game.

Either that or he'd forgotten how truly boring conversation at an English house party could be.

"Ah, as to that, Lord Portmire," he started to hedge, "I think—"

A strong hand landed on his shoulder. "Ah, there you be, laddie. Lord Reese and Lord Quarterman are wantin' to talk to you about something verrry particular, so ye'd better come along with me," Alec said in a hearty and entirely inconsistent brogue.

From the sour look on Lady Reese's face, she thought that keeping the host waiting was preferable to interrupting the hostess. But since Alec was the wealthy grandson of an earl, she finally managed to rearrange her elegant features in a stiff smile.

"Of course, Captain Gilbride, you and William mustn't keep my husband waiting. But before you dash off, let me introduce you to Lord and Lady Portmire."

Will had to hold back a groan when his cousin planted a flourishing kiss on the back of Lady Portmire's hand and paid her an extravagant compliment. Apparently, elderly ladies were no more immune to Alec's charm than the average deb or Spanish innkeeper's daughter.

"Oh, Captain Gilbride," Lady Portmire trilled, "you do look so dashing in your Scottish regimentals. And I love that, that . . ."

When she waggled a finger in the direction of Alec's groin, Will swore he could hear Lady Reese's molars grinding together.

"Sporran, my lady," Alec answered, giving the old woman a roguish wink.

Lady Portmire let out a surprisingly girlish giggle. "Oh, my dear captain, I do hope you're sitting next to me at dinner this evening."

Lord Portmire gaped at his wife, clearly stunned by her behavior.

"We can only hope, my lady," Alec replied. "And, now, if you'll excuse us, duty calls." With that, he took Will's arm and decisively pulled him away.

"I take it that Lord Reese does not, in fact, desire our company," Will said.

"Of course not," Alec said. "I was just saving yer arse."

"Will you please leave off playing the noble son of Arran? It gives me a headache when you do that."

"You're not the only one," Alec said. "But it does work wonders with the old ladies. Aye, and with the young ones, too."

"After that performance you'd best hope you're *not* sitting next to Lady Portmire at dinner. I suspect she'd have her hands all over your *sporran*."

"Thank you for the unnecessary warning, but I suggest we turn our minds to business. Have you talked to Beaumont yet? Because I haven't been able to get near the man. Miss Whitney seems to be guarding him like a mamma cat with only one kitten."

"I've yet to be introduced. Lady Reese has been parading me around the drawing room for the last half hour, as I'm sure you've noticed."

"I have." Alec swiped a goblet of wine off the tray of a passing footman. "You said she didn't like you, so that's a bit odd, don't you think?"

"I do think, but I can't worry about that now. I have to spend some time with Beaumont—and Evie."

"Let's deploy a new tactic. We'll circle round and come at them from opposing sides. Trap them in the gully, so to speak."

Will didn't much enjoy approaching Evie like he would an enemy, but he nodded his agreement. Alec wandered off at an angle, as if heading to speak to Lord Reese, before casually strolling around to come up behind Evie. Will, meanwhile, made a head-on approach.

When he was still several feet away, he could see Evie's shoulders go up around her ears as if she sensed him nearing, even in the midst of a serious conversation with Beaumont. She turned her head, snagging Will's gaze. Behind the glint of reflected candlelight on her spectacle lenses, her eyes widened with dismay.

Damn.

Aside from her evident distrust making his job more difficult, he hated the idea that she wasn't comfortable around him. He supposed it was inevitable given the years apart and the way he'd disappointed her, but he didn't share her unease. From the first moment he'd seen her today, he'd been overcome by a sense of familiarity so strong it had robbed him of breath. Was it merely a reactive instinct to returning to his childhood haunts? He'd not felt that way when visiting with Aunt Rebecca only a few weeks ago, but perhaps the sorrow over his uncle's death had mitigated the cheer of that particular homecoming.

Beaumont, noticing Evie's distraction, had broken off and turned to face Will with a puzzled look on his features. When their gazes met, Beaumont's head jerked back as if he had just sighted the enemy. He moved a step closer to Evie, one hand disappearing behind her back, and Will had little doubt that Beaumont's hand now rested protectively on her waist. Obviously, the man had good instincts where his almost-fiancée was concerned—a useful if unwelcome bit of knowledge.

"Wolf . . . Will . . . good evening," Evie stammered. "It's . . . it's nice to see you again."

Evie's awkwardness in company was nothing new. But awkwardness with *him* was. Will gave her a slight bow and the warmest smile in his arsenal.

Her smooth complexion pinked up with a pretty blush and her generous bosom rose and fell on a quick exhalation of breath, the plump mounds straining against her bodice. It took a great deal of willpower on his part to resist the temptation to take a longer glance down.

"I'm glad I accepted Matt's invitation," he said. "It's been like coming home, seeing Maywood Manor and all my old friends."

Her full mouth thinned into a narrow line as she transformed from flustered to annoyed in the space of one breath. "One could wonder that you didn't make the trip sooner, but never mind. I'm glad you're enjoying yourself. Certainly my mother seems happy to see you."

Ah, now that was a tidy detail. She obviously thought her mother was up to something too.

Beaumont glanced at Evie and cleared his throat in a pointed fashion. Her shoulders jerked even higher and her cheeks went from pink to red.

"Oh, dear, I'm forgetting my manners," she said. "Michael, allow me to introduce you to Captain William Endicott of the 1st Royal Dragoons. Will, this is the Honorable Michael Beaumont, a very good friend of mine."

After murmured acknowledgments of the introduction, silence held sway for a few seconds as the two men took each other's measure. Will might have been amused at the way Beaumont's gaze flicked over him in sharp assessment, as if sizing up a rival, if he didn't still have a hand on Evie's back. In fact, from Will's angle, he could see that it rested perilously close to the swell of her pretty arse.

Will ignored his growing irritation and focused on the man in front of him. Beaumont was almost as tall as Will but thinner and looked more the scholarly sort than a Corinthian. His style was respectable although hardly that of a dandy—his Oriental-style cravat and neatly brushed hair attested to that. He held himself with a quiet sort of confidence that Evie would probably find attractive.

More important was what he deduced from Beaumont's lean, clever features, and the brown eyes that shone with intensity and intelligence. If the sharpness in that dark gaze was any indication, Beaumont was a man who didn't miss much. If he *was* involved in a conspiracy, Will had the distinct impression he would be a formidable opponent. That meant that Evie—if she really was about to marry the man—could be in danger, after all.

Even a remote possibility of that was not acceptable to Will.

When neither man seemed inclined to break the uncomfortable silence, Evie let out an impatient sigh and attempted to fill in the breach. "Will is an old childhood friend, Michael. We practically grew up together."

Beaumont's smile transformed his features from ones of narrow suspicion to those of a man who clearly had warm feelings toward the woman standing before him. "Then the captain is indeed a lucky man, Evelyn. I wish I had known you when you were a little girl. I'm sure you were most charming."

When Beaumont's fingers inched a fraction closer to Evie's bottom, Will lifted a pointed eyebrow at the offending hand. Evie let out a tiny gasp and took a hasty step to the side.

"I'm sure I wasn't," she said with an uncomfortable laugh. "Wolf, er, Will could tell you that. Eden and I were both perfectly horrid little girls."

Beaumont looked a little embarrassed to be caught with his hand all but on Evie's arse, but he made a quick recovery. "I'm sure that's not true, at least in your case, as no doubt the captain must attest to."

"Evie was a sweetheart," Will agreed. "Now, Edie . . . that's a different story. You took your life in your hands when you embarked on one of her adventures. But Evie never had anything but the kindest of natures."

Evie's eyes went wide at his compliment. Will held her gaze, silently conveying that he meant every word of it.

But her reaction was not what he expected. Her expression grew pinched and anxious, and she moved in Beaumont's direction, as if looking for support. Beaumont rested a reassuring hand on her arm.

That made it clear there was some sort of understanding between them, and Will liked that as little as he liked the fact that Evie turned instinctively to Beaumont for protection . . . against him.

"How did you and Evie meet, Mr. Beaumont? Is *your* family old friends with the Reese family, as well?"

"I'm afraid we didn't have that pleasure until a few years ago," Beaumont said in a haughty tone. For a supposed radical, he could look down his aristocratic nose with the best of them.

"We met at a lecture at the Royal Society," Evie added with a forced-looking smile. "We discovered we shared an interest in Celtic history, and Michael was kind enough to loan me a number of books on the subject. That led to discussions of other matters of mutual interest."

Evie was interested in Celtic history? That was news to Will.

"And a fortunate day it was for me when I decided to attend that lecture," Michael said warmly, "and for St. Margaret's, as well. You were the saving of us, Evelyn."

A genuine, sweet smile curled her lips, making her look young and shyly pretty. Will's gut clenched with the knowledge that Beaumont could tease out of hiding the Evie of days gone by, when he couldn't.

Focus on the task. "St. Margaret's?" he asked with polite interest. "I'm afraid I'm not familiar with that."

"It's a church and a charity in St. Giles," Evie replied. "Michael is one of the patrons, and I sometimes help out. I'm sure it's nothing you'd be interested in, Will."

"I'm interested in everything you do, Evie," Will said in a gently chiding tone. "You should know that by now."

"Really?" she said. "I would have thought the opposite was true, given our history."

The unexpected riposte robbed him of speech for a few moments. Beaumont stepped into the conversational breach. "I'm sure you have no interest in our simple little charity, Captain Endicott. Anything we could tell you would surely pale in comparison to your military adventures in the Peninsula, for instance."

Will was tempted to grab the blighter by his cravat and pull him up on his toes, but Beaumont's jab had revealed something important. Evie had clearly talked to Beaumont about him, perhaps even explaining their falling out.

And now she'd gone back to looking awkward, as if she'd suddenly remembered how much she loathed conflict. "Michael, I'm sure it must be time to go in for dinner. Will you escort me in?"

Just as Beaumont turned to take her arm, Alec strolled up and smoothly inserted himself between Evie and her swain. "Miss Whitney, how delightful to see you again. I must tell you, I find your family completely charming. Your mother, in particular, has been most welcoming."

"That would be a change," Evie muttered.

Will finally gave in to his darker angels. "I'm sorry, I didn't catch that."

"Never mind," she gritted out. "Michael—"

"I don't believe we've met," Alec said, turning to Beaumont with an expansive smile. "Miss Whitney, will you do the honors?"

Evie sighed and then performed the most perfunctory of introductions. "The *Honorable* Michael Beaumont, Captain Gilbride."

She stressed the *Honorable* as if to suggest that Michael was above their touch. She obviously didn't know that Alec was heir to one of the wealthiest earldoms in Britain. Still, it wasn't like Evie to indulge in snobbery. It was more evidence of how rattled she was.

"Alec, we were talking about Mr. Beaumont's charity in London," Will added. "In St. Giles. It sounds a most worthy cause, which I am sure would interest you greatly."

His cousin needed no further prompting.

"Oh, indeed," Alec responded, appropriately enthused. "A man can't do enough to help the unfortunate poor, can he? You must tell me all about it, Mr. Beaumont. I'm indeed vastly interested."

Will had to swallow a laugh. As usual, Alec was laying it on rather thick. Evie's features displayed her skepticism, but Beaumont was peering at him with an arrested expression on his scholarly face.

"You take an interest in charitable works, Captain Gilbride?" he cautiously asked.

"Lord, yes, as does my grandfather, the Earl of Riddick. We're forever talking about where we can do the most good.

There's such a great need, especially in the stews, don't you agree? It's positively shocking what those poor devils there have to suffer."

Though Will initially thought Alec was overplaying his hand, he was wrong. From the gleam in Beaumont's eyes, the man was well and truly hooked.

"In that case, I'd like very much to tell you about the work we do at St. Margaret's," Beaumont replied.

"Splendid. I can't think of anything I'd rather talk about." Alec took Beaumont's arm and started to lead him away.

Beaumont seemed to recollect himself. "Evelyn, do you mind—"

"Not to worry, Mr. Beaumont, I'll take care of her," Will replied.

That brought the scowl back to the man's face, but Alec steered him toward the other side of the room, talking with obvious enthusiasm. In a matter of seconds, Beaumont was reengaged in the discussion and had apparently forgotten all about Evie.

Will had no intention of making the same mistake.

He turned back to her with a warm smile. She nervously flapped her lace fan against the side of her leg, looking worried and suspicious. "What are you up to, Will?"

He turned his back to the room, shielding her from observation. "Why should I be up to anything, Evie? I simply want to speak with my oldest and dearest friend."

Prettily flushed a few minutes ago, she now looked pale and strained. "Oh, is that what we are? Perhaps we have different definitions of friendship. In my understanding of the term, friends stay in touch with each other. They answer letters and make an effort to see each other when they come back home, for however brief a time. And they certainly don't abandon one of them to wonder what she'd done to deserve such shabby, hurtful treatment from her *oldest and dearest friend*."

For a moment, Will was too shocked to muster an answer. They stared at each other, the years and the distance falling away under the onslaught of her emotional pain. The hell of it was that he truly didn't *have* a good answer, for he'd done exactly that—abandoned their friendship. Not out of malice or disregard, but simply because he'd been too idiotically selfish to understand the impact it could have on someone as sensitive and loving as Evie.

Then she blinked, as she recalled her surroundings. Flushing a bright pink, she looked away. "I had no right to say any of those things, Will. Please forgive me."

He let out a heavy sigh. "You have every right to be angry with me. But I never meant to hurt you, sweetheart, and that's the truth. I was just too young and stupid to know any better. Or to know what I truly wanted."

She met his gaze, her cornflower-blue eyes big and bright with unshed tears. "And what do you want now?"

He wanted to tell her that he was sorry he'd been such a fool, and that he should never have turned his back so firmly on her. That he wanted them to be close again, as close as they'd once been.

But there was another truth staring him in the face. As much as he regretted hurting her and losing her friendship, he *didn't* regret his decision to enter the army. Oh, he'd been clumsy and could have done it better, but he'd found the life he'd wanted there. And, at the time, that life hadn't included her.

"Evie, I'm sorry." He grimaced at the inadequacy of his response. It was bad enough he had to lie to her about Beaumont and the real reason he was visiting Maywood Manor. Will refused to compound that ugly but necessary deception with vague promises he couldn't possibly keep.

The swift passage of pain across her face wiped away the precious glimpse of the sweet girl he'd once loved.

"Never mind," she said in a flat voice. "Both of us, as you say, were young and stupid, especially me. I should have known better than to expect anything from you."

Her bitter pessimism sparked him to anger. "Evie, I am truly sorry I hurt you, but I never once made a promise to you that I couldn't keep."

"No, you were always very careful in that respect, weren't you? God forbid you should accept any responsibility for your actions."

Evie started to move away but he lashed out a hand to grasp her wrist. She startled, and then tugged. "Let me go," she hissed, "before someone notices you acting like a bully."

"A bully?" he asked with disbelief. "I know I hurt you and I'm truly sorry for that, but I know how strong you were, too, despite your shy ways. You were *always* the strong one, much more so than Eden, in fact. You were happy, too, no matter what was going on around us. But now I barely recognize you."

She went so pale she looked ready to swoon. But when he reached out for her, she pushed his hand away.

"I'm sorry I don't live up to your expectations," she said, obviously fighting for control. "It must be such a disappointment to know that I've finally grown up. But you see, I now have better things to do than moon over arrogant, handsome boys, and trail behind them like a lovesick puppy."

"It wasn't like that, and you know it. I remember we were happy—with each other." God, even to his own ears he sounded like a fool.

"That is true," she said in a low voice, trying not to draw attention. Her tone seethed with resentment. "But what *I* remember is that the rest of my life wasn't happy or easy. I was running this household by the time I was fifteen, because Mamma couldn't be bothered to do it. But when I was with you, I tried to be what you wanted me to be— happy and carefree, the kind of girl I thought you would love. But it didn't work. You left me anyway and never looked back."

He wanted to protest, but she cut him off. "And once I got over the pain and shock of being summarily abandoned, I finally got the chance to be who I wanted to be. Not who *you* wanted me to be."

Before he could respond, he heard the soft patter of evening slippers rushing up behind him.

"Is everything all right, Evie?" Eden asked, barging past him.

"Yes, dear, everything is fine. Will and I were just reminiscing over old times."

There was no possible reply to that, so Will simply held his tongue.

Eden narrowed her eyes at him and leaned in a bit, apparently ready to jab him in the chest with her finger. Or slap him. "I'll be talking with you later, Wolf Endicott." It was definitely more threat than promise.

"I'll look forward to it," he responded dryly.

Eden let out a disgusted snort and took her sister's arm. "Come along, darling. Michael's waiting to take you in to dinner."

They marched right past Alec, barely deigning to notice him as he hastily stepped out of their way. Will glanced around, looking for a bare spot of wall against which to bang his thick skull.

"Looks like that went well," Alec observed as he strolled up.

"You can't even begin to imagine," Will said.

"I did my part, so it's not my fault you don't have your

head in the game. But it's not like you to let a pretty girl twist you in knots like that, Wolf." He paused for a moment. "Well, I suppose it was only to be expected."

"What the hell is that supposed to mean?" When Alec started to answer, Will waved a hand. "Never mind. How did it go with Beaumont?"

"The man has angels coming out of his backside, to hear him tell it. But I'll fill you in later." He nodded across the drawing room. "It's time for dinner, and you're to take in Miss Eden Whitney. I believe she's waiting for you."

Sure enough, Eden stood by the door, glaring at him like he'd just erupted from the depth of Hades in a belch of fire and brimstone.

"Good God," Will muttered. "What the hell have I done to deserve this?"

A mocking laugh from Alec was his only answer.

Chapter Six

Evie hovered outside the breakfast parlor, trying to work up her courage. Sooner or later she'd have to face Will and apologize for her rude behavior the previous evening. More than one person, including her mother, had seen her deliver him that unfortunate scold in the drawing room. Even Michael had noticed her bad temper. Not that she'd done a very good job of hiding it.

As for Will, she'd managed to avoid him for the rest of the evening, thanks to Eden switching the place cards in the dining room. Predictably, their mother *had* seated Evie next to Will, but Eden had shifted him next to garrulous Lady Portmire. Evie had read his annoyance in the tight set to his jaw, but he'd treated the elderly countess with faultless courtesy.

Mamma had been startled and clearly displeased by the switch but had done nothing but direct an angry glare at Evie, wrongly attributing blame to her, as usual. Not that Evie minded. She would happily accept a lecture if it meant saving her from the discomfort of having to spend hours sitting next to Will. After last night, she could almost wish never to see him again.

That proved Will's assertion that she'd turned into a coward, even if he hadn't expressed it quite like that.

"Is something wrong, Miss Evelyn?"

Swallowing a startled squeak, Evie turned to find one of the footmen standing behind her with a rack of toast in his hand.

"No, not at all," she said with a weak smile. "Here, let me get the door for you."

The young man looked appropriately horrified at the suggestion. "No, miss, that won't be necessary."

He scuttled around her to open the door. When she preceded him into the room, he breathed out an audible sigh of relief, leaving Evie to reflect on the fact that she was capable of upsetting even the junior footman with very little effort. She supposed it took a certain amount of talent to be able to offend most everyone she knew, except for Michael, who never took offense at anything she said or did. No wonder she liked him so much.

Ducking her head, she braced herself to face their guests, including Will.

Sunshine streamed through the Venetian windows and threw bars of light and shadow across the pink and green floral carpet. The breakfast parlor was one of the prettiest rooms in the house, with pale green walls trimmed with glossy black panels, and a set of lovely Queen Anne sideboards against the wall. Evie and Eden often whiled away a good part of the morning in this room reading their correspondence, planning the day's activities, or simply chatting. It was a pleasant, peaceful way to start the day.

It also had the added virtue of being the only room their mother rarely set foot in. Mamma invariably had breakfast in bed before she repaired to her private parlor at the back of the house. Unfortunately, she had chosen to come down for breakfast this morning, which meant she had something up her sleeve. Only in the case of a dire emergency did Mamma set foot out of her room before eleven o'clock, even when guests were visiting. The fact that she was down before ten today was alarming, to say the least.

"There you are, Evelyn," Mamma said from her place at the foot of the table. "I was beginning to think I'd have to send a footman up to fetch you."

Evie murmured an apology, though it wouldn't do a whit of good in deflecting her mother's ire.

A quick glance around the table revealed that only a few of their guests had joined them. The ladies hadn't come down, and some of the men had probably eaten earlier and then gone fishing with her father. Eden was there, of course, and Matt, along with Michael and Lord Portmire, who looked sleepy and befuddled, as usual.

Unfortunately, Will and Captain Gilbride were there too, which meant Evie's luck had completely run out.

The men all rose to their feet and bid her good morning, then Will pulled out the empty seat beside him for her. His rather stern mouth curved up in a polite smile that failed to span the distance to his riveting blue eyes. If one could be said to be smiling and scowling at the same time that was Will.

His eminently reasonable demeanor was better than she deserved, but she still had no intention of sitting next to him, if for no other reason than he might be tempted to *accidentally* dump his plate of coddled eggs and ham in her lap. There was no point in tempting fate.

"Come sit by me, dearest," Eden said brightly, patting the empty seat next to her.

Feeling like the worst sort of coward, she headed to the other side of the table, dropping into the seat between Eden and Michael with a barely repressed sigh of relief. Between her mother's glare and Will's narrow-eyed inspection, she felt like she'd been forced to run a gauntlet.

"Good morning, my dear," Michael murmured in a solicitous voice. Like Will, he subjected her to a close inspection, but his gaze conveyed concern rather than disapproval.

No wonder he looked concerned. After a sleepless night, Evie fancied she looked rather like Lady Alice, the pale, pinch-faced Elizabethan ancestor who peered down from her portrait in the upstairs gallery. Legend had it that Alice haunted the top floor, drifting around in an annoyingly insubstantial manner, frightening the maids. Evie felt rather stretched and insubstantial herself this morning, although no one with her sturdy frame could be accused of fading away. She could never truly play a tragedy queen, given that she was as healthy as an ox. She simply wasn't built for lying around on couches in dimly lit rooms, vinegar in one hand and smelling salts in the other.

"Can I make up a plate for you?" Michael asked.

"No, thank you," she said, forcing a smile.

It was time to stop feeling fragile. True, she owed Will an apology and that wouldn't be fun, but there was no reason to mope about simply because an old friend had stopped by for a visit. She should be happy to see him, and supremely grateful he had escaped the carnage of Waterloo unscathed.

"I'll just have tea and toast," she said. "Then we can spend the rest of the morning going over the books, if you'd like."

Michael had brought a great deal of paperwork with him, including the ledgers for the charity school at St. Margaret's and the other relief services the church provided to the local population. They also needed to write a series of letters to prospective donors, since their foremost patron, Lord Ellsworth, had died a few months ago. They had enough funds to keep things running for the rest of the year, but the financial situation would grow precarious after that. While Michael channelled a good deal of his own money directly into St. Margaret's coffers, that couldn't go on forever, as Lord Leger, his father, had recently made clear. Although sympathetic to the travails of the Irish immigrants, the earl believed his youngest son far too willing to spend his money on the *undeserving poor*.

"If you wish," Michael replied with a smile, "but it's a lovely day out. If you'd like to do something else, we can work on the books later."

"Now, Miss Evelyn, why would ye be wantin' to spend the morning with your head in a fusty old book?" Captain Gilbride said from across the table. "Surely we can do better, especially on a day as fine as this."

Evie peered at him, mystified by the captain's inconsistent brogue. Most times, his accent mirrored that of an English aristocrat who'd spent his formative years at Eton and Oxford. But once or twice last night he'd slipped into a Scottish accent heavy enough to make her think he might leap to his feet and commence dancing a reel. She was beginning to suspect that Gilbride affected the accent as more of a joke than anything else, although she couldn't imagine why. Her suspicions were confirmed by the incredulous lift to Will's eyebrows as he eyed his friend.

"No doubt you're longing for an excursion in the great outdoors," Will commented sardonically to Alec. "What do you have in mind?"

"I've heard about some bonny ruins no more than a half hour's ride away. An old abbey, I believe."

"That would be the Abbey of St. Osmund," Eden said in a bored voice.

Most visitors to Maywood Manor made the trip to the picturesque ruins, and Evie and her sister had been there at least a dozen times. As pretty as the ruins were, she had no desire to see them again.

"Yes, that's it," Gilbride said with a smile so charming that any woman but Eden would have dissolved into a puddle at his feet.

But Evie's twin simply shrugged, making her disdain for the suggestion abundantly clear. "It's an old Cistercian abbey that fell into ruins after the monasteries were shut down. It's pretty, but nothing unusual."

"Aye, but it sounds like the perfect way to spend the morning with a pair of lovely lasses such as you and Miss Evelyn," Gilbride said. "There'll be ample opportunity to wander among the ruins, I imagine, and no telling what a lad and a lassie might get up to."

The captain punctuated his outrageous comment with a broad wink at Eden. When he winced, Evie was certain Will had just kicked him under the table.

After several moments of highly fraught silence in which Eden seemed too stunned to respond, Mamma dredged up a strained smile. "I think that's a splendid idea, girls," she said. "You can either take the landau or ride with the men."

Of course.

This was what Mamma had been hoping for all along, probably intending to throw her together with Will. She had little doubt her mother had told Gilbride about the ruins in the first place.

"Thank you, Mamma," she answered, trying to sound appropriately regretful. "I'm afraid Michael and I have a great deal of work to do this morning. Perhaps tomorrow might serve."

Her mother put her teacup down with a decided click. "Evelyn, that kind of cavalier rudeness is something I particularly abhor. Captain Gilbride has gone out of his way to propose an entertainment that all the young people can enjoy. I'm shocked you would respond in so negative a fashion."

Evie froze. Rarely did her mother deliver her scolds in front of anyone but family members. To be castigated publicly, especially in front of Will, made Evie sick to her stomach. Then again, her mother had never treated Will with any special consideration, and it wouldn't be the first time he'd heard Lady Reese take her daughter to task.

Sure enough, when Evie snuck a peek at him, Will was regarding her mother with open disapproval. In fact, he scowled so fiercely that Evie began to worry that her mother would both take notice *and* offense.

Eden sprang to her defense. "Mamma, there's no need to poke up at Evie. I have no desire to go to the ruins, either." She switched her gaze to Captain Gilbride. "If you want to know the truth, they're a dead bore, and certainly not the way *I* want to spend the day." Her tone clearly indicated she found the captain a dead bore too.

"No one is interested in your opinion, Eden," Mamma said in a severe voice. "Evelyn, I will not have you spending the day locked up in the library with Mr. Beaumont, conspiring over that dreary charity of yours. For one, it's not healthy. For another, I don't approve of your associating with the type of unsavory and dangerous characters frequenting that part of the city. I've been meaning to talk to your father about it for an age, and I intend to do so as soon as possible."

Evie could feel Michael stiffen beside her. His reaction was understandable since Mamma's tone and expression made it clear she considered him one of the unsavory characters lurking around St. Margaret's.

"Mamma, that's unjust," she blurted out, her anger on Michael's behalf pushing her to respond. "Mr. Beaumont and I are doing wonderful work in St. Giles, and it's unfair to suggest otherwise. And I have no intention of giving up my work, no matter what you or Papa might think."

Her mother's gasp of outrage hissed through the awkward silence that had fallen over the breakfast parlor.

"Now you've done it," Eden murmured under her breath.

Already regretting her outburst, Evie cast a shamefaced glance at Will and Gilbride. But Will wasn't paying any attention to her or to Mamma. Instead, he studied Michael with a sort of focused interest, as if Michael's reaction to the ugly family scene was the only one that mattered.

"Well, this is a pickle," Gilbride said. "My dear Lady Reese, I do beg your forgiveness. It was foolish of me to assume that the ladies and Mr. Beaumont didn't already have plans for the day. I'm happy to postpone our outing until a more convenient time."

As upset as Evie was, she couldn't help noticing the captain's Highland brogue had disappeared—again. More to the point, his smile was so ruefully charming that even Mamma would have trouble withstanding it. Evie added thanking Captain Gilbride to her mental list of things to do that day.

"Not at all, my dear sir," her mother replied, unbending a bit. "I entirely support your idea to visit the ruins. As soon as I'm finished with my tea, I will instruct my housekeeper to have a picnic lunch made up." She leveled a stern glance in Evie's direction, one that said *and I'll deal with you later*. "The girls can be ready to go within the hour."

Eden let out a dramatic sigh. "Mamma, if Evie and Mr. Beaumont don't wish to go . . ." She trailed off when their mother's eyebrows crawled up her forehead.

"I think it a delightful idea," Michael said in a cheerful voice. "A lovely day such as this is not to be wasted." He nodded politely across the table to Gilbride. "Thank you for suggesting it, sir. I can't remember the last time I went on a picnic."

Gilbride looked startled but quickly recovered. "Capital! It's all set, then."

Mamma blinked several times, obviously torn between relief that she'd gotten her way and annoyance that it was Michael who'd smoothed things over.

"Are you sure?" Evie whispered to him. "I know how you detest that sort of outing. And we have so much work to do."

Michael gave her such a sweet smile that Evie remembered why she was going to marry him. She wasn't madly in love with him, but no man had ever treated her with such courtesy and consideration. That surely counted a great deal more than passion, or the quivery feeling one got behind the knees when a certain person walked into the room.

But even as Michael assured her that he was agreeable to the change in plans, Evie felt Will's gaze pulling at her, so familiar and strong that it frightened her. Reluctantly, she met it head-on, expecting to see sardonic amusement over this morning's domestic tempest in a teapot.

But it wasn't amusement or even mockery she discerned in his gaze. His expression was intent as he studied her, and when his gaze flicked over to Michael, it darkened with something that looked surprisingly like resentment. Or was it jealousy?

That, she told herself as she rose to her feet, simply couldn't be true.

Chapter Seven

Evie hurried through the entrance hall as she pulled on her gloves. She was woefully late since she'd been dragging her feet upstairs in the vain hope that the riding party would leave without her. In fact, she'd almost worked up the courage to defy her mother's orders when Eden had rushed in, determined not to leave without her.

"I know you don't want to see Will," her sister had said, "but you can't hide away forever. The war is over and we'll be running into him on a regular basis, so you'd better get used to it. Besides, Mamma will raise a horrid fuss and that benefits no one, especially Michael."

That annoying logic had punctured Evie's resistance. Drawing her mother's fire onto Michael's head was hardly fair, given the noble gesture he'd already made to deflect her ill temper.

Smiling absently at the footman holding the door open, Evie rushed outside but was forced to pause under the portico until her vision adjusted to the bright morning sunshine. The effect was always intensified by the glare off her spectacles' lenses, and it took a few moments until the motes dancing in front of her eyes began to clear.

"About time." Eden grinned at her from atop Castor, her bay gelding. "I thought we were going to have to send out a search party."

"They wouldn't have had to search very hard, would they?" Evie replied tartly as she descended the shallow marble steps.

Castor shook his head, obviously eager to be off. Eden settled him with an easy touch, totally in control of the large horse. She looked enchanting, as usual, in her forest-green riding habit and dashing feathered cap.

It always amazed Evie that her sister rode so confidently given the fact she refused to wear spectacles. Evie's heart leapt to her throat every time her twin took a hedge or soared over a ditch, but Eden never seemed to falter. She'd developed strategies over the years to compensate for her poor eyesight, one of which had been to find and train Castor until he was uncannily attuned to his mistress. It was the only thing that kept Evie from blurting out hysterical warnings every time her sister galloped out in her bold, fearless style.

She glanced around the small group on the gravel drive, mounted and ready for their expedition. Michael smiled down at her from one of the gentler horses from Maywood's stables, while Captain Gilbride allowed his gigantic black stallion to prance around the forecourt. Lord Deerling and Sir Reginald Baskerton, two of Eden's most persistent suitors, had joined them as well, flanking Eden as they vied for her attention.

But Will was missing, as was a groom with Evie's horse.

"Where's Pollux?" she asked, referring to her gelding. She didn't enquire after Will, since she had no intention of displaying any interest in him.

"Lady Reese thought you might be more comfortable riding in Will's curricle," Gilbride answered. "Capital idea, as I told your dear mamma. That way you can also bring the picnic basket. I must admit to already feeling rather peckish, despite this morning's excellent breakfast."

When that comment earned him an incredulous stare from Eden, Gilbride simply gave her a dazzling grin in return. The big Scotsman's smile could disarm any female, but right now Evie had to resist the impulse to throw her hat at him. Logic told her that it wasn't his fault she had to ride with Will—that was entirely Mamma's doing. Then again, Gilbride *had* been the one to suggest this morning's dreary little outing, so perhaps she needn't feel guilty for wanting to bash him over the head.

"I am, of course, pleased to be of assistance, Captain Gilbride," she said. "I had thought to ride today, but Lord knows we don't want you missing a meal. You might faint from hunger and fall off your horse."

Gilbride's eyes widened at her retort, which instantly made Evie feel better. Her riposte had been terribly ill-mannered, but she would be sure to say extra prayers at church on Sunday to make up for it.

"I'm sorry, darling," Eden said, trying not to laugh. "I tried to dissuade Mamma, but she was adamant that it would be *more fun* for you."

"I must remember to thank her," Evie responded dryly.

Oh well, at least she could use the opportunity to apologize to Will. And since they would be in an open-air carriage, surrounded by the riders, things couldn't get too intimate. Eden would try to stick close and no doubt Michael would ride next to the carriage whenever the width of the laneway allowed. Really, there was no reason for her heart to thump so erratically or for her palms to feel damp inside her tightly fitted gloves.

But a moment later, when Will's curricle appeared

beneath the stone arch leading from the stables, Evie knew there was more than a little cause for concern.

He drove a beautifully matched pair of grays, expertly wheeling them in a neat circle to the front of the house. As she might have expected, he handled the rig with skill and confidence, his impressive masculine form on full display since the warm September day obviated the need for a caped driving coat. His perfectly cut, form-fitting blue coat showcased his broad shoulders, and his biscuit-colored breeches clung like a second skin to his long, muscular legs. He rested one booted foot against the gently curving dashboard, smiling down at her as he brought the horses to a smooth stop.

"Your carriage awaits, my lady," he said, sweeping off his hat with an uncharacteristic flourish. His smile widened into a grin as roguish as one of Captain Gilbride's.

Though she'd been immune to the Scotsman's attempt to charm her, Will succeeded in raising a flutter of nerves in her belly. Evie realized, with no small degree of dismay, that no other man's smile— not even Michael's—held anything like the same power.

As she struggled to respond to this unfamiliar, debonair version of Will, his smile faded into a puzzled expression. "Evie, are you all right?"

"Um, yes, of course," she said.

Trying not to appear as flustered as she felt, she gathered her skirts and reached for Will's outstretched hand. But Michael had dismounted and rushed over to help her.

"Please, take my hand, Evelyn," he said in a kind voice at odds with the nasty look he directed at Will.

Will regarded Michael as if he were a lower order of species. Evie was sure his father, the Duke of York, could not have looked more arrogant than he did glaring down his nose at the other man. It almost appeared as if the two were marking their territory, for lack of a better term, and *she* was apparently the territory.

She turned her nose up at Will's outstretched hand in favor of accepting Michael's assistance. She gave her well-mannered beau a warm smile—partly to compensate for the instinctive, disloyal response that Will had so easily called forth from some idiotically feminine part of her.

"I hope you'll ride next to the curricle," she said to Michael, ignoring the clearly annoyed male sitting next to her. "Perhaps we can discuss a bit of business instead of wasting the entire afternoon in frivolous pursuits."

"If there's anyone who's earned an afternoon of frivolity, it's you," Michael replied in an earnest manner. "But I'm happy to keep you company. If, that is, Captain Endicott doesn't mind."

"I don't mind at all," Will replied with a rasp that sounded rather like a snarl. "If you can keep up, *that is.*"

He sprang the horses, enveloping Michael in a cloud of dust. Evie grabbed the side of the carriage, then twisted around to see her beau sneezing into his handkerchief. Eden and her escorts were already cantering in the carriage's wake, while Captain Gilbride politely waited for Michael to recover and mount his horse.

"That was rude," she said sternly to Will. "You almost knocked poor Michael off his feet."

His brawny shoulders lifted in an easy shrug. "He was annoying me."

"Well, *you're* annoying *me.*"

He again flashed her that simultaneously disturbing and appealing rogue's grin. "No, I'm not. I can always tell when you're truly annoyed."

She refused to dignify such a ridiculous statement, staring straight ahead as she adjusted her hat that had been knocked askew by their sudden start. Aside from the fact that Will *was* acting in an abominably rude fashion, Evie couldn't deny she felt just a tiny bit flattered. Men never brangled over her, and she had to admit it was rather fun.

Until she remembered how Will had chosen *not* to fight for her, all those years ago. In fact, he'd let her slip out of his life with barely a whimper.

The sun chose that moment to slip behind a cloud, and Evie shivered with a sudden chill. At least she hoped it was a chill, because the idea that Will still had the power to make her feel somehow lacking was a thoroughly depressing thought.

He glanced over. "Are you cold? I have a lap blanket under the seat. Would you like me to pull it out for you?"

"Of course not," she said. "It's a lovely warm day, and the sun will be out from behind that cloud in a moment." She glanced over her shoulder at the riders. "I do think you should slow down, though. The others are having trouble catching up."

He shrugged. "As you wish." His fingers moved slightly on the traces, but it seemed to have no discernible effect on the horses.

She resisted the impulse to shake her head at him, knowing he would do exactly as he pleased. There had never been much point in arguing with Will—she *always* capitulated in the end—so she turned her attention to the landscape around her as they bowled down the winding drive from Maywood Manor to the main road. To the west lay the tenant farms, their fields lush and golden with ripening grains. The home woods ran to the east and the south, and a wide turn soon brought the curricle under a magnificent stand of oaks that marched along the drive to the gatehouse.

It was all so blessedly familiar as, she had to admit, was the presence of the man next to her. And it was all too easy to mentally slip back to the days when she and Will had spent hours driving together in his little gig, so happy in each other's company.

He'd loved to tell stories back then, inventing tall tales about a boy named Ethelred Bracegirdle who'd run away from home, traveling to Egypt and the Orient to seek his fortune. Though ridiculous, most of the stories were so funny that Evie usually ended up collapsed with laughter. Only later, when Will had joined the army and left his old life behind, did she realize that those tales were the expression of his own longing for adventure.

She stifled a self-pitying sigh as she remembered how much she'd loved their times together, regardless of the disappointments that had come later.

As he slowed to pass the gatehouse and turn through the old stone gates into the narrow country lane, she had a vivid flash of the day he'd taught her to drive on this very lane. It had been in a little pony cart on a mild September day such as this. Though Evie had only been twelve, it was the day she'd started to fall in love with Will, as ridiculous as it was to say now. But as his hands had closed over hers, helping her to guide the pony, she'd felt an internal jolt she could still remember. And when he'd looked down at her, his silvery-blue eyes warm with affection and laughter, Evie had been lost. Since then, there'd never been another man who evoked the same feeling in her—a bright joy that seemed to spring from glorious, carefree days, and a summer that never ended.

Back then he'd been only a boy, but now he was a man— and a powerful, intensely attractive one at that. His big, Corinthian's body crowded her on the seat, and even though they drove under an open sky, the intimacy threatened to smother her.

She sucked in a deep breath to ease the constriction in her chest. God only knew the havoc Will would play on her emotions—on her life—if she let her guard down with him. Even worse, to allow an attraction to him again would be a terrible betrayal of Michael, a man who had gifted her with a renewed sense of purpose in life. What could she ever truly hope for from Will except heartache and disappointment?

"What's wrong, Evie?" he asked in a quiet voice.

She startled. "Nothing. Why do you ask?"

"I remember that particular sigh. It means you're not happy about something."

She sat up straighter, trying to put some distance between them. The blasted man was impossibly large, and the Lord knew she wasn't exactly a tiny thing. Between the two of them and the excess material of her riding habit, it was a miracle they were even able to fit into the curricle.

"I'm fine." She flashed him what she hoped was a nonchalant smile. "I hardly think you know me very well, given the passage of time since we were children. I've grown up, Will."

He glanced down at her, his gaze lingering on her face and then moving to her bosom. "You certainly have."

Her mind blanked, struggling to find an appropriate reply. Unfortunately, there didn't seem to be one.

Cautiously, she peered up at him. She hadn't been sure before, but now it did seem clear that Will was flirting with her. Not that she was adept at flirtation, or even in recognizing the signs. In fact, she was monumentally bad at it. But she surely wasn't mistaking the heat in Will's eyes that had made them darken like smoke curling up from a blue flame.

When his lips tilted up in an amused smile, she realized her mouth was hanging open. She snapped it shut and jerked her head forward. "Will, you should keep your eyes on your pair. This road is quite bad after all the rains we've had this summer."

His low laugh did things to her nerves and insides that defied description. It was beginning to dawn on Evie that what she'd felt for Will as a girl—as powerful as that had been—had lacked a full awareness of his potent physical attractions.

"Certainly, Madame Scold, whatever you say," he teased.

"When have I ever scolded you, William Endicott?" she asked, retreating behind a façade of exasperation. "As I recall, you always led me around by the nose. Really, I'm quite ashamed of my weak-willed behavior back then."

"If anyone did the leading, it was your sister," he said dryly. "And if memory serves, you gave me quite a scolding last night."

That comment gave her nerves another kind of jolt, one not nearly as pleasant.

"Yes, about that . . ." She threw a quick glance over her shoulder. Michael and Gilbride were catching up to the curricle, but were not yet close enough to eavesdrop.

Might as well get it over with.

Will's calm expression as he managed the traces suggested nothing more than a friendly disinterest in the conversation. But she knew him as well as he knew her. If she didn't miss her guess, most of his attention was still on her and not on his cattle.

"I owe you an apology, Will," she said quietly.

He cocked his head, still looking politely disinterested. "I'm sorry, what did you say?"

She raised her voice a notch. "I behaved rather wretchedly to you in the drawing room last night, and you didn't deserve it." *Well, not most of it, anyway.*

He looked regretful. "You'll have to speak up, Evie. I can't hear you over the noise of the carriage wheels and the horses."

The beast. He was going to make things difficult for her.

"I said I'm sorry," she practically yelled. "Which you heard the first time, you brute."

He laughed. "I am a brute, and for that *I* apologize. But I couldn't resist because you looked so guilt-ridden."

"I *am* guilt-ridden, and a gentleman would accept my heartfelt apology and be done with it," she grumbled, crossing her arms over her chest.

His glance flicked absently down to her bosom, and Evie couldn't help flushing. Then he returned his attention to the horses. "No apology is necessary, my dear girl. I earned that thundering scold. Not only for my behavior last night but for everything else, too."

"I'm not sure what you mean," she said, disconcerted by his switch in demeanor.

He remained silent for a minute or so as he navigated a curve that brought them under a fine stand of canopy trees. But the dappled sunlight and shadow failed to hide the tension in his shoulders, or the way a muscle ticked in his jaw. When he finally answered, it seemed as if he had to pry his lips apart. "That last summer I was home . . . I'm sorry for that, Evie. I've been sorry about it for a long time."

She resisted the urge to curl her shoulders forward, as if for protection against the memories of that last summer together.

Will had been away for months, enrolled in studies at the Royal Military College. She'd missed him terribly but knew that soldiering would suit him far better than a career in either the Church or the legal profession. Will, naturally, had been thrilled by the opportunity to join the army and please his father. Evie had only asked that he write to her whenever he had the chance.

He had written a few brief notes that communicated how busy and happy he was in his new life. But he'd also addressed her in the most affectionate terms and said he couldn't wait to see her again. Fool that she was, Evie had believed Will returned her feelings with equal ardor.

Will had returned home that summer to visit with his guardians, the Endicotts. He was almost nineteen and Evie was soon to turn seventeen as she prepared for her debut with Eden in the upcoming Season. Quite old enough, she had thought, for them to pledge their love for each other.

The first few weeks had been lovely, with Will seemingly overjoyed to see her. He'd told her about his father's plans to buy him a commission in the Guards, and Evie had listened with pride and happiness. She saw no reason why his military service should be an impediment to their future since many sons of the nobility served in elite army regiments and still went on to marry. With any luck, Will would soon be an officer, one who'd be able to support a wife. Between his income and her dowry they would be able to live a happy, if fairly modest, life. She'd never been put off by a lack of riches, and much preferred life away from the bustle of London and the whirl of the *ton*. Will and Eden were the only people necessary to Evie's happiness, and she'd had them both.

But it had all gone horribly wrong during a ball at the Endicotts' gracious manor house. She and Will had stood up together twice and he'd escorted her into supper, too. His eyes, his words, his touch . . . all had conveyed how much she meant to him. Evie had never been more certain that their happiness together was all but assured.

When Will escorted her out to the terrace for air after a particularly robust set, Evie's heart had thumped with excitement. Not at the notion that he would make any untoward advances, because he was too serious and proper for that. Nor would he think it right for an all-but penniless young man of questionable parentage to make the first advance, or put demands on her. So after careful thought, Evie had decided she had to take the first step, since Will likely never would. She'd thought about nothing else for weeks and it was finally her chance. With one bold act, she would show him how much she loved him.

As they'd leaned against the balustrade, gazing up into the night sky, she'd gathered her courage and gone up on tiptoe, pressing her lips to his mouth. She'd put everything she felt for Will into the shy, heartfelt kiss.

Will had startled, but then his arms had stolen around her and he'd pulled her into a tight embrace. She'd melted into him, reeling under the passion of his surprisingly expert kiss. Unfortunately, the kiss lasted mere seconds before he'd gasped against her lips and broken away.

In the light of the half-full moon, she'd seen the stunned—in a horrified way—expression on his face. For the first time in her life, Evie felt awkward and shamefaced in his presence.

But when she'd asked him what was wrong, he'd simply stammered out an incoherent apology and hauled her back into the house. They'd run into Eden in the hall—she'd come looking for them—and Will had handed Evie over with a shocking lack of ceremony. He'd avoided her for the rest of the night and indeed for the rest of the week, ensuring they were never alone together. She tried more than once to talk to him about the incident on the terrace, but he dodged her until it became painfully obvious that he found her company nothing more than a source of embarrassment.

When he left for London to take up his commission—leaving earlier than planned—Evie had almost been grateful. To be physically near him when he clearly wished to avoid her ripped her heart into ragged shreds. She'd spent the years following that humiliation trying to convince herself that Will's rejection had been the inevitable result of her childish, misguided infatuation.

Staring blindly down the lane, Evie swallowed hard against the memories that congealed like suet in the center of her chest.

"We were both young then, and I was silly." Evie tried to sound like a sensible woman instead of a heartbroken girl. "I had no right to expect . . . things from you."

Will's hands tightened on the reins. The horses broke into a canter, and for a moment his attention was fixed on the animals. When he'd settled them into a more leisurely pace, he looked down at her with a narrow, irritated gaze.

"Why are you scowling at me?" she protested. "I just told you it wasn't your fault."

"Of *course* it was my fault. And you had every reason to expect things from me."

She pressed a hand to her chest, nearly breathless. "What . . .what things?"

"Courtesy and respect, to begin with," he said from between gritted teeth. "And affection. I was a complete bounder to treat you in such a cavalier fashion."

He sounded so disgusted with himself that she had to smile. "You were, rather. It felt horrible."

"If it's any consolation, I felt horrible about it too. For a very long time." He blew out an exasperated breath. "I did try to apologize a few years ago, though, if you recall. You weren't very receptive to it."

She wanted to bury her burning face in her hands. But in some strange way it was a relief to be able to talk about what had happened between them. To be candid as they'd once been with each other.

"I wasn't ready to hear any apologies then," she admitted. "I was still mortified, and Eden was spitting mad too. I was so afraid she was going to bash you over the head with a vase that I just wanted to get her out of there."

A fleeting smile touched his lips. "I have a vivid memory of that encounter. There are few things more terrifying than your sister in full rage."

"I know. It's splendid, isn't it?"

One of Will's eyebrows moved in a skeptical lift, but he didn't contradict her.

"So, what's changed?" he asked a moment later. "Why are you able to hear my apology now?"

Evie stared down at her clasped hands, sensibly gloved in plain tan. She knew the answer to his question. What had changed was meeting Michael. His friendship and admiration had done so much to restore her confidence, and their work at St. Margaret's had helped her to realize she'd wasted too much time grieving over her first, foolish love.

But that felt much too private to explain to Will.

"I grew up, I suppose," she said vaguely. "And it seemed silly to fret so much about a kiss, especially one that was clearly so, er, distasteful for you."

Now it did seem silly, but at the time she'd been devastated. Aside from everything else, she must have been very bad at kissing, although she'd certainly enjoyed it. Will, however, had fled as if all the hounds of hell were hot on his trail.

He shot her an incredulous glance. "Evie, it was a *splendid* kiss, which was one of the reasons why I stopped."

She went stiff as a fencepost as they wheeled through the village of Barrington. Though her gaze took in the verdant green and the quaint Elizabethan buildings, her brain was fixated on trying to understand his shocking words.

"That makes *no* sense," she managed.

"It makes perfect sense," he retorted. "Good God, you were barely seventeen and entirely innocent. I had no business taking advantage of you or our friendship."

"If memory serves, I believe *I* was the one taking advantage of you."

That surprised a snort of laughter out of him. "I suppose that's true. Still, I had no business responding the way I did."

"I don't know," she mused. "I thought it was all rather lovely."

He met that remark with steadfast silence, concentrating on guiding his horses through the turn onto the long road that climbed the gentle hill to the abbey ruins.

"In any event," he said once he'd sorted the turn, "I was mortally embarrassed by my shabby behavior. I found it impossible to discuss it with you. After all, you were my dearest friend. It was a shock that I could think of you in . . . well, in *that* way."

And there it was—the depressing confirmation that Will had never loved her in the way she had loved him.

"I must say, though, that I did think about that kiss many times over the years," he said with a self-satisfied grin. "I'm exceedingly fond of that memory, Evie."

Now it was her turn to stare incredulously at him. "Then why did you never say anything to me? Or even write, for God's sake?"

The roguish glint faded from his eyes. "The short answer? I was terrified of hurting you."

She poked him in the ribs with her elbow. "Too late."

His mouth twisted into a wry, almost sad smile before he threw a quick glance over his shoulder. "I was a complete idiot, and I owe you a thousand abject apologies. But I'm afraid we must drop this particular topic for now, since we're about to have company."

Evie had been so riveted by this momentous revision of history that she'd failed to notice the sound of cantering horses. She twisted in her seat and saw Michael and Gilbride approaching the back of the curricle.

"Oh," she said, disconcerted. "Well, it doesn't matter anymore, I suppose."

Liar.

He shook his head, muttering something like *stubborn woman* under his breath. While she cast about in her head for an appropriate change in topic, he took the matter out of her hands.

"As I said, we'll drop this particular discussion. For now." Then his slight scowl smoothed into an easy, practiced smile. "So, my dear, tell me about this charity of yours. I must admit to being intrigued."

Chapter Eight

Will never minded propping up a column in a ballroom, not if there were enough pretty girls to watch on the dance floor. Tonight, however, there was only one girl at the Duchess of Campforth's ball who captured his interest, and that was Evie, making her way through another set with her annoyingly persistent partner, Michael Beaumont.

He couldn't blame Beaumont in the least since Evie was looking amazingly pretty tonight, even though the cut of her dress was modest compared to most other women there. Pale green folds of soft fabric clung to her curves, lovingly outlining her magnificent bosom and lush bottom. Her hair gleamed like a polished guinea, pulled into a simple knot on the top of her head and then allowed to cascade in streams of gold down the back of her neck. Her bow-shaped mouth curved up in an unconsciously sensual smile that had Will imagining things he had no business thinking about. Even her spectacles didn't detract from the beauty that most men were too stupid to see.

That so many were blind to her loveliness was partly Eden's fault, although the twins would be aghast to even voice something they would see as the ultimate disloyalty.

But there was no denying that Eden's vivacious personality and teasing wit tended to cast Evie into the shade. The fact that Eden had no qualms about displaying her abundant physical assets in one stunning dress after another made the difference even more startling. Whereas Evie usually hid behind spectacles and modestly cut, almost matronly clothing, her twin flaunted her charms and thoroughly enjoyed the attention she so easily attracted. Most men identified Eden as markedly prettier, even though the twins were truly two peas from one pod.

Will, however, had never shared that opinion, not even when Evie was a shy, gawky girl. Her twin might sparkle and flash but Evie quietly glowed, lit from within by a generous and loving nature. If other men couldn't see past her shy demeanor to her true worth, they were only to be pitied.

Beaumont, however, clearly *did* see past it. He was smitten with Evie, as his possessive manner both on and off the dance floor amply demonstrated. Watching the couple for the last hour or so, Will had grown increasingly irritated by Beaumont's open displays of affection. Every time the man's hands strayed close to Evie's rump, or his arm *casually* brushed the side of her bosom, it was all Will could do not to bound onto the parquet dance floor, spin him around, and lay him flat on his back with a solid uppercut to the jaw.

He sighed, repressing the impulse to bash his head against the marble of the column. His overblown reaction didn't just stem from a desire to protect his old friend. Ever since that outing to the abbey ruins, when Evie's lush form had been plastered against him during that ill-conceived carriage ride, Will had been acutely aware of why he'd walked away from her all those years ago. She posed an incalculable temptation to his self-control, and giving in to that siren call would be a disaster for both of them.

Will knew that Evie still harbored feelings for him. She might *think* she wanted to marry Beaumont, but he knew otherwise. Her emotions were evident in her soft, shimmering gaze when she looked at him and in the slight tremor of her voice whenever they spoke of days gone by. Will had quickly realized that Evie was on the verge of marrying a man she didn't love, and that his appearance on the scene had raised sudden complications. The way she'd been avoiding him for the last several days confirmed that theory.

If only she knew how complicated the situation truly was. While, technically, he was only spying on Beaumont, Evie's relationship with the man and her involvement at St. Margaret's also put her under the glass. And if she ever discovered the truth, Will knew she would never forgive him.

But there was no avoiding it, because that was why both he and Alec were here tonight—to sniff out Beaumont's friends and potential allies. Some among the wealthy and powerful always sought profit from chaos, and might be willing to provide Beaumont with funds to support his cause. That Beaumont was strident in that cause was no longer in doubt, as they'd easily discovered by shadowing him the past week. The young man wrote and published inflammatory pamphlets about Catholic emancipation and attended intellectual salons where the topics of conversation skated close to treason. While Beaumont's passionate outpourings might simply reflect an earnest and rather naïve worldview, he could easily be involved in something far more sinister.

A sardonic voice broke into his unpleasant reverie.

"Good Lord, you look ready to rip out the young pup's throat, and I have a notion it's not because of his politics."

Will pushed away from the column, scowling at the smirk on Alec's face. "It's about time you showed up. I've been trailing around after Beaumont and his friends for the last hour, trying not to look like a lunatic. The last time I dodged behind a potted palm our hostess looked ready to have me carted off to Bedlam." He was joking, of course, since his skills at discreet surveillance were as good as they'd ever been—despite the distractions Evie posed.

Alec, resplendent in his regimentals, cast a quick glance around them.

"No one is listening," Will said dryly. "You know I haven't lost my touch."

His cousin shrugged. "Can't be too careful, not with the cannonball this bloody assignment is turning out to be." His gaze fixed on Beaumont and Evie, just coming off the dance floor on the other side of the massive ballroom. "I spent some time with Beaumont last week. While you were capering about with Miss Evelyn, I was practically paying court to the fellow. God only knows what he must think of me."

"That you're an ardent philanthropist, no doubt. And, by the way, I was hardly *capering* with Evie. Except for that day in the ruins, she's treated me like I'm a leper, bells and all."

Alec folded his arms across his chest and smiled, conveying the appearance of a man engaged in casual conversation. He liked to give the impression that he was a genial and not very bright giant, but Will knew he had his eye on Beaumont, Evie, and probably twenty other people in the room at the same time. "I noticed that. What did you do to rattle the poor girl?"

"I'm not sure," Will said with a casual shrug. It was a lie, but Alec didn't need the gory details. "I suppose she hasn't yet forgiven me for abandoning her, as she put it."

"And yet you two seemed *quite* chummy in the carriage."

"I know it's difficult, but try not to be an idiot," Will replied in a tone of false sympathy.

Alec's laughing gray eyes flashed back at him. "Someone is certainly in a foul mood. You know what you need?"

"No, but I'm sure you'll tell me."

"A visit to a cozy little brothel. It's been much too long since you've had a good shagging."

"I think not, but feel free to carry on without me."

His cousin let out a soft hoot. "That's what I thought. You're still keen on the girl, aren't you?"

Will narrowed his eyes in warning. "I suggest we stick to business. We haven't had much chance to speak the last few days, since you've been busy with other things."

Before answering, Alec took the time to give a pair of pretty girls strolling by a flourishing bow. They both giggled, flirting behind their fans, before gliding away.

"I'm sorry, old son," Alec finally said in a vague manner. "What were we talking about?"

"Never mind." Will knew Alec had been dealing with matters relating to his grandfather's estate in Scotland, a topic his cousin was never keen to discuss. "Let's get back to Beaumont. What do you think of him?"

Alec shook his head. "The man's a living saint, as far as I can tell, and he's entirely devoted to his blasted charity. He nattered on about it for hours and certainly didn't seem reluctant to share information. I thought I might have to shoot myself to escape the endless parade of detail."

"It stands to reason since Beaumont is so devoted to helping the Irish poor. And why not plan sedition at the same time? The charity could be a good cover."

Alec nodded, frowning slightly. "True, but he struck me as full of honest enthusiasm more than anything else."

"Did he bring up the issue of conditions in Ireland, or Catholic emancipation?"

"Only in passing. He was more concerned with extracting money from me for the Hibernian Benevolent Association—

the charity connected to St. Margaret's Parish. He said they stand in need of new patrons."

Will once more propped his shoulders against the pillar, giving his friend an evil grin. "And was he successful in his efforts?" When Alec glared at him, he laughed. "You're such a soft touch."

His cousin was generous to a fault, always emptying his pockets to beggars, crossing boys, downtrodden prostitutes, and anyone else who needed help.

"I thought it would help me get through the front door," Alec answered defensively. "If I'm a patron I have a damn good reason to visit the place."

"Well done. I persuaded Evie to show me around St. Margaret's, too. I intend to make arrangements for that visit as soon as I can get her to speak to me."

Alec's only reply was a distracted grunt. Will followed his cousin's gaze to a shallow window alcove framed with blue velvet drapes, where Evie and Beaumont chatted with Eden and a trio of her ever-present swains.

He flicked an interested glance at Alec. "What do you think of Evie's sister? You spent time with her last week, too."

"Only because I had to run interference to keep her away from you and Miss Whitney," Alec said in a disgruntled tone.

"Yes, and I thank you for your help. Eden didn't seem all that keen on your company."

Alec let out a grudging laugh. "She thinks I'm a complete bore, what with me prosing on about charities and whatnot."

"Not to mention your loyal son of the Highlands routine. That seemed to put her off too."

"Pity. She's a bonny lass and that's a fact. But at this point I suspect she'd rather shave her head than hold another conversation with me. My little act apparently worked too well." He let out a dramatic sigh. "The sacrifices I make for Crown and country."

"Poor you," Will said. "But despite your trepidation, I think it best we spend some time visiting with the ladies and Mr. Beaumont. It will afford you the opportunity to find out just how much Eden dislikes you."

"Won't that be a lark," Alec replied sardonically.

An unexpected touch on Will's shoulder had him spinning around, instinctively starting to assume a defensive stance. When he saw who stood behind him, he winced.

"Stand down, Wolf, you're not in the Peninsula," Aden St. George said, trying not to laugh. "The only danger you face in this ballroom is from matchmaking mammas or rich widows on the prowl."

Will shot a glance at Alec, relieved to see he also regarded their newly arrived companion with a slightly embarrassed demeanor. He obviously hadn't noticed Aden sneaking up on them, either, though Aden was almost as tall and brawny as Alec.

Aden St. George had been one of England's most talented and lethal spies in the long war against the French, and the man chosen to be Dominic Hunter's replacement as Head of Section. He was also their cousin, and a by-blow of the Prince Regent himself.

Will shook Aden's hand. "I suggest you not sneak up on me again, or you might find yourself with an injury in a most unwelcome part of your anatomy."

Aden laughed. "My wife would have something to say about that. You cross her at your peril, I assure you."

Alec clapped Aden hard on the back, managing to jolt their big-framed cousin slightly forward. "We heard you'd gotten yourself leg-shackled. To the sister of the Earl of Blake, was it not?"

Aden's grin was so sheepishly happy it made Will blink.

His cousin had always been a grim, quiet man who avoided personal relationships. Apparently, the new Mrs. St. George had effected quite a change.

"Yes, Lady Vivien Shaw and I were married last fall. You'll have to stop by our town house in Cadogan Square and make her acquaintance."

Alec raised his dark eyebrows in pointed mockery. "You mean she lets you go out without an escort? Why the devil would she trust a crafty bugger like you to roam around town on his own?"

"The appropriate question is why would I let *her* roam around on her own," Aden replied. "She's more likely than me to get into trouble. But Vivien is now in the family way, and not feeling up to an evening in an overheated ballroom."

After the appropriate congratulations were exchanged, with Alec again pounding Aden on the back, Will cocked an enquiring eyebrow. "We're happy to see you, but why *are* you here tonight? Swanning around a *ton* ballroom is hardly your style."

"Only duty could force me to endure such a grim task," Aden replied. "The Duke of York, however, thought this would be a good opportunity for us to meet without drawing undue attention. He's waiting for us in the duchess's study, so we can have a private conversation before he comes upstairs to the ball."

"Oh, Christ," Alec muttered, grimacing.

Will agreed with the sentiment, since they had yet garnered little useful information to report. He'd met with Dominic yesterday to communicate their progress and apprise him of their plans to visit St. Margaret's as soon as possible, but Will's father clearly wanted to hear about their progress—or lack thereof—directly.

Aden gave a wordless shrug that perfectly conveyed his sympathy. None of the cousins had particularly comfortable relationships with their sires, and reporting to one of them made it that much trickier.

"Give it a few minutes," Aden said, "then join us in the study." He slipped away into the crowd, moving discreetly for a man his size.

"The bonny lassies will have to wait, I suppose," Alec said in a morose voice.

"We can only hope they'll refrain from planning any additional conspiracies in our absence." Will watched Evie as she shared a laugh with her sister. It was impossible to believe that she was involved in anything nefarious.

He and Alec strolled to the wide doorway leading from the ballroom to the upstairs landing of the mansion. Several people called out greetings or tried to engage them in conversation—in Alec's case, mostly women—but they made their excuses until they found themselves out in the hall.

A liveried footman waited for them at the top of the stairs. "This way, if you please," he said with a bow.

He preceded them down the stairs and toward the back of the house, ushering them to a door where Aden waited for them. Their cousin led them in.

The study was a handsome, oak-paneled room with bow windows that faced out into the duchess' famous rose garden. At this time of night, the windows only reflected the light from several branches of candles, a few lamps on reading tables, and the wavering image of the man sitting in a leather club chair in front of the fireplace, drinking a brandy.

"Good evening, sir," William said to his father.

The three cousins bowed to the duke.

"St. George, have a seat." York waved a vague hand at the chair next to him. "I'd tell you lads to fetch yourselves a brandy, but there's no point shilly-shallying down here. The fewer who know we're meeting, the better."

"Yes, sir," Will took the chaise opposite his father. Alec, who obviously preferred standing, moved behind the chaise to take up a position behind Will. Whether to cover his back or hide behind him remained an open question.

His father launched into it without fanfare. "I understand from Dominic that you've made very little progress." His thick brows pulled into a beetling scowl. "I trust neither of you needs me to point out the urgency of the situation."

If Will had been standing, he would have been forced to repress the impulse to shuffle his feet. A slight noise behind him suggested that Alec was doing just that.

As for Aden, the bastard lifted a mocking eyebrow but kept his mouth shut.

"No, sir, you don't," Will said. "And although Alasdair and I hoped to be further along in our investigation, we've made some progress."

The duke looked regally down his long nose. "Are you suggesting that Dominic mischaracterized your report?"

Will managed to hold in a weary sigh—barely. "Not at all, sir."

"Then it is *I* who misunderstand?" His father's eyebrows would have disappeared into his hair, if he still had any.

"Indeed no, and I would never suggest such a thing, Your Highness," Will said, throttling back his frustration. There was no denying his father was a resourceful and accomplished commander, but like many men in power, he was often impatient and quick to judgment.

"Will, perhaps you can summarize what you told Sir Dominic yesterday," Aden smoothly interposed. "That would be to my benefit as well, since I was unable to attend that meeting."

Will looked at his father who grunted his permission.

Swiftly, he recapped what had transpired at Maywood Manor, with Alec adding additional information parsed from his conversations with Beaumont. Even on a second hearing, Will had to admit it wasn't much of a report.

"So, we're not really very far along, are we?" barked the duke.

"Only insofar as we can't rule out Beaumont's involvement," Will replied as tactfully as he could.

"Can't rule it in, either. The man's a bloody saint, if you ask me," Alec added with regrettable bluntness.

The duke's eyes narrowed ominously. "What is *that* supposed to mean?"

"Only that Beaumont seems genuinely devoted to his charity," Will hastily interposed, "which obviously doesn't preclude him from involvement in a conspiracy. It just means he's sincerely passionate about what he believes in."

"Men who hold passionate opinions are sometimes revolutionaries or tyrants," the duke said, "as we saw all too unfortunately in France."

"Indeed," said Aden. "We can all agree that we don't have enough evidence to rule Beaumont in or out as a suspect. Perhaps it would be best if we decide on our next course of action."

"By *we,* you mean *us,*" Alec muttered. Will wanted to yank him down by the cravat and tell him to keep his mouth shut.

Instead, he nodded to Aden. "We have a plan to get closer to Beaumont. Alec has managed to convince him that he's interested in donating money and patronage to his charitable endeavors. Beaumont is enthusiastic and seems to have developed a degree of trust in Alec. My cousin will continue to work on that end of things while I poke around St. Margaret's."

"Poke around when?" the duke asked.

"Tomorrow, I hope. Miss Whitney has agreed to show me around the building and introduce me to some of her charity cases."

"Make sure that happens," his father said, rising. Will and Aden rose with him. "Our sources in Dublin are no less concerned than they were a week ago." The duke strolled for the door. "By the by, William, what's your impression of Miss Whitney? Any sense she's involved in this?"

"No, sir," Will replied. "She's completely innocent, I'm sure of it."

His father paused with his hand on the doorknob. "And what is the basis for that certainty?"

"I know her, sir." Will resisted the impulse to spring emphatically to her defense. That would only make his father suspicious.

"You'll have to do better than that, my boy," the duke replied with disdain before stomping from the room.

"Christ," Alec said after the door had closed. "That was a lovely little disaster."

"It could have gone better," Aden admitted. "But Dominic and I will handle the duke. You two just keep your noses to the ground and stick to the plan."

They discussed details for a few more minutes and then headed out to the hallway together. Aden took his leave from them at the front door. "I have a beautiful wife waiting for me, snugly tucked into bed," he said, when Alec teased him about his eagerness to return home. "And her company is infinitely preferable to yours." He flashed them a sardonic grin as he accepted his hat and cane from the butler. "Besides, I know how much you lads enjoy doing the pretty with the ladies."

"Bugger you," Alec called after him, shocking both the butler and the footman at the door.

Will started up the stairs. "I need to get Evie alone," he said to his cousin. "I suggest you try your winning ways on Beaumont and make some more progress on your budding friendship."

"Such a tough assignment for you," Alec mocked. "I know how much you hate spending time with such a lovely girl."

"You really are a complete ass," Will said.

He ignored Alec's mocking laughter as they plunged into the ridiculous crush of the ballroom. Duchess Campworth's affairs were always too crowded, even at a time of year when London was thin of company. But she served excellent victuals and champagne, encouraged deep play at the card tables, and had a tendency to invite anyone involved in the latest, most salacious scandal. It made for an unbeatable combination when it came to attracting a crowd.

Over the mass of waving feathers and gigantic turbans, Will scanned the crowd for Evie. Alec, a few inches taller, finally spied her. "At the top of the room, near the refreshment table."

Will wasn't much pleased to see Beaumont still hanging all over Evie, gazing into her pretty face with a nauseating expression of puppy love. Eden stood close by, laughing and flirting with the usual circle of idiots courting her favor. Evie all but ignored her sister, earnestly intent on conversation with Beaumont.

"Christ," Will growled. "Beaumont never leaves Evie alone for a moment."

"I'll take care of that," Alec said. "Should be a waltz coming up soon. Why don't you take Miss Evelyn out for a whirl and then down to supper. I'll keep Beaumont and the terrible twin occupied."

Will had to laugh at Alec's description of Eden. Evie's twin hadn't a bad bone in her body, but she had a knack for getting into mischief and keeping everyone around her in turmoil. It mystified him why she was so much more popular than Evie. True, Evie didn't flatter or flirt, but she was just as pretty as her twin and a damned sight easier to be with.

They reached their targets in good order, thanks to Alec's willingness to bull his way through the well-bred mob. As usual, Will followed in his wake issuing apologies, but for once he didn't mind. With perfect timing, he was able to elbow his way in front of Beaumont just as the orchestra struck up the waltz.

Ignoring Beaumont's mumbled protest, Will gave Evie his warmest smile. "Miss Whitney, may I claim the pleasure of this dance?"

She blinked up at him, her eyes wide and startled behind the lenses of her spectacles. "Oh, Will, when did you arrive? I haven't seen you all evening." Then she winced, obviously embarrassed that she'd all but admitted looking for him. That naïve declaration pleased him more than it should have, but he knew better than to let her see that.

"We arrived some time ago," he said vaguely, "but you were in a set. Besides, it's so crowded it took us forever to make our way to the front of the room."

"It is a crush, isn't it? That's why Michael suggested we beat a retreat to a quiet corner behind the refreshment table." She gave Beaumont, who was clearly fuming as he tried to edge around Will, an encouraging smile.

"Understandable," Will replied, taking a casual step to the side to block Beaumont from reaching Evie. "Although any corner that includes Edie and her pack of suitors can hardly be called quiet."

"I heard that," Eden said loudly. She shoved her way through the aforementioned pack, showing no more compunction about stepping on toes than Alec had. "And I don't believe your excuse for one minute, Wolf. You and your oversized shadow arrived almost an hour ago, and you didn't even attempt to come see us." She finished her complaint by directing an irate glare at Alec, whose only response was to give her an outrageous wink.

"Well, you're here now, and that's all that matters," Evie said, directing a reproving frown at her twin.

"Indeed we are." Will took her hand and threaded their fingers together. "Now about that dance."

"Captain Endicott," Beaumont began in an irate voice, "I'm afraid that Miss Whitney—"

"Mr. Beaumont!" Alec exclaimed, cutting him off. "Just the fellow I wanted to see. Why, only a half hour ago I was talking to a friend about the Hibernian Benevolent Association. He posed me several interesting questions about the services you provide to the poor unfortunates of St. Giles. I've a mind he might be willing to donate a tidy sum if we can satisfactorily answer his questions."

Alec's slight emphasis on the word *we* and his chummy *we're in this together* manner did the trick.

Beaumont perked up. "Who is this person?"

Alec tapped the side of his nose. "Don't want to bandy his name about yet, but I can assure you that he's very plump in the pockets." He leaned forward, affecting a conspiratorial whisper. "And he might be willing to speak to others on our behalf too."

"Splendid," Beaumont said. "After this dance with—"

Alec emphatically shook his head. "Don't think we can afford to let this one slip away." He clapped a friendly but clearly restraining hand on Beaumont's shoulder. "We need to discuss this *immediately.*"

Beaumont cast a doubting glance at Evie, who seemed to be inspecting the toes of her dancing slippers. Then she lifted her eyes to cast a shy glance at Will. That look told him she wasn't the least bit averse to dancing with him and leaving her suitor to Alec's tender ministrations.

"Not to worry, Beaumont," he said, gently pulling Evie to his side. "I'll take care of Miss Whitney."

"Oh, I, I . . ." she stammered as he swung her into the waltz.

As he twirled her around, Will caught a last glimpse of Alec leading Beaumont away by the elbow, while Eden—whose suitors were drifting away—directed a killing glare at Alec's back. Will had to stifle a laugh. Yes, it was rude of them to abandon her so precipitously, but Eden had left legions of suitors in the dust. The little jab to her pride would likely do her good.

When he moved through the next turn, Evie's full breasts brushed his chest, a lush slide of silk and soft, tempting flesh, and all thoughts of Eden blew away like mist before a strong wind. And when he looked down at Evie's pretty face, taking in her flushed cheeks and slightly parted lips, his mind seemed to go fuzzy around the edges.

It took him a few moments to figure out why—all the blood was apparently draining from his head, heading rapidly for points farther south.

Chapter Nine

Evie sucked in a deep breath that pushed her bosom right into Will's broad chest. When a cascade of sensations sizzled through her body, she didn't know whether to faint from humiliation, snuggle in closer, or try to pretend she wasn't the least bit affected by his embrace. Obviously, choice number three was the only sensible course of action, though her body disagreed with that assessment.

Oddly, Will also seemed disconcerted, peering down at her with a puzzled look. A faint flush glazed the hollows of his cheekbones. She could swear his pupils had dilated, making the light blue of his gaze stand out in dazzling contrast. It also took her a moment to realize he was holding her much too tightly. If she needed any confirmation, the shocked expressions on the faces of elderly chaperones as Will swept her down the dance floor provided it.

She winced. As lovely as it felt to be in Will's arms, she hated being fodder for gossip.

When she tried to insert some space between them, he resisted. Startled, she glanced up at his face. A smoldering intensity had replaced the puzzled expression in his eyes, and he stared down at her now with an almost predatory gaze. Everything inside her seemed to go still, as if something momentous was about to happen. She felt like a bird or small animal anticipating the advance of a mighty storm, one that had the power to change the landscape forever.

As Will swept her through another turn, the crowd parted in a garish whirl of color, and she caught a glimpse of Michael and Captain Gilbride. Eden trailed in their wake with a cross expression on her features. As if Evie had called out to her, her twin's head whipped around and their eyes locked. Evie could see a flare of alarm in her sister's eyes, and Eden's right hand came up in a short, choppy wave. Then the dancers swirled together again, cutting Eden and the others off from view.

But the warning from her twin had been clear. *Trouble ahead, Evie. Ignore at your peril.*

And she suddenly remembered that Michael would soon be asking formally for her hand in marriage, which meant she had *no* business feeling anything but friendship for Will. How many times did she need to be reminded of that?

Then she also remembered how dreadfully awkward she felt whenever she waltzed. The feel of a man's arm encircling her body had always been disconcerting—especially since her lamentably generous bosom showed a tendency to get in the way, invariably leading to much tripping over her own feet. Even with Michael she could never feel entirely comfortable, despite his being a most decorous and careful dancer.

But to her vast surprise, she'd forgotten how poorly she waltzed as soon as Will took her in his arms. She felt so light that dancing with him seemed to come as naturally as breathing.

Of course, a moment later and all too predictably, she stumbled badly.

Will quickly righted her and slowed the pace. "Evie, are you all right?"

She'd managed to stub her toe against his rock-hard shin, but she repressed a groan.

"I'm fine," she said, trying to again force a few inches between them. Now that she'd come to her senses, she was painfully aware of the heat burning between them at every point where their bodies connected.

Irritation pulled his brows together into a scowl. "For God's sake, stop wriggling around like an eel. Either something is wrong or you're a considerably worse dancer than I remember."

That pulled a startled laugh from her throat. As enjoyable as it was to have Will's arms around her, especially with that exciting but altogether too dangerous look in his eyes, she found it much easier to manage him when he acted like the Will she'd always known—a familiar friend rather than a lover.

But when he tried to pull her tight into his muscular form again, she hissed, "You're holding me too close. People are beginning to notice."

Sure enough, she caught a glimpse of her mother on the edge of the dance floor, with her fan paused in mid-wave as she stared at them. But instead of throwing daggers at her with her eyes, Mamma tilted her head and gave Evie a sly smile. That look so alarmed Evie that she tripped over her feet again.

Will heaved a sigh and steered them toward the edge of the dance floor.

"We don't need to stop dancing," Evie said. "You just need to stop squeezing me so tightly."

An oddly speculating look darkened his gaze, but he didn't answer until he'd maneuvered them past an enthusiastically oblivious couple. "If I don't get you off this floor, I'm afraid you're going to kill yourself. Or me."

"I'm not that bad," she grumbled.

She hated that she was so clumsy, and she hated the rush of heat to her face even more. Will must think her little changed from the awkward schoolgirl he'd rejected so many years ago. That wasn't the case, even if he couldn't see it. Too bad she couldn't find a way to communicate that fact without sounding like a complete ninny—or like she wished for him to make advances to her.

"No, you're not," he said, easing her into a fortuitously empty space by a marble column. "In fact, you were doing beautifully until a few minutes ago. What threw you off your feed?"

"What a remarkably inelegant way of expressing your point. What put me *off my feed* was the way you were squeezing my ribcage until I could barely breathe."

A lazy grin curled up the corners of his mouth. Evie *did* feel breathless, even though he was no longer touching her.

"I liked squeezing you." His purring voice sent fairy fingers dancing down her spine. "I must say, you felt very nice in my arms."

It took all her willpower not to gape at him. "Will Endicott, surely you're not flirting with me," she asked, trying to sound severe. Though she should be aghast—for a hundred reasons—at the moment she found it difficult to work up the appropriate outrage.

The tiny part of her brain that remained rational, however, buzzed in circles, trying to understand why he was acting so out of character.

When Will's gaze deliberately flicked down to her bosom, Evie was painfully aware that her nipples were doing their best to poke through the thin fabric of her undergarments and dress. Not that her nipples seemed to mind his notice. In fact, her brain had obviously disconnected from her body the second he had taken her into his arms.

"And would you mind if I were?" he asked in a husky, altogether unfamiliar voice.

Evie had to resist the temptation to slap her palm against her ear, wondering if her hearing had gone bad.

Before she could formulate a semi-coherent response, Will's head jerked up and his smiling lips rolled in on themselves, stretching tight and thin as Evie became aware of a commotion behind her. It was substantial enough to compete with the strains of the orchestra, the chattering voices, and the clicking of shoes on the dance floor.

As Will snapped to attention, one of his hands came to her elbow to gently turn her around. When she did, she found herself staring straight at the medal-covered chest of a rotund figure, clothed in an imposing dress uniform.

"Good evening, sir," Will said, bowing to the Duke of York.

Evie stared, blinking like a simpleton. She knew, of course, that the duke was Will's natural father but she'd never met him, only seeing him from a distance at reviews and the occasional ball. The usual responses seemed to twist in on themselves and her mind went completely blank.

Will's elbow nudged her from her daze.

"Y-your Royal Highness," she stammered, dropping into a deep curtsey.

As she rose, she cast a nervous glance around her. The duke was accompanied by several officers and his hostess, but they hovered some feet away as if to give them a modicum of privacy. She sensed, however, that they were clearly all straining their ears to eavesdrop.

"Captain, introduce me to the lady," the duke barked.

Evie repressed the instinct to flinch and smiled politely as she forced herself to gaze up into the duke's round, florid face. It took all her discipline to resist taking an involuntary step back, since His Highness regarded her with something like antipathy.

Why, she hadn't a clue.

"Of course, sir," Will replied calmly. "This is Miss Evelyn Whitney, the daughter of Viscount and Lady Reese."

If anything, the duke's scowl went from bad to worse after the introduction. Evie dropped into another deep curtscy, just to be on the safe side.

"Are your parents about?" the duke asked in the same blunt manner. "Perhaps you can find them while I have a chat with Captain Endicott."

Evie flinched, staggered by the rude dismissal. Will went stiff beside her, silently radiating disapproval of his father's tactics. The fact that the duke's followers were listening with avid eagerness made the situation doubly distressing.

She struggled to maintain a semblance of dignity. "Of course, Your Highness." She nodded a good-bye to Will, trying not to show how rattled she felt. But when Will's hand again grasped her elbow, pulling her up short, she let out a little gasp.

"I should be most happy to speak to you, sir," he said quietly, "after I have escorted Miss Whitney back to her party."

The duke's narrowed gaze signaled how little he appreciated his son's defiance. "I'm sure Miss Whitney can find her way back to her mamma, William. She's not a chit of a girl, after all."

That last bit was clearly not a compliment.

Evie glanced nervously at Will, and her heart sank when she saw his jaw go rock-like. She mentally groaned at the idea of him defying his powerful father in public—and all out of a misguided sense of loyalty to her. She honored him for it, but neither of them would benefit from the gossip that would surely follow on the heels of an ugly little scene.

As if sent from heaven, Gilbride appeared through a small gap in the crowd, moving to stand next to Evie. For a big, dominating man who seemed to bull his way through life, he had a remarkable ability to move with cat-like stealth.

"Your Highness," he said, giving the duke a respectful bow. Then he smiled down at Evie. "May I escort you back to your party, Miss Whitney? Your mamma sent me to fetch you." He cocked what looked like an ironic eyebrow at Will's father. "With your permission, sir."

The duke waved an impatient hand. "Yes, yes, go on."

Forcing herself not to look at Will, Evie took Gilbride's arm and let him lead her away through the crowd. He chatted amiably all the while, sounding like a featherhead, even though Evie was coming to conclude he was far from it. His arrival had been too well timed to be anything other than deliberate, and he'd handled the situation with polite efficiency. When she was no longer choking back a dreadful sense of humiliation, hoping the floor would open up and swallow her, she would make a point of thanking Gilbride for his welcome intervention.

Halfway up the ballroom, she could no longer resist looking over her shoulder. Will and his father stood where they had left them, although the duke's entourage had widened the circle around them. Apparently, at that point they feared a prince's displeasure more than they wished to overhear his conversation with his son.

Evie's heart sank as she took in Will's stone-faced expression. He listened politely to his father, and nodded his head once in agreement. But she knew what that blank expression meant. He was furious, but as embarrassed by the little scene as she was. That she had caused the scene, however unintentionally, made her stomach cramp with dismay. She and Will had just started to heal the wounds between them and this episode would surely destroy any chance of reconciled friendship.

Without Will ever having to tell her in so many words, she understood how important it was for him to please his father. Years ago, when the duke had decided to pay for his schooling and his commission in the army, Will had been overjoyed. His father's private acknowledgment had been one of the defining milestones of his life. Openly defying the duke out of loyalty to her, even over something so inconsequential, would surely have repercussions.

"It's not your fault," Gilbride said in a quiet voice as he steered her around a clutch of languid dandies. "You did nothing wrong, and neither did Wolf."

It took a moment to swallow the lump in her throat before she could answer. "Thank you for your kindness, sir. I'm not sure why the duke was so gruff with us, but I would hate to be the cause of any unpleasantness between Will and his . . . and the duke."

Gilbride let out a sardonic snort. "Most members of the royal family excel at unpleasantness, at least the dukes do. One eventually gets used to it."

"But—"

He gave her a reassuring smile. "Truly, Miss Whitney, you have nothing to worry about. Wolf is more than adept at handling his father. You needn't be concerned."

He gave her another one of his winks, though this one seemed friendly rather than flirtatious. Evie thought she rather liked the big Scotsman, no matter what Eden might say about him.

But as they rejoined her family and friends, Gilbride's jesting persona reasserted itself. She was now more than half-convinced he was playing some sort of role. That hardly sounded rational, but there seemed to be no other explanation for his rapid shifts in behavior.

"Hallo, hallo," he exclaimed in a booming voice that made her sister grimace. "Look who I stumbled upon in my stroll around the room. I knew Miss Evelyn would be as eager as I am to snabble up the lobster patties at supper, so I convinced her to toddle back with me." He finished his clownish speech by giving Mamma, who was staring at him with her mouth slightly open, a buffoonish grin.

"Oh, for God's sake," Eden muttered, taking Evie's arm. She made a shooing motion at Gilbride with her free hand. "Thank you for retrieving my sister, Captain, but there's no need to waste another minute on us."

Gilbride showed his blinding white teeth in a broad grin. "Nay, lassie, you'll no' be getting rid of me that easy. I have every intention of assisting you ladies down to the supper room."

As gloomy as Evie was feeling about the ugly episode with Will and his father, she couldn't stifle a spark of amusement. Gilbride's brogue seemed to be a matter of convenience for him, adopted when he wished to annoy or tweak someone.

Like her twin.

"That's entirely unnecessary," Eden responded in a blighting tone. "Evie and I will go down together, and Mr. Beaumont will escort my mother."

"Oh, of course," Michael said, suddenly springing to life. "It would be my honor to escort Lady Reese to the supper room."

He peered at Evie with a perplexed expression on his face, and she felt a stab of guilt that she'd practically forgotten his very existence. She made a silent promise to stop thinking about Will and focus on the blessings right under her nose.

"It would be lovely if you took Mamma down," she said, smiling at Michael. "I, for one, would be happy to sit and chat in a quiet corner for the rest of the evening."

"Well, I wouldn't," her mother said huffily. "But I suppose we should go now if we want to find a seat that isn't in a draft. Her Grace's public rooms are exceedingly drafty, I'm sorry to say." She bestowed a gracious smile on Gilbride, pointedly ignoring Michael. "Captain Gilbride, I would be most pleased if you escorted me to the supper room. Mr. Beaumont can follow with the girls."

Even Gilbride looked a little nonplussed by her mother's rudeness. Michael simply shrugged and gave Evie a small, understanding smile. Despite Gilbride's inanities, Mamma obviously found an heir to a Scottish earldom preferable to a younger son of a Catholic aristocrat—even if that younger son came from a wealthy and distinguished family.

Gilbride recovered quickly. "I'd be delighted, your ladyship." He moved with alacrity to her mother's side, but smiled at Michael as he did so. "And perhaps while we're having a bit of refreshment, Mr. Beaumont and Miss Evelyn can tell me a bit more about their charitable endeavors."

Mamma rolled her eyes but refrained from commenting as she took the captain's arm.

When Eden linked her hand through Evie's right arm, Michael moved around to her left. They fell into the slow-moving stream from the ballroom to the supper room, following in their mother's wake.

"I quite like Captain Gilbride," Michael said in a musing tone. "He strikes me as a genuinely kind man."

"He's a complete oaf," Eden huffed, sounding alarmingly like their mother. "I don't know how you can stand to spend so much time in his company."

"He's not an oaf," Evie said. "He just wants us to think he's one."

Michael nodded. "I would agree with your assessment. I wonder why he would wish anyone to think him so clownish."

"Because he is a clown?" Eden commented.

Evie frowned at her sister. It wasn't like Eden to be so ungenerous, even toward someone who annoyed her. She was impetuous and sometimes impatient, but never mean-spirited.

Her twin sighed. "Don't mind me. I'm just annoyed that the Duke of York so roundly snubbed you. It was awful of him."

Blast.

"You saw that from across the room?" Evie asked.

"It was quite evident to anyone watching," Michael said. Oddly, he didn't sound put out about it.

"And I'm *truly* annoyed with Will for not escorting you back," Eden said. "Whatever could he have been thinking?"

"It wasn't his fault," Evie said. "The duke all but ordered Will to stay with him."

"A true gentleman would have seen to your comfort first," Michael said.

His tone confirmed he saw Will as a threat, and that made Evie feel guilty all over again. She held her tongue, swallowing her instinctive urge to defend Will.

"I will give Gilbride some credit in this situation," Eden said. "He obviously figured out the problem and took it upon himself to act. I wouldn't have thought a big dolt like him could move so quickly."

Evie darted a nervous glance forward. They were separated from the captain and their mother by only old Lady Hanson and her two daughters. Fortunately, Mamma seemed to be happily chattering away with Gilbride, claiming his full attention.

"Don't be silly, Evie," her twin said, knowing, as usual,

what she was thinking. "They can't hear anything we're saying."

Just then, Gilbride glanced over his shoulder, straight at Eden. One of his eyebrows lifted in what could only be described as a sardonic tilt.

"Well, I'll be damned," Eden muttered under her breath.

Evie hushed her, but her sister simply grinned. Still Evie did notice that Eden flushed a bit, probably with embarrassment.

They made their way down the broad staircase and turned into the supper room, two large drawing rooms normally separated by pocket doors but now open to create a space large enough for the necessary number of small and medium-size tables, covered in crisp white linen. At least half were already occupied, but Gilbride deftly steered them to a larger table by a set of French doors that lead to the terrace.

With a sigh of relief, Evie sank into one of the little chairs grouped around the oval table, and glanced around. "Where did Mamma go?"

"Lady Reese wished to speak with Lady Castlereagh," Gilbride said, nodding to the other side of the room. "She said she would join us shortly." He snagged an empty chair from a nearby table and placed it next to Evie. "There, we'll save that for Will. No doubt he'll be along any moment."

Evie had just started to relax, but that notion sent her nerves jumping again. She didn't know whether she wanted Will to join them or not. Probably not, given the exciting but disturbing question he'd asked her just before the duke interrupted them.

Eden glanced toward the door. "Yes, I see him coming." She frowned, squinting. "Who is that with him? I can't tell from this distance."

Evie turned in her chair, praying he wasn't with the duke. Then she froze, realizing the truth was much worse.

Will was escorting Lady Calista Freemont, daughter of the Marquess of Corbendale and one of the nastiest people Evie had ever met. She'd attended Miss Ardmore's Select Academy for Young Ladies with Calista and had frequently been the target of the older girl's mean-spirited pranks.

Though Calista was both pretty and rich, her gruesome personality kept her from making a spectacular match. Will, unfortunately, wouldn't know that, given all his years spent abroad. Right now he seemed fairly enamored, smiling down at Calista as she batted her eyelashes in bold flirtation.

"Oh Lord, not her," Eden groaned.

Gilbride had been talking to Michael, but Eden's comment brought his head up. He craned his neck forward like a turtle coming out of its shell, then sat back and shook his head with disapproval.

"Idiot," he muttered.

Evie sent up a fervent prayer that Will and Calista would sit somewhere else, but Michael got to his feet and waved his napkin, drawing their notice.

"Doesn't he know what a shrew Calista is?" Eden hissed to Evie.

"He knows," Evie replied with a scowl.

Will caught sight of them and waved back, and Evie's faint hope that she'd be spared another humiliating scene died with a whimper. After tonight, she *would* do her best to avoid Will, since he'd obviously developed a knack for pitching her into dreadful situations. And why he was flirting with Calista—and he clearly *was* flirting—after doing the same with her less than a half hour ago was a mystery. She'd never thought of Will as the sort to play fast and loose with a woman's feelings, but perhaps she was wrong about that.

Just like she'd been wrong all those years ago when she thought he was in love with her.

As Will and Calista approached, Gilbride got up and took the seat next to Evie, the one he'd set out for Will only a few minutes ago. He leaned close and murmured. "Just ignore him when he's acting like a clodpole, Miss Evie. That's what I do."

She gave him a weak smile, startled by the revelation that he obviously knew something about her embarrassing history with Will. Even worse, Gilbride seemed to think it still mattered to her.

Which, unfortunately, it did.

"Good evening," Will said with a smile. "May we sit? We don't want to put you out, but most of the tables are full."

"Of course they won't mind," Calista said with honeyed malice. "Evelyn and I are old friends, are we not? And Eden, as well."

Eden eyed Calista like she was a poisonous viper about to strike. Fortunately, her twin held her fire, for once deciding not to raise a fuss.

Michael and Gilbride came to their feet.

"You are most welcome to join us," Michael said with alacrity. He gazed down at Evie with an encouraging smile. "You don't mind, do you?"

Evie had to clear her throat before she could answer. "Of course not."

Will fetched an empty chair from an adjacent table, and they all shuffled to make room. Michael resumed his seat next to Evie and spoke to her in a quiet tone. "I didn't realize you were friends with Lady Calista. I'm happy you have the chance to spend some time with her."

"I'm not, on both counts," Evie ground out between clenched teeth.

"Oh, well," he said vaguely. "Captain Endicott seems quite chummy with her though, don't you think?"

Evie couldn't muster a polite response and didn't even try.

"Beaumont's jealous of Wolf," Gilbride murmured from her other side. "That's why he's acting like a ninny."

Evie held back a sigh. Either Gilbride was a great deal more perceptive than most people gave him credit for, or she was ridiculously transparent. Neither thought provided any comfort.

"He has no reason to be, I assure you," she replied in a cool voice.

"Lady Calista tells me that you and Eden attended school with her," Will said in a hearty voice, obviously trying to restart the conversation. "I didn't know that."

Since Eden's only response was to cross her arms over her chest and glare at Calista, it was left to Evie to answer. "There was no reason for you to be aware of that fact."

Will's eyebrows shot up at her terse reply. His gaze jumped to Eden and then back to Evie. He pressed his lips into a grim line and shook his head, recognizing he'd blundered into another uncomfortable situation.

"Oh, yes," Calista trilled in a treacly voice. "We had such a gay time, didn't we, Evelyn? You *were* a clumsy girl, forever tripping over things, much to everyone's amusement. I do hope you've grown out of that unfortunate malady."

"Speaking of clumsy," Eden said in dulcet tones that would have warned anyone who knew her, "I recall an incident where you ended up with your head in a wash bucket. Or have you forgotten that, Lady Calista?"

Since Eden had been the one to engineer that particular result, it was a good bet Calista hadn't forgotten. It had been in retaliation against Calista and her friends—all haughty, insufferable girls—after they'd placed a bucket of greasy slops against the door to the room where Evie and Eden slept with two other girls. When Evie opened the door, the bucket had tipped over and the slops had gone everywhere. She'd crashed to the floor in the slippery mess, accompanied by gales of laughter from Calista and her band of harpies. Furious, Eden had filled the bucket with ice cold water from the outside pump and dumped it on Calista's head. Evie was sure Calista's outraged screams had been audible for miles.

"I haven't forgotten *anything*," Calista snapped, her big brown eyes sparking with rage.

"I say, who's for champagne?" Gilbride interjected, leaping to his foot. He waved down a passing waiter and then practically dragged Will up by the collar, claiming they would fetch some cakes from the refreshment table. Gilbride seemed to be lecturing Will as he dragged him off, who didn't look happy to be at the receiving end of a scold.

While Eden and Calista continued their glaring match, Evie turned to Michael and began talking about some financial details regarding the charity's ledgers. She didn't give a hang about the ledgers at this moment but desperately needed something to talk about that did not involve Calista. Fortunately, Michael gamely threw himself into the discussion, finally recognizing he'd committed a capital blunder when he'd invited Calista and Will to sit with them.

A few minutes later, they were joined by Will and Gilbride who unloaded plates full of sweets on the table. When the men were reseated and cakes dished out, Evie returned to her low-voiced conversation with Michael, determined to ignore the hideous little flirtation Calista tried to carry on with Will. Fortunately, Will was having none of it, adopting a stone face that seemed to bring Calista up short.

Unfortunately, that prompted Calista to once more turn her ire on Evie.

"Evelyn, *must* you and Mr. Beaumont go on forever about that boring charity of yours? It hardly seems like polite conversation for a supper party." She turned to Will and gave him what she must have thought was a charming smile. "Not that our dear little Evelyn was ever adept at polite conversation."

When Will's only response was to lift an imperious eyebrow, the dreary woman faltered for a moment. But she quickly recovered, redirecting her malicious gaze back at Evie.

"But you clearly disdain such mundane social endeavors because you have much more important things to do, like spending your time with Papists and those dirty Irish peasants you seem so fond of. No wonder you have so few suitors." Calista's cold gaze flicked to Michael. "Except for ineligible ones, of course, according to poor, dear Lady Reese."

Calista's venom shocked them all into silence for a good five seconds, making the gay chatter and clinking of crystal and china around them sound inordinately loud.

Will recovered first, speaking in low tones that vibrated with anger. "Lady Calista, I hardly think your opinion on such matters—"

"Never mind, Will," Evie said, cutting him off. She stretched her arm across the table, picked up a plate of strawberry shortcake, and flipped the contents onto the bodice of Calista's primrose-colored, cambric gown. One strawberry bounced and lodged itself in an elaborate knot of lace at the center of her bodice.

With everyone gaping in astonishment, Evie leveled a sugary smile at Calista, who was sputtering with incoherent fury. "Dear me," she said, "you are *so* right, Lady Calista. I am the clumsiest creature on the planet."

Still smiling, Evie glanced at Will. When their gazes

locked, his mouth clamped into a tight line that began to quiver suspiciously, as if he were repressing laughter.

"Well done, Miss Evie," Gilbride murmured, "but prepare to take heavy fire in return."

When she followed the direction of his pointed stare, her heart sank. Standing behind Will's broad shoulders was Evie's mother, her face taut with anger. Beside her, as terrible luck would have it, was Lady Corbendale—Calista's mother.

Chapter Ten

Evie rummaged in her jewelry case for her garnet earbobs, though she had little desire to get dressed this morning. She had even less desire to sit with her mother and wait for the callers who would surely arrive to salivate over last night's debacle. The scene with Calista wasn't the most salacious of scandals but would provide at least a week's worth of embarrassing gossip.

Mamma was furious that she'd been forced to utter an abject apology to Lady Corbendale, one of the haughtiest doyennes of the *ton*. But Evie had to give her mother credit. After the apology had been offered up, she'd acted as if nothing untoward had occurred. Mamma had taken Gilbride's arm with a dignity even the queen couldn't match, smiling graciously at their acquaintances as they left the supper room. Naturally, tittering remarks had followed in their wake, but Lord Bromley, for one—a shy but very nice man—had given Evie a thumb's up as she passed. Another dashing young man by the door had murmured a *well done, Miss Whitney,* as she walked by.

And Will, she discovered, *had* been trying not to laugh. He'd escorted her and Eden downstairs to the carriage, and she could feel his big body shaking with repressed laughter the entire way. Eden had then started to giggle, and Evie had been forced to hiss at both of them to be quiet.

But no one laughed once they got into the carriage. Not even Will's affectionate good-bye—he'd kissed Evie's hand before helping her step up into the barouche—had done much toward staving off the shame she felt under the lash of her mother's tongue. Mamma had made it clear that she'd had enough of Evie's inappropriate social behavior and all but forbade her from seeing Michael. When Eden had mounted a vigorous defense, Mamma had ordered her to hold her tongue.

When they reached home, their mother had sent them straight upstairs, forbidding them from even talking with each other. Normally, she and Eden ignored that sort of edict, but Evie was feeling too low at that point to talk to anyone, even her twin.

The worst was that she still didn't know how she felt about Will. He'd run frustratingly hot and cold all evening. One moment he seemed to be flirting with her, the next he was ignoring her. After that, he was finding her an unparalleled source of amusement. The confusing end to a horrible evening had included—least she be tempted to forget—a public snub by a royal duke.

She sighed as she inserted the bobs in her earlobes and then turned on the padded chair at her dressing table when the connecting door to Eden's room opened.

"Well, you certainly look like you lost your best friend," her sister commented. As always, she looked perfect in the floating muslins that fluttered around her neat ankles and pretty pink shoes.

"If Mamma has anything to say about it, I think I will have," Evie said.

Eden threw her a quizzical look as she flopped down in

the armchair in front of the fireplace, still managing to look graceful. "I thought *I* was your best friend."

Evie frowned. "You're more than that. You're part of me, and I couldn't live without you."

"Just checking," Eden said. "You mean Michael, I suppose, but you're not to worry about him. I already talked to Papa about last night, and he promised to take care of Mamma."

Evie perked up. "He did? What did he say?"

"At first he was inclined to be annoyed with you, but when I explained what actually happened—" She paused to peer through the open door, checking for eavesdroppers before continuing. "Suffice it to say that Papa found the entire episode rather hilarious. He suggested that you keep your head low for a few days and try not to irritate Mamma further. Of course, we all know how easy that will be."

The tight feeling around Evie's chest eased for the first time since last night. She adored her father. He never thought her silly for preferring books and charity work to flirting with young men, and had never failed to deflect Mamma's temper when it became necessary. He quite liked Michael, too, although the jury was still out when it came to his granting permission for them to be married. Despite Papa's easygoing nature, last night's episode would not advance Michael's case.

"That's a relief," she said. "Everything is a bit easier to bear knowing Papa isn't angry with me. I hope Mamma won't hold on to it for too long, especially when it comes to Michael."

"I wouldn't bet on that," Eden said. "You know what the old girl's like. She loathes being humiliated, especially in front of someone as high in the instep as Lady Corbendale."

Evie dropped her forehead into her palms. Her sister was right. Her mother would no doubt put her foot down, both about Michael and her charity work. Even before this Mamma barely tolerated her *little hobby,* as she called it.

Eden came to kneel beside her, sliding one arm around her shoulders. "Evie, you worry too much."

She met her twin's sympathetic gaze with a grimace. "I made such a mess of things. I know what Calista is like, and I should have ignored her."

Her sister sat back on her heels and grinned. "I'm just relieved that it's not me causing the scandal. And tipping that plate down Calista's scrawny bosom was a splendid moment. I only wish I'd thought of it."

Evie wrinkled her nose. "I wish you had too."

Her sister scrambled to her feet and pulled Evie out of her chair. "Listen, darling, it's not a bad thing to kick over the traces now and again. You're much too serious. Sometimes you act like an old lady, as if your life is already over."

"I do no such thing."

"You do, and as much as I like Michael, he's not much better. You bring out the worst in each other."

Evie tugged her hands away. "I prefer to think we bring the best out in each other."

Her sister's response was a derisive snort.

"Well, what do you want me to do?" Evie asked defensively. "I'm not you. It's not like I have suitors lined up around the block."

"You need to give Wolf a chance," Eden said.

Evie stared at her sister, wondering if she'd heard her correctly. She had to swallow twice before she could manage an answer. "You're wrong if you think Will is courting me. And I wouldn't want him to, anyway."

"Oh, really?"

"Yes, really, and this is a stupid conversation." Evie headed to the door. "I'm going down. I'm sure Mamma is waiting for us in the drawing room."

"She is, and we've already got a visitor."

"But it's not even eleven o'clock." Clearly the news about last night's incident was traveling about town even more quickly than she expected.

"This is a *special* visitor, one you will surely wish to see."

Evie could hear the note of mischief in her sister's voice. "Who is it?"

Eden grinned. "It's Wolf, and I do believe he's most eager to see you."

Will was beginning to regret his choice of seating. Every time he moved the delicate chair squeaked alarmingly beneath him, as if about to collapse. But Lady Reese had not given him much choice. She'd waved him to it while she ensconced herself in the middle of a much sturdier chaise covered in Chinese-patterned silk. Not that he had any intention of complaining, since he'd half been expecting Evie's mother to bar him from the premises. He wouldn't blame her if she did, since he was ultimately the author of Evie's current plight.

But Will's father had stolen a march on him last night, insisting on introductions. It had been the first step on the path to disaster. Logic had dictated the necessity of keeping Evie as far away from the duke as possible until the conspirators had been exposed and the plot against the government thwarted. If Will had been thinking logically, he would have whisked her away to some quiet alcove or even to the supper room as soon as Alec distracted Beaumont. Then, he could have extracted a commitment from her to visit St. Margaret's as soon as possible.

Instead, he'd asked her to waltz with him, and that had been his undoing. Because once he'd pulled Evie into his arms, his logic had collapsed as soon as those soft, generous curves had nestled against him. Keeping his eyes pinned to her face hadn't made rational thought any easier, since she seemed to get prettier every time he saw her. He'd forgotten how gloriously big and blue her eyes were behind those spectacles. Along with her sweet face and her thick, honey-colored hair, it added up to an enchanting package.

As for her lush pink mouth . . . all Will had been able to envision were her lips on his body, kissing their way down to his—

"May I refresh your tea, Captain?" Lady Reese enquired. "Or perhaps you'd like me to ring for a cool glass of lemonade. You look rather flushed."

Good God.

What the hell was he doing, sitting in the Reese drawing room having fantasies about Evie with her mother not three feet away?

"No, thank you, my lady," he said, dredging up a smile. "It is rather warm out, but I do believe it's perfect weather for a carriage ride."

That bit of idiocy had her ladyship casting a doubting glance out the window. Though it was mild enough, the heavily overcast sky threatened rain.

"I'm sure Evelyn will be delighted to go out driving with you," her ladyship said.

That was doubtful after last night's multiple social disasters. Evie had barely been able to meet his gaze when he'd handed her into the carriage, and his heart had ached at the combination of shame and defiance warring for dominance on her face.

Lady Reese peered out the window again. "Perhaps Evelyn should take an umbrella, as it does look a little showery. Not enough to cancel your proposed drive, however," she added hastily. "I'm sure my daughter won't mind a few raindrops."

Will made a noncommittal sound of agreement, wondering why Lady Reese was so bloody friendly. It was such a marked departure from her usual treatment of him. Only her husband's close friendship with Will's uncle had enabled her to endure his regular visits to Maywood Manor. But while he didn't know what had changed, he intended to use it to help Evie.

He put down his teacup and cleared his throat. When Lady Reese lifted a haughty eyebrow, it brought back a flood of childhood memories. No one else could intimidate so effectively with just a lift of a brow. In some ways, he found her just as formidable as his father.

"My lady, I must apologize for the incident in the supper room last night. I was Lady Calista's escort, and while I am loath to criticize so fashionable a young lady, her behavior was insulting, especially to Evie."

Lady Reese put her teacup and saucer down with a decided click. "I am aware of that fact, Wolf. However, Evelyn had no business acting in so outrageous a manner, regardless of the provocation. I was mortified, especially since Lady Calista's mother had been gracious enough to escort me back to our table."

It took Will a moment to respond as he tried to cope with the fact that Lady Reese had just addressed him by his nickname. She'd never done that before. He inserted that interesting development into a mental slot marked *what the devil is going on* and focused on the subject at hand.

"I know it looked bad, but I'm sure Evie's reaction was instinctive more than anything else." He flashed what he hoped was a charming smile. "My only real surprise is that Eden didn't get there first."

The flesh across Lady Reese's cheekbones stretched tight

with disapproval. Clearly, she would brook no criticism, good-natured or otherwise, of her favorite child.

"In any event," he added, trying to recover lost ground, "I had no right to intrude on your party. I regret being the vehicle for so unfortunate a scene, and I sincerely apologize."

Lady Reese tilted her head, studying him with cool regard. As a boy, that look had unnerved him. She no longer held that power over him, and he simply returned stare for stare.

Truth be told, he'd always found her interesting, if for no other reason than she was so unlike her daughters. The girls took after their father, a sturdily built man with wheat-colored hair and a kind manner, rather than Lady Reese who was slender and elegant, with a handsome face and chestnut hair barely touched by gray. She carried herself with a prickly sense of dignity that he'd eventually realized masked a sense of inferiority. Lord Reese might be a viscount and a well-liked one at that, but his fortune was merely respectable. His lordship aspired to nothing more than a pleasant life in the country, taking care of his tidy holdings.

Lady Reese, on the other hand, had always wanted more for her children than she'd received from her own marriage.

"I am aware," she finally said, "that Calista is an ill-tempered girl allowed free rein by an indulgent mother. But Evelyn should have held her temper, knowing that most of the injury resulting from the gossip will fall on her. I only wish to protect her from that."

"Do you? Sometimes I wonder."

Lady Reese sucked in a startled breath, but Will decided he didn't give a damn about offending her. He'd spent too many years watching Evie suffer at the receiving end of her mother's ire and realized he'd had enough.

After a long moment of weighty silence, her ladyship finally pried her lips apart. "I do as I see fit with my children, and I will not apologize for that. But believe me when I tell you that I do not hold either you or Evelyn primarily responsible for last night's incident. I know *exactly* who is to blame for the unfortunate change in my daughter's behavior."

Will was all ears to hear more, but the door to the drawing room opened and Evie rushed into the room. She looked both flustered and adorably shy.

He couldn't help smiling as he rose. She'd never been shy with him before, and he was convinced the change resulted from her unsuccessful attempts to repress her attraction toward him. He should probably be doing his best to help her in that particular endeavor but had to admit the idea held little appeal.

"Good morning, Will," she said, trying for a brave smile. "I hope you haven't been waiting too long. Edie only just told me you were here."

Will took her outstretched hand, forestalling her curtsey by bringing her fingers to his lips. When his mouth touched her sweetly scented skin, he felt her shock in the slight jerk of her hand.

Lady Reese clucked her disapproval, although apparently not at him. "I will speak with your sister, since I expressly told her to send you down immediately."

"I'm sorry, Mamma," Evie said, extracting her hand from Will's hold. "I didn't expect callers this early."

"After last night's escapade, I expect we'll have many callers today," her mother responded tartly.

When Evie's shoulders went stiff and straight, Will had to fight the urge to draw her into a comforting embrace.

He wanted to kiss the delicate white skin on the back of her neck, sweetly exposed by the upsweep of her thick hair into a simple knot. Evie might be fairly short and have a pleasingly plump figure, but she had a long neck that cried out for kisses.

"I know," she said. "I'm sorry for that, Mamma. I'll do my best to deal with them today, I promise."

"You won't, because I'm sending you off with William for the rest of the morning. Your sister can receive with me today. She's almost as much at fault for last night's unpleasantness, since she had the bad manners to show her amusement at Lady Calista's humiliation."

Evie's mouth dropped open. Will knew it was a rare day in hell when Lady Reese criticized Eden.

Then Evie obviously took in the fact that her mother had all but ordered her to spend the day with him. She cast him a startled glance, her cheeks turning a bright shade of pink. He would have enjoyed her charming display of nerves but for the fact that she'd obviously rather spend the day at the receiving end of nasty gossip than in his company.

"Mamma, I really think I should stay," she protested. "After all, this is my fault."

"There is more than enough blame to hand around, young lady," her mother replied. "Now, go upstairs and get ready."

"But—"

"Go," Lady Reese said, pointing an imperious finger at the door.

Evie rolled her eyes and threw Will an irate look, a sure indication that she was rapidly recovering from her bout of shyness. She marched out of the room, shutting the door with a decided snap.

Lady Reese gave him an apologetic smile, but the frosty cast of her eyes worried him.

"Please don't be too hard on Evie, your ladyship," he said after a moment's consideration. "I think she's having some trouble adjusting to my . . ." He struggled to sum up their complicated history.

"To your precipitous return to her life after breaking her heart all those years ago?" Lady Reese asked. Clearly, *she* had no trouble defining that history.

Still, her blunt response surprised him. "That was never my intention. And forgive me if I'm wrong, but it appeared at the time that you would not have approved of our marriage."

"No, not then," she said.

That gave him another jolt. "You mean you would now? What's changed?"

"You have," she replied in the same, startling vein of candor. "You've established a sound military career and you have influential patrons. Lord Reese, for one, expects you to do quite well."

Ah.

Lady Reese had always found Will's parentage distasteful, but his father's support over the last several years had obviously changed her opinion.

Unfortunately, her ladyship couldn't know that the duke would have his hide if he even so much as suggested he wished to marry Evie. His father had made it clear last night that she was to be the subject of an investigation and nothing more.

"You need to find a wife who will support your career and social standing, William," the duke had said in a blighting tone. "The Reese family is well enough, but the girl consorts with radicals and has, at best, a modest dowry.

Besides, she's damned awkward. No style or conversation, from what I understand."

His father had then pointed him in the direction of Lady Calista, all but ordering him to take her down to supper.

And look how well that turned out.

"I'm not rich," he said to Lady Reese. "I can provide comfortably for a wife and family but certainly not in the style Evie's accustomed to."

"Not yet," she said with pointed emphasis.

Will shook his head, trying to control his exasperation. None of this made any sense. "I thank you for your confidence, my lady, but the subject appears to be moot. Evie has no notion of marrying me. In fact, it would appear she's all but engaged to Mr. Beaumont."

Lady Reese's dark, elegant brows snapped together in a fierce scowl. She rose to her feet like an avenging fury. "She will *not* be marrying that man. Not if I have anything to say about it. He's been a most regrettable influence on her. Not only is Mr. Beaumont a Catholic, he has radical tendencies. I refuse to allow my daughter to marry that sort of person."

Will pondered whether to bark at her for her cold-hearted bigotry or applaud her for an instinctive sense that something was off-color with Beaumont. He decided on the former. Beaumont came from one of the oldest and most distinguished families in the land, but there was still a great deal of ill feeling toward Catholics. He found it ironic that both Lady Reese and his father shared a mutual antipathy for Beaumont.

Evie, unfortunately, would suffer the consequences even if Beaumont were to be found innocent.

"Michael Beaumont is a wealthy son of a distinguished earl," he pointed out. "And he is clearly fond of Evie."

"I don't trust him." She sounded like she was grinding

rocks between her teeth. "He's going to bring her trouble. I just know it."

Now, *that* was interesting. Lady Reese might be lamentably narrow-minded, but she was an intelligent and perceptive woman. Did she sense something about Beaumont that was a genuine threat, or was she simply another anti-Papist?

"Are you suggesting Evie is in some sort of danger through her association with Beaumont?" he asked in a deliberately skeptical voice.

Lady Reese gave her head a tiny shake, as if throwing off her uncharacteristically emotional display. She resumed her seat with her usual dignity. "I'm saying that you have an obligation to my daughter, William, one which I consider to be of long standing. I expect you to act upon it, as any gentleman would."

There was no response to that statement that wouldn't toss him into a pit full of snakes. Fortunately, he was rescued by Evie's return.

"I'm ready," she said, sounding more resigned than annoyed. Perhaps she'd decided that an outing with him *was* preferable to spending the day as the *ton's* current target of gossip.

Will made his bow to Lady Reese and went to take Evie's arm. She'd garbed herself in a well-cut, royal blue pelisse that shaped her luscious curves and brought out the color in her eyes. With the faint blush in her cheeks, her sweetness made his mouth water.

"You look pretty," he said, starting to enjoy himself.

She wrinkled her nose as if she didn't believe him. "Where are we going?"

"I'll tell you when we're outside."

"Have a nice day, my dears," her mother called after them. "Don't forget to take an umbrella."

"Oh, thank you, Mamma," Evie responded. She glanced at Will as he led her to the entrance hall. "Why do you think she's acting so . . . nice?"

He shrugged as he took an umbrella from a waiting footman. "I haven't the foggiest idea."

Chapter Eleven

As Will handed her up into his dashing green curricle, Evie struggled to calm her flustered nerves. She felt horribly awkward after last night's scene with Calista, despite Will's evident amusement with the ghastly episode. And then there was her mother who was apparently doing everything she could to throw Will at her, as if she truly did believe he'd come courting.

All those tangled-up emotions scattered when he sprang into the carriage and sat next to her. Left in their place was a heightened awareness of his muscular body plastered against her—shoulder, arm, hip, and thigh. So much contact and so much heat that all but threatened to turn her brain to mush.

He smiled, his knowing gaze partly shaded by the brim of his hat. "Are you comfortable, or do you need a lap blanket?" He peered up at the sky, a high overcast that turned the gleaming white of the neat town houses lining the street to a dull, pale gray. "I don't think it's going to rain, so we'll keep the umbrella stowed under the seat for now."

"I don't need a lap blanket, but perhaps this isn't the best day for a drive in the park," she said, hating that she sounded so breathless. "We wouldn't want to get rained on if you're wrong."

He cut her the rogue's grin she was beginning to like too much. "I'm not wrong. Besides, we won't be spending much time in the park."

With no explanation of that cryptic remark, he set the curricle bowling down the street, expertly negotiating the tight corner at the top of Upper Brook Street moments later to bring them into Park Lane.

"Well, where *are* we going?" she finally prodded. "I hope you didn't plan anything too elaborate, since I'm hardly dressed for it."

His gaze flicked down over her body, lingering on her chest for long seconds. "You look just fine," he said in a low, rumbling voice that made her go suddenly weak. Of course, that feeling might also be the result of being wedged so tightly against his brawny frame.

She tried to put an inch or two between them, disconcerted by his apparently deliberate flirtation. "That's not what I asked," she said in a prim voice.

"First I need to say something."

Evie glanced at him, puzzled by the sudden switch from easygoing flirtation to an almost somber tone. She'd always been able to read Will—except for their spectacular misunderstanding years ago—and he'd never been prone to capricious changes in behavior. Now, he seemed different in ways she barely recognized.

But she supposed the same could be said about her. Although never as carefree as her twin, Evie hadn't always been a pattern card of buttoned-up spinsterhood. She remembered a childhood full of laughter and games and the silly adventures children engaged in when they had no one to please but themselves. Bit by bit, she'd lost that sense of fun. Sometimes, when she looked at Eden, so full of curiosity and eager for life, she felt little better than a pale copy, leached of color and interest.

She blew out an exasperated breath, impatient that she would think, much less act, with such inflated drama—as she'd done last night. She had a perfectly good life, with friends and family that loved her and work that truly meant something. It was simply Will's sudden reappearance in her life that had made her begin questioning herself.

It was a bellwether warning to keep him at a safe distance.

"Evie, are you listening to me?"

She jerked, blinking in surprise as she realized they'd already turned onto Piccadilly and were driving past Green Park Lodge.

"Um, yes . . . that is to say . . ." She grimaced. "I'm sorry, Will. My mind must have wandered for a moment."

"Well, that puts me in my place," he said sardonically.

When she maintained an uncomfortable silence, he made a scoffing noise and turned into the laneway leading to the Reservoir, pulling up his horses under a stand of trees.

"I thought you said we weren't going to the park," she said.

"We weren't, but I need your full attention when I say this," he said, setting the brake and turning to face her.

Evie darted a glance around. Green Park was mostly deserted this early in the day, devoid even of nannies with their young charges, no doubt kept inside by the lowering sky. In fact, she thought she'd just felt a drop or two of rain but had no intention of pointing that out. Not when Will was looking at her with an expression suggesting she had more hair than wit.

He did seem to have a marked effect on her ability to think rationally.

She crossed her hands on top of her reticule and gave him what she hoped was a placid smile—one that a schoolmistress might give to her prize pupil. Or one that encouraged but also suggested the answer didn't really matter all that much.

Will tipped her chin up with a leather-gloved finger, forcing her to look straight into his riveting eyes. Eyes that had always been able to see clear into her heart. In the old days, Evie had found that enchanting. Now his close inspection inspired conflicting impulses—to melt into his arms, or to leap down from the carriage and take to her heels, heading for the uncertain safety of Hertford Street.

A wry smile curled up the corners of a mouth that was both hard and generous and utterly masculine. Evie could remember every detail of how that mouth tasted—even after only one kiss under a moonlight sky years ago.

As if in response to the vivid memory, his fingers moved to gently cradle her jaw. He barely touched her, and yet his touch held all the heat and emotion of a lover's embrace.

"You *are* going to drive me mad, aren't you?" Will murmured.

The intensity of his gaze struck her full-force, making her heart pound with a heavy beat that rushed blood through her body. Evie began to tremble deep inside, and it radiated out until even her fingers shook.

"Will," she managed to croak. "What are you about?"

He finally shifted his gaze, casting a quick glance around. His hand, however, remained on her chin a moment longer, finally drifting away in a soft slide along the underside of her jaw. As hard as she tried, she could not repress a shiver.

Then he turned forward and put a few inches of space between them. "God knows what I'm doing," he muttered, as if to himself.

"If you don't, *I* certainly can't tell you," she said, annoyed with yet another mercurial change in his behavior. If this was the new Will, she wasn't sure she liked this version all that much. Well, in all honesty she was forced to admit she'd liked his gentle touch on her face, though she would certainly never tell him.

Fortunately, he laughed, dissolving some of the tension.

"I'm trying to apologize for that scene in the supper room last night," he said. "I didn't intend to make things difficult for you."

He picked up the reins, although he didn't set the horses in motion. In fact, he stared straight ahead, a frown marking his handsome features.

"Is there something else?" she asked, poking his bicep. Even under the fabric of his coat it felt like she'd tapped an iron bar.

He grimaced. "Yes. I need to apologize for my, er . . . for the Duke of York's behavior last night. I had no expectation he would act so rudely to you. I'm truly sorry, Evie. It was awful for you."

That was certainly the truth, but Evie knew it had also been awful for Will. She heard the shame and frustration in his voice, and silently cursed his father for humiliating him so publicly. But she sensed that too much sympathy on her part would only embarrass him further.

"What I'd *really* like is for you to apologize for talking to Calista in the first place. I suppose you didn't know how truly awful she is, but that's no excuse," she said in a rallying tone.

One corner of his mouth edged up in a reluctant smile. He released the brake and deftly turned his horses, wheeling out onto Piccadilly once more. "You're right, I didn't know. But I can assure you that I now entirely share your opinion. Lady Calista got everything she deserved last night."

Inside, Evie breathed a sigh of relief. The very idea of Will caught in the clutches of a shrew like Calista made her stomach cramp. Not with jealousy, she firmly told herself, but because she hated to see a friend fall prey to a budding harpy.

"How *did* you find yourself trapped in Calista's claws?" she asked. "You don't even know her." She'd lain awake half the night worrying over that—along with a dozen other things—and she was still curious.

He hesitated, as if weighing how to answer. "You can put that down to the duke, as well," he finally said. "He all but threw her into my arms."

"Really? It looked to me like he was reading you a lecture."

"That came before the throwing."

Evie suddenly felt the need to fuss with her reticule. She shouldn't ask but couldn't help herself. "I assume the duke lectured you about me?"

He flashed a look full of regret. "Was it that obvious?"

She turned a hand, palm up, in silent answer.

He sighed. "I had hoped it wasn't *too* obvious."

"Only Captain Gilbride and I noticed, I think," she said, determined not to mention Eden's assessment that half the room had likely discerned the snub.

He cursed under his breath.

She touched his sleeve. "It's nothing to stew about, Will. I'm simply curious to know how I offended him." She gave him a wry smile. "I'm rather famous for offending people, but this is the first time I've pulled it off with royalty."

That won her a grudging laugh. "It wasn't you, *per se*," he said. "My fa . . . the duke—"

"You can call him whatever you want around me," she

interrupted. "He *is* your father, and the relationship is important to you. As it should be."

"Thank you," he said quietly. "It's hard to speak of him in that way. Even harder to think of him as my father, if you want to know the truth. My uncle raised me and was always there for me, not the duke."

"Yes, I imagine it's been awkward sorting out those conflicting loyalties. But stop stalling, Wolf." She deliberately used the old nickname. "I'm going to badger you until you tell me what that lecture was about." The fact that he was so obviously loath to tell her had both piqued her curiosity and made her worry—for him.

"I'd forgotten what a scold you can be, Evie. No, wait. I hadn't."

"Do I need to bash you over the head?"

"No, stop. I'll tell you. Head-bashing is *not* recommended while driving through Mayfair."

They'd reached the outskirts of Mayfair already, heading toward Leicester Square. She'd barely noticed, too interested in their conversation to pay much attention to the bustle of the streets of London.

"My father," he said in a careful manner, "has taken a considerable interest in my future."

"Well, that's all very good, isn't it?"

"In some ways, but it would appear he's turned into something of a matchmaker."

It only took Evie a few seconds to decipher his vague statement. "Of course. He would wish you to marry an heiress, preferably one who is both accomplished and beautiful and will help you establish yourself socially. The opposite of someone like me, from the duke's point of view."

He glanced at her with a reluctant smile of appreciation. "You were always quick as the devil, Evie."

"For all the good it does me. I hope you made it clear to your father that I was not casting lures at you."

He shook his head. "It would seem he thought *I* was the one doing the casting."

Her throat constricted. "You must have told him how silly that was." Her voice came out on a squeak.

"He never gave me the chance. The lecture was followed immediately by the introduction to Lady Calista." He gave her an ironic glance. "You know the rest."

It struck her that his answer was little more than a dodge. But wisdom dictated she not pursue that avenue of thought, for a thousand reasons she would no doubt shortly remember.

Because of Michael, you birdwit.

It astounded her how easily she forgot about her almost-fiancé whenever she was anywhere near Will.

"I hope you're not too offended, Evie," he said in a concerned voice. "I'm sure the duke doesn't dislike you in a personal way."

Evie had formed the opposite impression last night, though it seemed odd since she'd never spoken to the Duke of York. But he clearly disapproved of her on some level, and if Will *did* know he would wish to spare her feelings and not tell her.

She gave his arm a brisk pat. "Your father has only your best interests at heart, and I understand that. But if I may give you some advice, it would be that you not consistently defer to him. Yes, he's a prince *and* your commanding officer, but he needs to understand he can't order you about, at least not when it comes to domestic matters."

He raised mocking eyebrows. "And is that the advice you follow when it comes to dealing with your mother?"

"Ouch," she said, giving an exaggerated wince. "Very well, I've learned my lesson and will no longer provide any commentary on your private life. I would ask, however, that you afford me the same courtesy."

"Yes, of course," he said in a rather formal tone. "If that is what you wish."

She almost groaned. "I was joking, Will. Now, I suggest we not ruin the rest of the day by talking any more about our tiresome parents. And since you've made your apologies in an appropriately abject fashion, will you now tell me where we're going?"

She had an idea, though it seemed a strange choice for a social outing. But when the curricle turned onto Coventry Street, with its gold and silversmiths and jewelry shops, her suspicions were all but confirmed.

"Surely you've guessed by now?" he asked with a smile.

"You're taking me to St. Margaret's."

"Indeed. I'd like to see what you do there."

"Why?" She'd assumed his earlier questions about her work had been nothing more than the polite interest of an old friend.

"I'm not entirely a frippery fellow," he said in a wounded voice that didn't fool her a bit. "I can be serious now and again."

"You're actually the least frivolous person I know. Or, almost," she amended, thinking of Michael. "But why in heaven's name do you want to spend the afternoon poking around a charity school? Won't you be bored?"

Will kept his attention on his horses while he navigated the curricle around two carts whose drivers were engaged in a shouting match. He didn't speak again until he'd negotiated their safe passage, and Evie couldn't shake the feeling he was composing his answer.

"Nothing you could do would ever bore me," he said. "This is important to you, so it's important to me."

She fiddled with the delicate brass chain on her reticule, not sure what to say. The idea that she was important to him raised more questions than it answered.

"Besides," he added, "Alec is interested in supporting the place, so I thought it made sense for me to take a look. He's a bit of a soft touch, if you want to know the truth, and I wouldn't want him taken advantage of."

She twisted in her seat to glare at him, her flustered worries dissolving under a flare of anger. "William Endicott, are you suggesting that *I* would do such a thing?"

"Dammit, Evie," he said. "That's not what I meant and you know it."

"I don't know how I could take it any other way."

"It's not you I'm concerned about," he growled.

She let out a heavy sigh. "Michael. I really don't understand why you don't like him. He's a thoroughly decent, honorable person who's invested a great deal of his own money into St. Margaret's and the Hibernian Benevolent Association."

"If you can't deduce why I don't like the man, I'm certainly not going to tell you," Will said in a dry voice. "But we'll save that discussion for another time. For now, be assured that I'm most sincere when I say that whatever interests you, interests me."

Part of Evie *did* wish to explore why Will had conceived such a dislike for Michael. She could almost believe he was jealous, as silly as that seemed. But since Michael had quite clearly developed a corresponding dislike of Will, she couldn't think of any other explanation that made sense. However, that was a topic fraught with danger and she decided to agree with Will and let it drop.

"Very well," she said, "what would you like to know?"

"How did you come to be involved with St. Margaret's?" He slowed the curricle to turn into Princes Street.

"Through Michael, of course. As you know, I met him at a lecture at the Royal Society, and we soon realized we shared a number of common interests."

A grunt from Will told her how little he liked that answer.

"In any event," she hastily carried on, "he introduced me to St. Margaret's and the Hibernian Benevolent Association. The work is worthy and the need great, I assure you. I was happy to become involved."

"I can imagine," he said coolly. "How do your parents feel about your spending so much time in St. Giles?"

"Mamma hates it, of course," she said gloomily. "Papa is better, although he worries it's dangerous for me to go into the Holy Land as much as I do."

Will threw her a startled glance. "Christ, please don't tell me you actually go into the rookeries."

She shook her head. "I'm not a complete idiot, Will. But I certainly would if I thought I needed to."

"I would strongly advise against it under any circumstances," he said with a thunderous scowl. "It's more dangerous than you can imagine."

She didn't tell him that she *could* imagine, since she'd had to venture into the stews on two occasions to deliver food and supplies to ailing families of parishioners. But she'd only done so in the daytime, escorted by Michael and one of the local men who used their services. It hadn't felt especially dangerous, though the conditions in the tenements had left her feeling tremendously sad and rather hopeless.

Still, she had no intention of sharing that information with Will. Only Eden knew the extent of what she did at St. Margaret's, and her sister would never betray her.

"I repeat—I am not an idiot."

"I never thought you were," he said, sounding frustrated. "But you do have an exceedingly kind heart and a tendency, on occasion, to be a tad bull-headed."

She rounded her eyes in mock indignation. "Are you sure you're not talking about Edie? I'm the absolute pattern card of caution."

He snorted. "You used to be. I'm not so sure about that now."

She rather liked that assessment. She no longer wanted him to think she was the meek little miss of long ago, too cautious to venture outside her small circle of friends. Working at St. Margaret's—and with Michael—had helped her overcome the most bothersome elements of her lamentably shy nature.

"Tell me more about your work," he prompted.

As he guided his horses through the busy streets, moving closer to the teeming warrens of St. Giles, she described the work she did at St. Margaret's, which was mostly with the charitable association attached to the parish rather than with the church itself. But both were intertwined, since the church also ran a charity school for the local children and most of the adults who came for help were first and foremost parishioners.

"Not that being a faithful attendant to services is a prerequisite," she said with a tiny sigh. "If that were the case, we certainly wouldn't be able to help nearly as many people as we do."

"Ah, problems among the faithful?" he asked wryly.

"Life is very hard for them, and most don't have much time for church. That and other things tend to keep them out of the pews."

"Like drinking?"

She grimaced. "Yes. Beer, mostly, but gin can still be a problem. Not that it's only the Irish immigrants who are plagued with the vice. You mustn't think that."

Since she'd started working at St. Margaret's, Evie had come to better realize just how much bigotry still existed against the Irish, both for their nationality and their religion. That bigotry was something she had to fight on a regular basis as she tried to extract support from potential benefactors. More often than not she failed, and since the death of Lord Cardwell, the charity's most generous patron, she and Michael had been finding it ever more difficult to raise the necessary funds.

Will gave a sympathetic nod. "The Irish are no more predisposed to that particular vice than Englishmen. It's ridiculous to think otherwise."

"Your view isn't shared by many in the *ton,* I'm afraid."

"I'm guessing you've had some difficulty raising money for your work?"

"The charity school doesn't really have a problem," she said. "It's generally supported by some of the more prosperous shopkeepers and merchants of Irish descent in the city. They provide for most of the upkeep of the church, too."

He nodded. "I take it you're not that involved with the school or the church itself."

"Michael and I are both stewards of the school, but we're primarily involved with the activities of the Hibernian Benevolent Association."

"With a name like that," Will said dryly, "I can understand why you have trouble raising money from the *ton.*"

"How true," she said, wrinkling her nose. "But I can't get Michael to change it. He's devoted to the cause of justice for the Irish and says it's important we not be afraid to speak out on the issue."

Will slowed the carriage almost to a crawl as he avoided yet another pair of overloaded carts jostling for the right of way at a crowded corner. Once they'd maneuvered past the knot of bystanders thoroughly enjoying the verbal brawl between the carriers, he resumed the conversation.

"And what about you?" he asked. "What do you think about the plight of the Irish?"

She frowned, again wondering why he was so interested. "I'm deeply concerned about their living conditions, and I want to do everything I can to alleviate their distress. But if you're asking if I have a specific political opinion on either the Union or Catholic emancipation, I don't. I know those issues are exceedingly important, but I'm more concerned with feeding starving children, putting a roof over their heads, and helping their parents find work."

He glanced down at her, a faint smile tipping up the corners of his mouth. Evie couldn't help feeling like she'd just passed some sort of test.

"That's what you do?" he asked, the smile warming his voice. "Feed the starving and succor the poor? Well, it's certainly what I would expect of you."

"You make me sound like some sort of dreary medieval saint," she said, trying to cover up the fact that his praise—and the expression on his face—made her insides flutter with pleasure. "I do, however, try my best to help when I can."

He nodded, once more switching his attention to the bustling street. "And I understand you do that by helping people find respectable work, some of them within the households of the *ton*."

"Yes. Did Michael tell you that?"

"No, Alec did. He and Beaumont have been talking about St. Margaret's quite a lot, as you may have noticed."

She realized she was clenching her reticule in an anxious grip. "I do hope Captain Gilbride is serious in his interest. Believe me when I tell you that we could use the help. It's become discouragingly difficult to raise new funds."

"He is, as am I. But I'm surprised to hear *you* sounding so discouraged."

"Unfortunately, I don't have adorable English orphans to use as fodder to appeal to our donors. I have adults—mostly illiterate and sometimes ill-spoken or inebriated. Or both," she said, deciding to be candid. "Add in the fact that they are both Irish and Catholic, and you can imagine the usual response to my requests."

"Yes, but it's not like you to sound so downtrodden about it, Evie."

She jerked slightly in her seat. Had she? She thought she was simply being honest. "I suppose you don't know me that well anymore, do you?" she said, trying—and failing—for a light tone.

He transferred the reins to one hand and reached over to cover her clenched fists. "Then I'm very pleased to acquaint myself with the new Evie. And happy to help you in any way I can."

Pleasure mingled with confusion as she peered up at him. She used to be able to understand what he was thinking just from the fleeting expressions that crossed his face. But now . . . well, she supposed they were *both* new to each other. Given the passage of time and all that had occurred between them, it made sense that he would find her greatly changed from their more carefree, childhood days.

But before she could say anything, he released her hands and turned the curricle into the paved yard behind St. Margaret's Church. Well into the tangle of streets that radiated out from Seven Dials, Will had unerringly guided them to their destination without once asking for direction from her. She frowned, again thinking it odd that he took such an interest in the place, and in her affairs.

He pulled up in front of the low, warehouse-like building attached to the small church. "Shall we go in? I'm most eager to see what you've been working on."

As he handed her down, she tried to shake off the sense that Will was up to something. She might not be able to read him as well as she used to, but a little voice inside insisted she hadn't entirely lost the knack.

Chapter Twelve

Evie fussed with the skirts of her carriage gown, avoiding his gaze. That added to Will's certainty that she was hiding something. Something to do with her work at St. Margaret's.

But what?

Every instinct told him she knew nothing about conspiracies or assassination plots, especially after her response to his probe about the Irish question. It was just like Evie to focus on the practicalities of the situation rather than the politics. Even as a young girl, she'd always confronted the problem that lay directly before her, whether it was a tenant's sick child or a stray dog caught in a poacher's trap. Her twin, on the other hand, took on the larger battles. Eden had a force of character and personality that would have ensured her a career as a politician if she'd been a man. Evie, however, much preferred to address the smaller problems of daily life, caring for those around her with a quiet, endearing concern. She was born to be a wife and mother, bringing order and comfort to all within her orbit.

She was passionate about her work but wasn't a radical. And she sure as hell wasn't an assassin. Nor would she ever involve herself in a cause that hurt another human being. But that didn't mean that Beaumont—or someone else—wouldn't try to take advantage of her kind nature. Evie might think herself an experienced, even cynical woman of the world, but at her core she was still the affectionate, trusting girl he'd always known.

"If you'll wait here," she said with a hesitant smile that made Will want to kiss her, "I'll fetch one of the boys to look after the horses."

As she crossed the yard, he took a few moments to enjoy the enticing sway of her backside before she disappeared into the building attached to the church. In the years since he'd last seen her, he'd almost forgotten how splendidly built she was. Some might call her plump, but he thought her perfectly proportioned, with a slender neck, a long, graceful back ending in a sweet, round arse, and generous curves calling out for attention from a man's hands. In fact, he was beginning to find it disturbing how much he wanted to be the man— the only man—who would have the privilege of sampling her physical charms.

He let out an impatient snort, mentally shaking off the image of a naked Evie in his bed. That was unlikely to happen—would *never* happen, if he had any brains—and he was here for a set purpose. That purpose was certainly not to be distracted by lurid thoughts of Evie. He'd already been forced to lie to her and had no business making things worse by salivating over her or by acting like a jealous fool with Beaumont. Yes, he'd tried to convince himself it was simply a part he played, but he was grimly aware of just how thin that excuse was starting to sound. While he could certainly get Evie to trust him as a friend and only as a friend, every time he was with her he wanted more. Much more.

Focus, you idiot.

Murmuring absently to his horses as he held them in check, he ran a practiced eye over the church building and the surrounding area.

St. Margaret's was tucked away on a small street off Monmouth, only a few blocks from Seven Dials. It was on the edge of the rookery—too close for Will's comfort given how much time Evie spent here. Still, this street seemed safe enough with its narrow houses and two-story shops. The structures were shabby, to be sure, but seemed respectable enough, with a coffeehouse, a few old clothing stores, and a boarding house or two lining the short street. A few men loitered in front of the coffee shop, apparently in a genial argument as they smoked their pipes. A woman dressed in plain but neat garb hurried by, carrying a basket of produce.

As for St. Margaret's, it was a modest but tidy red-bricked affair with a slate roof, capable of holding no more than a hundred congregants, he judged. Larger, and surprisingly so, was the building attached to the back end of the church, the one into which Evie had disappeared. It consisted of two stories composed of lime-washed brick, with several window bays. A blue, four-paneled door in the center was topped by a patterned fanlight. Will guessed it had once been a warehouse, now converted to other uses, including as a church hall.

The air of respectability surrounding the place reassured him too. The yard was swept clean, the windows were free of soot, and two large pots with red geraniums flanked the door, lending an unexpected splash of color. The flowers were almost certainly Evie's idea because she'd always loved flowers, particularly geraniums. It would be just like her to impart so domestic and cheerful a note, even here in a back alley of St. Giles.

The blue door opened and Evie strode out. An errant

breeze swept through the yard, plastering her skirts to her body, and displaying both the outline of her legs and the sweetly rounded notch at the top of her thighs. Will forced his gaze up, trying to ignore the bolt of sensation to his groin.

Christ. He would likely be crippled with lust before completing this mission.

"Is something wrong," she asked as she came up to him. "You look . . . pained."

"No, but I suspect I might soon have reason to be," he said, eyeing two urchins trailing in her wake, devilment written all over their grubby little faces. "Please tell me those two aren't going to look after my cattle."

Actually, the beautifully matched pair and the curricle were Alec's, and Alec was notoriously touchy about his animals. He would no doubt look with extreme disfavor on little boys handling them.

"Aw, go on, guv," one of the urchins piped up. The engaging, freckle-faced boy had a shock of red hair sticking out from under his cap. "Me and Benny looks after Mr. Beaumont's horses all the time."

Will widened his eyes at Evie, who was struggling not to laugh. It took a few moments before she could compose herself enough to answer. "Will, I'd like you to meet Peter McGuire and his brother Benjamin. Boys, this is Captain William Endicott. You'll do just as he says and take good care of his animals, will you not?"

Benjamin, who looked younger than Peter, split his mouth open in a good-natured grin that revealed he was missing his two front teeth. With the size of his smile, Will could almost see down to the boy's tonsils.

"Aye, Miss Evie, we will," Peter said. "You can count on us, guv—true blue, and that's a fact."

Will narrowed his gaze at Evie.

"Honestly, Will," she said, "you can trust them. They do look after Michael's horses on a regular basis. There's a stable over in the next street where Peter and Benjamin are training to be grooms. They will look after your horses splendidly."

Will heard the slight note of anxiety in her voice and saw the pleading look in her eyes behind the polished glint of her spectacles. Glancing down, his gaze collided with two earnest pairs of eyes, also pleading with him.

"We'll take good care, sir," Benjamin said in a squeaky voice as he gazed longingly at the beautiful grays. "Promise."

Will capitulated. Alec would kill him if anything happened to the pair, but he found himself unable to disappoint the boys—or Evie.

"Very well." He extracted a shilling from his vest pocket and flipped it to Peter, who seemed to be in charge. "Walk them up and down, and come fetch me if you have any trouble. There's another shilling in it for you if you take good care of them."

The boys babbled their thanks, tripping all over themselves with excitement. Fortunately, they calmed down when they approached the horses. Will lingered a few moments to see how they got on, but they handled the pair with a maturity beyond their years. Then again, the children of the rookeries grew up quickly, forced into work, begging, or thievery at an early age.

"Thank you," Evie murmured as he took her arm.

"They seem like smart boys. Do they attend the school?"

"When their parents let them. They have four other mouths to feed, and Mr. McGuire makes very little money as a day laborer. He sometimes sets the boys to begging with their baby sister. If we can train the boys to be grooms,

I'm confident we can find places for them in a few years. It would make a real difference for the entire family."

He ushered her through the door into a low-ceilinged, narrow hallway that appeared to run the length of the building. "Is that one of the things you do—train children for useful employment? I thought St. Margaret's only ran a charity school?"

"Many parents in the parish see little use for book learning, so we try to combine school with training for a useful profession." She glanced over her shoulder as she led him along the passageway. "We help the parents find employment too. As I mentioned, I'm a steward for the school, but my primary focus is on assisting adults who come to us for help. I work very closely with them."

Will nodded politely, hiding his surprise. He'd thought her involved in the typical sort of charity work for women of her class—such as helping to raise funds for indigent children or perhaps occasionally teaching a class to little girls. Her involvement at St. Margaret's was much more significant than he expected.

She showed him into a large room with benches and a few tables, a globe on a stand at the head of the room. "This is where we hold classes for the children in the mornings and on Sunday afternoon. We occasionally hold classes in here for the adults, although we have workrooms upstairs, too. Those are mostly for teaching the women fine needlework and other useful skills. Father Kevin O'Kelley, St. Margaret's pastor, lectures on Sunday afternoon and also conducts classes for the men." She grimaced. "Although attendance is often a little spotty."

"I imagine it can be difficult to persuade them to give up what little free time they have to come here and sit through a lecture."

She closed the door and gestured for him to follow her down the hall. "Yes, but Michael has devised a way to encourage participation. He holds informal discussion groups afterward, and we provide food and drink." She threw him a wry smile over her shoulder. "It's amazing what a cup of beer and a few meat pies will do. Sometimes the discussion can get quite lively, especially when Michael decides to give a political lecture."

Will maintained his expression of polite interest. "Indeed? How often do those informal discussions take place?"

"Usually once a week on Friday night, although there's a great deal of activity on Sunday, too. The men often prefer to leave the churchgoing to the womenfolk and the children, and congregate over here to smoke their pipes and *'ave a chew,* as they call it. Some days the air is blue with smoke when they finish."

He couldn't help smiling at her bang-on imitation of an Irish accent.

At the end of the passage, a set of steps led up to the second floor and another passage branched off to the right, leading to another wing.

Evie pointed up the stairs. "As I mentioned, the other workrooms are upstairs, along with bedrooms for Father O'Kelley and his housekeeper and her son. We can go up if you like, but the rooms are similar to the classroom I just showed you. Although there are no classes in session now, you're welcome to return on Sunday when things are busier."

"I'm impressed, Evie," he said. "I expected a small charity school, but these facilities are quite expansive."

Leaning against the window frame next to the staircase, she untied her bonnet and took it off with a little sigh of relief. Even in the dull light of an overcast London day, her hair, pulled into a thick coil at the base of her neck, glowed like warm honey.

"We're very fortunate that Michael was able to purchase this building a few years ago and donate it to St. Margaret's."

He ignored the tightening in his gut at the warmth that infused her voice whenever she talked about Beaumont. He even hated the fact that she constantly used his given name, since it spoke to an intimacy that Will was beginning to actively resent.

"That was good of him," he replied in a neutral voice. "What used to stand on these premises?"

Her lush mouth kicked up into a little smile. "A gin house and distillery."

He couldn't help a laugh. "Ah, I thought I caught a faint trace of something."

"No doubt it's the lingering scent of the juniper and alcohol. They're very difficult to scrub out, although we've certainly tried."

She pushed off from the window frame. "Let's finish the tour, shall we? The offices and kitchen are along this passage."

He followed her, his gaze fastening once more on her bottom, gently outlined beneath her soft blue skirts. Will seemed to be developing an obsession with her arse, one that might prove difficult to break.

The truth was that he was fast growing obsessed with *Evie,* which took some getting used to. They'd been close as children, and he'd always loved her. But the feelings she aroused in him now had nothing to do with childhood friendships and everything to do with the fact that he was a man and she was a desirable woman.

A woman he admired and cherished, he reminded himself,

and one he'd sworn to protect. *That* was what mattered, not his surprisingly strong physical attraction to her. His first and only job was to get to the bottom of the conspiracy that threatened not only the government, but Evie, too.

"The kitchen is through there." She pointed to a door at the bottom of a shallow flight of stairs. "That's Mrs. Rafferty's domain. She's the housekeeper, although she also does some cooking for Father O'Kelley as well as for the meetings we hold for the men. And here," she said with a proud little flourish, "are the offices of the Hibernian Benevolent Association."

Opening a door opposite the steps to the kitchen, she led him into a sort of anteroom that clearly served the function of a small drawing room. The walls were whitewashed and plain, hung with a few innocuous paintings of landscapes and religious scenes in simple wooden frames. A battered armchair sat in front of a small coal grate, and a green velvet chaise that looked like it had come from a lady's dressing chamber stood against the opposite wall, a low table in front of it. A sturdy-looking teapot surrounded by mismatched cups and saucers was the table's only adornment. The decidedly shabby room had a sort of coziness that was enhanced by pots of flowers. Geraniums, again, clustered on the sill of the window that looked onto an alley.

Will smiled. Even here, Evie did what she could to introduce some color and beauty.

"I know it's not much," she said, wrinkling her nose as she gazed about the room, "but it does allow us some privacy and a more normal setting when we meet with some of our charity cases. The men can get quite intimidated when they have to face Michael across a desk. Or me, in the case of the women. Most times, they find it hard to ask for help."

"For anyone with a shred of dignity, it would be." He nodded to a door behind the chaise. "What's in there?"

"That's Michael's office, although I use it when he's not here." She walked over and opened the door. "It's where we keep correspondence and the ledgers relating to the charity. Michael takes care of most of that, although I handle some of the correspondence with our patrons."

Will took a quick glance into the small room, noting the plain furnishings—a large desk and chair, fronted by two cane chairs. The desk was angled toward the door, revealing cubbyholes and drawers, one of which had a keyhole. That presumably locked drawer piqued his interest. "Do you keep any monies on the premises?"

"No. The funds are with Michael's bankers, or kept at his rooms. We both carry only small amounts when we come here and leave nothing in the offices."

Will needed to search that mysterious locked drawer once he got Evie out of the way. "You mentioned that you help find positions for your charity cases. How does that work?"

She watched him with a puzzled smile. "Will, are you truly interested, or simply doing some footwork for Captain Gilbride?"

He wanted to put her question down to an understandable assumption that he would find talk of charity work boring—as would most men of the *ton*—but he suspected such was not the case. Though her smile had a teasing cast to it, it didn't reach her eyes. Behind her spectacles he thought he read a clear skepticism of his motives.

Not good.

Evie's quiet manner had fooled many into thinking her less perceptive than she was, but Will knew she had a mind like a good magistrate— sharp, inquisitive, and prone to suspicion. That last trait was newly developed and one he needed to factor into his calculations.

"As I said, I promised Alec I'd look into things," he answered with an easy smile. "But I wasn't exaggerating when I said that what is important to you is also important to me."

"I'm glad," she said, sounding a little breathless.

Her shy, grateful smile tore through him like buckshot and made him feel a complete cad. He *was* interested in the place for her sake, but not for the reasons she'd take from his words. Will made a promise to himself that once this was all over, he'd make as sizeable a donation as he could—and ensure Alec did too—to support her work at St. Margaret's.

If the place didn't turn out to be a center for deadly conspiracies. He dreaded that possible outcome. Even if he could keep Evie from harm or suspicion, she'd never forgive him for spying on her once the truth was known.

"If you'll have a seat, I'll explain how we do things," she said. Then she clapped a hand to her chest. "Oh, I'm sorry, I've been terribly rude. Would you like some tea? I can step into the kitchen and ask Mrs. Rafferty to make some."

He shook his head, smiling. "I thought I'd take you to Gunter's when we're finished here. After last night I owe you a treat."

Only after the words were out of his mouth did Will realize that her suggestion would have afforded the perfect opportunity to get her out of the room so he could do a quick perusal of Beaumont's desk. But her rueful grin almost made up for his blunder.

"You obviously haven't forgotten that I could never resist ices."

"I've never forgotten anything about you, Evie," he said quietly.

That was the simple but earth-shattering truth. For years,

he'd allowed the pressing concerns of his life in the military to overshadow his feelings for her. But now that he was with her again, he realized she'd always been there, quietly waiting at the back of his mind and deep in his heart. In some mysterious way, she'd been a lodestone during the difficult years of the war—invisible but always exerting a subtle pull of memory, one that spoke of peaceful, happier days.

She stared at him, wide-eyed and uncertain. Her hand drifted up to rest gently against her pretty mouth. An overwhelming urge to kiss her flooded through him, and it took a forceful effort not to haul her into his arms and taste her sweetness, searching for the love she'd once had for him and hoping it was still there.

Footsteps clattering in the hall startled them both. Evie's gaze darted to the door. Her cheeks flushed pink and she made a funny little grimace, as if she'd just thought of something unpleasant. Then she seemed to shake it off, along with the fraught intimacy of the previous few moments.

"Have a seat," she said, waving to the chair. "I'll see who that is."

She opened the door to the hallway but didn't step fully out while she talked to whoever was standing there. Will's gaze drifted to Beaumont's office, but there was no chance of getting in there while Evie lingered close by. He suspected that he and Alec would need to make a midnight expedition to St. Margaret's sooner rather than later.

Rather than take a seat, Will tuned his ears to Evie's conversation. There were at least two people in the hall, one a man and the other a woman, both with heavy Irish accents. If he leaned over slightly, looking around Evie, he could see the edge of a bonnet and a slender shoulder and arm clothed in drab but serviceable fabric.

Will jerked fully upright when Evie turned around with a smile. She blinked, as if surprised to see him still standing in the center of the room.

"Will, I'd like to introduce you to these people. They live on the other side of King Street and have been coming to St. Margaret's for over a year." She lowered her voice. "I thought speaking to them might give you a better sense of what we do rather than simply listening to me. Would that be all right?"

King Street was in the heart of the Irish rookery in St. Giles. Will was most definitely interested in meeting them.

"That sounds like a fine idea," he said.

Evie opened the door wide and ushered the couple into the small space. Will moved behind the leather armchair to stand next to the hearth.

"I'd like to introduce Miss Bridget O'Shay and her brother, Mr. Terence O'Shay," Evie said, smiling kindly at the newcomers. "Bridget, Terence, this is Captain William Endicott."

He wouldn't have needed the introduction to know they were siblings, although Terence O'Shay towered over his sister and had massive shoulders and stevedore hands. Bridget, who didn't look much older than Evie, was slender, fine-boned, and very pretty, despite her plain servant's garb and the drab bonnet on her head. They both had the pale complexion, dark hair, and blue eyes of the Black Irish. Their strong features included a chin that, on the young woman, was determined, but on the man looked stubborn and sullen. Bridget dipped into a curtsey, giving him a friendly smile, while Terence narrowed his eyes, only grudgingly taking off his rough woollen cap when his sister nudged him.

"It's a pleasure to meet you," Will said in a friendly voice.

"I doubt that," Terence muttered. Bridget cast her brother a stern warning glance before returning her attention to Will.

"Thank you for your kindness, Captain," she said. She had a pleasant, low voice, softened by the lilt of her accent. "Miss Whitney just said you was interested in what we do at St. Maggie's and asked if we would mind chattin' with you."

"I am indeed, if you don't mind."

"Please, everyone, take a seat," Evie said. "Terence, would you mind bringing in one of the chairs from Mr. Beaumont's office? That way we can all be comfortable."

"I'll be standin'," came the surly reply. "I won't be stayin' long enough to bother meself with fetching the seat."

His sister let out an exasperated sigh, sending Evie a little grimace of apology. Will had the impulse to shake the man for embarrassing his sister.

"As you wish," Evie responded in a cool voice that made her displeasure abundantly clear.

Will found it interesting that Evie's habitual shyness had been replaced by a manner that signaled how clearly she was in charge. It wasn't brassy or false but seemed to slip easily over her, as if she were in her natural element. It stemmed, no doubt, from her need to manage the world and make it a better place.

She turned her back to Terence and ushered his sister over to share the chaise with her. Will waited until they were seated then took the armchair.

"What would you like to know, sir?" Bridget asked in a bright tone. The girl had an engaging and well-spoken manner that immediately disarmed.

"I was curious as to when you came to London, and what part of Ireland you hail from," he replied.

"We come from Londonderry, sir, in the north. We arrived in the city two years ago this September."

"And why did you come?"

"Because there ain't no work back home, thanks to you bloody English," Terence growled. "Why else do you think we'd be leavin' our home and kin?"

"That's enough, Terry," his sister rapped out. "If you can't be keepin' a civil tongue in your head, you'd best be quiet and let me do the answerin'."

"That's the best idea you've had all day, girl," Terence said, his mouth turning down with an ugly sneer. "Have your little chat with the swells. I got other business to attend to."

On that trenchant note, the man slapped his cap back on his head and stalked out of the room.

Bridget's cheeks flew bright red flags against her pale skin. "Miss Whitney, I'm that sorry you had to see that. You too, Captain Endicott." She grimaced. "Poor Terry hasn't been himself lately, what with the problems with work and all."

Evie patted Bridget on the shoulder. "You're not to worry, dear. We completely understand." She glanced at Will. "Terence lost his job last week, the third time in as many months. It's been very frustrating for both of them."

"He's a good man, he is," Bridget said earnestly, "but he's plagued by the blue-devils, and then he starts drinkin' and missin' work. Father O'Kelley's tried talkin' to him, but Terry just tells him . . . well, it wouldn't be proper to repeats what he says."

"I'm sure you're doing your best to help him," Will said.

Bridget pulled off a shabby glove to rub her temple, as if

it pained her. "I try, but he ain't makin' it easy. I keep tellin' him we're that lucky to be here in London when things are so bad at home. But he won't hear none of it. He misses it, you see. Ireland," she finished, her voice breaking.

"And I respect him for that," Will said. "It's hard when you miss your home and your family."

"But you've done well, Bridget," Evie said with an encouraging smile. "You've made a splendid go of things, and you've been very helpful around St. Margaret's as well. We so appreciate everything you do." She looked at Will. "When Bridget first came to us, she assisted Mrs. Rafferty with the cleaning and the mending. She still helps out on her day off, and whenever else she can."

Bridget gave him a shy smile. "Mrs. Rafferty taught me all sorts of things, and Miss Whitney helped me find a position."

"We're very proud of Bridget," Evie said. "She's a maid in Sir Gerald Milbank's household, and we have every expectation that she will one day become a lady's maid or even a housekeeper."

"I hope so, miss," Bridget said. "I'm workin' hard to get there someday."

Will had been nodding and smiling while the women talked, but the name of Bridget's employer had pricked up his ears. Sir Gerald was a wealthy magistrate with strong connections to the current government. Will knew he often held dinners for senior ministers like Peel or even the prime minister. Those men were not sympathetic to the cause of Irish republicanism, and it made him wonder if Bridget had any idea of the politics of the man she worked for.

He asked the girl a few more questions about her employment and where her brother lived—which was in a St. Giles tenement, not surprisingly—but made no objection when Bridget excused herself, saying she had to speak to Mrs. Rafferty before returning to work.

"What do you think?" Evie asked after Bridget had taken herself off.

"She seems a bright, capable young woman who stands to do you proud," he said. "I take it that this is the main focus of your work—trying to secure gainful employment for your charity cases."

Evie nodded. "That's the first thing we try to do. The men often find work as day laborers or unloading ships on the docks, but it's harder for the women. The only option sometimes is working in the mills. They're dreadful places, but the other choices are worse." She shook her head, looking infinitely sad. "We've lost more than a few women to prostitution and thieving, I'm sorry to say."

"But fortunately not Bridget."

She brightened. "Yes, I'm so proud of her, because she's worked very hard from the day she first came to us, training with Mrs. Rafferty and taking as many of our classes as she could. I was thrilled when we were able to find her a place in Sir Gerald's household."

"How did you manage it?"

"I know Lady Milbank, Sir Gerald's wife. Her grandparents on her maternal side were Catholics, so she's fairly sympathetic to our cause." She wrinkled her nose. "Unlike much of the aristocracy, I'm sorry to say."

"Is your primary strategy to find work for the people you sponsor in the homes of the aristocracy?"

She nodded. "And in any decent household with servants. For the women, certainly, since those are the best jobs for them. But we try to place everyone who comes to us in a position that will ultimately lead to them acquiring a skill or profession. If not as a servant then in some useful trade, or working in a shop or one of the shipping companies. There are a fair number of shopkeepers and businessmen of Irish descent in London who assist us in that regard."

Will was more than impressed with all Evie had accomplished. With part of his mind, he listened intently for anything that might be remotely suspicious or indicate that Beaumont was involved in conspiratorial activities. Nothing he'd seen or heard today provided any evidence, although it was clear that St. Margaret's warranted further investigation. Terence O'Shay and his open resentment indicated that such was the case, since it was impossible to imagine he would be the only one of the church's charity cases to harbor antipathy toward the English.

But another part of him had to acknowledge that damned growing fascination with the new Evie. She'd thrown her heart and energy into her charity work, coming to life with a glow that lit up her beautiful eyes and brought vibrant color to her cheeks. Will remembered that look from their youth, though in those days it had been for *him* that she glowed.

He was petty enough to admit to some satisfaction that he hadn't seen her sparkle like that around Beaumont, except perhaps when they talked about their work. Still, it was Beaumont who would eventually be the lucky recipient of her full affections, not him, and that stuck in his craw like a piece of rancid mutton.

He kept silent, digesting everything he'd seen and heard, until Evie gave him a verbal nudge.

"Is there anything else you'd like to know?" she asked, a faint but amused challenge in her voice. "Or do we pass muster?"

He forced a smile. "I'm very impressed, and I'm sure

Alec will be too. You're doing wonderful work here, Evie. Even a frippery fellow like me can see it."

She scoffed. "Nonsense. There's nothing frippery about you, and you know it."

"Perhaps I'll surprise you one of these days."

She tilted her head, giving him a puzzled smile. For a moment, he thought she was going to pursue the lead he'd just tossed her, but then she gave a small shake of the head. "If there's nothing else," she said, rising to her feet.

"Just one more question," he said, standing. "Are there many hard cases like Terence O'Shay? I don't much like the idea of you dealing with a man like that, to tell you the truth."

"Now you sound like my mother," she said dryly.

Will clutched his chest. "Cut to the quick in one fell swoop."

She laughed, but sobered enough to answer. "Terence is a very difficult case, I'm afraid. He holds on to a great deal of anger against the English, despite our concerted efforts to convince him we're not all monsters." She sighed. "There are a few others like him, I must admit, but Terence is about the worst."

Anxiety rustled through him. "You're never alone with those men, are you?"

She waved a dismissive hand. "Goodness, no. Michael generally deals with the men, or Father O'Kelley. I work primarily with the women and the children." She smiled. "I enjoy that very much."

"I'm glad to hear it. Now, I think I've made you work quite hard enough, and I'm also honest enough to admit that I'm beginning to fear for my horses. Who knows what those two scamps of yours have gotten up to?"

Evie laughed. "I'm sure they're fine, but I agree that I've

bored you enough for one day." Her lush mouth curved into a surprisingly flirtatious smile that set the pulses hammering in his veins. "Now, Captain Endicott, I do believe you promised me an ice, did you not?"

"I did, madam, and I intend to keep that promise."

Will flicked another glance into Beaumont's office, noting the placement of the window and the desk before he followed Evie out of the room.

He'd be back soon.

Chapter Thirteen

Evie smiled at her sister as she accepted a cup of tea, although she suspected her smile looked more like an anxious grimace. Ever since Will arrived for her mother's dinner party this evening, looking outrageously handsome in his regimentals, she'd been struggling to repress the shivers that danced along her nerves and weakened her knees. And when she thought she'd finally managed to get them under control, she'd found herself sitting next to Will at the table. Then the shivers had turned into flushes that burned up her neck to her cheeks. If she didn't know better, she'd think she was coming down with the ague.

"Wolf's making you nervous, isn't he?" Eden murmured from her spot next to Evie on the damask chaise tucked into a corner alcove. They'd retreated there as soon as their mother led the women into the formal drawing room after dinner, hoping to avoid conversation with anyone. Evie needed to be left in peace so she could reorder her thoughts before Will, Michael, and the other men joined them for tea.

She'd already spent most of dinner stammering like a fool every time Michael glowered at her from the other end of the highly polished table. Mamma had deliberately placed her next to Will, as far from Michael as she could. It wasn't Evie's fault, and she had every intention of telling Michael that as soon as possible. It did him no good to glare at her when she merely talked to her dinner partner, as basic manners dictated. Michael obviously thought she was flirting with Will though she was doing nothing of the sort. She wouldn't dream of it.

Except that she *had* dreamed of it, along with all sorts of other unnerving things since their outing to St. Margaret's a few days ago.

"Is it that obvious?" she asked in a resigned voice.

Eden pointedly looked at Evie's right knee. Evie glanced down and winced to see it jiggling up and down like mad, rather like a puppet on a string. She clamped her knees together to stop.

"Don't let Mamma see that," Eden said. "She'll make you wrap a scarf around your legs."

That thought made Evie's dinner—what little she'd managed to force down—churn in her stomach. As a child, she'd had a terrible habit of jiggling her leg when nervous. When she hadn't been able to lecture Evie out of it, Mamma had finally resorted to tying a woollen scarf around her knees, under her dress. Since Mamma had embarked on this corrective course in the middle of August, it had proven beastly hot and dreadfully unpleasant. Evie had shed more than a few tears over it but she had to admit it worked. Within two weeks the habit was broken, rarely to return.

Only when Evie was truly rattled.

"Perhaps I can persuade her to use a silk scarf this time," she said in a half-hearted jest.

"I'm joking, darling," Eden said. "Mamma isn't going to do anything so horrible, but she *will* lecture, which is never fun."

Eden cast a swift glance around to make sure no one was

listening. Fortunately, the other ladies—eight in all—had clustered around Mamma at the other end of the room. It was a small party tonight, mostly family friends who knew each other well. They happily chattered away, accepting cups of tea and drifting to seats in the luxuriously appointed room freshly hung with wallpaper in a Bloomsbury Square pattern. Mamma had been most eager to show off her re-design of the room, thankfully leaving the twins to fend for themselves until the men joined them.

"You know," Eden said in a conspiratorial voice, "if you want to stay out of trouble, just spend the rest of the night talking to Wolf. For some reason, Mamma has taken a real shine to him since he's returned home."

"That's got nothing to do with Will and everything to do with Michael. She's no doubt hoping I'll transfer my affec-tions." Evie scoffed. "As if I'd be so disloyal to poor Michael."

Eden's eyebrows went up in a comical tilt. "Far be it from me to criticize, but you've been doing a rather good job of ignoring *poor Michael* so far."

Evie couldn't help starching up. "I haven't been ignoring him. Good Lord, Mamma hasn't let me near Michael all evening. Before dinner, she had Lady Montrose monopo-lize him, and then she placed him at the other end of the table and Will right next to me. I *had* to speak with my dinner partner, of course, particularly since he's an old friend."

"But you didn't have to moon at him, now did you?"

Evie gaped at her sister, scandalized. "I was doing no such thing! Was I?"

"Well, yes, you were, if you want me to be honest about it. Not that *I* blame you," Eden said. "Wolf is frightfully good-looking and has a smashing set of shoulders."

"Not quite as smashing as Captain Gilbride's, as you have apparently noticed," Evie responded in a tart voice.

Her twin batted that comment away with the flick of her wrist. "I'd have to be blind not to notice that, but it's rather like admiring a prime piece of horseflesh. I enjoy looking, but I'm not necessarily inclined to ride him."

"I cannot believe you just said that." Evie was torn between horror and laughter. "If Mamma heard you say something so risqué, she'd lock you in your room for a week."

"I'd never say it to her, now would I? But back to Wolf—"

Evie held up a restraining hand. "I don't want to discuss him. He's simply an old friend, and that's the end of it."

"You are such a pitiful liar, darling. Ever since your little outing with him the other day, you've been fluttering around the house like a schoolgirl with a crush on a handsome officer. It's like something out of a bad novel. You'd better watch yourself, Evie, or you'll find yourself in a spot of trouble."

"You make having an ice at Gunter's sound like a lewd encounter in the shrubberies at Vauxhall Gardens, when of course it was nothing of the sort. The primary purpose of the outing was not enjoyment, as you well know. Will wanted to see St. Margaret's, and that's where we spent most of our time."

The corner of Eden's mouth turned down in a skeptical twist. "Ah, yes. Wolf was acting as an agent for Captain Gilbride, who has suddenly developed a great interest in the deserving poor. I'm telling you, Evie, I don't trust that oversized Scotsman. He seems the least likely philanthropist I can imagine, and I don't believe for a minute that he gives a hoot about St. Margaret's or the unfortunates you help."

Evie shook her head. "That's hardly fair. We know little

about Captain Gilbride's charitable leanings, and there's no reason not to take him at his words. Goodness, why would he spend so much time with Michael if he didn't truly want to help?"

"I can think of one good reason."

"And that is?"

"He's diverting Michael's attention away from you in order to give Wolf a clear opening."

Evie stared at her sister. Although her mind instantly rejected that conclusion, her ill-mannered heart apparently wanted to mull it over. There could be no other explanation for why it started to pound like a drum.

She had to swallow a few times before she could answer. "That's ridiculous. Will has no interest in me other than as a friend."

Eden adopted an expression of pity. "Keep on telling yourself that, if it helps."

Evie, in fact, had every intention of continuing to tell herself just that, even though she'd spent the last few days grappling with the notion that Will did appear to be, well, almost courting her. Though apparently genuinely interested in her work, his manner at Gunter's and in the carriage afterward had seemed exactly what her sister was suggesting—flirtatious. Will had never flirted with her before, not even when they were younger. He wasn't the sort of person to engage in that sort of thing. Not with her, and not with any other girl, as far as she could remember.

But that was a long time ago when he was little more than a boy. Now, as Evie was painfully aware, he was a man.

She'd started to halfheartedly argue with her sister when the door to the drawing room opened and the men followed Papa into the room. The women revived like flowers that had just received a refreshing mist of water, and some of the younger ones did everything they could to attract Will's and

Gilbride's attentions. Evie certainly couldn't blame them, because they were by far the handsomest men in the room.

Probably the handsomest men in London. Especially Will, and how unfair was that?

"Don't look now," Eden murmured, "but here comes Michael. Oh, and how surprising, Gilbride is in hot pursuit."

Evie fixed a smile on her face as Michael and Captain Gilbride joined them. It was not an easy task when one was clenching one's teeth.

"Evelyn, is this seat taken?" Michael's tone suggested he wasn't quite sure of his welcome. He nodded at the empty cushion next to her on the chaise.

"I was saving it for you," she exclaimed, patting the seat. A lie, but surely only a little white one. "Please join us. I've barely been able to exchange two words with you all evening."

He pulled the tails of his evening coat aside and sat down. "You've been much engaged," he said with a casual and rather false laugh. "I did not want to intrude."

He spoiled the easy affect he was obviously hoping to convey by shooting a glare across the room at Will, currently engaged in conversation with Evie's mother.

She repressed a sigh. Whatever Will was up to, it did seem to be making Michael jealous. Turning her back on her sister, who was already verbally sparring with Gilbride, Evie set about soothing her beau's ruffled nerves.

A brief discussion of their plans to expand the charity-school classes to include adults restored Michael to his usual gentle humor. Gilbride pulled up a chair to join the discussion, asking one or two decidedly intelligent questions that had the effect of launching Michael into an enthusiastic explanation of plans to extend the reach of the Hibernian Benevolent Association over the next several months. Evie had to give the captain credit because he gave not the slightest indication that his attention was anything less than genuine.

While the two men engaged in a passionate debate about the best way to "squeeze money from the nobs," as Gilbride put it, Evie turned to her sister, unable to keep from crowing a little bit.

"I told you the captain was sincere in his interest," she whispered.

When her twin simply inspected the captain with a suspicious gaze, Evie rolled her eyes. It was clear there was no pleasing Eden when it came to Gilbride. Eden normally got along well with almost everyone, but for some reason Evie couldn't fathom, such was not the case with the charming Scot. And her dislike seemed to be growing rather than diminishing over time.

Her twin's gaze shifted from the two men, and Eden suddenly went poker-stiff. "Oh, blast. Mamma's got Will between her claws. She's on her way over, and she doesn't look very happy, either."

"Oh, confound it," Evie blurted when she saw her mother marching toward them, practically dragging Will in her wake. Mamma's trenchant gaze was, unfortunately, directed at Michael.

"I'm sorry, my dear, did you say something?" Michael asked, looking rather startled as he turned from his discussion with Gilbride.

She gave him a weak smile. "I simply said Mamma was approaching."

"Oh, was that it?" Gilbride said with a roguish twinkle. "I must get my hearing checked, because I could have sworn you said something rather different."

"I wish you would go get it checked right now and leave the rest of us alone," Eden muttered.

Evie cast her sister a scandalized glance but then turned her attention to her mother.

And to Will, who bore a long-suffering expression on his face. Clearly, Mamma had been bending his ear about something.

"Goodness! Why are all the young people congregating here in the corner?" Mamma asked with a mien so fierce she looked like a bird of prey. The effect was enhanced by her dark hair with its dramatic streaks of white at the temples. "My dears, this is hardly polite to the rest of our guests, is it?"

Her hawklike gaze fell upon her daughters. "You mustn't keep Captain Gilbride and Mr. Beaumont all to yourselves, girls. And you, Evelyn, have quite abandoned William. Is that any way to treat an old friend?" She cast a treacly smile at Will, who looked distinctly nonplussed.

And no wonder, since her mother's reformation when it came to Will constituted a stunning reversal.

Michael and Gilbride had risen to their feet at Mamma's approach. The captain spread his arms wide, giving his hostess a wry and enormously appealing smile. When Eden sucked in a startled breath, Evie darted a glance her way.

Her twin had gone rather pale, as if she'd just received a nasty surprise. Evie made a mental note to ask her about it when the party was over.

"Ah, Lady Reese, you must put the blame on me," Gilbride said in a voice of rueful apology. "I've been having a wee chat with Mr. Beaumont and the ladies, monopolizing their attention. You must allow me to make amends. Simply command me, and I am yours."

Mamma was not entirely immune to the captain's charms. She slapped him lightly on the arm with her fan and let out a surprisingly youthful laugh. "Save your flirtatious ways for the younger generation, my dear captain.

Your wiles will not work on me. In any event, it is not up to you to entertain the other guests. My daughters should be exerting themselves in that regard instead of tucking themselves away in a corner."

Or, daughter, as the case may be, Evie thought. Predictably, her mother's gaze jumped to her, signaling that she was the target of her ire, not Eden. She braced herself for another lecture about neglecting her *old friend* Will.

"Actually, I'm to blame for monopolizing Captain Gilbride's attentions," Michael swiftly interposed, "and I do apologize. The good captain had some questions about the work we do at St. Margaret's, and I thought to enlighten him—with Miss Evelyn's assistance, of course."

He gave Mamma a sweet smile, one Evie thought no less charming than Gilbride's and a great deal more sincere. The dear man was trying to draw her mother's fire away from her, but she knew with a sinking heart that it would only make things worse. Unfortunately, he either didn't understand or didn't care, because he chattered away as if Mamma wasn't glaring at him with poorly concealed antipathy.

"I tend to get carried away with enthusiasm when discussing my work," Michael said cheerfully, "so you must place all the blame on me and not your daughters."

The stiff, square set of Mamma's shoulders now reminded Evie more of a scarecrow than a bird of prey—one that would soon come down off its peg and chase them around the room.

"Really, Mr. Beaumont," her mother snapped, "I hardly think a social occasion is the appropriate venue for talking about *your work*, as you term it. I believe there is no one more charitable than I—"

She stopped to level her scarecrow gaze on Evie, who hadn't been able to hold back a small, choking noise.

"—than I," her mother repeated. "But I have heard quite enough discussion of those Irish persons that you and my daughter insist on aiding. I really must ask that you refrain from any more talk on that topic whilst under my roof."

"And certainly no one can blame you, Lady Reese," Will smoothly intervened. "As Captain Gilbride has already noted, you must place the blame on us. Mr. Beaumont was simply doing a kindness by answering our questions."

Evie, whose stomach was now so twisted she thought it might never unknot itself, dredged up a grateful smile. When Will nodded back, his blue gaze also transmitted a clear warning message.

Stay out of it.

"Your generosity is commendable, William," Mamma said, sounding like she didn't think it commendable at all. "But Mr. Beaumont knows how I feel about this subject." She flicked a quick glance in Evie's direction that seemed full of calculation. "And I must insist he not raise the issue again, or he will no longer be welcome in my house."

As it so often did when she was annoyed, Mamma's voice rose to the level of a clarion call, drawing the eyes of several guests. Evie stared at her, aghast, and with a mounting anger that her mother could be so rude. Even though she understood how little Mamma cared for Michael, her behavior this evening had been mean-spirited and beyond the pale.

"Mamma, that's hardly fair." Evie barely could speak past a throat gone tight with anger. "Michael is the soul of charity, and he doesn't deserve your disapprobation."

Eden hissed out a breath and squeezed her hand in warning, but Evie was too furious and too humiliated to heed the signal. She was used to her mother needling her, too often embarrassing her in public. But to attack Michael directly— the kindest man Evie had ever met—seemed to tap into a foul brew of shame and resentment she could no longer repress.

"I think it's simply *awful* the way you treat him, and I won't stand for it a minute longer," Evie exclaimed, barely registering the appalled looks on the faces of the others. She only had eyes for her mother, whose features turned as hard and unforgiving as a basilisk's.

"Do not deign to lecture *me,* my girl," her mother said. "I will not stand for it."

Evie jumped to her feet, anger propelling her upward. "What are you going to do about it, Mamma? Throw me out to the street?"

Michael let out a distressed *tsk* and took her elbow in a gentle grip after he came to his feet. "Evelyn, your mother has every right to decide what topics are suitable for her daughters to discuss. I'm only sorry that I have offended her so deeply."

Evie gaped at his apologetic, hang-dog expression, and then shook her arm free. "How can you say that? Her behavior toward you is disgraceful. I simply don't understand how you can stand there and take it, day in and day out."

Will shook his head. "Lady Reese, why don't you allow me to—"

"Stay out of this, Will," Evie warned, jabbing a finger in his direction.

Much to her surprise, he rolled his eyes and then nodded, as if giving her permission to carry on.

"Evelyn Whitney, you will not say another word," her mother rapped out. "If you do—"

"Goodness me, what a lively discussion," a cheerful voice interrupted.

Evie choked back a relieved gasp at the sight of her father's face popping up behind her mother's shoulder.

"Oh, thank God," Eden muttered.

"I can only assume you are discussing politics," Papa said jovially, even though his round, pleasant face was wrinkled with concern. "Really, gentlemen, must we bother the ladies with so dreary a subject?"

Mamma turned an offended gaze on her husband. "My dear sir, if you only knew—"

"Yes, my love, in a moment," Papa interrupted, resting a gentle hand on her shoulder.

Mamma pressed her lips into a tight line, clearly choking on the hasty words she'd been about to utter. Evie's father was a mild, genial man who rarely intervened with his wife and children, or interfered in the domestic affairs of the household. But on the infrequent occasions when he felt called upon to do so, Mamma had always known better than to contradict him.

"Evie," Papa continued, giving her a warm smile, "I've been telling Lord Templeton about that edition of *Gulliver's Travels* I recently acquired. Would you please fetch it for me from the library?"

In the wake of her father's timely intervention, Evie's anger began to drain away, replaced by horror as soon as she realized how thoroughly she'd embarrassed herself. She loathed making scenes and calling attention to herself, and yet she'd behaved just as rudely as her mother. All she could do was nod in response to her father's request, pathetically grateful that he'd given her a means of escape.

"Take your time, my girl," her father added.

"I'll go with her," Eden piped up, rising to take Evie's hand.

"You will stay with your mother," Papa said. His mild tone nonetheless brooked no opposition. "Now, go on, Evie. As I said, take your time."

"Thank you, Papa," she whispered.

She couldn't bring herself to look at Michael. He must

think her as great a shrew as her mother. But she did cast an involuntary glance at Will as she brushed past him. The sympathy and worry etched on his face almost made her burst into tears.

Blinking rapidly to clear her vision, she walked at a moderate pace toward the door. The room seemed enormous as she passed the other guests, all looking at her with gazes mingling sympathy and amusement. Thank God they were intimate friends of the family and knew very well that Mamma was not averse to raising her voice in company. Still, there would be no avoiding some gossip and teasing as a result of their quarrel, especially since it involved Michael. It would be a long time before Evie's mother forgave her for that, and there would be consequences. That was doubly unfortunate, since Michael already had enough enemies in the *ton*—people who would be only too eager to tarnish his name. She felt sick with shame at her mother's mean-spirited behavior and at her own lapse in good manners.

But Evie couldn't help wishing Michael would defend himself just once when Mamma treated him with such disdain. Though he could be passionate about the things he believed in, it irked her no end that he wouldn't stand up for himself when he became the target of insults. Tonight seemed little different from the incident at the Duchess of Campworth's ball, when Evie had been forced once more to come to his defense.

Then, again, why did she have the right to expect anything different from Michael when she rarely stood up for herself?

Finally, she reached the wide double doors. Their senior footman opened them, casting her a slight, sympathetic grimace. Evie forced a wan smile, grateful for his kindness but embarrassed that even the servants felt sorry for her.

She paused in the hallway, pressing her hands to her flushed cheeks as she wondered what to do. Neither Papa nor Eden—nor Michael—would be annoyed if she didn't return to the party. In fact, they probably expected her to scurry away and hide like she so often did. Telling her to fetch the book had simply been Papa's way to defuse a nasty situation and allow her to leave the room. Evie knew for a fact that Lord Templeton had no desire to peruse old editions of books, since he only cared about his horses and his next meal. She should just go upstairs, crawl into bed, and wait for Eden to come up and report on how she and their father had smoothed things over. That's how it usually worked when her mother was angry with her.

But as she hovered at the staircase, trying to decide whether to go up to her bedroom or down to Papa's small library, an image of Will's face, with that warm, accepting look in his eyes, swam in her vision. He hadn't been the slightest bit embarrassed by the scene and had even seemed to encourage her with that nod of his. More than anyone but Eden, he understood what her mother was like, and he'd told Evie more than once when they were children that she should stand up for herself. That Mamma would respect her more if she did. How ironic was it that she'd given Will the exact same advice about his father the other day? Now, here she stood, on the verge of sounding the retreat.

Yes, she'd been dreadfully disrespectful to her mother, and she would apologize for that lapse. But this time, she would *not* bear the fault for causing the scene in the first place, or allow her mother the satisfaction of effectively chasing her away to her room. Evie had done too much running already, and it was past time she stopped responding that way to every little crisis. Because she'd grown up afraid of her mother's disapproval, she'd learned to fade into the shadows when it came to expressing her true feelings and standing her ground. But she found herself growing heartily sick of retreat, and equally sick of people thinking she was a coward.

Starting with Will. She'd been a coward with him, too, and she refused to behave that way any longer.

Taking a deep breath, she lifted up her skirts and marched down the staircase to the library. A small voice in the back of her mind questioned why it was so important to show *Will* that she wasn't afraid—not Michael. She knew she should have the courage to face that question head on but told herself there were only so many battles she could fight in one night.

Determined to ignore—for now—the indisputable and inconvenient fact that she was annoyed with Michael and *not* annoyed with Will, she opened the door to the library. She paused a few seconds to allow her eyes to adjust, since only an Argand lamp on her father's desk and a small fire in the grate lit the room. Crossing to the fireplace, she extracted a spill from a brass container and used it to light a wall sconce as well as a branch of candles on the small occasional table next to her father's reading chair.

As she started to peruse the shelves for the Swift volume, Evie breathed in the welcome scents of leather, parchment, and her father's snuff. She loved this room and spent as much time there as she could. Although not nearly as large or well stocked as the library at Maywood Manor, it held a fine collection of poetry, novels, and the classics. At her father's insistence, the big leather chairs were comfortable rather than fashionable, and the Wilton carpet was plush enough to lounge on in front of the fireplace and while away the afternoon with a book. Most importantly, the library was her father's domain, a refuge from her mother's bothering and fuss.

She spied the requested book on one of the uppermost shelves and was reaching for it when a slight stir of air fluttered the hem of her dress. A moment later she heard the door close. Sighing, she came down on her heels, knowing her moment of respite was over.

"Can I help you with that?" His deep voice sent flutters dancing low in her belly.

As Evie spun around, she almost lost her balance and had to make a grab for one of the shelves. "Wolf," she exclaimed, startled into blurting out his nickname. "What are you doing here?"

In the soft light, he did look rather like a wolf. His hair was a rough gold and his high cheekbones and rugged jaw lent a hard, almost fierce, cast to his features. As he prowled across the room, she had to resist the temptation to press a hand over her pounding heart. There was no reason for Will to make her nervous, and she needed to start believing that *right now.*

When he stopped just a few inches from where she'd plastered herself against the bookshelves, the slow, devastatingly attractive smile that curled up his oh-so-masculine mouth sent her pulse racing like a runaway horse. He stretched out an arm, resting a big hand on the mahogany shelf next to her head. It effectively caged her in.

"Why, Evie," he said in a voice that made her shiver, "I've come to see if you need help."

Chapter Fourteen

Will braced a hand next to Evie's head, taking in the sweet flush that gave color to her pale, perfect skin. Her golden eyelashes fluttered as she cast her gaze down toward the vicinity of his feet. When she slowly sucked in a breath, the tops of her generous breasts lifted in tempting white mounds over the modest neckline of her dress. All he had to do was dip his head and he could easily trail his tongue across that glorious expanse of feminine flesh.

Christ.

What the hell was he thinking? He'd come down here to see how she was, not to seduce her. Eden had lobbied to be allowed to follow her sister, of course, but her father had prevented that with only a few soft-spoken words. Lord Reese rarely threw his weight around in his household, but when he did, everyone paid heed. His lordship had then taken Beaumont off to speak with Lord Templeton and Mr. Garvey, while Lady Reese had commanded Alec and a protesting Eden to join the other guests. She'd sailed away with the two of them in her wake, pointedly leaving Will to his own devices.

And leaving him in a quandary, as well. Lady Reese's

actions had clearly indicated that he was to follow Evie in another obvious effort to throw them together. And as much as her agenda made him wary, following Evie was *exactly* what he wished to do. He'd seen the sweet girl's fury give way to hurt and shame, and he'd seen the tears start to well up in her big eyes, only half-hidden behind the glint of her spectacles. At that point, he'd wanted to take both Lady Reese and Michael Beaumont by the scruffs of their necks and knock their bloody heads together. Evie's mother was a harridan *par excellence*, and Beaumont didn't have the good sense to know when to keep his fool mouth shut.

It had taken him only moments to decide what to do, Lady Reese and her blatant attempts to match-make be damned. Evie was his oldest friend, and the image of her alone in the library, crying her eyes out over her mother's cruelties, gutted him like a rusty blade.

Alec, naturally, had tried to stop him. In fact, he'd even attempted to follow but Lady Reese had clamped onto him like a bulldog with a bone.

Will wasn't overly concerned with her ladyship's clumsy attempts to turn him into an eligible suitor for Evie because Will knew nothing of the sort would happen. He would simply comfort his friend and escort her back upstairs when she was ready to return to the party.

But that was before he saw her, the candlelight turning her hair into a gold waterfall and softly outlining the lush body that was clad simply in a dress of pale green silk. She'd turned with a gasp when he came into the room, but then stilled, her shoulders pressed into the bookshelves as if she unconsciously sought to brace herself. Though he told himself she couldn't possibly guess his thoughts, that shy, downcast gaze and the slight tremble of her pretty mouth contradicted him.

More than any desire he'd ever felt, Will wanted to lean

down and cover that mouth with his own, drinking deep of her sweet, gentle nature and innocent sensuality.

Instead, he pried his fingers from the bookshelves and forced himself to take one step back. And then another.

Evie's gaze lifted from the floor and she blinked a few times, as if to focus on him. Then she expelled a tiny breath—of relief, he thought—and let her shoulders relax.

"Will—I—" She stopped and frowned. "What are you doing here? Did Mamma send you after me?"

He shrugged, trying for a casual smile. "She certainly didn't seem to mind that I came, but that's not why I followed you."

She looked troubled by his answer. "Why, then?"

He rolled his eyes. "Evie, you nit, I was worried about you."

The teasing endearment brought a wry twist to her gorgeous mouth. He'd always liked her mouth, with its classic, rosebud pout that seemed so at odds with her shy, serious personality. But now he had to admit he was becoming captivated by it, spending more time staring at it then actually listening to the words that issued from her lips.

As if to prove that point, she pushed the bridge of her spectacles up and frowned again. "Will, did you hear what I just said?"

"Of course," he said. "You just thanked me for coming to check on you." Thank God at least some part of his idiotic mind had been paying attention. As an intelligence agent, he'd always had impeccable discipline, but Evie was proving almost fatal to his focus.

She gave her head a tiny, doubting shake, and Will suddenly remembered how good she was at reading him. He needed to remember that, and to remember he had a job to do too.

"I also said you didn't have to do it," she said. "I'm fine. Truly, I am."

He studied her face for a few seconds. When she arched her eyebrows in a silent, ironic commentary, he let out a reluctant laugh. "Yes, so I see."

She leaned back against the bookcase but this time simply appeared to be getting comfortable.

"I'm not a child any longer, you know. I'm not going to fall apart and cry whenever Mamma scolds me." Then she gave a self-deprecating grimace. "Well, not very often, anyway."

He glanced behind him, then took a third step back to settle on the edge of her father's desk. "No one could blame you if you did. Your dear mother deserves a thundering scold herself for her abominable behavior tonight."

Again her mouth pulled into a wry, adorable twist. "Don't worry. Papa will take care of that."

"I find that a little difficult to imagine."

She laughed at his sarcastic tone. Evie had a beautiful laugh—rich and soft, like a velvet scarf drifting through the air. He suddenly had a compelling urge to hear that laugh issue from her throat while she was naked in his arms, with him buried deep inside her sheltering body.

That image had the unfortunate consequence of turning him hard. He shifted uncomfortably, mentally issuing a stern warning to his randy member.

"Oh, you'd be surprised," Evie said, blessedly unaware of his silent struggle. "He was most displeased tonight. I'm sure he and Mamma will be discussing it after the guests depart."

"For all the good it will do." A moment later, Will wished he'd held his tongue, for her smile died and the humor fled from her eyes.

"Mamma will behave a tad more nicely for a day or two,"

she said somberly, "but then everything will return to normal."

"Good God, Evie, how does your father put up with her? He's the mildest man anyone could hope to meet."

She frowned thoughtfully, as if genuinely pondering the question. "Well, it's not generally a problem for him or the others. I'm the one who drives her so distracted." She sighed. "Mamma can't seem to help picking at me, and I can't seem to help annoying her."

Will rose off the desk and took a long stride in her direction. His hands twitched with the need to pull her into his arms, but he resisted, even though every impulse in his body urged him to do so.

"Evie, you've done nothing wrong. You've *never* done anything wrong, and your mother is entirely at fault. The failing is hers that she cannot see the sweetness of your nature." He couldn't touch her, but he put as much honest emotion as he could into his voice.

She stared up at him, blinking as if stunned by his outburst. Then her lips parted in a tremulous smile. "It's kind of you to say so, Will. I try to get along with her, but nothing I do seems satisfactory."

She gave a bewildered shake of the head that cut his heart in two. When he was a lad, he'd fumed in silence when her mother scolded and bullied, but now it seemed worse. For so many years, he hadn't been there to try to protect her, to soothe her battered feelings or joke her around as he'd done in the past. Where had it all gone so wrong between them?

Evie's gaze slid away from his, and she flushed a faint pink. "She's been worse these last few months, and I don't know what to do about it. It's . . . mystifying."

To Will, there was nothing mystifying about it. Michael Beaumont's courtship was the cause. Will didn't want to push her too hard, though. Not when she was obviously feeling fragile.

He rested a finger along the curve of her jaw and nudged a bit until she, reluctantly, looked at him. "You do know the reason for her ill temper, don't you?" He softened his probing with a smile.

She wrinkled her nose, which made her spectacles tip slightly askew. He couldn't help thinking again that she was the most adorable thing he'd ever seen.

"I do, and you're a beast to make me acknowledge it," she said with a sigh. She reached for his hand, moving it away from her face. She squeezed his fingers for a moment, then let go and wandered over to the antique globe on a mahogany stand next to her father's desk. Slowly, she set the ball spinning, staring absently down at it. Will followed but simply stood by her, waiting for her to answer.

"It's Michael," she finally said. "She can't stand him, and it's so unfair. He's a terribly nice man. If she'd just give him a chance."

Will had no right to be jealous, but the ugly twist in his gut at the warm tone in her voice mocked that idea. Still, *terribly nice* wasn't exactly a ringing endorsement of love, was it?

"Your mother has always been the worst sort of snob, Evie," he said. "I'm not defending her by any means, but wasn't it predictable that she would object to Beaumont's Catholic heritage and beliefs?"

When she scowled at him, he held his hands up. "You know it's the truth."

"But Papa doesn't object to Michael's religion."

"That's because the Beaumonts are rich. Your father is both a kind and practical man."

"That's a perfectly horrible way to put it," she said indignantly. "You needn't make Papa sound so . . . so mercenary."

Will dragged a frustrated hand through his hair. The last thing he wanted to do was discuss Evie's impending engagement to a man who might be a traitor. At least he assumed that's what they were talking about. Perhaps it was time to find out, once and for all, about the nature of her relationship with Beaumont.

"Evie, I don't mean to pry—"

"Then don't," she interrupted.

He dredged up a rueful smile that he hoped made him look both charming and harmless. But the way her eyes narrowed with suspicion told him he'd failed.

"I care about you, Evie," he said. "I don't want to see you get hurt."

Now her eyes popped wide open. "You think Michael Beaumont would hurt me? That's rich, coming from you."

Now he wanted to tear his hair right out. Instead, he finally gave in to the overriding impulse and gripped her by the shoulders. She startled under his hands and her mouth formed a surprised oval.

"Just tell me the truth," he growled. "Are you going to marry Beaumont, or not?"

She flushed a bright pink, and managed to look both embarrassed and annoyed. "Not that it's any of your business, but Michael has not, as yet, asked for my father's permission to court me."

He scoffed at the dodge. "Trust me, Evie, he will."

Because she couldn't deny that, she simply glared up at him. He found the obstinate set to her jaw and her refusal to be honest with him completely infuriating. He'd been closer to Evie than anyone but her twin. Surely that gave him the right to know exactly how she felt about Beaumont.

Plus, it was his job to keep her out of danger, as he could never forget. That was the true reason for his ire.

Keeping telling yourself that, you idiot.

"If—*when* he does make it formal," he ground out, "are you going to say yes?"

She tilted her head, searching his face. The light from the lamp on the desk glinted off the lenses of her spectacles, obscuring the expression in her eyes, and suddenly she seemed opaque to him.

He gave in to another misbegotten impulse, plucking the spectacles from her nose and placing them behind him on the desk.

"What are you doing?" she demanded, trying to reach around him to reclaim her frames. He clamped his hands back on her shoulders, preventing her.

"Answer the question, Evie."

She stared up at him, her cornflower-blue eyes dark and huge in the muted, flickering light. They held a measure of defiance but also an intense vulnerability, as if he'd somehow stripped her naked.

God, he only wished he could.

She spluttered at him for a few moments and then tilted her chin up at a defiant angle. "Why *shouldn't* I marry him? He's a kind, generous man, and we share many interests. And he's devoted to me."

The part of his brain that processed her words balked at her response. The other part, the part that had nothing to do with his mental capacities, was caught by the sensation of warm, bare skin under his hands. He spread his fingers wide over her shoulders, nudging them under the narrow strips of lace at the top of her puffed sleeves. It would take only a flick of his hands to push those ridiculous little bits of fabric down, fully exposing her shoulders and the tops of her breasts.

"William Endicott, what are you doing?" she asked, trying to sound outraged.

He wasn't fooled. Not when he felt small shivers coursing through her muscles and saw the flutter of her golden eyelashes.

"Yes," he replied, ignoring her question. "I've noticed how Beaumont follows you around like a lovesick puppy."

Evie stiffened. She whipped a hand between them and pointed it up at the tip of his nose. "Now, you listen to me—"

He cut her off. "Do you love him?" Her little tirade died on her lips. She drew in a stuttering breath, too shocked to answer.

Some evil part of him whispered that she didn't want to answer the question, because she didn't *know* the answer.

"I . . . I . . ." she stammered.

"It's an easy question," he murmured, letting his fingers drift in slow circles along her naked shoulders. "Do. You. Love. Him?" With each word, he let his hands slip a little deeper under the fabric of her sleeves.

Her gaze darted away, and she grimaced. "You can't ask me that, Wolf," she whispered. "You don't have the right."

He hated seeing that look on her face. Hated the idea that their past—and the hurt he'd inflicted on her—might be part of the reason for her pain in the present. He wanted to do whatever he could to correct the mistakes of the past and take that pain away.

"I don't," he whispered back. "Just like I don't have the right to do this, but I'm going to do it anyway."

He moved one hand to her jaw, cupping it while tilting her head back. Her mouth opened; whether in protest or shock, he couldn't tell. But it didn't matter, because he finally gave into the desire he'd been battling from that first moment he'd seen her on the lawn behind Maywood Manor. Bastard that he was, he took ruthless advantage of those parted lips to slip inside, taking her mouth captive. She made an odd, squeaky noise before freezing in his grip.

Her paralysis lasted but a few moments as he desperately searched for the girl who'd never shut him out before. Who'd once kissed him with a shy, innocent fervor he now realized he'd never forgotten. And when she finally responded relief flooded through him, as honest and true as what he'd felt on the battlefield when he realized he lived to fight another day.

As her arms stole up around his neck and she trembled within his embrace, the echo of their sweet, youthful kisses faded in the clamor of blood pounding through his veins and his heart hammering against his ribcage. Because it wasn't a girl he pulled close—it was a woman. And it wasn't just the lust-inducing feel of her generous breasts pressing against him that inflamed his senses, it was the way she opened up to him, responding to his invasion with an enthusiasm that both startled and thrilled him.

If he'd ever needed confirmation that Evie was not the young girl he'd once known and that she was all grown up, this was it. Anything that had ever happened between them in the past couldn't begin to compare with this moment.

He groaned deep in his throat and staggered backward against the desk, lifting her right off her feet as he moved. She gasped but didn't lift her mouth from his, instead twining her soft arms more tightly around his neck. Years of holding back—for both of them, he reckoned—fell away, replaced with a voracious need that blotted out every rational thought, every distraction.

Will managed to sit down on the corner of the desk, bracing his legs wide and pulling her between them. He slipped his hand from her jaw, gliding it down to her hip. God, he could feel the heat and softness of her body right through the thin layers of her dress and chemise. Spreading his fingers, he nudged her forward, until she was plastered against his cock. The notch at the top of her thighs framed him perfectly, and he couldn't help groaning into her mouth.

She went still again and Will mentally cursed. He'd pushed too far, but every instinct drove him forward, telling him it wasn't nearly enough.

Her lips came from his, allowing a breath of space between them.

"What are we doing?" she whispered in a bewildered voice. She sounded close to having second thoughts, but her arms were still wrapped around his neck and she held herself tight against him.

"I should think it obvious," he said, swooping down to sweep a hot lick across her rosy mouth. She moaned, and her eyes went soft and sleepy-looking.

"I'm kissing you, silly girl," he murmured as he trailed his mouth along her jawline. Her skin was as smooth and finely grained as satin. He wanted to see it all, every inch of her beautiful body exposed to his sight and touch. His hands followed the thought, carefully pushing down her sleeves to more fully expose her shoulders and chest.

"Yes, I know," she said, her voice coming more strongly even as she trembled under his roving fingers. "But I think—"

Will never got the chance to know what she thought, since the next sound he heard was the library door opening.

"Evie, I've been looking—"

Beaumont chopped off his words, and the brief, fraught silence that ensued was like a bucket of cold water to Will's face. On a strangled cry, Evie pulled up straight in his embrace. Since Will's fingers were still caught in her sleeves, it had the unfortunate effect of pulling the fabric even farther down her arms, exposing the top of her stays and the generous breasts they barely contained.

"Oh, God, let me go," Evie exclaimed as she struggled in his grip.

"Stand still," Will growled. He was trying to get her damn dress back up where it belonged, but her wriggling wasn't helping. She was so frantic to escape from him that she didn't notice she was half-undressed.

You've done it now, you stupid bastard.

"Let go," she snapped.

For good measure, she aimed a kick at his shins. Will barely felt it but was afraid her struggles would send her tumbling to the floor.

Cursing God, fate, and Michael Beaumont, Will pulled his hands away. When Evie whipped around to face Beaumont, her bodice sagged below her stays. Will supposed he must be in some sort of shock, because the only thing he could seem to focus on was how voluptuous and tempting Evie looked in her pretty linen stays topped with pink lace ribbons.

"Michael, this . . . this isn't what it looks like," she stammered.

She still had failed to notice the epic disaster afflicting her bodice. Beaumont had, and his furious gaze snagged right onto Evie's breasts.

Taking a step closer, Will tried to tug her dress back up from behind.

"Stop that," Evie hissed, twisting around to slap his hands.

It was only then that she finally noticed the thoroughly debauched state of her clothing, and she sucked in a gasp of dismay that echoed through the room.

Beaumont remained nailed to the floor, his face frozen in a horrified mask as he studied her. His dark eyes held such a look of betrayal that Will had the impulse to toss

Evie over his shoulder, throw open the French doors to the garden, and carry her off into the night.

Sadly, no such fortunate escape awaited any of them.

"Michael, I swear, it's not what it looks like," Evie said in a choked voice as she struggled with her bodice. The despair and panic in her normally sweet tones made Will's throat close up.

She took a step forward but almost tripped over the hem of her sagging gown, prompting Will to reach out and catch her by the shoulders. So focused was she on Beaumont that she didn't even seem to notice.

"Say something, Michael," she pleaded.

Before anyone could say a damn thing, a swift clatter of heels heralded the arrival of another participant in their ghastly little drama. Any hopes Will had harbored of explaining the situation to Beaumont—taking all the blame, naturally—died when Lady Reese marched into the room.

"Mr. Beaumont," she announced in ringing tones, "I specifically asked you—" She stumbled to a halt as her evening slippers slid over the polished floorboards and made contact with the thick Wilton carpet that covered much of the library floor. She pitched forward and was forced to grab Beaumont's shoulders to keep from going down in an inelegant heap.

Not a drama, a farce.

"What in God's name is going on in here?" Lady Reese screeched.

"Nothing, Mamma, I swear," Evie said, still struggling with her bodice. Her hands trembled too badly to make much headway.

Heaving a sigh, Will reached around her, yanked the bodice up over her stays, and then pulled her ridiculous little sleeves back up on her shoulders. He mentally cursed those frivolous bits of fabric since they were responsible for his—and Evie's—downfall.

Evie wrenched out of his grasp again. "Will was helping me look for Papa's book," she said. "And then we just started talking."

"You call that talking?" Michael exclaimed, finally breaking free of the shock that had apparently held him immobile. He sounded almost as screechy as Lady Reese, and looked a great deal more upset.

Evie shook her head so hard one of the floral pins in her hair flew out and dropped to the floor. "It was nothing. I swear to you, Michael, it didn't mean anything."

Bloody hell.

Will did *not* like the sound of that. "Now, hang on just a minute, Evie—" He choked back his words when he realized how supremely stupid his intervention would be.

Holding his silence, he reached behind him to retrieve Evie's spectacles then handed them to her. She put them on with trembling hands, looking dazed.

By that time, Lady Reese had shoved Beaumont out of the way, obviously recovered from her shock. In fact, if Will didn't know better, he'd say that her horrified expression of a few moments ago had been replaced with one of infinite deviousness.

That tears it. We're in for it now.

He waited for his doom to fall upon him. To fall upon both of them, since Evie would share it.

Lady Reese marched up to her daughter. "Evelyn, were you and Captain Endicott . . ." She declined to finish the phrase, instead waving her hand in a windmilling motion.

"It's not as bad as it looks, Mamma," Evie said, her voice breaking. "I swear."

And that made Will's heart break. He wanted to sweep her into his arms and soothe her, telling her that all would be well. That's what he'd done when they were young, whenever her mother would tear a strip from her and Evie would flee to him for comfort. He'd always been able to make her laugh—to make her believe the sun would shine tomorrow. Damned if he didn't want to keep playing that role in her life.

"Evelyn, you've been alone with William for a considerable time *and* your bodice was practically down around your waist," her mother retorted in a strident voice. "How do you intend to explain away that unwelcome fact?"

Evie cringed and took a step back, bumping into Will's chest. When he rested his hands gently on her hips to steady her, this time she didn't pull away. He had a feeling, though, that her response was instinctive, seeking comfort from a familiar source. If Eden were there, she would no doubt have gone to her.

Eden came rushing into the room as if conjured up by that stray thought. Alec, for some demented reason, followed in her wake. Will began to think they might as well invite the entire party down to the library and get it over with.

"What's going on?" Eden darted a worried look at her twin. "Everyone wants to know where you all are."

"I was just about to find out what has transpired in this room," Lady Reese said. She switched her gorgon-eyed gaze from Evie to Will. "On your honor as an officer and a gentleman, William, I expect you to provide an honest recounting of what occurred between you and my daughter."

"It's not necessary to call my honor into question, my lady," Will responded in a calm voice. "I will truthfully answer any question you wish to ask." He glanced at Alec, now leaning against the doorframe and shaking his head with evident pity.

Lady Reese nodded. "Very well. Then please tell me if you were kissing my daughter."

"Certainly I was."

As soon as the words left his mouth, a weight lifted from Will's shoulders. He and Evie had nothing to be ashamed of—well, they did, but he'd be damned if he apologized for kissing her. There was a sense of inevitability to this night's work, since he and Evie had spent years ignoring the unfinished business between them—quite obviously to their peril. This was not the result he had foreseen or would have chosen, but nor was it truly a surprise.

Evie clearly didn't feel the same way because she pulled from his light embrace and went straight for her sister. Eden met her in the center of the room. She wrapped her arms around Evie and gently led her to the chaise in a reading nook nestled between two bookshelves, murmuring in a soothing undertone.

Lady Reese flicked a glance at her daughters but came back to focus on Will. "And I take from what I saw when I came into the room that matters had progressed quite a bit beyond kissing."

Alec made a snorting sound that he turned into a cough. When Will glared at him, his cousin held his hands up and gave him a wry little grin.

Will added *kill Alec later* to the mental list of tasks he was already compiling.

"Matters had progressed further than they should have," he said, trying to hedge for Evie's sake. She was sitting on the chaise, trying not to cry. Right now, all he could hope was to spare her as much embarrassment as possible. "But I assure you I would not have continued in that vein. I have the greatest respect for your daughter, Lady Reese, as I believe you know."

Well, that was probably a lie—not the respecting part,

but the stopping part. If Beaumont and the others hadn't interrupted them, God knows where he and Evie would have ended up.

On the chaise with her legs wrapped around my hips.

Will clamped down hard on that image and kept his focus on his future mother-in-law. The full realization that her ladyship was soon to be one of his nearest relations was appalling enough to wipe the enticing image of a naked Evie from his brain.

"That may be so," Lady Reese carried on triumphantly, "but I think you will agree that quite a bit of damage has been done as a result of your actions. Since you *do* respect my daughter, I trust you understand your obligations to her."

Will bowed. "Indeed. I will call on Lord Reese first thing in the morning, if that meets with your approval."

"No, that's ridiculous," Evie cried, jumping up from the sofa. Eden pulled her back down and commenced whispering to her in an urgent tone.

Beaumont once more came to life, heaving a great sigh. Will didn't think he could ever like the man, but now he felt a reluctant sympathy. There was no doubt he cared for Evie a great deal. Not only had he suddenly lost her, he'd just been thoroughly and publicly humiliated.

With immense dignity, Beaumont walked over to the chaise. Evie looked up at him, her face chalk white. Tears trickled from beneath her spectacles.

"Evelyn, I must ask you a question," he said in a gentle voice. "And I beg, like your mother, that you tell me the truth."

She sucked in a breath and nodded. Will's gut pulled tight at the dawning of hope on her wan-looking features. Surely she didn't still want to marry the man, not after what had just happened?

"Ask me anything," she said.

Beaumont paused for a moment, as if collecting himself. "Are you in love with Captain Endicott?"

Evie's mouth dropped open. Clearly, that had not been the question she was expecting.

"Evelyn, I need your answer," Beaumont gently prompted after several long seconds of tense silence.

She glanced at Will, looking both flummoxed and distraught. He forced himself to remain impassive, not letting her see how much he wanted her to say *yes*. She had to make this decision for herself. He would *not* press or force her.

In truth, he didn't have a clue what he should say anyway, even if she did want his guidance. The entire situation was the biggest mess he'd ever found himself in, including being captured by the French back in the Peninsula.

Evie blinked a few times and then looked back at Michael. "I . . . I don't know how to answer that," she said.

Beaumont's head bowed for a few seconds, then he gave her a small, sad smile. "You just did, my dear. Evelyn, allow me to express my undying loyalty and respect. I will always honor our friendship, and I hope you will do the same."

Without waiting for her to respond, he turned to Will. "Captain Endicott, let me be the first to congratulate you. I only hope you truly deserve so fine and noble a lady as Miss Whitney."

That gracious response stunned Will into silence. He managed a bow, although he suspected he looked like a dumbstruck fool.

After a polite nod to Lady Reese, Beaumont left the room, his dignity intact. In his wake, Evie was practically vibrating with furious tears, Eden was dividing her evilest glares between Will and her mother, and Lady Reese was smiling at Will with odiously triumphant satisfaction. As for

Alec . . . he was taking in the whole mad scene like he was watching a performance at Astley's.

Evie moved first, throwing off her sister's arms and jumping to her feet. She propped her hands on her hips and glared at her mother. "I'll never forgive you for this, Mamma. I could have smoothed things over with Michael. Instead, you made fools out of all of us."

Lady Reese starched up to her haughtiest stance. "You are beside yourself, Evelyn, and don't know what you're saying. I'm doing my best to save your reputation, something you seem to have little care for yourself."

"Oh, curse it," Evie shouted, stamping her neatly shod foot. It was so unexpected and so bloody endearing that Will almost burst into laughter.

"Eden, take your sister to her room," Lady Reese snapped. "Stay with her until I come up."

"I don't need a blasted escort," Evie raged. She whirled on her heel and ran from the room, not sparing even one glance for Will. Though that rather stung, at least she didn't seem to be blaming him for the evening's debacle. At least not yet.

Eden threw Will an enigmatic glance and swiftly followed her sister. As she went through the doorway, she deliberately shoved past Alec.

"Out of my way, you great lummox," she ordered. Alec hadn't even been in her way, but he politely murmured an apology nonetheless.

"Captain Endicott," Lady Reese said, once more resorting to formalities. "I will tell my husband to receive you at ten o'clock tomorrow morning. Is that acceptable to you?"

"Yes, my lady, it is."

She seemed to breathe out a tiny sigh of relief, and her hauteur gave way to a tentative smile. "Thank you. Welcome to the family, William. I will see you tomorrow."

Will could only gape after her, stunned by her rapid-fire changes in demeanor. It seemed to be a trait shared by all the ladies in the family, now that he thought about it.

Alec pushed off from the doorframe and strolled into the room, now deafeningly quiet after the exit of the combatants. "Well, that was entertaining," he said. "I suppose I should offer you congratulations."

"I'd rather you offered me a drink," Will said. "Let's get the hell out of here."

"Splendid idea. And while we're having that drink, perhaps we can chat about the best way to break the happy news to your father. That and how to tell your new fiancée that you're spying on her."

Will shot a glare at his cousin. "Bugger off, you great lummox."

Alec laughed and followed him from the library.

Chapter Fifteen

"You're certain you can do this?" Evie tried not to sound as skeptical as she felt.

Eden curled her lip. "Really, Evie, do you think anyone would believe *I* would wear this gown?"

"It's rather rude of you to put it quite that way. You look perfectly lovely to me."

Eden peered at her reflection in Evie's dressing-table mirror, grumpily adjusting the high-cut bodice. "Oh, well, it'll have to do," she said with a sigh. "I'd better join Mamma before she gets suspicious. She wanted to leave for Lady Talwin's gala by nine o'clock."

Strictly speaking, *Evie* was joining their mother, since Eden was supposedly laid up in the bed with a sudden and severe cold. Evie had tried earlier to convince Mamma to allow her to stay at home this evening, but Mamma had refused. She'd assumed, rightly, that Evie was doing everything she could to avoid Will. She also assumed, rightly, that Evie would do everything she could to repair her relationship with Michael, including slipping out of the house to see him.

Thwarted at every turn, Evie had finally come up with a

plan. It was a desperate one to be sure, but the circumstances called for it.

"Turn around and let me do a final check," Evie said, twirling a finger in the air.

Eden rolled her eyes but complied, spinning in a slow, graceful arc that made the skirts of the pale blue gown bell out around her ankles. As far as Evie was concerned, it was a perfectly lovely dress—cut to flatter without revealing an excessive amount of bosom, dignified without being dowdy, its color pleasing without screaming for attention. It was one of her favorites, but the long-suffering look on her sister's face made her opinion of it clear.

Eden tended to favor gowns with low-cut bodices in jewel-like tones that made her stand out from the crowd. Her style of dress, coupled with her vivacious personality, all but ensured that Eden would draw everyone's eye and guaranteed a cluster of suitors hanging about, ready to be plucked like low-hanging fruit. Evie didn't begrudge her twin's popularity for a moment, but she sometimes wondered how they could be so much alike and yet so different.

Rising from her dressing table, Evie tucked an errant lock of hair back under the silver-spangled band that helped to contain Eden's thick hair in the smooth chignon at the back of her head. Evie squinted—her second-best pair of spectacles tended to blur at the edge of the lenses—but finally nodded her approval.

"You'll do," she said. "Even Mamma won't know it's not me."

Eden snorted as she pushed Evie's best pair of spectacles higher on her nose. "When we dress and act the same, Mamma can never tell us apart. Neither can Papa. Only our dear brother and a few of the staff at Maywood Manor have ever developed the trick of figuring out who's who." She picked up the cream silk shawl draped at the end of Evie's bed and flung it over her shoulders. "Just remember to stay in my bed for at least fifteen minutes after we're gone. You know how often Mamma forgets her reticule or fan and makes poor John Coachman return to the house to fetch it."

Evie nodded. She was wearing one of her sister's extravagant, lace-trimmed dressing gowns, although she'd kept her stays, chemise, and stockings on underneath. And she'd already given their lady's maid the night off, just to be safe.

"And be careful," Eden added in a stern voice. "What will you do if Michael isn't at his rooms at Albany House? It's one thing to go sneaking through Mayfair, but it's quite another to go into St. Giles at night alone." She tugged on her lower lip, suddenly looking worried. "I don't know, Evie. Perhaps you shouldn't do this."

"You would do it without a second thought."

"That's different."

Evie tried not to feel *too* annoyed. Her sister only wished to protect her. "Different because you're brave and I'm not?" she asked, trying for a wry smile.

Eden dropped her gloves and fan on the bed and rushed over to take Evie's hands. "Darling, you're the bravest person I know. You have to be to put up with Mamma's constant harping and still carry on with your charity work. I just meant that I'm a bit worldlier, and able to respond more, er, actively, if anything should go wrong."

Evie didn't point out that all the time she'd spent in the stews had exposed her to things Eden probably couldn't imagine. But there was no denying that her twin was physically braver and stronger. When they were children, it had always been Eden who'd taken the dare, climbed the trees, or even bested their brother or one of his friends in a physical contest—despite, perhaps even because of her bad eyesight. Eden might fool most people into thinking she was a beautiful featherhead, but Evie knew differently. Her sister had a strength and depth of character evident to all who knew her well.

"Don't worry," Evie said, giving her sister's hands a quick squeeze. "I borrowed the housekeeper's stout parasol. It will come in handy should I need to beat someone off." She grinned to show her sister that the idea of anything like that happening was far-fetched. "I'll be sure to pick a hackney driver who looks respectable, and I'll pay him to wait for me. If worse comes to worst, I can ask Mrs. Rafferty to escort me back from St. Margaret's."

Eden reluctantly nodded and let her go. She went back to the bed and started to collect her things but sank down onto the soft mattress instead, frowning at Evie over the top of her borrowed spectacles. "I still think you should have talked to Wolf this morning when he came to see Papa. You could have at least tried to explain things to him."

Evie pressed her forearms tight against her stomach, as if she could hold in the feelings of shame and panic that overwhelmed her every time she thought about last night. Not only her betrayal of Michael, but how she had let Will kiss her in the first place. She still couldn't quite fathom how it had happened or why.

Well, strictly speaking, that wasn't true. Once Will took her into his strong arms and his lips covered hers, all rational thought had dissolved under his touch. She'd been swept away into a beautiful fantasy come true, one she'd been dreaming about for a very long time.

She had to swallow hard before she could answer. "There was no point. I know Will, and there would be no talking him out of it. The only way I can save both of us from an enormous mistake is if I beg Michael's forgiveness *and* convince him that we should still be married."

"Mamma won't be happy about that," Eden said dryly. "She seems thrilled that Will has agreed to marry you."

Her mother's hypocrisy made Evie's stomach burn with acid. "It's so unfair. She barely tolerated Will, and yet now she's pretending to like him because she can't stand the idea of me marrying Michael. I assure you, he would not last long in her good graces once we were married."

"Oh, I don't know about that," Eden said. "Will has a future, you know. When I was skulking about downstairs this morning, I heard Mamma and Papa talking about it. He's not rich like Michael, of course, but even Papa seemed pleased."

Evie waved a dismissive hand. "He was only trying to placate Mamma."

"I wouldn't be so sure about that. Papa always liked Will."

"Eden," she said with exasperation, "Will has no desire to marry me. It would be completely wrong to leg-shackle him because of one little kiss."

Her sister let out a derisive snort. "It didn't sound like a little kiss, from what Mamma said. According to her, your bodice was practically down around your waist."

Evie's cheeks turned fiery. That moment when she realized her disheveled state had been one of the worst in her life, especially with the look of anguish in Michael's eyes. That it had followed several of the loveliest moments of her life was truly ironic.

"Will does *not* want to marry me," she said doggedly.

Her sister studied her thoughtfully, then gave a brisk nod. "Want to know what I think?"

"No."

"I think you're still in love with Will, and you should marry him."

Evie gaped at her. "I am not, and I most decidedly *should* not."

Her sister began swinging her foot like she didn't have a care in the world. "The thing is, Sis, since Wolf's been back, you seem so much more . . . well, alive, I suppose. Things happen around you now. I hate to be critical, but you do rather act like an old lady when you're with Michael. Don't you want more excitement in your life than that?" She waggled her eyebrows in a salacious manner. "Wolf knows how to have fun."

"That's one way of putting it. No," she said, raising a hand to forestall her sister. "I don't want to discuss it anymore. I need to try to explain things to Michael, and this is the only way I can think to do it on such short notice. His note said he would be leaving for his father's estate tomorrow, and goodness knows when he'll be back."

The first thing Evie had done this morning was send a note around to Michael's rooms, but he replied that he was not yet ready to see her. She simply *had* to speak with him tonight, before Mamma got a chance to tell the entire world about her engagement to Will. Evie had managed to convince her parents to wait a few days before they did that, arguing she needed time to get used to the idea. She hated tricking them but what other choice did she have? Will didn't love her, and Evie couldn't imagine anything worse than forcing him into marriage. He'd resent her for the rest of his life—possibly even causing a breach with his powerful father—and that would simply kill her.

"Edie, please, please do this for me," she begged. "I know it's wrong to involve you in such a deception, but I must see Michael tonight."

"Oh, silly, don't worry about me," Eden said, collecting her things. "I get to have all the fun tonight *and* wear your spectacles. I cannot tell you how much I will enjoy being able to see people's faces for once. Although with some of my suitors that's rather more a curse than a blessing."

Evie had been trying for years to get Eden to wear spectacles in public, but her sister simply refused. Eden was a splendid person in more ways than she could count, but she was just a wee bit vain. "Thank you, darling," she said. "I will be forever in your debt."

"Pish. As I said, it'll be fun."

But as she came to kiss Evie good night, Eden hesitated, looking worried.

"What now?" Evie asked in a resigned voice.

Eden grimaced. "I hate to throw a damper on things, but what if Michael doesn't want to marry you? You have to marry someone, Evie. There was considerable gossip after you and Will *and* Michael didn't return to the party last night. It was rather obvious that something strange was going on, especially since you and Will were gone for quite a spell."

Evie was well aware of the possibility that Michael would still reject her. "I'll just have to convince him that he doesn't have a choice."

Her sister shook her head. "I can't wait to hear how you manage that."

Will took refuge behind a pillar at the far end of Lady Talwin's baroque ballroom. In the last hour, no fewer than three matchmaking mothers had shown a surprising amount of interest in him, and their daughters had tried to engage him in a flirtation despite the fact that he'd shown not a particle of interest. Perhaps he should blame it on his dress regimentals, which sometimes appeared to have an odd effect on young ladies' mental processes. It certainly wasn't his fortune, since everyone knew he didn't have one. It also didn't help that Alec was going around telling anyone who would listen that Will was a war hero.

In any case, interest from eligible maidens or their mammas was no longer relevant. Not since his haphazardly managed engagement to Evie.

Every time he thought about it, which was reliably every few minutes, a jolt of amazement arced through him. He might be tempted to call it *surprise,* but it wasn't, because in some way it felt ordained. The only surprising part was how easily he'd accepted his change in status, and how some part of him had welcomed it with both relief and anticipation. Evie was not the girl he had expected to marry, but it felt entirely right that she was.

His father, of course, would be irate. Evie would bring only a respectable dowry and very little in the way of useful connections. And she was involved with an organization that could possibly be a hotbed of conspiracy and sedition.

Of course, Evie had not yet agreed to marry him. She'd refused to come downstairs when he called on her mystified father this morning, and that gave Will some cause for concern. Lady Reese had explained it away with glib words about a headache, but that was bollocks. The situation was so bloody awkward it was a miracle they'd been able to discuss the settlements like rational human beings. But Lord Reese had been pleasantly surprised with Will's financial situation—which wasn't a fortune, but certainly a decent competency—and Evie's mother had been downright ecstatic.

After they'd finished, Lady Reese had assured him that Evie was looking forward to seeing him at Lady Talwin's ball. Will knew that was bollocks, too. Evie was furious with him, and it would take a good deal of work to bring her around. But, somehow, he'd do it. He'd work his arse off to give her the happy life she'd envisioned with him as a girl, a life that she richly deserved.

The only remaining problem, as he saw it, was the fact that she might be inadvertently caught up in a conspiracy. If Evie found out he'd been spying on her, she would brain him with a poker and that would be the end of their future together.

Like a mischievous Scottish hobgoblin, Alec loomed out of the crowd with a smirk on his face.

"Hiding away from the adoring multitudes, are we?" he said, jabbing Will in the shoulder. "Wise man, especially since your fiancée should be arriving at any moment. Don't want to give her a reason to back out of it, now do you?"

"She has yet to back *into* it, as you well know," Will retorted. "And the only reason I'm garnering any attention is because you keep telling people I'm a war hero. I wish you'd bloody well stop it."

"No need to thank me," Alec said with an airy wave that looked ridiculous coming from a man his size. "Besides, all that will stop as soon as your future mamma-in-law starts gabbing about the impending happy event."

"Oh, joy." Will loved Evie, but Lady Reese as a mother-in-law was a truly daunting prospect.

"Well, enough larking about." Alec reached out a long arm to snatch a goblet of wine from a passing footman. "Aden is waiting for us by Lady Talwin's greenhouse. He says he has some news."

Will shoved off from the column. "About time we got something from the Intelligence Service. I only hope it's information we can actually use."

They slipped through a convenient door behind them into a corridor that ran lengthwise along the side of the mansion. It led to the back of the house and away from the kitchen and other service rooms, which accounted for the quiet that quickly enveloped them.

Will glanced at his cousin. "Let's not mention my impending nuptials to Aden. I need to break the news to my father before he hears it from someone else."

In fact, he'd asked Lord and Lady Reese to refrain from any kind of announcement until he'd had a chance to talk to the duke. He'd also assumed Evie would be grateful for a pause before the madness began, which Lady Reese had reluctantly confirmed.

Alec grimaced with sympathy. "I don't envy you that conversation, old boy. When do you intend to pull the trigger?"

"I thought I'd try him at the Horse Guards tomorrow. Might as well get it over with."

Alec stopped him with a touch on the arm. "For what it's worth, I think you're making the right decision, not only for her sake but for yours. Evelyn is a splendid girl, and I suspect she will make you a splendid wife."

"Thank you. I can only hope my father will share that opinion," Will replied dryly. Still, he was moved by his cousin's words, and by his loyalty.

"Bugger him," Alec said. "And if you ever need help, you know you only have to ask."

Will nodded. "I know, and I thank you, but I'm sure we'll be fine."

He didn't mention his doubts about a whole host of other issues, such as where they would live and what he would be doing for the rest of his life. Though marrying Evie would diminish his chances of garnering his father's support for any career advancement, Will could still hope that Wellington thought enough of him to ignore that problem.

They cut down a corridor that led to the greenhouse. Just outside its glass doors, Aden waited for them, lounging in a wrought-iron chair, his long legs thrust casually out before him.

He rose to his feet, looking rather grim. "Dominic's source in Dublin—"

"Isn't that now *your* source?" Alec interrupted.

Aden flashed a brief grin. "I'm still getting used to the change."

"No doubt. Now, about that source," Will said, already impatient to get back to the ballroom. A niggle of worry about Evie had started to form. Why was she so late?

Aden nodded. "Our source in Dublin has managed to get his hands on a letter from Michael Beaumont to Daniel O'Connell, who as you already know is an ardent advocate of both Catholic emancipation and dissolution of the Act of Union."

"Yes, Dominic told us that O'Connell and Beaumont had corresponded," Will said. "How did their relationship develop in the first place, by the way?"

"They know each other through Beaumont's mother, Lady Leger. Her family is Irish, and distantly related to the O'Connell family," Aden replied. "Beaumont is apparently an admirer of O'Connell's politics."

Alec grimly shook his head. "So Beaumont has Irish relatives? Unfortunately for him, that puts him under even greater suspicion."

"Anything of use in their correspondence?" Will asked.

"It regarded the aborted duel between O'Connell and Robert Peel," Aden said. "Beaumont expressed concern for O'Connell's safety and pleaded with him to avoid taking any further risks."

"That's not exactly damning," Alec protested. "The opposite, I would think."

"True," said Aden. "But Beaumont went on to write of the importance of O'Connell's leadership in *the cause,* and how they couldn't afford to lose him. Who *they* are remains a mystery, as does the exact nature of their cause."

Will shook his head. "Many people support Catholic emancipation, or even breaking up the Union, but they would never resort to violence to achieve those aims."

"Which is why we need information before we can act," Aden said. "Without solid evidence, we can hardly start arresting random Irish immigrants or people who hold what some might consider radical views. The prime minister of course is greatly concerned that we avoid a repeat of the Gordon riots. If rumors were to get out that a group of Irish radicals was fomenting treason, the results could be dire. Most of all for the innocent Irish and other Catholics of London."

Will glanced at Alec. "We're making some headway, at least in terms of getting into Beaumont's office at St. Margaret's. I'll break in later tonight, or tomorrow night at the latest. Alec is going to see about searching Beaumont's apartments at Albany."

Aden nodded. "Keep me apprised of everything you find—decisive or otherwise. I've got the Home Office and Peel breathing down my neck."

"Understood," Will said, eyeing Aden's breeches and top boots. "I take it you won't be joining us in the ballroom tonight?"

"No. My wife is rather under the weather, and I'd like to get home to her."

Will frowned. "Again? Nothing too worrying, I hope."

Aden shook his head. "Simply the usual stomach ailments that afflict women in her condition."

"Maybe I could develop a stomach ailment," Alec said in

a sour tone. "Barely back in London, and I'm already sick of haunting these bloody balls and soirees. Don't know how anyone stands it."

"Poor you, having to keep all those eager society widows at bay," Will scoffed. "Best regards to your wife, Aden." He took Alec's arm and started to propel him down the hallway.

"One more thing, Will," Aden softly called.

Curbing his impatience, Will turned back and lifted an enquiring brow.

"Congratulations on your engagement," Aden said. "Miss Whitney is a lovely girl. I'm sure you'll be very happy." Then he gave a slight bow and disappeared into the greenhouse.

"How the hell did he know about my engagement?" Will exclaimed, exasperated.

"Well, they did ask him to replace Dominic," Alec said, "so he must be good at his job."

"Spies," Will said in disgust as they strode down the hall. "They're the worst bloody gossips of them all."

Alec grinned but didn't reply, since some guests had wandered out of the ballroom and into the hall. One, an acquaintance of Alec's, hailed him into a conversation. Will nodded and kept going, determined to track down Evie. If she hadn't yet arrived, he'd already decided to leave the ball and pay a call at her home. It was late, but he'd be damned if he'd allow her to put him off any longer. They needed to settle a number of things—tonight.

Circling the edges of the crammed ballroom, he avoided getting drawn into conversation. Halfway down the room, he finally spotted Evie standing quietly by her mother, who was speaking with a pair of elderly women.

He paused, frowning as he ran a quick, assessing gaze over his fiancée. She looked pretty in her sweet but unassuming gown, with a new hairstyle a tad more ornate than usual. Had she done it to impress him? He didn't think so, because Evie didn't give a whit about her coiffure. Something else seemed off, too, although he couldn't put his finger on it. Perhaps it was the way she flicked her closed fan against her thigh, as if she was irritated or impatient. And had she just rolled her eyes at her mother? Evie tended to go still and quiet at large social functions, trying to fade into the background. She didn't wriggle her fan or generally look like she was ready to jump out of her skin.

Perhaps she was just nervous about seeing him. He'd do what he could to calm her jitters, assuring her that everything would work out for the best.

"That's odd," Alec said, popping up next to him. "I didn't think Miss Whitney wore spectacles in public."

"Are you top-heavy?" Will asked. "Evie always wears her spectacles, regardless of the occasion."

"I know that, you idiot, but that's not Evelyn. That's Miss *Eden* Whitney."

"You've gone completely daft," Will snorted. "Eden would never dress like that, and she doesn't wear spectacles in public."

Alec shrugged as he turned an ironic eye in Evie's direction.

Disconcerted, Will took another good look at his fiancée.

And then another.

Christ.

Eden was pretending to be her sister. His instincts had told him that just a few moments ago, if he'd only been paying attention. When they were young, the girls had enjoyed teasing their family and friends by switching identities. It had worked with almost everyone—including him on more than one occasion. Their parents had rarely been able to tell them apart when they played their little charade.

Eden hadn't fooled Alec, though, which was both interesting and annoying.

Will muttered a curse under his breath. What the hell was Evie up to, trying to pull something like this? Suddenly, the worry that had been dogging him all night began to make acute sense.

"Oh, I see," Alec said with the ghost of a laugh. "Miss Eden has stepped in for her sister. How amusing, but I wonder what's going on?"

"Let's go find out," Will said grimly, thrusting his way through the mob.

Chapter Sixteen

"Sure you don't want me to stick around, miss?" The hackney driver rolled a wary eye around the deserted street. "This ain't exactly the best part of town for a young lady like you."

Evie smiled at the burly man as she handed him the fare. "Thank you, but no. I have friends inside who can see to my safe return home."

He gave her a shrug, but stuffed the money into his pocket without further comment.

As the driver pulled out of the yard, Evie scurried to the back entrance of St. Margaret's. A damp breeze swirled dust around her ankles. The air smelled dank and the night sky hunched over the city, the occasional flicker of lightning illuminating ugly black storm clouds. With her luck, she'd get a good soaking on the way home.

The door was unlocked. She breathed a sigh of relief that someone was still working in this part of the building and prayed it was Michael. She'd already wasted time waiting outside Albany, cooling her heels in the hackney after tipping the night porter to fetch her as soon as Michael returned to his apartments. After forty-five anxious minutes, she'd decided to proceed straight to St. Margaret's. The cabbie hadn't much liked driving into the London stews so late at night, and Evie certainly shared his trepidation. But, at that point, there'd been only one other choice for her.

That other choice was not one Evie was willing to accept, at least not yet. She would not allow Will to be bullied into a relationship he clearly didn't want, despite his decision to do the honorable thing. He might enjoy kissing her, but Evie was certain he wouldn't enjoy what came next—a marriage to a woman he'd rejected once already. Michael's forgiveness was still her best chance to prevent disaster and spare Evie the humiliation of a husband who didn't love her or want her.

She pulled the heavy oak door shut and hurried down the long corridor to the office. All was quiet, and her heart sank when she saw no light coming from under the parlor door. Just to be certain, she opened it and peeked in.

Blast.

Michael's office was dark, as well. It would be just her vile luck to cross paths with him as he returned home to his rooms in Mayfair.

As she closed the door and waged a silent debate over her next steps, she heard the low murmur of voices drift up from the kitchen. Her spirits lifting—because Michael usually made tea when he was working late, often stopping to chat with the housekeeper—she hurried along the corridor and down the stairs, pushing through the swinging door into the low-ceiling room.

She paused on the threshold, one hand on the door, surprised to see Terence and Bridget O'Shay, along with three other men, seated around the scrubbed pine table in the center of the room. One man was vaguely familiar but the others were strangers—large, rather grim-visaged strangers who looked decidedly unhappy at her sudden appearance. Michael wasn't present, nor was Mrs. Rafferty.

Evie frowned, disconcerted by the veiled hostility she sensed in the room. It felt as if she'd somehow interrupted some sort of dispute. The housekeeper never allowed meetings to be held in her spotlessly clean kitchen, since *that's what the classrooms are for* she'd pointedly made clear on more than one occasion. Why would she allow this group, some of them strangers, to meet here, especially with neither Michael nor Father O'Kelley on the premises?

Bridget jumped to her feet, eyes wide and cheeks flushed a rosy pink. "Miss, I . . . we didn't expect to see *you* tonight!" She made it sound like an accusation.

As Evie stepped down into the kitchen, Bridget hissed at her brother to stand up, jabbing him in the shoulder when he didn't comply. A fierce glare directed at the other men had them loudly clattering their chairs back on the stone floor as they hastily rose. Terence merely sneered at Evie and crossed his hands over his shabby jacket. It was the sort of behavior she'd come to expect from him.

"I'm sorry if I'm disturbing you," Evie said with a polite smile. "I was looking for Mr. Beaumont. Or Mrs. Rafferty. Has she already gone to bed?"

"Aye, she has gone up, Miss Evelyn," said Bridget with a shy smile. "But she said she'd lock up once we finished." She jabbed her brother in the shoulder again. "We were just leavin'. Ain't that right, Terry?"

The big man scowled at his sister and shambled to his feet. "Aye, we was. Nothin' more worth talkin' about, as far as I can see." His gaze flickered to the other men, and Evie got the distinct impression he was as unhappy with them as he was with her.

"Before you go," Evie said firmly, "can you tell me if Mr. Beaumont was here this evening?"

Bridget bobbed her head like a nervous quail. "That he was, miss. In fact, he was the reason we was meetin' tonight."

Evie frowned. "Really? He never said anything to me, and I saw no mention of it in the meeting book." Evie and Mrs. Rafferty shared responsibility for scheduling meetings for St. Margaret's and the Hibernian Association. Very little took place that they didn't know about.

Bridget shrugged. "I can't say nothin' about that, miss. You'd have to ask Mr. Beaumont."

"I will," Evie said, forcing a smile. She couldn't avoid the feeling that something wasn't right. It seemed out of character that Michael would leave the building while these people remained. Although most who used their services were hard-working, honest folk, there was the occasional hard case who could not be trusted.

Like Terence O'Shay.

"Can you tell me when Mr. Beaumont left?" she asked.

"About twenty minutes ago, miss," said the man Evie thought she might have met before. He gave her a friendly smile.

Evie pondered what to do for a few moments, then decided to let all this pass until she could speak with Michael. "Well, if you're finished with your meeting, I'd be happy to lock up."

Bridget nodded. "And you'll tell Mrs. Rafferty, miss? I wouldn't want her bein' angry with Mr. Beaumont for leavin' early."

"Of course—" Evie broke off when she heard the door swing open behind her. She glanced over her shoulder and almost fainted when she saw a man come stalking down the short flight of steps.

Will.

In his dress regimentals, he looked overdressed and

incongruous in the humble setting but still managed to seem bigger and more dangerous than all the other men in the room, including Terence O'Shay. His blue eyes were as cold and unforgiving as a January sky, and his already-hard mouth pulled into an even harder line. Will had never been the sort to blow up when he got angry, preferring to reason his way out of arguments, but she was learning he could be a grim and formidable man when something displeased him.

Clearly, *she'd* displeased him a great deal.

"Will, er, Captain Endicott! How did you get in here?" she blurted out.

He came to a stop, toe-to-toe with her, looming in what she felt sure was a deliberate attempt to intimidate her. Evie's anger began to stir as she remembered she had just as much cause to be annoyed with him as he had with her.

"You helpfully left the back door open," he said sarcastically. "I was able to waltz right in without a lick of trouble."

She winced. "Oh, yes, I suppose I forgot about that."

His eyebrows crawled up his forehead. "You *suppose?* Have your wits gone begging? What if you'd been alone and someone besides me had decided to wander in? Someone harboring ill intent?"

"There's no need to be rude," she huffed. "Everything is fine, as you can see. And I'm not alone." She glanced at Bridget and Terence. "I think you will remember Captain Endicott."

"Oh, aye. He's engraved on me bloody memory," Terence drawled in an insolent tone.

Bridget shot her brother a stern look and dipped into a curtsey. "Yes, miss. Good evening, sir."

Will gave her a slight jerk of the head that barely counted as a nod. "Having a meeting, Miss O'Shay? I hope I didn't interrupt anything."

The blatant suspicion in his voice had Evie darting a nervous glance around the room. Terence and the other men radiated waves of resentment. The sudden spike of tension in the room was disturbing, and it certainly hadn't been a tea party before Will's arrival.

She supposed she couldn't blame these poor fellows. An army officer would likely make them uncomfortable, given the unfortunate history of those who frequented St. Margaret's. She understood the travails their families had suffered under the boot heels of the king's army, especially during the years of rebellion. She knew how long their memories were too.

"They were just leaving," she said firmly. "Good night, everyone."

The strangers practically scrambled over themselves to leave, but not Terence. He strolled out with an arrogant, almost carefree air that had Evie swallowing a sigh. No wonder the dratted man couldn't hold on to a job. He apparently had a dreadful attitude toward every Englishman he met.

As Bridget scampered by, Evie stopped her with a touch on her arm. "I'll see you this Sunday evening for sewing class, I hope."

"Aye, miss, you will, and that's a fact," the girl all but babbled in her haste to be gone.

Evie nodded and let Bridget follow her companions. Their footsteps clattered on the stone floor of the corridor, then the slam of the back door signaled their departure. Silence fell over the room, broken only by the ticking of the small clock on the fireplace mantel and the hissing of banked coals in the grate.

She reluctantly met Will's eye, not because she feared his temper but because she hadn't seen him since that fraught scene last night. She'd been hoping to avoid him until after she'd had a chance to mend the breach with Michael and could assure Will that honor had been satisfied. Now, she was facing off with the man who assumed they would soon be wed. The fact that he was also the man who'd seen her half-dressed, her bosom overflowing her stays, didn't help matters.

Shifting from one foot to the other, she tried not to feel like a child found guilty of bad behavior. "How did you find out where I was?"

"Edie told me." He propped his hands on his lean hips and shook his head with disgust, exactly as if she *were* a naughty child needing discipline. "What the hell were you thinking?"

"About what, exactly?" She would hedge her bets until she could determine how bad things were—such as whether Mamma had also discovered their ruse.

He scoffed. "What do you think? About switching identities with your lamentable twin. Edie's idea, I suppose."

"Actually, it was mine."

His eyes reflected his surprise, giving Evie a tiny surge of satisfaction. With Will, she usually felt two steps behind.

Not that her little victory truly mattered with disaster looming before her. "Does Mamma know? You didn't say anything, did you?" She couldn't keep a quaver of anxiety from her voice.

He shook his head and some of the tension seemed to drain from his big body. "Of course not, goose. I would never expose you in so reckless a manner to your dear mamma. The consequences don't bear thinking about." The look of genuine horror on his face almost made her laugh.

Almost.

"In fact," he continued, tilting his head to peruse her from head to toe, "I almost didn't see it myself. Edie's very good at impersonating you, although her manner wasn't entirely accurate."

Evie was suddenly aware of how wobbly her legs felt. It probably resulted from a combination of anxiety and lack of sleep. She tottered to one of the kitchen chairs and sank into it. "We haven't done it since we were girls, so she's probably lost the hang of it."

Will barked out a derisive laugh. "It was good enough to fool just about everyone, I assure you."

"Then how did you know?" She knew her sister would not have betrayed her unless forced to.

"Alec saw it," Will said, sounding disgusted. "Unlike me, he spotted the ruse right away, and from across the room, too."

Evie widened her eyes. "How extraordinary. I must ask him how he managed it. His observations might come in useful next time."

Will's eyes narrowed dangerously. "There had better not *be* a next time, Evie." When she started to protest, he held up a hand. "We can quarrel about that later, if you like. By the way, what were that lot doing here tonight? Were you meeting with them?"

He'd gone back to sounding hard and suspicious rather than immensely irritated. She peered at him, puzzled by the switch.

"Evie, what were they meeting about?" he asked with exaggerated patience when she didn't respond right away.

She frowned. Why would Will even care? "Actually, I have no idea. I didn't ask."

"That's just perfect," he said. "Do you have any idea of what actually goes on around this place?"

She bolted up at that, anger giving her a fresh jolt of energy. "Of course I do, and I don't know how it could be your business, anyway."

"Everything about you is my business, now that we're

about to be married." He sounded like he was strangling on the words. "Or have you forgotten that?"

"I haven't forgotten anything, but I do not agree with your assessment of the situation," she said in a haughty voice. Then she glanced at the clock and felt light-headed again for the second time that evening. It was terribly late, and she needed to get home before her mother and sister returned from the ball.

"Confound it," she said, sighing. "Will, I need to get home. Since you're here and acting so ridiculously protective, you might as well take me."

"I have every intention of doing so, but first—"

She heard his muttered curse when she slipped past him up the stairs and out the door. She made it halfway down the hall before he caught up with her.

"Not so fast, my dear," he said. "We're not going anywhere until we have a few things sorted out."

He clamped a gentle but firm hand on her arm, ignoring her protests as he steered her into the parlor, shutting the door to lean against it. She fumed silently even as she acknowledged that a big, irate, and very handsome man whom she was desperately in love with was a very effective means of blocking her escape.

Desperately in love with? Oh dear, that didn't sound good, even in her head.

"This is ridiculous," she said in a thin voice, trying to rally. "We have nothing to talk about."

He gave a hoot of derisive laughter. "Try another one, my sweet."

She crossed her arms, which brought his gaze flickering down to her chest. It also brought the blood rushing to her cheeks. She dropped her arms and planted her hands on her hips instead. Sadly, that failed to solve the problem because now Will's gaze traveled slowly over her entire body, his eyes turning dark with heated interest.

Drat, drat, drat.

"All right, I suppose we do need to talk," she said in a grumpy voice, trying to ignore her body's response to the sensual intent she saw in his eyes. "But I simply must get home before Mamma and Edie are back from the ball. Can't we do this tomorrow?"

His gaze came back to her face and the heat faded. She didn't know whether to be glad or sorry.

"No, because you'll slip out first thing in the morning in another misguided attempt to speak with Beaumont," he said. "I'm not letting you out of my sight until we reach an agreement."

"The only agreement we're going to reach is that we're *not* getting married," she retorted.

"To repeat, try another one, Evie. Because we certainly *are* getting married. I've discussed it with your parents, and they agree with me."

She flung her arms out wide. "Well, you haven't discussed it with me," she shouted.

"Good God, you haven't given me the chance," he said, exasperated. "I've had to resort to hunting you down like a hound after a fox."

She had to swallow hard against the tight feeling in her throat. If she'd needed any confirmation that he didn't want to marry her, his words and the tone of his voice served quite well.

"And I'm beginning to feel like the fox, although it would appear that the hound isn't actually very eager to catch her." She pressed her lips tightly together, hating that she sounded so wounded. The scene held humiliating echoes of a moment she'd spent years trying to forget.

Will stared at her for a few seconds then let out a weary sigh. Only then did she notice the drawn look to his lips and the exhausted, hollow expression in his eyes. He looked as unhappy as she did, and that only made things worse.

He pushed away from the door and came to her. It took all her nerve not to retreat—or throw herself in his arms, seeking comfort. Long ago, the latter was what she would have done, at least until he'd gone away and forgotten her.

Reaching down, he took her hand, threading their fingers together. "Sweetheart," he said in an infinitely gentle voice, "where in God's name did you get that silly idea? I would think that after our encounter in your father's library, you would understand the exact opposite is true."

His voice—that warm, low voice she'd always loved—had her swallowing tears. "You don't want to marry me and you know it. Everyone knows it."

He made a scoffing noise and pulled her hand up to his mouth. When he turned it over and pressed a kiss to her wrist, right on her madly pounding pulse, Evie felt her knees go wobbly again.

"Not true," he said. "I do want to marry you." A ghost of a smile passed over his mouth. "I'm a little surprised by how much, to tell you the truth, but I suppose I shouldn't be."

She wasn't sure what he meant by that remark but decided not to pursue it. For now.

"I'm supposed to marry Michael. You realize that, don't you?" she asked in a tight voice. "We've been planning it for a long time, and now I've hurt him terribly."

"I do realize that," he said in a patient voice. "But you're going to marry me instead. I'm sure Beaumont is quite clear about that."

She winced. Every time she thought of the horrified look

on Michael's face, she felt sick with shame. "He was so upset last night. I hate that he saw us . . . that way."

"I know, and I regret that I placed you both in that situation. And you *should* apologize to him. We both should, after things are settled between us."

She tried to pull her hand away, but he held on tight. "No, Will. I'm going to tell him that last night was simply a . . ." She trailed off at the sardonic lift of his eyebrow.

"An aberration," she forged on. "A result of too much emotion and distress. I'll beg Michael to forgive me, and then he and I will go on as before. You'll be free of any obligation to me, since Mamma and Papa will have to allow me to marry Michael in order to preserve my reputation."

A cold blue flame lit up Will's eyes. "I think not."

Evie refused to be intimidated. She yanked her hand and this time succeeded in freeing it. "Why are you doing this, Will? It's ridiculous." She averted her gaze, struggling with a myriad of conflicting emotions that threatened to overwhelm her.

Will took her chin and nudged it up so she had to meet his gaze. "Tell me the truth, Evie. Do you love Beaumont?"

She stared into his amazing eyes, eyes she'd once lost herself in for hours at a time. She'd never been able to lie to him—not that she'd ever wanted to. "I care for him a great deal. Besides, we share much in common. Our work, the charity . . ." She wavered to a halt when he stroked a finger across her lips.

"That's not what I asked, sweetheart. I asked if you love him."

"How can I begin to answer?" she said, despairing of making him understand. "It's so much more complicated than that."

A wry smile touched the edges of his mouth, and she had

to fight the urge to reach up and kiss first one corner and then the other.

"Then let's try another question," he murmured. "Do you love me?"

His features—cherished for so long—blurred as she blinked back tears. Despair and a relentless inevitability pounded through the last of her barriers.

"Don't you know the answer to that?" she whispered.

"I do." Will made it sound like a vow. "And for that, I am exceedingly grateful."

Then he bent and took her mouth, ravishing it like the wolf that he was.

Chapter Seventeen

Evie's knees buckled under the onslaught of Will's fierce kiss. His arm snaked around her, drawing her in until she was plastered against him, shoulder to thigh. Even through the layers of clothing, his hard chest pressing on her breasts made her nipples tingle. She gasped as his tongue swept into her mouth. The kiss was so much more than the brief taste of last night's unexpected embrace. This was a devouring, and the ravishment she'd been dreaming so hopelessly about for so long.

Whimpering with helpless pleasure, she wrapped her arms around his neck and went up on tiptoe. The kiss was as hot as a lick of fire across her lips, and her body softened, yearning for more, growing damp and eager in the secret, feminine places. Every part of her seemed to be giving way, toppling in the path of his seduction. She was where she wanted to be—straight in front of him, her arms open wide. She'd waited a lifetime for this, and her heart rejected any notion of pulling back. To do so would be madness.

But so is this, whispered a voice in her head.

She stilled in his arms, trying to remember the reasons

she should be saying no. She'd come into the room expressly to say no. But with his mouth on hers, demanding total surrender, Evie could no longer formulate a reason to deny him what he wanted.

What *she* wanted.

He released her mouth. Her eyes fluttered open—she hadn't even realized she'd closed them—and she looked up into his burning gaze. She read a thousand sensual demands in those familiar depths and sensed the barely restrained predator in the rocklike tension of his body.

"Stop thinking, Evie," he said as he swiftly untied her bonnet and tossed it onto the nearby table.

His husky growl made the back of her knees turn to water. After he disposed of her hat, his hand slid to her bottom and cupped her, nudging her forward to connect with his aroused body. His hard length intruded through her thin skirts, pressing into her mound with a seductive, terrifying temptation that seized the breath in her lungs.

"I . . . I feel like I *should* be thinking about what we're doing," she said, trying not to pant. "But you're making it awfully difficult."

His lips parted in a feral smile. "Ah, then we're heading in the right direction."

As if to make good on his point, he lowered his head and nipped her earlobe—she'd never imagined *that* could make one feel like swooning with pleasure—then trailed hot kisses down her throat. When he nipped her again, sucking the tender skin at the base of her neck, every muscle in her body went slack.

Slow down. Be sure this is what you want.

She clamped her fingers into the fabric of his coat to hold herself steady. "Will, are we really going to do what I think we're going to do?" Her voice was so squeaky she barely recognized it.

His other hand moved down to cup her bottom as well, and he gently ground himself against her mound. Evie arched up on her toes, her body instinctively reacting to the bolt of sensation his movement created.

Will groaned and his eyes almost closed as he flexed his hips once more. "Christ, I hope so. I feel like I've been waiting forever."

"Do you really want this? Want me?" she whispered, afraid to hope. She wanted so much for that to be true.

His eyelids lifted, and Evie's heart skipped a beat at the passion that lit his eyes with a blue fire. "I want you, Evie—in my arms, in my bed, in my life."

Those were the words she'd longed to hear. The walls she'd built against him, year after painful year, were crumbling into dust.

He pressed a searing kiss to her mouth, robbing her of breath and making her restless for more.

"I want you naked beneath me," he said when he released her lips. "And I want you on top of me, my cock driving up into you while I play. I want *you,* Evie. Mine, forever."

Oh, dear. Who knew that sort of wicked talk could be so exciting? Evie knew she should be shocked but couldn't seem to muster the slightest sense of indignation.

She tightened her grip, trying to still the trembling in her body. "That sounds nice," she managed to get out.

He smiled as he moved his hands up to her hips. He held her gently, no longer grinding against her, but still holding her tight against his arousal.

"What part?" he said. His deep rumble held a hint of amusement.

She wrinkled her nose at him, suddenly shy. "All of it, although some of it does sound rather awkward," she said, trying to make a joke.

But she did want more from him, so much so that her

body practically vibrated with yearning. It was, however, also dawning on her how little she knew about lovemaking. She'd never thought much about it in terms of Michael. Truthfully, it was hard to even imagine with him. But everything was different with Will. She could indeed imagine it and had many times when she was younger, if rather vaguely. Evie was aware of the generalities but fell down when it came to the details.

"Do you mean about being on top, with me inside you?" he asked.

His eyes glittered and a dark flush glazed his cheekbones. It would certainly appear that Will did want her, and very much, and that went a long way to assuaging Evie's shyness.

"Yes, that part. I'm having trouble imagining it," she replied, slightly shocked by her boldness.

"Shall I show you, my sweet?"

The dark tone to his voice had her toes curling and her stomach doing funny flips. What he suggested was wicked and depraved and entirely outrageous, and if she had a brain in her head she would deliver him a severe scold and then insist he take her home. But this moment was everything she'd ever wanted. How could she walk away from it? From him?

His gaze softened, and an understanding smile curled up one corner of his mouth. "You're allowed to want it, Evie. It's not wrong, I promise you. I want it too."

She let out a soft sigh of surrender—to herself as much as to him. "I never could say no to you, could I?"

"Don't say no to *me,* Evie. Say yes to *us.*"

She saw the quiet promise in his expression, heard it in his voice. This was the Will she'd always known and loved, the Will she trusted. This man would never hurt her.

"Well, you *have* made me curious," she admitted. "About the, um, mechanics of things."

"Then let me give you a demonstration." He clamped his hands back on her bottom and lifted her straight off the floor, cradling her against him.

She gaped at him as he pivoted on his heel and took a step back to the sturdy old chaise in the corner. "Here? You're going to show me here?"

He carefully lowered himself onto the low chaise, forcing her to shift and scramble into a position straddling his thighs.

"No time like the present," he said with rakish insouciance.

Evie was about to register a half-hearted objection when his mouth came down on hers again. Her protests were annihilated by the hot, slick glide of his tongue and the strength of his arms holding her snugly against him. For several minutes he simply held her on his lap, gently ravishing her with his lips and tongue, giving her the time to sink into a shimmering haze of boneless pleasure. With every kiss she felt the imprint of him on her mind and body and knew there was no going back. There was no one else who could draw forth the yearnings of her heart, nor would there ever be again.

Will broke the kiss. "Are you comfortable, my sweet?" He glanced down. "You seem rather tangled up in your dress."

Now that he called attention to it, she took in the way her skirts had twisted around her legs, trapping her in an awkward position. Reaching back, she tried to pull them free and almost toppled off his lap.

He steadied her, laughing. "Here, let me. Lift up a bit."

When she did, he pulled her skirts free, but instead of draping them over her legs, he pulled them—and her chemise—up above her hips, exposing almost everything from the waist down.

"What are you doing?" Then she winced at the screechy tone in her voice.

He let out a dramatic sigh. "I can't demonstrate the mechanics if you can't see anything."

"Oh, that makes sense, I suppose," she said doubtfully.

He dropped a quick kiss on her nose. "Trust me, Evie, all right?"

She nodded, giving him a hesitant smile.

"Good. Now, let's get rid of this."

This was her spencer. He made short work of getting it off then started on her bodice, reaching around her to undo the buttons.

Evie leaned forward so he could reach the lowest button. "Aren't you going to take some of your clothes off too?"

He flashed a wicked grin. "That won't be necessary, at least not tonight." He plucked her spectacles from her nose and placed them on the table with her bonnet.

"Well, I suppose you're the expert," she said, blinking as her vision readjusted.

He was about to reply but apparently lost the thread of the conversation when he eased her sleeves down her arms. Evie wriggled her hands free, blushing as he studied her bosom with an avid gaze.

"God, Evie," he whispered, tracing a finger along the top of her stays. "You're so beautiful."

She'd always thought herself as too abundant in that area to be considered fashionable, and had never thought of herself as beautiful—nor had anyone else, for that matter. Not even Michael had ever called her that. Only Will.

"Thank you," she whispered.

He tipped her chin up and brushed a kiss across her lips.

"You don't have a clue how lovely you are, but I'm going to show you."

His hands moved to her stays, unlacing and easing them down. Her breasts, white and full, spilled out, her pink nipples already puckering. She heard a hiss escape from between his lips, and then his hands closed around her breasts.

Evie gasped when he began to massage her nipples. They immediately hardened into tight points, tingling deliciously. She pushed into his hands, trying to increase the pressure.

"Do you like that?" he murmured.

She could only moan her reply. Deep between her thighs, her flesh went soft and damp, and she instinctively pressed down against his arousal.

"You have gorgeous breasts, Evie," Will said as he continued to play with her. "They're like sweet candies, just waiting to be sucked."

His shocking, exciting words made her squirm.

"Oh, oh," she gasped, when the sensitive spot between her thighs rubbed against his hard length. Small, lovely spasms rippled through her, deep inside, and she had to grab his shoulders to maintain her balance.

Will watched her through narrowed eyes, his hands still teasing her nipples. "That's it, move against me. I don't want you to hold anything back."

She couldn't have remained motionless if she'd wanted to, not with his clever fingers stroking her breasts and torturing her stiff nipples with delicious play. Evie gave herself over to the unfamiliar sensations as she moved against him. She *loved* the sight of his long, tanned fingers on her breasts, tweaking and gently pulling the beaded points until she thought she would go mad. When he flattened his hands on her and dragged his calloused palms over her nipples, she rose up on her knees, arching her back as pleasure bolted from her breasts to her womb.

"Oh, yes," Will growled. One hand went to her shoulder, pushing her back in a deeper arch. That thrust her breasts up high. He dipped down his head and sucked a breast into his mouth, his tongue wrapping hot and wet around her throbbing nipple.

"Oh, God!" The words were wrenched from Evie's throat. She writhed against him as her inner flesh throbbed with a deep ache that begged for relief. Will held her in a merciless grip sucking on first one breast, and then the other. He nipped and teased, tonguing each nipple into a tight, aching peak. The sensation drove her mad. Though it was just shy of pain, she wanted him never to stop.

But even that still wasn't enough to soothe the rising demand within her that cried out for more.

"Will," she pleaded. "Please do something."

He swirled his tongue around her nipple once more, then leaned against the back of the chaise, pulling her upright. He kept one hand on her breast, massaging it as he watched her. His silvery-blue gaze and his rough golden hair, gleaming in the dim light, reminded her why she'd nicknamed him Wolf when they were children.

"What is it, Evie?" he asked in a low, masculine rumble. "What is it you need?"

She wriggled in his lap, trying to press closer to soothe the ache between her thighs. That pulled his lips tight in a predatory smile, and one of his hands settled on her hip, pressing her down to maintain contact. But it still wasn't enough.

"That's just it," she complained, throwing her arms wide. "I don't know what I need."

When he laughed, she focused her eyes enough to glare at him. "I thought *you* were the expert," she said in a grumpy voice. "Why are you acting so beastly?"

He leaned close to plant a gentle kiss on her lips.

"I'm sorry, my love, but you look so delightfully undone that I couldn't resist teasing you. But I know exactly what you need, and I'm going to give it to you," he said, his voice dropping to a lower, rougher register.

He pulled her skirt and chemise up to her waist, opening her completely to his gaze.

Evie couldn't help glancing down. Since she straddled him with her legs spread wide, he could see her blond curls and even the plump flesh they only partly obscured. Blushing, she looked at him from under her lashes. His gaze, intent and focused, followed the path of his fingers as he traced patterns on her upper thighs, brushing against her damp curls.

"So pretty," he said in a hushed voice. "Those sweet golden curls and your wet little cunny."

She jerked when his fingertips brushed over her. His touch was gentle, almost reverent, and that proved a heady combination when combined with his profane language.

"You are wet, aren't you?" he murmured.

She nodded, even though she suspected the question was rhetorical. She was wet—hot and damp and wild for his touch.

"Will, please," she moaned.

He made a rough sound low in his throat, and then slowly pushed his fingers between her folds. Evie let out a strangled wail and rose up high, stunned by the fierce, gorgeous contraction of her inner flesh. That brought her breasts right up to his face and Will didn't hesitate. He pulled her in with a hot suck, alternately laving and flicking the stiff point of her nipple with his tongue. All the while, his hand worked between her thighs, massaging her inner folds, gently circling the tiny knot that ached and burned for his touch.

Evie grabbed onto his shoulders, fighting for balance. Helplessly, her hips pushed into his hand. His other hand came to her bottom to guide her in a gentle, grinding rhythm that drove her pleasure into a tight coil. Her breath came in sobs as she moved against him, her body lashed with pleasure by his expert manipulation. She felt him everywhere—his tongue curled around her nipple, his beard-roughened jaw sending shivers of delight across the tender skin of her breast. One hand squeezed and massaged her bottom, and the other rubbed between her folds, teasing her sex until she thought she would scream.

When tiny ripples of pleasure began to pulse deep inside, Evie almost did scream. She pushed down, trying to deepen the contact, desperate to ride the building wave of desire that flowed from her womb.

Almost purring against her breast, Will pulled his hand away. Shocked, Evie dug her fingers into his shoulders, her body throbbing with unfulfilled need.

"Will, don't stop now!" she yelped.

His head lifted, his gaze gleaming with passion and— blast him—amusement. "I'm not stopping, love, I'm joining you. I want to be inside you when you come."

She tried to catch her breath. Evie wasn't entirely sure what he meant, but she did very much want him inside her since she was beginning to think that was the only way he could assuage the frustration and need pulsing between her legs.

"Lift for a second," he ordered.

Awkwardly, she pushed up, letting him slip a hand to the front of his trousers. He quickly undid his fall and freed himself.

Evie glanced down, but when she saw the size of Will's arousal she almost wished she hadn't. Not that she felt inclined to call a halt to the proceedings—not at all. She just felt even less sure about the mechanics than she had before.

Will tipped up her chin to look at him. "Trust me," he whispered.

She leaned forward and touched her forehead to his. "I do. I'm just being silly because it's my first time."

"And I'm honored by that, my love, more than you can know. But I suppose I'd best get busy and help make you ready for it."

"Funny, I thought that's what you were already doing," she joked.

"Oh, there's more," he murmured. "Much more."

Then he rubbed two fingers through her folds again, slicking through her moisture, before slowly pushing them inside her. Evie bit her lip at the slight burn as he pressed into her tight passage, but she couldn't deny how lovely it felt too. When he began stroking and massaging her inner muscles, she moaned and started to move again.

"That's it, my beautiful girl," he whispered. "Do whatever you want."

Will twisted his hand, bringing the base of his palm against her tight bud while keeping his fingers buried inside her. Evie rode him, eager for more. She clung to him, rubbing her naked breasts against the fabric of his coat, making her nipples tingle and ache. She couldn't help looking down at their bodies, relishing the erotic contrast between her white, naked flesh and his soldier's garb. His big hands were everywhere, teasing, guiding and building her pleasure to unimaginable heights. It was wicked and forbidden, and she should and no doubt would feel thoroughly ashamed when it was over.

But it was also the most exciting thing that had ever

happened to her. It was Will, and she'd wanted him for so long. She wanted to imprint him on her body and her soul, so the memory of this moment would never fade.

Tiny contractions once more rippled through her channel, her inner flesh contracting around his fingers.

"God," he groaned. "You're so ready for me."

She gave a jerky nod, beyond any kind of verbal response. He withdrew his fingers, then tilted her up and forward a few inches. A moment later, she felt the broad head of his erection slip into her, forging into her tight channel. She hissed out a breath and went still.

Will murmured soothing words as he gently guided her body. Then he flexed his hips, nudging into her at the same time as she started a long slide down his thick length.

It burned like fire and yet felt wonderful at the same time. She sucked in a breath, holding it as she desperately searched his eyes. His gaze was heavy-lidded and gleaming, his cheekbones flushed with pleasure.

"Christ, Evie," he rumbled. "You feel like heaven."

She touched his cheek, smiling tentatively as he urged her down the last few inches until her hips were flush against him. Evie couldn't begin to describe how she felt—amazed, terrified, filled in a way she never could have imagined, both physically and emotionally. To be joined so intimately with him after she'd thought him gone from her life forever seemed impossible to fathom. She clutched at his shoulders, almost afraid to draw breath for fear she'd wake up and find it all a dream.

Then again, dreams didn't usually sting in such sensitive places. Evie wriggled a bit, trying to ease her discomfort. Perhaps it was her lack of knowledge regarding the mechanical details that contributed to the problem, although Will's size surely had something to do with it too.

His pleasure-dazed expression faded as his gaze sharpened on her. "Too much?"

She tried not to wince as she shifted again. "Well, it's very nice, but not quite what I expected."

"It's your first time, love. There's always some pain."

"I'm sure it will be better next time," she said stoutly.

He laughed. "It's about to get better right now."

And then he slipped a hand between their bodies to find the knot of flesh hidden in her curls. He began teasing it with slow, tantalizing movements. Warmth radiated from beneath his fingertips, seeping into her core. It seemed only natural to start moving again, rocking against him as he massaged her. When her excitement once more began to build, Will surged into her, stroking her inside and out.

Sensation rose in a golden spiral that flowed through her body. Her movements were jerky, unpracticed, but Will steadied her, silently guiding her to move with him. Their fractured breaths broke the silence, uneven and hurried. But their bodies moved together in glorious rhythm. Will touched her everywhere—holding her back, urging her forward, but always keeping her with him.

He flexed his hips, growling out his own pleasure. "Come for me, love," he rasped.

Now she understood. Evie stretched up, reaching for the bright burst of pleasure just beyond her grasp. When Will flicked his fingers over her tender flesh, she broke. She arched her back as the sensation pulsed within her, a luxurious spasm then seemed to go on forever.

Will clamped both hands on her bottom and surged one last time, high and hard, his strong thighs lifting her as he groaned out his release. His eyes were closed, his features pulled tight with passion. She clung to him, her own eyes filling with tears of gratitude and emotion as his powerful body shook under her hands.

As he finally came to rest beneath her, his eyelids rose and a slow, sensual smile curled his lips. With trembling hands, Evie brushed her fingers through his dishevelled golden hair.

"My Wolf," she whispered, and then collapsed in his arms.

Chapter Eighteen

Will stroked a hand down Evie's back, his barely sated senses relishing the feel of her soft skin under his fingertips. As he cradled her trembling body in his arms, his reason grappled with the enormity of what had just happened between them. The enormity of what he had just done.

He'd taken her, an innocent maiden, on a creaky old chaise in a shabby little parlor at the back end of a church in the slums. Hardly the stuff of romance and certainly not the act of a man of honor, one duty-bound to protect the reputation of his bride. If anyone were to find out about this salacious little episode—and it had been deliciously salacious, he must admit—Evie's good name would suffer, regardless of their impending marriage. He should be thoroughly ashamed of himself for ravishing her in so primitive a fashion. The fact that he'd brought her to climax shouldn't be a source of satisfaction to him at all. He should be on his knees, begging her to forgive him for acting like a voracious brute.

But he wasn't the least bit sorry it had happened. The idea of going onto his knees before her had simply planted another image in his brain—Evie with her legs spread wide or draped over his shoulders, opening her tender flesh to the play of his mouth and hands.

Next time, he promised himself. Right now, he had to get Evie safely home before anyone found out she was even gone.

Turning her face to nuzzle into his neck, she heaved a sigh replete with satisfaction, pushing her lovely breasts against him. Will had always known that Evie hid a lush, welcoming body behind her plain spinster clothes. To say her form was spectacular was no exaggeration, and he could only thank his stars that the men of the *ton* were too stupid to realize the prize hiding behind that shy façade. Will had only begun to explore the bounty Evie had to offer, but he intended to devote a good part of his energies over the next several months to doing just that.

After, of course, he and Alec completed their mission and proved, among other things, that Evie had nothing to do with any criminal conspiracy.

That dreary thought broke through the warm cocoon they'd spun around each other in the quiet room. He needed to get moving, transporting Evie home and making a quick return to St. Margaret's so he could search Beaumont's office. It should be easy enough to filch the keys from her reticule once he had her in a hackney. All he had to do was kiss her until she was too distracted to notice what he was doing.

"Evie, my love," he murmured, "I'm reluctant to make you move, but I think we'd best be going. We need to get you home before Lady Reese and Edie return from the Talwins' ball."

"Oh, drat," she muttered.

She pushed herself upright, wincing as she sat up straight

in his lap, her legs still straddling his thighs. She gave him a shy smile as she rested her hands on his shoulders, her eyes shining as she met his gaze. Will's heart turned over at the joy he saw in her expression. The Evie he'd known had come back to life before him, with her love open and honest and no barriers between them. That's what it had been like before he'd taken her dreams and crushed them under the heel of his boot as he'd marched off to find adventure.

In one sense, she terrified him, because so much of her happiness seemed dependent on him. But he realized now what a gift that was, too, a much greater gift than even the ample pleasures of her body or her innocently sensual response to his lovemaking. The true gift was Evie's heart, which would now be forever his. She might not be the most beautiful woman he'd ever been with, and she wouldn't bring him riches or social influence. What she would bring was herself—her kind and generous nature, her gentle perception, and her loyalty. Marriage to Evie would come with a price, but it was a price he found himself more than willing to pay, given all she would bring him in return.

"You had to mention Mamma, didn't you?" she said with a rueful smile. "I can think of no better way to destroy any inclination I might have for pleasure, even with you."

He let out a soft laugh. "I'll have to remember that. No referring to your mother when I intend to make love to you."

"That would be wise," she said as she struggled to pull up her stays.

She was gloriously disheveled, with her satiny smooth breasts and full pink nipples enticingly propped up by her undergarments. Letting out a regretful sigh, Will dropped a good-night kiss on one rigid tip and then reached to help her.

"I'll do it," she said in a soft voice. As she slipped her hands under his to rearrange her bodice, she avoided looking at him, instead keeping her gaze on her fingers as she restored herself to some semblance of order.

Will tipped her chin up with a finger. "Are you feeling shy, Evie? There's no need, you know, not with me."

She twisted her mouth in a wry smile, her cheeks faintly flushing pink. "It's silly, isn't it? I wasn't at all shy when we were, well, you know." She waved a vague hand. "But now I can't help feeling rather . . . awkward."

When her glance darted across the room to avoid his, Will knew something else was troubling her.

He grasped her gently around her ribcage, letting her breasts rest on his hands with a lovely, heavy weight. He might not have the time to take her again tonight, but he wouldn't rush her, not after the step they'd just taken together.

"Out with it, my girl. What's bothering you?"

Her nose twitched, as if something had tickled it, then she tilted her head and looked at him from under her golden lashes. It was so unconsciously sensual that his cock started to twitch back to life.

"I can't help thinking that this isn't truly what you want," she said. "Last night was . . . not what I intended to happen between us. I'm afraid you're only doing this out of a sense of obligation to me, not because you wish for it."

If she'd said that to him a week or two ago, he might have agreed. But with every passing moment Will was convinced that taking Evie for his wife was the right decision for both of them. "No one forced me to do anything. I'm doing exactly what I want to do."

She worried her lower lip with her teeth, the sparkle in her eyes replaced by doubt. He hated that she questioned herself—and him—but given their past he couldn't blame her.

He flexed his pelvis, nudging into her with his stiffening cock. At this rate, he might never get her home.

When she gasped, her eyes going wide, he flashed a wolfish grin. "Does this feel like you're forcing me to do something I don't want to do?"

She gripped his shoulders. "N-no, but—"

He leaned in and brushed a kiss across her plump lips. "But what?"

"Well, Mamma once told us—"

"I thought we were leaving your mother out of this."

She scrunched up her nose in an adorable grimace. "Sorry, you're right. You should just ignore me."

He smiled. "That would be impossible. I can, however, guess what your mother said. She told you that men were insatiable brutes who would fornicate with any woman under any circumstance."

She let out a sheepish laugh. "Well, yes. She was trying to warn us away from dangerous situations."

He nodded. "Very wise of her, and for some men it's probably true. But not for me. I don't pretend to be a saint, Evie, but I'm not a rake, either. Especially when it comes to you."

He moved his hands from around her body to capture her face between his palms. Her misty eyes gazed back at him, vulnerable and full of hope. Emotion rustled through him, along with the conviction that he must never betray that hope. "Evie, I've never cared about another woman the way I care about you, and I never shall. You are more important to me than anyone on this earth."

Her eyelids fluttered down, the thick lashes a silken shield hiding her expression. Then she looked at him, and the happiness that blazed forth from her gaze rendered him speechless.

"Do you truly mean that?" she whispered.

He had to work to get the words past his tight vocal chords. "I promise that I do."

She rested her cool fingers over the backs of his hands and pressed a soft kiss to his lips. He tried to deepen it, but she suddenly murmured something against his mouth and pushed up.

"As happy as that makes me," she said with a little grimace, "and as delighted as I would be to stay here forever with you, I must regretfully say that my knees beg to differ. In fact, if I don't get up soon I might end up crippled. I don't think *that* would be a very good start to our marriage."

He laughed. "Indeed not, and it would be deuced awkward to explain how you ended up that way. Here, let me help you."

He grasped her around the waist and lifted her up, and mentally sighed to lose the clasp of her luscious flesh around his cock. Evie wobbled a bit as her feet hit the floor, and he kept a firm grip until she was able to steady herself.

"I think my foot fell asleep." She rested her hands on his shoulders and lifted a foot in the air, rotating it at the ankle.

"I'm sorry, Evie. Your mother was right—men are brutes. I promise that next time we're together, I'll make proper love to you in a bed." Given his state of arousal as he watched her hobble over to retrieve her spencer from the chair, he could only hope that would happen as soon as possible.

As she restored her clothing to some semblance of order, he began to calculate how quickly they could wed. Evie didn't strike him as the type of girl who wanted an elaborate wedding or who needed to wait for a large trousseau, but her parents would find marriage by special license to be rather slipshod. Still, that might be the way to go in any case. Not only would he get Evie into his bed sooner rather than later, it would be less likely to irritate his father if they were married with little fanfare.

He came to his feet, absently putting himself to rights as he thought of all the things he needed to do over the next week or so—stopping a deadly conspiracy, breaking the news of his impending marriage to his surely annoyed father, and planning a wedding. Oh, and finding suitable accommodations for his bride. After he knocked all those items off his list, he could then turn his mind to how he would support his wife in the fashion she deserved.

Evie was struggling with the small buttons at the top of her bodice, so Will went to help her.

"I can't see a thing in this dratted light," she said with a sigh, standing like a little girl as he finished dressing her. "I do hope we didn't sit on my glasses while we were, er, you know."

"Never fear, my love, they're right here." He retrieved the rather battered silver frames from the small table. "Although these do look a little worse for wear."

"They're my spare pair." She settled them on the bridge of her nose. They were slightly askew, giving her a rather comical air. "Edie's wearing my good ones."

"Ah, yes, about that," Will said, remembering that he was annoyed with her. "I do hope—"

"Now, Will," she interrupted, "you're not going to be one of those husbands who is always scolding his wife, are you?"

"As I was about to say, I do hope you won't be one of those wives who continually hares off on crazy adventures."

Her eyebrows tilted up over the rims of her spectacles. "You *do* know who I am, don't you?" She pointed a finger on her breastbone. "I'm Evelyn, the quiet one."

"Well, I suppose I can forgive you this time, but no more midnight trips into St. Giles. Are we clear?"

"Will—"

"Evie, I need your promise on this," he said quietly. "I won't be able to manage if I have to worry that you're running off into danger."

Her mutinous look faded, and she went up on tiptoe and kissed him on the chin. "I suppose I can understand that, given that I've spent years worrying that you would be blown to bits on some battlefield."

He grimaced. "Ouch. All right, I understand. And I also understand how committed you are to your work. But I expect you to keep me apprised of what you're doing and to keep yourself out of danger at all times."

She nodded, but he had an uneasy sense she was only listening with half an ear.

"Will, I still need to speak with Michael," she said bluntly. "He deserves an explanation and an apology."

His gut pulled tight. "You weren't engaged to the man, Evie. You don't owe him an apology."

Aside from the fact that he was learning that he was the jealous sort who didn't want his prospective bride spending private time with any man but him, Will wanted to keep her as far away from Beaumont as possible. After what he'd seen of that highly suspicious meeting in the kitchen, he was convinced that something dodgy was happening at St. Margaret's. If that was the case, it made sense to assume that Beaumont was involved until evidence indicated otherwise.

Evie made a scoffing noise and laid a hand on his chest. "You know that's not true. Michael is a good man, and he deserves to know why I've changed my mind."

"He already knows why," Will growled.

She rolled her eyes. "I knew you were going to be difficult. I won't put up with that, even from you."

He was trying to formulate a response to that annoying

statement when the small clock on the mantelpiece chimed out the hour.

"Oh, good God," Evie gasped. "I didn't realize it was so late. We'll have to continue this later."

"Fine," Will said, resisting the urge to clench his teeth. He glanced around the room. "Where's your reticule?"

When he looked back at her, she'd gone beet red.

"Actually," she said, "I need to, um, freshen up a bit, if you don't mind. Could you wait while I visit the . . ."

"Privy?" he supplied for her, feeling a bit guilty. He really *had* been acting the brute. Of course she would want to attend to her personal needs. "Certainly, my love, take your time. And don't worry about your mother. I'll handle her, if need be."

She gave him a grateful smile then hurried from the room, murmuring that she would return in a few minutes. He listened to her soft footsteps patter down the hall, the sound fading into silence. He waited for several more seconds, but all remained still.

It was too good a chance to miss.

Will opened Beaumont's office door wide, letting the light from the parlor spill across the desk. He made a quick search of the desk drawers and cubbyholes, keeping one ear open for Evie. As far as he could tell, paperwork and ledgers he quickly glanced through detailed the legitimate business of the Hibernian Benevolent Association. He'd need more time to follow any money trails that surfaced, but if he found what he thought he was likely to find, that sort of work could wait for later.

His search revealed only the one drawer that locked. He paused, straining his ears again for Evie's footfall. Surely she would take at least five minutes to conduct her feminine business, which meant that he still had a little time.

He dug into his waistcoat pocket, extracting the small

picklock he always carried, and went to work on the lock. It yielded almost instantly. If Beaumont really was trying to hide something of significance in his desk, he wasn't doing much of a job.

A small packet of letters—four in all—filled the small drawer. Three carried postmarks from Dublin and the other from Ulster. The Dublin letters were from O'Connell, and the Ulster letter was from a man whose name Will didn't recognize. That last missive contained a short list of names, along with a brief explanation that the men listed could not return to Londonderry given their *unfortunate history*, but were *well suited for the work already detailed* in previous letters. Terence O'Shay's name was on the list.

As far as Will was concerned, combined with the reference to past troubles, that made investigation of the names on the list an imperative.

He refolded the list and shoved it into the inside pocket of his coat, then opened the first letter from O'Connell. A quick perusal indicated that the Irishman was thanking Beaumont for his support in the *business with Peel,* which Will assumed was a reference to the aborted duel between O'Connell and the chief secretary. O'Connell also thanked Beaumont for his generous donation of time and money to *the cause which we both so ardently support*, despite whatever *hardships might befall them in the course of seeking justice.*

Will breathed out a soft curse. The letter wasn't decisive by any means, but it certainly pointed in an unpleasant direction for Beaumont. Logic dictated that he take the missives with him to show Aden. If Beaumont was guilty, as Will was beginning to suspect, he could hardly raise the alarm when he discovered the theft of his letters. In fact, his response one way or another could be instructive.

A quick footfall in the parlor brought his head up with a jerk. "Will, where are you?"

A moment later, as he finished relocking the drawer, Evie appeared in the doorway. A bewildered frown marked her features. "What are you doing?" Her gaze jumped to the surface of the desk, and the envelopes lying upon it.

Will had to bite back an entire string of foul curses as horrified understanding dawned on her face.

"You were searching Michael's desk." Her flat voice left no room for denial. Whatever Banbury tale he came up with, there was no room for pretending he hadn't been doing exactly what it looked like.

Her gaze snapped up to meet his, disbelief and the first hints of betrayed trust darkening the blue depths. It was the look that had haunted him for years, and it made him sick at heart to see it again.

"Why were you doing that?" Her voice rose to a thin, high note.

He took a step toward her, but she scuttled back, her elbow banging into the doorframe. She let out a muffled exclamation of pain but held up her other hand to hold him back.

"No, don't touch me." She sounded like something was strangling her. "Tell me why you were searching his desk." Her gaze darted to the small pile of letters on the desktop. "Is that Michael's correspondence? Will, you have no right to touch that!"

She made a move forward, trying to scurry around him, but he whipped out a hand to grasp her forearm.

"Evie, stop for a minute and listen," he said. "There's a reasonable explanation, but let me take you home first before your mother discovers you missing. We can talk about it there, I promise."

She wrenched her arm free. "Hang my mother. I'm not going anywhere until you tell me what you were doing."

He let out a frustrated sigh. "I would rather explain this to you later, once you've had a chance to recover from the, er, activities and emotions of the evening." And once he came up with a halfway reasonable explanation for what he'd done.

She stared at him like he'd lost his mind, then her mouth sagged open. "Is this about my relationship with Michael? Are you looking for letters between us that you think might prove embarrassing?" A fierce little scowl pulled her eyebrows together. "Because if you are, I assure you that no such correspondence exists. I suppose I should be flattered by such jealousy on your part, but I'm not. I find it indicative of a lack of trust in me that I do *not* deserve."

Will grabbed the unexpected lifeline. He dredged up what he hoped was both a sheepish and proprietorially male expression. "Guilty as charged, sweetheart. You have every right to give me a thundering scold, and I promise to give you ample opportunity to do so—after we get you home."

She peered up at him with a suspicious gaze. "Are you telling me that you *still* don't trust me with Michael? Even after what happened between us tonight?"

Will felt his eyes pop wide. "God, no, nothing like that. It's just that . . ." He trailed off, knowing how idiotic his explanation must sound. "It's just that when it comes to you, I find that emotion seems to overcome my logic." Some sardonic part of him inwardly laughed at how true that statement was. Loving Evie seemed to blow the rest of his life to smithereens. "I promise it won't happen again."

He finished off that canard with an apologetic, rueful smile he could only pray would charm her and allay her suspicions. The Evie he'd once known would never have questioned him, instead accepting everything he said as gospel truth. He could only hope that, in that way at least, she hadn't changed.

His hope died when he saw her gaze go flat and cold.

"You're lying," she said. "Don't lie to me, Will, not after everything we've been through."

Christ.

Clearly, she was no longer the innocent girl who'd once worshiped the ground he walked on. After tonight, she'd likely never speak to him again.

He swiftly ran through his options, weighing the conflicting loyalties that battered away at him. If he told her even some of the truth, how would she react? Would she warn Beaumont? Given her loyalties to the man, that was certainly a risk.

But what about her loyalty to me?

It was a fair question. Once he apprised her of the facts, might she not understand why he'd done what he did? And since she loved him, should he not expect her to be loyal to him, even if it meant betraying Beaumont?

They stared at each other, frozen in a horrible tableau as the moments ticked by. Evie broke first. Her lips started to tremble and she was suddenly blinking away tears.

"Evie, sweetheart," he started, feeling desperate.

When she clutched his arm, whatever he'd been about to say died on his tongue.

"Please, Will," she begged. "Just tell me the truth. You trust me enough to do that, don't you?"

Trust.

That word, that concept, was at the heart of their relationship, as was its opposite—*betrayal*. But to whom did he owe his trust first? His country, his father, or Evie? He knew what he *should* do, he knew what his duty was, but the stark plea in her vulnerable eyes made only one choice possible.

He'd betrayed her once, and he wouldn't do it again. "You're not going to like it."

"I don't care. Just tell me."

Tersely, he outlined the situation, trying to hold back the depth of the manipulation he'd practiced on her. He'd done it to protect her, of course, but she wouldn't see it that way. For now, he stuck to the basics and hoped that her sense of duty to England—and her love for him—would carry the day.

For a minute or two, she clutched at his arm, her eyes growing wider with every second that passed. When he touched on his father's role in the affair, she flinched. Then, as he explained what he'd been doing tonight, she jerked her hand away, staring up at him with horror.

"You're all insane," she said in a hoarse voice. "Michael would never do anything like that. He would never betray his country or his king."

Will ached to take her in his arms and comfort her, but he forced himself to maintain a calm, logical demeanor. There was enough emotion swirling about the room without him adding to it.

Besides, she'd probably box his ears if he dared to touch her.

"I wish that were true, Evie, I sincerely do. But the evidence against Beaumont is unfortunately . . . fairly substantial." He held up a hand when she started to rip up at him. "I'm not absolutely asserting guilt, and of course he will have the opportunity to state his case. I'm simply explaining why Alec and I took the actions we did."

She clenched her hands into fists, clutching them against her middle. It was a habit from her youth, an unconscious, protective instinct. "Why didn't you just *ask* Michael? I'm sure he could explain everything to your satisfaction."

Will hesitated, trying to think of an explanation that wouldn't offend. A moment's thought told him it was impossible. "If he *is* guilty, we would be giving him advance warning. We need to track the conspirators down and stop them, not allow them time to escape."

Evie had now gone dead white with shock and looked barely able to keep on her feet. She stumbled over to one of the rickety chairs in front of Beaumont's desk and sank into it. Will took a step toward her, every instinct urging him to comfort and care for her.

"Stay back," she said. "I don't want you touching me."

He flinched, more at her tone than the words, although they sliced through him like a corsair's blade.

She sucked in a few deep breaths before coming back at him. "Why you, Will? Why did your father ask you to take on this horrid task? You're a soldier, not a spy."

He grimaced. This was one thing he'd hoped never to be forced to reveal, but he wouldn't lie to her any longer. "That's not entirely accurate. I'm what the army calls an exploring officer, which is for all practical purposes an agent for military intelligence."

Her expression went blank. "You are a spy," she said slowly, as if she had trouble processing the information. "Is Captain Gilbride a spy as well?"

"Yes."

She let out a pathetic thread of a laugh, one that held absolutely no amusement. "I cannot believe this. Did you ever intend to tell me you were a spy?"

"It's not exactly information I'm eager to share," he said dryly.

She snapped upright from her slumped position. "I'm to

be your wife, William Endicott. Did you not think I deserved to know this?"

Well, at least she wasn't speaking of their impending marriage in the past tense. He supposed he should take that as a good sign. "I probably would have told you eventually, but it's not something I ever wanted touching you. Spying is not a gentleman's game. It's ugly and dirty and dangerous, and I wanted none of that coming near you."

"And yet you had no trouble using me to get to Michael, did you?" Her voice was heavy with disgust.

He gave a resigned shrug. "I had no choice, Evie. I was given no choice. Besides, I thought it was the best way to protect you."

She batted that away with an impatient wave. "I don't need your protection, but that's beside the point. This is really about your father, as I should have deduced. He was the one who assigned you this task, was he not?"

Will simply nodded. There was no point in lying about that, although he wouldn't go into details. Still, his father would probably toss him into the Tower and throw away the key if he ever found out how much Will had already revealed to her.

"And I know how very important it is for you to please the duke," she said.

He blinked at the arrogant sneer in her voice. Her mother couldn't have done any better.

"I'm doing it because it's my duty," he said in a voice as haughty as anything she might produce. After all, he might be a by-blow, but he *was* the son of a prince. "There's going to be an assassination attempt on a member of government, or possibly even one of the royals. Or don't you care about that?"

When she shrank back, Will was immediately swamped

with guilt. None of this was Evie's fault, and it was all a terrible shock to her. He needed to remember that.

"I'm sorry, my love," he said in a quiet voice. "I had no cause to speak to you in so rude a manner."

"I suppose I understand," she said in a colorless voice. "And if you had come to me at the very first and explained to me what you needed, I would have done everything I could to help you."

He didn't answer because he had trouble believing it. She knew it, too, and her gaze grew so bleak that his heart seemed to stutter.

"But you didn't trust me—again," she said in that same lifeless tone.

"Evie—"

"Tell me something," she ruthlessly cut in. "Is what is happening between us simply a means to an end? A way to complete your mission and gain your dear father's support? Because if you succeed, you'll be a hero, and that should greatly advance you in his good graces—perhaps even win you a knighthood."

The cynical question, which seemed so wrong coming from her sweet lips, made something inside Will twist into a dark, ugly shape. He stalked over to her chair and gripped her shoulders, lifting her straight out of her seat.

"You couldn't be more wrong," he growled. "Marrying you will not help gain my father's patronage or advance my career. You are—or were—involved with a man suspected of treason, which is hardly a point in your favor. And as you so trenchantly noted yourself only a few days ago, your dowry is merely adequate, and you have no social influence to speak of. My father specifically warned me away from you, so if you want to know why I'm marrying you, it certainly has nothing to do with currying favor with him or anyone else."

By the time he finished his tirade, her face had flushed a healthy pink and her eyes were sparking with fury. He belatedly realized that he'd done nothing but insult her rather than convince her that his mission had nothing to do with their impending marriage.

She stood as rigid as a block of stone under his hands. "How unfortunate for you, then, that we were discovered the other night in such embarrassing circumstances. But not to worry, William, since I release you from any obligation to me. God knows we wouldn't want to disappoint your esteemed father."

Her words were caustic, but he could see the anguish in her eyes. He'd failed her in every way possible, and likely destroyed his mission, too.

"Evie, that's not what I meant and you know it."

"Then perhaps you'd better clearly explain why you want to marry me."

He pressed his fingertips into her shoulders, willing her with all his might to understand. "Why do you think, my sweet goose? Because I want to take care of you, and protect you. You're the most important thing in the world to me, and—"

She whipped her hands up to his chest and shoved him hard. He wasn't expecting it, so he staggered a bit, losing his grip on her shoulders.

"Oh, get off me, you big oaf," she yelled. "I don't want to hear any more of your empty promises."

Then she twisted sideways, escaping from his grasp. She darted from the room and clattered into the hall, running at full speed.

"Goddamn it, Evie," he yelled. "Wait for me."

Knowing she wouldn't, Will snatched up the packet of letters and raced after her.

Chapter Nineteen

Will jogged down the steps of the Reese town house and climbed into Alec's waiting curricle with a muttered oath. It seemed he'd been cursing nonstop since his argument with Evie, and the stream appeared likely to continue unabated today.

"Let me guess," Alec said as he started the horses down Hereford Street. "Miss Whitney declined to wait for you and has already departed for St. Margaret's."

"Along with her devil twin. I'd like to lock them in their rooms for a month." Will pressed the heels of his hands to his eyes, which felt like they'd been scrubbed with sand. He couldn't remember the last time he'd had a decent night's sleep. "I suppose it was entirely predictable."

After catching up with his reluctant fiancée halfway down Monmouth Street last night, Will had hailed a hackney and hustled her into it, crowding her so thoroughly she had no chance to escape.

Naturally, their argument had continued, since she'd truly wound herself up in the two minutes it had taken him to run her to ground. She'd shredded his manners, his morals, and his intentions toward her, one moment threatening to box his ears and the next bursting into tears. That had been the worst part, but when he'd put his arms around her to console her, she'd kicked him in the shins. It had hurt, too, because she'd worn a sturdy pair of boots. The hackney driver had clearly thought they were killing each other, since he'd stopped the coach, pulled open the door, and threatened to throw them out into the middle of Oxford Street.

Fortunately, that had taken some of the wind out of her sails, after which Will had done his best to talk sense into her. He'd told her that he had no intention of turning over the evidence against Beaumont until he'd had a chance to speak with him. He'd also invited her to join him when he questioned Beaumont, which calmed her even more.

By that point, he'd concluded he had no choice but to speak with the man. Short of locking Evie in her room— and Will was tempted to do so—there was simply no way he could prevent her from telling Beaumont everything. She believed in the man's innocence and would consider herself duty-bound to warn him. It stuck in Will's craw that she didn't trust him enough to let him handle the situation, but he supposed he couldn't blame her. He couldn't help reflecting that it had been a poor start to a life of wedded bliss.

Provided that Evie still intended to marry him.

After Will extracted her unwilling cooperation, Evie had fallen into resentful silence for the remainder of the carriage ride. He'd tried again to apologize for not telling the truth to begin with, but she'd stuck her fingers in her ears and refused to listen to him. Though he'd been tempted to laugh, he'd known that would be ill-received, too.

When they'd finally reached their destination, she'd allowed him to hand her down from the hackney. She'd then stalked up the steps to her parents' house, used her key to open the door, and tried to slam it in his face. He'd barely managed to insert his foot before the door shut.

"Evie," he'd said in a stern voice as she glared back at him. "I will pick you up tomorrow morning. Do not leave the house until I arrive, or I will be forced to tell your father about our suspicions regarding the Hibernian Association."

He'd had no intention of doing that, of course, but figured the threat would keep her in line. Evie had turned her back on him and marched off, leaving a startled footman to scurry forward to shut the door. Wondering how he'd managed to create such a cock-up, Will had returned to his apartments and downed an exceedingly large brandy, which no doubt accounted for his headache this morning.

"Entirely predictable," Alec replied in a loathsomely cheerful voice. "And no doubt the Whitney girls have apprised Beaumont of everything, and with a high degree of exaggeration and color. I foresee an entertaining meeting."

"It won't be very entertaining if we don't manage to snuff out this plot," Will said. "Aden sent me a message this morning. My father is growing impatient."

Alec grimaced as he wheeled his pair onto Park Lane. "You're right about that, laddie. I can't decide whether to wish for Beaumont's guilt so we can finally nail down a promising lead or hope for his innocence."

Will crossed his arms over his chest and simply grunted in reply. He'd finally come to the conclusion that he, too, hoped Beaumont was innocent, for Evie's sake. If he was guilty she would be devastated by his betrayal, and by the fact that she'd been unwittingly used to foment sedition.

Of course, if Beaumont was innocent, Evie's anger would land squarely on Will, and he worried that their relationship would never recover. She'd probably break their engagement and do her level best to talk Beaumont into forgiving her. After last night, Will had no intention of allowing that to happen. Evie now belonged to him, and he'd make that fact abundantly clear to Beaumont, her family, the duke, and anyone else who needed to have the situation explained.

First things first, though. Aden's note this morning had outlined that it wasn't simply the Duke of York's impatience they needed to be concerned about. All indications from their Dublin sources were that the assassination attempt was imminent, possibly even within the next week. Time was running out and frustrations within the Intelligence Service and the government were rising. Agents were scouring the stews of London for information, particularly in the immigrant communities of St. Giles and Whitechapel. But without more concrete information, the search was all but useless.

After all, it wasn't called *intelligence work* by chance. One needed specifics, and guesswork rarely sufficed.

They took Oxford Street to Broad, and a short time later pulled into the yard behind St. Margaret's. Someone had obviously been keeping an eye out for them, because the carriage had barely pulled to a halt before the two young lads who'd taken care of the curricle a few days ago came dashing out the door.

Only this time they weren't smiling. The boys gave respectful tugs of their caps—and of course took Alec's money—but their little faces were grimly set and they looked much older than their years.

Alec glanced over his shoulder as he and Will headed to the door. "Are they trustworthy? They look none too happy to see us."

Will nodded. "I expect no one will be happy to see us, but your cattle will be fine."

But at this point, he wouldn't care if the urchins took the horses out for a joyride around the city. He needed to see Evie and prove to her that he wasn't the bastard— figuratively—that she thought he was. Never had he taken less satisfaction in a mission, and he mentally cursed his father for putting him in so untenable a situation.

Silence greeted them when they entered the building, and no one waited to escort them. Will led the way to the parlor, taking the half-open door as an invitation to enter.

He paused for a moment at the threshold, taking in the sight of the neat, empty room where he and Evie had made love only a few hours ago. His gaze jumped to the low chaise by the empty fireplace grate, and the image of her luscious body straddling him, arched in passion, made his teeth clench.

He forced his mind to focus. There were already too many emotional distractions on this mission, and having sex with Evie was the last thing he should be thinking about now.

When Beaumont appeared in the doorway of his office, it killed any lingering effects of last night's sensual encounter.

"Gentlemen," he said in a somber tone, "please come in."

Will nodded but didn't waste time on social pleasantries. He had to give Beaumont credit. He looked pale and tired and his brow was creased with worry, but he still nodded graciously to both Will and Alec as he ushered them into the room.

Beaumont returned to his seat behind the desk. Evie and Eden glared up at Will and Alec from the two chairs in front of it. The room was small to begin with, and Will supposed one could argue there was no room for additional seating. But he felt relatively certain that a tactical decision had been made to leave them standing.

From the stubbornly determined look on Evie's face, Will sensed that she'd made that decision, and that would suggest they were going to war.

Will crowded Alec over so he could close the door. Alec

took in the phalanx of resentful stares, and shrugged before propping his shoulders against the wall.

"So sorry you have to stand," Eden said in a mocking voice. "But perhaps it will help keep this meeting as brief as possible."

"Och, lassie, no chance of that," Alec said with a cheerful smile. "And you're not sorry at all, now, are you?"

Eden scowled and started to retort, but Will cut her off.

"Good morning, Evie," he said in a quiet voice. "I'm sorry you didn't wait for me as I asked."

She raised an imperious eyebrow, though it was obvious how rattled and upset she was. Her bonnet sat rather askew, the ribbon tied in a lopsided bow, and it looked like she'd grabbed the first dress that had come to hand. Lady Reese would have shrieked to see her wearing that faded blue gown outside the house. A green shawl that clashed with the dress was tossed carelessly over her shoulders, and her gloved hands held her reticule in a death grip.

Her face made his heart contract with worry and regret—cheeks pale, eyes weary and haunted-looking. He could tell she struggled to keep her lips from trembling. Still, she made a valiant show of strength.

"I do not answer to you, Captain Endicott," she said in a sharp voice. "I needed to speak to Michael before you started tossing around unwarranted accusations."

Will nodded. "Since you have apprised Mr. Beaumont of at least some of the facts, we might as well get started."

He took a step toward the desk so that he loomed over the man seated behind it. When Beaumont shifted uncomfortably, his eyes darting around the room, Will's hopes for his innocence sank. Perhaps the man wasn't guilty of treason, but he was clearly hiding something.

"Mr. Beaumont," he began, "the Crown has reason to believe that you are involved in a plot that would see the assassination of one, or possibly more, high-ranking members of government. That being the case, Captain Gilbride and I need you to answer some questions."

That brought Beaumont's head up, and this time he met Will's with steadfast defiance. "And if I do not answer those questions to your satisfaction, Captain Endicott? Will you have me arrested?"

Evie let out a gasp, smothered behind her hand. Eden patted her sister's arm and clucked that everything would be fine, an assertion belied by the daggers her eyes tossed at Will.

Will shook his head. "That is not my decision to make. But the evidence I found last night should have already been turned over to the appropriate authorities. We did not want to take that step, however, before speaking and hearing any explanation that could ameliorate our suspicions."

"Oh, how generous of you," Eden said sarcastically.

Evie threw her an impatient look. "Edie, hush. This is too serious for jokes."

Her sister subsided with an apologetic grimace.

"Do you refer to the so-called evidence you took from my desk last night?" Beaumont challenged. "You had no right to invade my privacy, Endicott."

"It was regrettable but necessary," Will said.

Beaumont bristled. "My father will not—"

"Your father can bring his complaints to the prime minister or to Peel if he feels it necessary to do so," Will cut in. He had no intention of letting Beaumont control the discussion. "Your correspondence with Daniel O'Connell clearly indicates your support for his particular brand of politics, and you've obviously been contributing funds to his *cause.* Would you care to explain where that money has been going?"

Beaumont's expression lightened. "Well, as to supporting my cousin's cause, as you term it—"

"That's how you term it as well," Alec broke in. He and Will often double-teamed, since it was an effective technique for rattling a suspect or informant.

"For God's sake, let the man speak," Eden snapped.

Evie cut her a sharp look but held her tongue. It appeared that the twins used much the same tactics in a difficult situation as he and Alec.

Beaumont threw Eden a grateful smile before continuing. "Very well, Captain Gilbride. I do support Mr. O'Connell's causes, both for breaking the Union and for Catholic emancipation." He lifted a haughty brow. "I do not suppose it is illegal to express such opinions?"

"You do more than express opinions," Will said. "You provide funding. Now, please tell me specifically what those funds are used for."

"For completely legitimate purposes," Beaumont said. "I gave Mr. O'Connell, as a friend and distant family member, a small loan to deal with the expenses he acquired in an, er, situation he encountered last month."

"That would be the aborted duel between Peel and O'Connell," Will said.

Beaumont paused, obviously startled. "Yes. There were financial costs for that affair, which, by the way, I am exceedingly happy did not come to fruition. Since O'Connell is not a rich man, I offered to assist him. He would only take a small loan, which I have no doubt he will pay back in full."

"And the other sums, what were they used for?" Will was flying blind to a certain extent, not having seen Beaumont's financial records. But the man seemed willing to talk, at least for now.

"Primarily to support the work of this charity," Beaumont said. "The situation in Ireland is dire for many Catholics, especially those in the rural areas. Between Peel's police force, which harasses and abuses locals, and the tenant laws, which lead to a disgraceful number of evictions of families without the means to support themselves, there are many who need our help. The funds that I provide—as do others sympathetic to our work—help us to bring many of those unfortunate families to England, where they may find opportunities." Beaumont grimaced. "Naturally, it is not their first choice to leave the land of their birth, but what can they do? They either emigrate or starve in the hedgerows. And I can assure you that many already have."

"I understand." Will couldn't blame Beaumont for his frustration, since the plight of Irish Catholics had been grim for years. Under any other circumstances, he would have been entirely in sympathy.

"And whatever is left over from that money," Evie interjected earnestly, "goes to helping the immigrants once they arrive in London. The donations support our classes and workshops and help buy food and medicine. That's what we do here, Will. We do not encourage sedition."

Her gaze so clearly begged him to believe her that he had to steel himself against it.

"And will your financial ledgers support that?" he asked, switching his attention back to the man behind the desk.

Beaumont nodded. "Yes. I will be happy to turn them over to you and anyone else who wishes to see them."

That was a good sign but obviously not decisive, because Beaumont could be keeping a false set of books. "That will be helpful," Will replied.

"Those ledgers are at my rooms," Beaumont said. "But you or Captain Gilbride can escort me back to Albany House after this meeting, if you deem it necessary."

Will didn't miss the sarcastic tone in Beaumont's voice but refused to feel guilty. It *was* necessary, if for no other reason than he needed to convince his father that they'd done everything properly in investigating Beaumont. But there were still several remaining issues.

"One of O'Connell's letters used an odd turn of phrase," Will said. "He spoke about 'hardships that might befall you' in the course of seeking justice. What did he mean by that?"

Beaumont looked slightly incredulous. "I should think it rather obvious."

Alec stirred from his position by the door. "Not to me."

"Color me surprised by that," Eden quipped.

Alec narrowed his eyes on her but refused to rise to the bait. Will had seen that look before, and it boded ill—for Eden. If she kept baiting the bear, she might not like the response she would eventually provoke. He could almost wish he were around to see it when it finally occurred.

"I would like to hear your explanation of that phrase, Mr. Beaumont," Will said.

Beaumont let out an aggrieved sigh. "For me, the hardships are more social than anything else. I'm sure you can imagine the displeasure of my parents, and I frequently find myself on the receiving end of slights from my acquaintances." He lifted an ironic eyebrow at Will. "You have seen the results of that yourself. Lady Reese, for instance, was resistant to my attempts to overcome her prejudice against me. Everyone in this room is fully aware of the outcome of that."

Will was surprised that Beaumont would speak so freely about such an awkward subject. He cut a swift glance to Evie, now flushed a high shade of pink and gazing at Michael with a look of regretful embarrassment. Will had to clamp down on the jealousy spiking deep in his gut. Had Evie begged Beaumont's forgiveness already? Was she even now trying to repair her relationship with her former suitor?

"As for Daniel O'Connell," Beaumont continued, "his

beliefs and his steadfast pursuit of them—by nonviolent means, I hasten to add—have an impact on his livelihood as a lawyer and bring him under the scrutiny of the authorities at Dublin Castle. As this very situation amply demonstrates." Beaumont leaned forward and jabbed a finger in Will's direction. "But I swear to you that neither Daniel nor I would participate in any sort of violence or seditious plot against the government. To even suggest such a thing indicates how little you know of me, or him. Daniel has always been vocal in his refusal to countenance violent means of change."

"Except for dueling," Alec commented sardonically.

Beaumont scowled. "An aberration, I assure you."

His words held a ring of truth, but Will didn't fail to note that Beaumont said he wouldn't *participate* in acts of violence. But what if he'd heard rumors about such planned acts or knew those willing to engage in violent conspiracies? Would he agree to turn that information over to the Crown?

"Thank you for speaking so frankly, Mr. Beaumont," Will said. "I just have one other question before we accompany you to your apartments to retrieve your ledgers."

Beaumont nodded slowly, suddenly looking less confident. He glanced nervously at Evie. She peered back at him with a perplexed frown.

"There were four letters in your desk," Will noted, "including one from Ulster. That one contained a short list of names, one of which was Terence O'Shay. There was also a brief commentary regarding the 'difficult history' of the men on that list and their suitability for the work detailed in previous letters. Would you care to explain what that means?"

Beaumont's features remained calm. But the hand he had

placed on the desk had clenched into a fist. Will suspected it was an instinctive—and revealing—reaction.

"That list contains the names of some men from the Londonderry area," Beaumont responded. Will had the sense he had to struggle to keep tension from his voice. "They've had some difficulty in adapting to life in England, so I have been discussing with some of our patrons in Ulster a way to address their situations."

Londonderry. If Will's memory was correct, that particular county had been the scene of some fierce fighting only a few years ago between Catholics from rural areas and the Orange Order, a sometimes violent organization that supported the interests of England. Had O'Shay and the other men on the list been part of that fighting? Had they brought their grievances to England?

Will placed his hand on Beaumont's desk and leaned in a bit. "Ah, Londonderry. An interesting place, that. And what solution did you and your patrons arrive at for these men? Are they also working for your cause?" he asked softly.

Evie jumped to her feet and took a hasty step toward Will. "What are you suggesting?" she asked, alarm ringing in her voice.

Will saw fear in her eyes, and that told him she'd also picked up on Beaumont's nervous reaction.

Alec came away from the wall. "Miss Whitney, please take a seat," he said, laying a gentle hand on Evie's shoulder. "We should be finished soon."

Now Eden surged to her feet, elbowing her sister out of the way to confront Alec. "Unhand her, you brute," she said, going toe-to-toe with Alec as she glared up at him. Eden was no slender, fragile miss, but next to Alec's brawny frame she looked like an outraged kitten confronting a mastiff.

Alec's eyebrows crawled up his forehead with polite incredulity. "Or what, Miss Eden? You'll beat me to a bloody pulp?"

Evie let out a muffled exclamation that sounded surprisingly salty. "Sit down, Edie, will you? Let's just get this over with." She pulled her sister back to her chair as she directed a reassuring smile at Beaumont. "It's all right, Michael. Please just answer Will's question."

By this time, Beaumont had partially recovered. "Of course, Evelyn. As I mentioned, Captain Endicott, these men have had difficulty adapting to life in London. It seemed sensible to consider providing them with passage to the Americas, most likely to Boston or Philadelphia, where there are already a number of Irish who have emigrated."

Will slowly nodded. That made sense, but his instincts still told him Beaumont was holding something back. "That certainly sounds reasonable."

When Beaumont let out a barely audible sigh of relief, Will went in for the kill. "That being the case, I'm sure you'd have no objection to telling me where I can find the men named on your list. We would like to speak to them— simply to clear them of any suspicion."

Beaumont flinched—not much, but enough for Will to pick up. The man's lips also thinned into a tight line, and he took several seconds answering.

"Michael, surely that's not a problem," Evie said. "I'm sure Terence and the other men would be happy to speak with Will if it would clear your name."

"I don't need them to clear my name, Evelyn," Beaumont responded sharply. "Nor, I imagine, would they wish to be subjected to an interrogation by a pair of English officers, or any other sort of authority that represents their oppressor." He directed a suddenly cold look at Will. "I will not give you that information, Captain. I've seen enough English justice to know that it does not work for the Irish. Those men are guilty of nothing but love for their country and a deep dissatisfaction with their lot in life. No thinking person could blame them."

Christ.

Now Will was almost certain Beaumont was lying. He might not be actively participating in a conspiracy, but he certainly knew someone who was, or had his suspicions. Either way, he was protecting them, which also made him guilty.

Will crossed his arms over his chest. "I'm afraid I must insist, Mr. Beaumont."

The man jerked up to his feet, shoving back his chair so hard it crashed into the wall. "Or you'll do what, Endicott? Arrest me? Hunt down those poor men like rats in the gutter? I'll take no part in that, I promise you."

Beaumont took a step forward, his hands clenching into fists as he glared at Will. Will simply lifted an eyebrow, maintaining his composure. Beaumont was unlikely to take a swing at him, but he was ready for him if he did.

"Better that we talk to them now, Beaumont, if they're innocent," Alec said in a warning voice. "Because one way or another, they'll be found."

"And then what?" Beaumont challenged. "You'll inflict your rough justice on them? Drag them through a sham of a trial, and you'll have those poor men swinging from the gallows before the week is out? If I don't protect them, who will?"

"Are you saying you're a sympathizer with Irish radicals, Beaumont? Even ones who support revolution against your own countrymen?" Will asked.

When Evie sucked in a horrified gasp, he made himself

ignore it. But never had he loathed his work more than he did at this moment.

"If by that you mean defending those who've been robbed of their natural rights and treated no better than starving dogs, then, yes. I'm a sympathizer, and proudly so," Beaumont shot back.

"Michael," Evie exclaimed, waving her arms in frustration, "don't give them any more fuel to throw on the fire."

Will gave her a warning scowl, frustrated that she would still charge to Beaumont's defense. Obviously, she believed the man innocent of treason, but surely even she saw that he was holding something back—if not outright lying about what he knew.

Beaumont drew in a harsh breath and made a visible effort to calm himself. He finally managed to give Evie a wavering smile. "You're right, Evelyn, I forget myself." Then he met Will's stare. "Captain Endicott, I must ask you and Captain Gilbride to leave my office now. You have distressed the ladies quite enough for one day."

"Distressed? Ha!" Eden retorted. "I'd like to beat them with my parasol."

Alec shook his head in disbelief.

"I sincerely regret if we have distressed them," Will said, "but I must insist you allow us to escort you to your apartments in order to retrieve your ledgers."

"I'm afraid I'm no longer willing to do that. I will, however, see that they are delivered to your rooms later today," Beaumont replied. "If you object to my manner of handling this situation, I suggest that you take it up with my father, Lord Leger."

Beaumont had obviously decided to dig in his heels, which would only make things worse for him—and for all of them, starting with Evie. He and Alec could certainly drag Beaumont out by the collar but that would serve no good purpose right now.

"As you wish," Will said.

He glanced at Alec, who was still shaking his head, probably over the whole lot of them. Never in all Will's years in military intelligence had a mission gone as badly as this one seemed to. Of course, it was predictable, given that the Reese twins were involved.

And given that Will's objectivity was completely shot to hell by his feelings for Evie.

After a curt nod to her, he followed Alec from the office. A moment later, the quick patter of footsteps sounded behind him in the hall.

"Will, please wait."

He turned to meet Evie rushing toward him, a look of anguish on her pretty face. He'd hoped to spare her all of this, but he'd been thwarted at every turn—by himself and by her.

She grabbed his arm. "What are you going to do?" Her voice was high with nerves.

"He's left me no choice, Evie. I have to turn all this information over to my superiors."

Her nails dug into the fabric of his sleeve. "Surely you don't believe he's guilty of treason!"

"Perhaps not, but he's guilty of something." When she flinched, he nodded grimly. "You know it, too, don't you?"

When she refused to answer, he gently pried her fingers from his arm. "Beaumont has until three o'clock this afternoon to turn over the ledgers and give us the information we need about the men on that list. Otherwise, I'll be forced to act."

All the color leached from Evie's face, and Will thought

she might actually faint. "Please don't do this," she whispered. "If you feel anything for me, don't do this."

Will had already steeled himself to resist her pleadings. To resist *her.* But he heard Alec curse under his breath.

"It's not about you, Evie," Will replied in a gentle voice. "I wish you could understand that."

But from the look of pain and betrayal in her eyes, it was clear she didn't. He had no choice but to turn on his heel and leaving her standing there, forlorn and alone.

Chapter Twenty

"If you'd like to wait, miss, I'd be happy to run up and fetch the captain," said the day porter as he disapprovingly eyed Evic over his shoulder. He paused halfway up the back stairs of the building that housed Will's set of rooms. "Don't know if he'd be too keen on you traipsing up like this, in case someone was to see you."

Evie resisted the urge to shriek with frustration. "Captain Endicott will be very happy to see me, I assure you. I'm his betrothed."

The porter looked singularly unconvinced, and Evie couldn't blame him. What respectable woman would visit her fiancé in so have-cavey a manner? This block of buildings on the edge of Mayfair held only bachelor apartments and rooms, and Will would no doubt pitch a fit at the possibility of even more scandal ensuing if her visit came to light. Fortunately, it was early enough in the day that most of the inhabitants were likely still asleep. The tulips and rakes of the *ton* had probably staggered home only a few hours ago and wouldn't leave their beds before noon.

Except for Will, of course, who would no doubt return to the stews in search of villains after snatching but a few hours' sleep. She'd already sent him three urgent missives over the last two days, asking to see him. He'd finally replied with a curt note an hour ago that he was too busy to call but would do so as soon as he had news to report to her. In the meantime, he'd all but commanded her to proceed with the plans for their wedding, including ordering any necessary trousseau.

After reading that spectacular bit of idiocy, she'd slipped out of the house and had quickly hailed a hackney. She'd fumed the entire way over, wondering how he could even *think* of getting married with Michael's fate hanging in the balance. Everyone else might assume their future together was all but an accomplished fact, but not Evie. Not that she didn't love Will—she did, with all her heart. But when he turned on his heel and walked away from her at St. Margaret's, she'd known there was no chance for them until they could get clear of this situation.

Clear in a way that did not end with Michael hanging for a crime he didn't commit.

Her head swam at that hideous thought, forcing her to stop for a moment and lean against the wall of the narrow staircase. She'd spent most of the last two nights pacing the floor of her room or trying to talk things through with her sister. At this point, she supposed she was functioning on only nerves and coffee.

"Miss, you ain't going to be fainting, are you?" The porter's pleasant, round face wrinkled up with concern. "Do you want me to fetch Captain Endicott?"

Evie took a deep breath and flapped her hand. "No, I'm fine. Please lead on."

She wasn't fine, and in fact was dreading this confrontation with Will. Though he would be furious with her, it was imperative that he hear the information Michael had finally— and reluctantly—imparted to her.

The thought of seeing Will again made every muscle in Evie's body go weak with both longing and dread. Those moments in the parlor at St. Margaret's had been both the best and the worst of her life. She'd given her heart and body so willingly to him and had even believed that he truly loved her. Despite the challenges their life together might present—and despite the hurt she had inflicted on Michael—being with Will had been a dream finally realized. Never had anything felt as right or as true.

And nothing would ever match the betrayal she'd felt when she caught him going through Michael's desk. To learn that he was a spy, one who apparently had little compunction in using their relationship to his own ends . . . well, she wondered if they could ever get past that, regardless of how much she loved him.

Of course, it seemed evident that Will was feeling betrayed as well, since he was clearly angry with her for choosing to support Michael instead of him. As much as she didn't want to, she could even understand his point of view. Will might have been a bounder for keeping the truth from her, but she knew his intentions were honorable. He was doing his sworn duty to king and country, after all. She only wished he could have trusted her enough to confide in her. That was the part she wondered if she could ever forgive.

When they reached the third floor the porter scurried ahead of her down the hall. The building where Will resided was not of the first stare, but it was neat and well maintained with at least three or four sets of rooms per floor. She followed the porter to the end of the hall, where a narrow window fronted onto the street.

The man rapped sharply on the door. When several seconds passed with no answer, he rapped again and spoke out. "You've got a visitor, Captain. It's urgent."

Evie heard a quick tread from inside the room, and then

the door swung open. Will appeared, rubbing his wet head with a towel. He was naked from the waist up. Every nerve in her body started to flutter at the sight of his imposing chest and shoulders. Only a few days ago, she'd gripped those brawny shoulders as she'd come apart in his arms.

"Is that you, Alec?" he growled, shaking the damp hair out of his eyes. "Why the hell—" He stopped, gaping at her as if he didn't believe the evidence of his eyes.

Evie gave him a weak smile and a wave, her mouth so suddenly parched she couldn't utter a word. Her idiotic response seemed to jolt Will back to life.

"All right, Hansen," he snapped. "I'll take it from here."

"I told her it weren't the done thing, sir," the porter said with an exaggerated roll of the eye, "but the young lady weren't inclined to listen."

Will barked out a harsh laugh. "Yes, I've noticed that about her. Not a word about this to anyone, Hansen, do you understand?"

The porter started to back down the hall, babbling nervously that he wouldn't whisper a word. Evie couldn't blame the poor man, because Will looked fierce and predatory—more like a lion than a wolf with his hair ruffled up in a golden mane around his head.

"Get in here, you." He pulled her into the room and slammed the door behind them. He braced his feet wide and planted his hands on his hips, scowling at her. "Have you gone mad, Evie? What the hell were you thinking?"

Like a witless girl, she stood there, her gaze helplessly trailing from his irate features, down over his broad chest to the trim waist and hips only partially hidden by his half-buttoned breeches, and then further down to his big, bare feet. He was, quite simply, the most magnificent thing she'd ever seen, and she wanted nothing more than to throw herself into his arms.

Which only illustrated the demented state of her intellect, given how furious she was with him.

Will let out an exasperated sigh and shook his head. "Oh, for God's sake." He grabbed her by the elbows and hauled her against him, taking her mouth in a ravishing kiss that was over almost before it had begun.

"Now that we've got that out of the way," he said, steering her over to a comfortable-looking armchair by the hearth, "sit down and wait quietly while I put on some clothes."

He practically shoved her down into the seat. She was so breathless—from rushing about, she told herself—that it took her a few moments to respond.

"Don't bother on my account," she said in a sarcastic voice as he retreated into what she assumed was his bedroom. "I've seen it before, as you no doubt recall."

He whipped around to stare at her, his blue eyes heating with what she thought was irritation, but she couldn't be entirely certain. The look on his face set her heart to thumping all over again.

"You haven't seen anything yet, I assure you," he said, growling like the lion he resembled.

"Don't brag, Will," she retorted. "It's immodest."

He braced his hands high on the doorframe, giving her an excellent view of the spectacular muscles in his chest and arms. "You are going to drive me completely insane, do you know that?"

She tried to think of an appropriate response to that insult but finally settled with sticking her tongue out. A childish response, given the horrid predicament they faced, but it made her feel marginally better.

Will snorted out a disbelieving laugh before disappearing into the other room.

Sighing, Evie propped her elbows on her knees and

rested her aching head in her palms. Fighting exhaustion, she tried to order her thoughts. Words swam through her brain in choppy, incomplete sentences as she struggled to frame Michael's information in its most positive light. It seemed an impossible task, given that he had lied to her, too. She'd been sadly gullible when it came to the men in her life.

"Evie, can I get you something?" Will's voice seemed only a few inches away.

She jerked upright, her eyes popping open. She blinked to see him crouched down in front of her, dressed in a shirt and waistcoat, and with his boots on. She must have dozed off because she hadn't even heard him enter the room.

"N-no, I'm fine," she stammered. "I'm just tired."

He frowned with concern as he covered her hands with one of his. "Which is why you should be at home resting instead of dashing about town risking even more scandal. I don't mean to lecture, sweetheart, but what are you doing here? Could anyone besides the porter have seen you enter the building?"

"No, I was very careful." She was impatient with what seemed like pointless social considerations, given the gravity of the situation. But she told herself that Will was genuinely concerned for her well-being, and that chased some of the chill from her heart. "I paid your porter very generously to keep what he saw to himself."

"I'll make certain of that." Will stood and pulled her to her feet. "But we've got to get you home as soon as possible, before anyone is up in this building. If we're seen on the way back to Reese House, we can just tell your mother we went for a morning stroll."

Evie resisted his efforts to pull her toward the door. "I'm not leaving until we've had a chance to talk."

He started to look thunderous again. "Evie, I told you the other day—"

"I've spoken with Michael," she interrupted. "He's told me something you need to know."

His face went blank for a moment, then his brows gathered in a disapproving frown. "What do you mean you spoke to him? He's under guard at his father's house with no visitors allowed until this mess is sorted out. The Duke of York made that condition very clear to Lord Leger when he agreed to allow Beaumont to be confined at home, not hauled off to prison under suspicion of treason."

"Yes, I know," she said tartly. "Lord Leger made that clear to *me* last night when I called on him. Besides, you needn't act as if you and the duke were granting Michael any favors. I know very well that you decided not to bring charges at this point because you feared Michael's arrest would warn his fellow conspirators. Not that he has any conspirators," she hastily added.

He stared at her, incredulous. "Lord Leger told you all this?"

She nodded.

"Unbelievable. And then he let you see Beaumont, against the duke's express orders."

Evie waved that detail away. "You make it sound worse than it was. I simply told him that Michael was withholding information you needed to know, and that I was the only one who would be able to get it out of him."

Will took a step back, putting distance between them. "So, you knew Beaumont was lying, didn't you?"

She nodded reluctantly, hating the austere look that came into his eyes.

"And when did you realize that?" he asked, sounding every inch the spy, not the man who professed to care for her.

"About the same time you did, I imagine. When he lied about the names on that list you found."

"And yet you said nothing," he said, shaking his head. "In fact, you defended Beaumont, even knowing he's up to his neck in this. How could you choose him over your country, Evie? Over *me?*"

She forced herself not to overreact. After all, she'd anticipated this response from him. "It's not what you think. He *might* know something about this alleged plot. Might," she emphasized, holding up a hand to stop his objection. "He certainly isn't part of it, and he doesn't condone it in any way. That's why he finally agreed to tell me what he knew. He's innocent, I swear."

Will reached up and started rubbing the back of his neck, which did lovely things to his brawny shoulders under the thin fabric of his trim-fitting waistcoat. Good Lord, the man was a study in masculine power and grace. Yet again, Evie wondered what he could possibly see in her.

Stop being a nitwit.

"We'll let others decide whether he's innocent or not," Will said, although he did sound a bit less annoyed than a minute ago. "For now, just tell me everything you know."

"Of course, but I would be grateful if you didn't loom over me in such a threatening manner, as if you're ready to gobble me up if I say the slightest thing to annoy you."

His stern face cracked with a rueful smile. "I'm more likely to gobble you up if you say something nice to me. But I take your point."

That remark made her blush, but by the time he dragged her back to the armchair, she'd recovered her composure. He pulled over a chair from a small writing desk by the window and crossed his arms over his chest. Looking stern as a judge, he lifted a brow as if to say, *proceed.*

"You would make a splendid magistrate, in case you're

wondering about a future career," she said. "Very well. It was clear to me during that horrible meeting at St. Margaret's that Michael knew nothing about any treasonous conspiracies."

"So you said, but just how do you know that?" Will rapped out.

"Because I can always tell when he's lying. He's not very good at it, as I'm sure you noticed. Beyond that, I've come to know him very well in the last few years—"

She stopped when Will's eyes narrowed, practically shooting blue sparks at her.

"Not *that* well," she said with exasperation, "which should be clear to you after what happened in the parlor the other night."

He didn't look particularly mollified. "Then perhaps you can explain exactly what you mean by *knowing him very well*."

Evie threw her hands up. "We were planning on getting married, you foolish man. Do you think we didn't talk about what we expected our lives to look like? We are very good friends, or we were until you came along and blew everything up."

He shrugged, not looking the least bit sorry.

"You are incorrigible, Wolf Endicott," she sighed.

Will gave her a lopsided smile. "I know, my sweet, but you'll just have to put up with me. Go on with what you were saying."

"Michael is not a devious or secretive person. Rather, he's ardent and open about what he believes in, and very principled. He's also a man of . . . elevated sensibilities, for lack of a better word. He abhors violence and killing." She wrinkled her nose. "In fact, he's rather squeamish about it. He even refuses to hunt."

"Huh," Will grunted, not sounding very impressed.

"That's all very well, but what if someone else is doing all the dirty work?"

"No," she replied in a firm voice. "Michael would never become involved in something like that. Besides, I am just as much engaged in the business of the Hibernian Association as he is. I doubt he could hide evidence of a conspiracy from me even if he wanted to."

"And yet he lied about the list," Will said in a skeptical voice.

"Yes, that is the one thing he's lying about, at least in terms of what he *thinks* the list might indicate in addition to what it truly means."

Will frowned. "I don't follow."

"The list is exactly what he said it was—the names of four men who are having difficulty adapting to life in London. Michael takes very seriously the notion that those men have no future in England and would be better off in America somewhere, like Philadelphia or Boston. Michael even approached Terence O'Shay with the idea a few weeks ago. Terence turned him down flat, I might add."

Will pondered that for a moment. "We'll get back to that detail. Let's say for the sake of argument that the list is what Beaumont says it is. What, then, is he holding back? Something's got him worried, or he wouldn't have acted the way he did."

Evie drew in a long breath, marshaling her thoughts. This would be the trickiest part of the discussion. "Have you ever heard of the Battle of Garvagh?"

"I'm afraid I haven't."

"But you have heard of the Ribbonmen, I'm assuming, by your reaction to the information that the men on Michael's list were from Londonderry."

Will's mouth twisted up in a wry smile. "That was very perceptive of you, Evie. Yes, I know who the Ribbonmen are—a secret society of rural Catholics, mostly in the north of Ireland. They fight tenant laws and evictions by Protestant landlords. I couldn't help wondering if the men on Beaumont's list were members. Are they?"

"I'll get to that in a minute after I tell you about the battle. In 1813, at the conclusion of a county fair in Garvagh—which is part of Londonderry—fighting broke out between hundreds of Ribbonmen and members of the Orange Order. Michael calls the Orange Order loyalist volunteers, for lack of a better term."

Will nodded. "I'm familiar with the Orange Order. They were as guilty of atrocities as some of the radical Catholic groups."

"Correct. There has been brutality on both sides, with very ugly results, as you know." She'd heard stories from women at St. Margaret's. Despite all the hardships they faced in London, she couldn't wonder that they'd sought to escape the tragic violence of their ancestral homeland.

Will leaned forward, resting his forearms on his thighs as he searched her face. "That list of names . . . the men were all from Londonderry, I'm assuming."

"Actually, they're all from Garvagh," she said softly.

Will jerked upright. "Good God, are you telling me that *all* the men on that list are Ribbonmen, and that they're here in London?"

She winced at the bark in his voice. "Michael isn't sure they would identify themselves as such, especially now. But they left Ireland after that unfortunate episode because, well . . ."

"Because they were fleeing arrest?" Will asked sarcastically.

Evie couldn't help feeling defensive on their behalf. "It doesn't necessarily mean they're guilty of anything, either in Ireland or here in England. According to Michael, some simply seem to have gotten caught up in the brawl."

"What about O'Shay?"

"Michael says Terence makes no effort to hide his allegiance to the Ribbon Order—or his hatred for the English."

"Yes, I noticed that," Will said dryly. "So, Beaumont knew these men were fugitives and yet he chose to withhold that information. That doesn't sound promising for him, I'm sorry to say."

"It's not like that, Will," she exclaimed. "He had no inkling of any sort of conspiracy or plot until we told him."

"Then why the hell didn't he just tell me the truth?"

"For one," she said, trying to be patient, "he had no indication that any of those men were involved in some sort of assassination plot. He only knows their personal histories and the fact that they're unhappy in their new lives."

"And is there a second reason Beaumont chose not to share his concerns with me?" he asked, clearly disgruntled by her reasoning.

"He's worried that the men will never get a fair hearing. That they'll be arrested and hanged for treason on the basis of nothing more than rumors and wild conjecture."

Will started to argue, but Evie held up a hand. "Surely you realize how much prejudice and hatred exists for Irish Catholics, especially here in London. Many are treated little better than animals. Can you blame Michael for worrying about them?"

"I understand all too well," Will said with a grimace. "And I sympathize. But why didn't Beaumont at least share his concerns with me? I would have assured him that I would do my best to gain fair treatment for those men."

Evie weighed her words, but there was no getting around it. "Michael doesn't trust you. That's why he didn't say anything."

Will's eyes narrowed to irritated slits. "Because I'm a soldier, or because I'm going to marry you?"

She stared at him, astounded that he could be so dense. "He doesn't trust you because you lied to me. You betrayed and manipulated me, and it's not the first time you've done it, either."

He flinched, but then a slow wrath heated up his gaze. "Evie, did you really tell Beaumont about what happened between us in the past? That's *our* business, not his."

She mentally winced, knowing she'd overplayed her hand. "Never mind that now. Please just tell me what you're going to do next."

He rose, looking impatient to be off. "I'm going to take you home, and then I'm going to talk to Beaumont and get him to tell me where those men have gone to ground."

Evie shook her head. "He doesn't know. You can check the church records, but I doubt it'll do much good. You know what a rabbit warren St. Giles is."

He gave her a hard stare. "Are you sure Beaumont isn't holding anything back? Or you, for that matter, to protect him?"

Evie jumped up, outrage blasting away the lingering remnants of her exhaustion. "Of course I'm not holding anything back! Do you know how difficult it was for me to come here like this? To trust you when you so patently did not trust me?"

He didn't look the least bit put out by her tirade. In fact, one corner of his mouth kicked up in a wry smile. "I trust you, Evie. It's myself I worry about."

"I have no idea what that means."

"Don't you? Then never mind. Come, we must be on our way. I need to track down Alec and then take another run at Bridget O'Shay. This new information might shake something loose about her brother."

Evie had already heard from Mrs. Rafferty that Will and Gilbride had spoken to Bridget. The girl, understandably, had dissolved into hysterics at the idea that her brother was involved in a treasonous conspiracy.

When Will reached to take her arm, she stepped back.

"You will help Michael, won't you?" she asked, unable to keep the anxiety from her voice.

He shook his head. "Is that the only reason you came here? To save Beaumont's hide?"

His hard demand flustered her. "Of course not! I want this to be over for your sake, as much as anything. But Michael is innocent, Will. Surely you see that. I need you to help him."

"And what if I don't? What could you possibly do about it?" he asked in a cold voice.

For a moment, Evie felt like she couldn't catch her breath. Then she remembered how well she knew the man standing before her. "Don't make idle threats, Will. It doesn't become you."

He took a stride toward her and grabbed her by the shoulders. "Goddamn it, Evie. I don't want to see an innocent man dragged into this, but Beaumont is in trouble—have no doubt about that. I don't even know if there's anything I *can* do."

She placed her hands on his chest, sensing the frustration and anger vibrating through his big frame. She'd been furious at what she saw as his betrayal, but he'd been under enormous pressure—not only from his father but from the very nature of the threat that loomed over them. If Will and Gilbride weren't able to prevent the threatened assassinations, the results could be dire for all of them. It would surely shadow them for the rest of their lives, and then what chance would she and Will have?

She stretched up on her toes and pressed a soft kiss to his chin. "I know. Please just do what you can, for my sake."

When he lifted her off her feet, bringing them face to face, she could only gasp. His eyes blazed and his features were taut with a complex mix of emotions she had trouble deciphering. "Are you in love with Beaumont, Evie? Tell me the truth, once and for all."

She felt her eyes pop wide. "What? No, of course I'm not. Didn't you learn anything from the other night, you stupid man?"

He didn't drop her to the floor, although she'd half-expected that given how she'd just insulted him. Instead, he mashed her against his brawny chest and took her mouth in a smothering kiss.

Chapter Twenty-One

Evie tasted the wildness in him. She answered it, grabbing the edges of his waistcoat and hauling herself up to fight for the kiss. To fight for him.

Her nails dug in as she tugged, and she heard a rip. Will dragged his mouth away on a choked laugh. "No need to rip my clothes off, Evie. You simply have to ask."

She shut her eyes, humiliated to be acting in so unladylike a fashion. Ripping one's fiancé's clothing hardly seemed appropriate behavior regardless of the provocation. And she *hadn't* really been trying to undress him, although the idea certainly appealed to her. But Will had made it abundantly clear that she needed to return home, and he needed to continue his search.

When she felt his fingers under her chin, swiftly untying the ribbons of her bonnet, she cracked open an eyelid. "What are you doing?"

"Undressing you." He tossed the bonnet behind her.

"Why?"

"So I can make love to you," he answered as he stripped her out of her spencer. He then spun her around and attacked the back of her dress. Faster than any lady's maid, he soon had her out of it and the dress joined the growing pile of clothes on the chair.

"But I thought you were in a hurry," she said. As protests went that was a weak one, she had to admit. Not that she actually wanted him to stop what he was doing—not with the delicious heat starting to pool between her thighs.

He loosened her stays, then spun her back to face him. Evie's heart stuttered at the possessive, almost feral expression pulling his face tight.

"I *am* in a hurry," he growled. From the way his gaze devoured her, Evie knew he wasn't talking only about the search that awaited him.

He swept her up in his arms, holding her high against his chest.

"Now what are you doing?" she asked.

"I'm taking you to bed." He strode through to his bedroom. "I'll be damned if I make love to you in a chair again."

Evie cast a quick glance around the plain but rather elegantly furnished room. The four-poster bed looked comfortable with its high mattress and thick quilt.

"Oh, I suppose that will make a nice change, won't it?" she said as he gently put her down.

When he laughed at her foolish reply, she couldn't help wincing. "Don't mind me," she said with a sigh. "I'm just being an idiot again."

Will paused in the middle of stripping off his waistcoat. "Evie, you do want this, don't you?"

She wasn't quite sure what she wanted at this moment except for Will to be safe and Michael to be free. And making love to Will, in her limited experience, did tend to complicate matters. But the avid, almost desperate desire that colored his gaze and the tension that gripped his big body clearly told her how much he needed this. Needed *her.*

As much, she hoped, as she needed him.

She gave him a tremulous smile. "Of course I do, silly."

"Thank God," he murmured. A wry smile eased the lines that bracketed his mouth. "Because I need to feel my cock deep inside you, Evie, and I need that now."

"Will Endicott," she gasped. "That's an outrageous thing to say."

Of course, she was the one standing there in nothing but her shift and stays, so she supposed she didn't have much business scolding him.

He dropped his waistcoat to the floor and reached for her. "Sweetheart, I'm just getting started."

Quickly, he pulled the stays from her body, leaving her clad only in her shift, stockings, and shoes. He picked her up and tossed her onto the bed, ignoring her halfhearted protest. In fact, she found it all unbearably exciting, and his extravagant display of masculine power wound her insides into a knot.

As Evie came up on her elbows to steady herself, Will pulled his shirt over his head. He unbuttoned the fall of his breeches, freeing his erection, then climbed onto the bed and straddled her.

She eyed his gorgeous, half-naked body and his straining arousal. "You're still wearing your boots, and I'm still wearing my shoes. And my spectacles."

He plucked the spectacles from her nose and placed them on the bedside table. "I wouldn't worry about your shoes, Evie," he said in a distracted voice.

"That's hardly the point," she replied, fighting an urge to moan as his hands came to her breasts. "It's not very—"

She broke off on a gasp when he dipped down and took her in his mouth, sucking her in through the linen of her chemise. When his tongue flicked over her nipple in a stimulating rasp through the fabric, she let loose a moan and arched her back off the bed.

He pulled the wet fabric taut over her nipple, avidly inspecting the stiff point. "I assure you, love, our footwear will not prove to be an impediment."

His hands cupped her, shaping her curves into plump mounds, and then his head bent again. For a few delirious minutes, he sucked, teased, and tormented her breasts until Evie was writhing beneath him. She could feel herself going slick and soft, and tiny contractions had already started deep in her womb. It didn't seem possible, but she thought she might climax even before he touched her more intimately.

Abruptly, he sat up, his pale eyes glittering with a heat she felt dancing across her skin.

"It's not enough," he said.

Evie came up on her elbows. "What's not?"

Instead of answering, he grabbed the hem of her chemise and shoved it all the way up to her neck. She squeaked, startled to be so quickly and thoroughly exposed, and in broad daylight, no less. Yes, he'd seen much of her the other night, but the room had been dimly lit and she'd still been partially clothed. Now, every part of her was visible to his hot gaze, painfully so in the morning sun. Her full breasts and pink nipples were on display, as was her unfashionably round body. Evie felt a flush start at her heels and move up her body in a swift tide of warmth.

"Christ, you're gorgeous," Will growled.

He was looking rather flushed himself, and his expression was decidedly approving. Evie gave him a tentative smile, feeling slightly less embarrassed. Still, she couldn't help slipping her hands to the top of her thighs in an instinct to cover herself.

"Ah, none of that," Will admonished.

He gently pushed her hands out of the way and then did the most astonishing thing. He nudged her wide open and pushed her knees up, then slid down the bed and settled between her legs. Evie came farther up on her elbows to peer at him, completely mystified.

"Good God, Will, *now* what are you doing?"

His lips curled up in a rakish smile. "I'm being outrageous."

He clamped his hands on her inner thighs as if to hold her still, then he came down on her. When his tongue slicked between her folds and dragged over her taut bud, Evie let out a startled cry and arched her body, almost lifting straight off the bed.

No wonder he'd gripped her so firmly. Sensation stormed through her in an overwhelming wave. As his mouth caressed her, she found herself unable to do anything but give herself up fully to it.

Not that Will gave her any choice. His broad shoulders wedged her wide and his hands held her in place while he feasted on her. Evie fell back onto the pillows, her eyes closing as he lavished her with one delicious sensation after another. She squirmed in his grip, instinctively pushing into his mouth, trying to deepen the contact on the part of her that throbbed under his deft tongue.

Will's head came up. "God, how beautiful you are."

In a daze, Evie came up on her elbows. Her stomach clenched at the sight of Will's golden head between her thighs. He played with her, his fingers drifting through her curls then spreading her soft folds wide to expose her sex. All of her was open to him—body, heart, soul—waiting for him to claim her.

He used her own moisture to stroke her, gently rubbing.

"So pretty, Evie. Everything about you is so pretty." His voice was a husky rumble that knifed through her.

"Will," she whispered, her voice breaking with need.

His hot glance flicked up to hers, then he swooped in and fastened his mouth tightly on her sex. He sucked her into his mouth and Evie came apart in a sudden, explosive climax. She let out a high-pitched wail and curled up to grab his shoulders, clutching at him with shaking hands.

A moment later, Will surged up her body, bringing her hands up and clamping them over her head. He pushed into her, spinning her climax to impossible heights. Evie threw her arms around his neck, holding tight as her channel tightened and throbbed around his erection.

Will groaned, pounding into her with fierce possession. Straight-armed, he loomed over her. His gaze, heavy-lidded and almost feverish, bored into her.

Evie could feel her eyes start to sting. "Wolf," she whispered, her voice fracturing with emotion.

"Yes, love," he said, in a tight voice. "I'm right here with you."

She gripped his shoulders, staring into his gaze. She felt like her heart was splitting wide open.

"I love you," she said.

He closed his eyes and came down on her, surging into her one last time before letting himself go, shaking in her arms as he found his release. Evie wrapped her legs around his hips, wishing they could stay connected forever.

After exhaling a shuddering sigh, Will slowly sucked in a few deep breaths before rolling onto his back, taking her with him. Evie rested, splayed inelegantly on top of him in a delicious, boneless daze.

After perhaps a minute, he lifted his head. "Are you all right?" He sounded cautious.

"Hmm," Evie muttered into his chest. She was beginning to wonder if she'd ever be able to move again.

"Are you sure? I wasn't exactly . . ." Will trailed off.

She sighed and lifted a bit, meeting his gaze. "Gentle? No, you were a perfect beast. A wolf best fits the description."

When concern flared in his gaze, she gave him a lazy grin. "But I thought it was rather splendid, if you must know."

He let out a relieved sigh. "Thank God."

She lowered her head back to his chest, enjoying the slow stroke of his hand down her spine. "You worry too much, Will."

His hand stilled on her bottom. "Evie, why did you stop calling me Wolf back then?"

She thought back to their last summer together when she'd made a deliberate decision to start calling him Will. "Wolf was your childhood nickname and I didn't want us to be children anymore." She sighed, thinking how foolish she'd been. "I was in such a hurry to grow up."

To grow up and be with him as wife and lover, or so she'd hoped.

"I don't mind if you still want to call me that," he said.

She pushed herself up, stacking her hands on his broad chest and resting her chin on them. "No, I like your proper name. It means resolute protector. Did you know that?"

He propped his hands behind his head, perhaps so he could see her better. She missed them on her bottom but had to admit the position showcased his muscular shoulders and arms.

"I did, and I intend to live up to my name, at least when it comes to you."

She subsided onto his chest again. "Perhaps we can resolutely protect each other."

He made a slight scoffing noise. "Yes, I'm sure."

"Will Endicott—"

He swiftly cut off her scold. "I know the meaning of your name, too. Evelyn means light."

The emotion in his voice had her looking up again. "Will?"

He reached down to cradle her cheek. "You are my light, Evie," he said in a husky voice. "You've always been my light."

She smiled at him, her throat too tight to speak. But then he let out a sigh, and she sensed a change come over him. Their brief respite from the perils of the world was about to come to an end.

"I'd like to spend all day in bed with you, love," he said, "but—"

"I know, it's time to get up," she said regretfully.

Evie slid off the high bed and found her spectacles. Will followed, retrieving a shoe for her that had ended up on the floor and helping with her stays.

He leaned down and kissed her nose. "You go in the other room and finish dressing. I'll be with you in a minute."

As he strode to the washbasin in the corner, she made her way to the front room to retrieve her clothes. She struggled into her dress, leaving undone the buttons she couldn't reach. She then slipped her spencer on over it, knowing it would preserve her modesty. Her bonnet disguised her messy head, thank God, but she suspected she looked a wrinkled mess.

Evie made a few more attempts at smoothing her skirts, hoping she didn't look *too* much like she'd spent the morning doing exactly what she had been doing. She also hoped she'd be able to get herself down the stairs without falling, since her legs still felt shaky from her explosive encounter with Will. Right now, she longed for a hot bath and the time to think through exactly how she felt about things—including assassination plots and her impending marriage.

Will strode from his bedroom, cravat neatly tied and not a button out of place, blast him. Next to him, Evie felt like an undignified shambles.

"I don't mean to rush you, sweetheart," he said as he took her by the elbow, "but I've got to get on O'Shay's trail before it goes any colder."

She allowed him to tow her to the door. "And you'll do what you can to help Michael, won't you?" Though Will would never be unfair, Michael *had* deliberately impeded his investigation. Evie couldn't entirely repress her anxiety over that.

Will's eyes narrowed to irritated slits. "Evie, I certainly hope this . . . episode wasn't some benighted attempt to manipulate me."

She spluttered. "Of course not! How can you even think that way?"

"How can I *not* think that way, given our history?" He shook his head in disgust. "God, we're a fine pair, aren't we? Do you think we'll ever be able to simply tell each other the truth?"

"Now you're just being beastly," she said, trying to hide how his words wounded her. "Besides, I'm not the one who's been doing all the manipulating around here. That would be you."

"I don't have time for this." He grasped her chin between his long fingers and gave her a hard stare. "Get one thing straight, my love. You and I *will* be getting married, whatever happens to Beaumont. At this point, I really don't care if the man spends the rest of his life in the bowels of Newgate prison."

"Don't you dare threaten me, Wolf Endicott," Evie huffed. "I have no—"

"There's another thing you should know about me by now," he said, cutting her off. "I never make idle threats." And then he hauled her, still protesting, from the room.

Chapter Twenty-Two

Will stalked down the deserted alley, automatically flicking his attention from one potential trouble spot to another. He paid particular attention to the doorways cast in shadow by the encroaching dusk and the overhanging roofs of tenement buildings. The houses of St. Giles leaned into each other, crowding out light and air and any sense that there was life beyond its prison-like walls. No wonder the Irish who lived in the stews—and anyone else who had the misfortune to abide there—hated those who didn't. Mayfair was only a few blocks away, with its gleaming white mansions, prosperous shops, and well-fed residents, but it felt like another country so acute was the difference. Given the circumstances, Will could hardly blame those who sought to destroy their masters.

But if years of war had taught him anything, it was that violence carried consequences that shadowed a man for the rest of his life. Even when necessary, it stained the soul and destroyed the innocents who stumbled into its path. If Will and Alec didn't stop this conspiracy, innocents would surely be harmed, including Evie, Bridget O'Shay, and even

Michael Beaumont, who now seemed guilty of little more than misguided compassion.

He passed a gin house with a few rough-looking characters clustered in the dank doorway puffing on their pipes and eyeing him with interest. Will slipped his hand inside his coat to grasp his pistol, making it obvious he was armed. That movement, combined with the glare he directed their way, did the trick. Two of the men melted back into the tumble-down shop. The remaining cove returned him a toothless sneer that would have been comical but for the hatred that deformed his narrow features.

Who could blame the poor devil? Will's boots alone could probably keep the man and his family in food—or drink—for a year.

He cut through a laneway that led to Vine Street, then through the Charlotte Mews to Woburn. Dusk had now fallen heavily from the sky, bringing premature darkness to St. Giles. Fortunately, he'd always had good night vision, and his eyes quickly adjusted. His passage was aided by the occasional gleam of a lamp or candlelight from a window of one of the many tenement houses, or from the gin shops and pubs that dotted the narrow passageways through the rookeries.

Over a day had passed since Evie provided him with the information she'd gleaned from Beaumont. Will, Alec, and Aden's men had spent almost every moment of that time searching the stews, trying to track down O'Shay and the other suspected Ribbonmen. Will had also questioned Bridget O'Shay again, a weepy affair with passionate denials that her brother was involved in any plot. Her tune had changed, however, when he brought up the Battle of Garvagh and the role of the Ribbonmen. The girl had gone quiet and still for several moments, her sobs cutting off in midgasp. With a little more prodding, she'd finally admitted that her brother *had* been involved in the incident at Garvagh but swore he'd promised to leave that all behind when they moved to England. Then she burst into tears again, babbling something about him *getting involved with bad men*.

Will hadn't enjoyed it, but he'd pressed Bridget hard for a possible location where O'Shay and the others could be hiding out. Obviously afraid of losing her employment or bringing the law down on her own head, the girl had finally pointed him in the direction of a particularly noxious warren of tenement buildings in the heart of St. Giles. It wasn't much to go on, but it meant they could focus the search. And only a half hour ago, Alec had sent a message to Aden's house reporting that they'd found the tenement where O'Shay was holed up. Will had been consulting with Aden when the note arrived. He'd immediately left to join Alec, who'd promised to hold off on taking action until he arrived.

He rounded a corner into a small square fronted on all sides by three- and four-story houses, most looking on the verge of collapse. Will melted into the deeper shadows of a convenient doorway, ignoring the scuttle of what was likely a rat across the top of his foot. He stood motionless, taking in the scene and analyzing possible escape routes, as he waited for Alec to find him. A foolish charge across the square would announce his presence in the clumsiest of fashions. O'Shay might not have thought to post lookouts, but a stranger would be noticed in an instant. Word would pass swiftly enough through the tenement to give anyone wanting to flee a head start.

A minute or two later, Alec's form seemed to dissolve and detach from the wall of the building across the square and ghost around the perimeter to meet him. He loomed up before him like a grim specter, wearing plain, black clothing and sporting an unshaven face and a low-slung cap that made him look as disreputable as any of the criminals who lurked in the dark. Despite his size, Alec had a tidy knack for adapting to his environment. No one who saw him tonight would believe he was heir to a wealthy earldom.

"Are we sure it's O'Shay?" Will murmured.

"Aye, and he's still there." Alec leaned against the rough plaster wall of the building behind him, as if settling in for a chat with one of the locals. "He's on the third floor, toward the back." Will caught a quick gleam of Alec's white teeth when he grinned. "I managed to get up there and grab a quick glance at the bastard before he disappeared inside his room. Based on your description, it's almost certainly him. Even better, there's only the one stairway in the building. He'd have a hell of a drop if he tried to escape by the window. Still, I put two of Aden's men around back, just in case."

"Who's watching him now?"

"Carrington has his eye on the stairs. O'Shay is alone, from what I can tell, so the three of us should be able to easily handle him."

Will nodded. "Let's get to it, then." The hairs were starting to bristle on the back of his neck. All his instincts told him they were running out of time.

And he couldn't help worrying about Evie. He'd extracted a halfhearted promise that she would stay clear of St. Margaret's and the Hibernian Association. She'd protested that the church and its buildings were perfectly safe, what with Father O'Kelley and Mrs. Rafferty in residence and with a constant stream of congregants, but Will didn't want to take any chances. Since Evie's agreement had sounded grudging at best, he knew he couldn't count on her staying safely at home. Certainly not if someone at her blasted charity needed help. She'd be off like a shot then, and there wasn't a damn thing he could do about it short of tying her to a chair. Even then she'd probably manage to slip away. She'd grown into the most stubborn, principled person he'd ever met, and he knew she'd make any personal sacrifice if she thought it was the right thing to do. Those qualities were going to try his patience, but they were some of the very reasons he was so bloody in love with her.

He stumbled, disconcerted by the simple, sheer force of the thought that had slipped so easily into his mind. He did love Evie. He'd *always* loved Evie, though he'd allowed himself to think it was something else, and not what it truly was. Apparently, he'd not been wise enough to admit it until now, when it was almost too late.

"What's wrong?" Alec whispered.

"Nothing. I just realized something, but it doesn't matter."

"Are you sure?"

Will smiled, even though he doubted Alec could see it in the enveloping dark. "It matters a great deal, actually, but I'll tell you about it after this is over."

"That sounds ominous."

A moment later, Alec motioned for silence as they approached the doorway of the building where O'Shay was hiding. He cocked his head, then pulled Will into an alley that ran between the dilapidated structure and the one next to it. It couldn't have been more than a foot wide, so they were forced to cram themselves in.

Will held his breath when footsteps sounded. A couple exited from the building. The man held the woman by the arm, talking to her in a genial Irish accent about their children. They hurried across the square and were swallowed up by the black maw of the laneway.

"How many people live in this building?" Will asked as he slipped from their hiding place. Alec's broad shoulders, however, were wedged in so tightly that Will thought he might have to yank him out. But his cousin finally wriggled free, grunting a low curse when the sound of ripping fabric accompanied the movement.

"Dammit, and this is one of my favorite coats," he complained.

"Remind me never to use your tailor. Now, stop being an idiot and answer the question."

"I'd say there are at least four or five families per floor, but let's hope they have the brains to stay in their rooms. They should, I expect. Once nightfall comes to St. Giles, sane people generally stay indoors."

They crept around to the front of the building and slipped through the battered door, which hung loosely on creaky hinges. St. Giles smelled like dung, urine, and rotting garbage at the best of times, but the outside air was as fresh as May in the Kentish countryside compared to the foul atmosphere they encountered inside the tenement house. Will resisted the impulse to gag at the clashing smells of bodily waste, mold, tobacco, and cooked cabbage.

"Awful," Alec said with a grim shake of the head. "Makes you wonder how anyone can survive it."

"I can only suppose the alternative was worse," Will said. He had to wonder exactly how bad Ireland could be to make the stews of London a better choice.

A tall, lean man appeared from under the staircase. He was dressed in black and moved with the silent economy that marked him as one of the brotherhood of spies.

"Anything?" Alec asked, not bothering to make introductions.

"Just the couple you saw a few minutes ago," Carrington replied in a low murmur. "I slipped back upstairs to check on O'Shay. He's still in his room, and I'm sure he's alone."

Will nodded. "Then let's get to it."

The three men moved as quietly as possible up the old

staircase, although they couldn't prevent the occasional creak or groan warping up from the decaying wood. Fortunately, the hallways were far from silent. Behind closed doors babies wailed, mothers yelled at their children, and thumps and clattering crockery signaled the making of evening meals. They probably could have charged up the staircase bellowing drinking songs for all anyone noticed.

O'Shay, however, would be a different story. The man might well know by now that he was being hunted and be straining to hear even one sound out of place.

They made it to the third floor without encountering any of the inhabitants and crept down the hall to O'Shay's room. They'd agreed on a plan on the way up—Alec would kick in the door and Will would go in first, hoping to immediately take down O'Shay. The others would pile on, if necessary. Given what a bruiser O'Shay was, Will assumed it *would* be necessary.

He counted off, one, two, three with his fingers, and then Alec's boot lashed out to deliver a shattering blow. The door crashed open, half-coming off its hinges. Will went in swift and silent, taking in O'Shay's dumbfounded face as the man tried to lumber up from a low bed in front of a small grate. Will caught the Irishman in the midsection before he could make it all the way to his feet. They crashed heavily into the bed, Will's shoulder connecting painfully with the wooden frame, and then rolled together onto the floor. Fighting with vicious desperation, O'Shay's huge hands grappled for purchase around Will's throat.

Will wedged his palm under O'Shay's chin, shoving up and snapping his head back. For a moment, the big man's hands loosened from around his throat, and that was all the time Will needed to twist enough to knee O'Shay in the gut.

He heard the *oof* when his knee connected, and O'Shay doubled over. A moment later, Alec and Carrington were dragging the Irishman off him. O'Shay continued to struggle, but he was gasping for breath and it took but a half a minute for the two men to slam him down into the wobbly cane chair—the only other piece of furniture in the dismal, low-ceilinged room.

By then, Will had his pistol pointed straight at O'Shay. "Stop fighting," he snapped. "Because I'll have no trouble putting a bullet in your knee to slow you down. And I'm bloody sure a wound like that won't stop the hangman from doing his duty."

His threat halted O'Shay in mid-struggle, and he sat fairly still while Alec tied his hands with a length of rope he extracted from an inner pocket. But that didn't stop the Irishman from uttering a low string of curses as he glared at Will, his dark eyes glittering with hatred. O'Shay might be guilty of treason, but he didn't look the least bit intimidated by his capture.

"Good. Now we'll have a little chat." Will stowed his gun in his pocket. "And I suggest you answer my questions with a great deal of frankness if you want to avoid the noose."

"No chance a' that, I reckon," O'Shay retorted. "You bastards have already made up your mind that I'm guilty, and that's the end a' it."

Will met Alec's gaze, both aware that Beaumont had made the same point.

"We might be able to argue for clemency if you tell us who your intended target is and give up your coconspirators," Alec said.

O'Shay rolled his eyes at them. "I don't *have* any coconspirators, you bleedin' idiots. Whatever it is you're after, you got the wrong man."

Will pulled Beaumont's letter from his pocket and held it up in front of O'Shay's face. "Then why is your name on this list?"

O'Shay leaned forward to peer at the piece of paper. Then he jerked hard against the rope that bound his wrists to the back of the chair. Will had to admit that if the man was playacting, he was doing a damn fine job of it.

"Do you know these men?" Will asked.

"Aye," came the reluctant answer.

Alec jabbed him in the shoulder. "You'll have to do better than that, man."

O'Shay bared his teeth in a snarl. "Sod off, you bleedin' Scotsman."

"Now, that's cut me to the quick," Alec said.

"We know you're a Ribbonman," Will said, "as are the other men on this list. You all had to flee Ireland after the Battle of Garvagh."

Even by the light of the miserable fire in the grate and a guttering tallow candle on the mantel, Will could see the color drain from O'Shay's face. "Who told you that?" he slowly asked.

"Your sister, for one," he replied.

Anguish flashed across the Irishman's features. He swallowed noisily before he could get the next question out. "What else did she say?"

"That she was worried about you. That she was afraid you were caught up in something you couldn't handle."

O'Shay's head drooped. He stared at the floor, looking stunned. Beaten, too, if Will didn't miss his guess. When he looked up again, Will was startled to see tears forming in the big man's gaze.

"Did she tell you where to find me?"

"She didn't want to," Will said. "But I didn't give her much of a choice."

"Did she tell you?" O'Shay gritted out from between clenched teeth.

Will and Alec exchanged wary glances. Something was

off, but Will couldn't yet figure out what. "Not this exact location, no. But she did tell us where to look."

O'Shay let out a harsh laugh, shaking his head. "Aye, and I bet it's kept you jumpin', hasn't it? She knew exactly where I was, but she's too clever to let you find me too soon."

Alec jabbed him in the shoulder again. "Stop speaking in riddles, man. Your sister is obviously trying to protect you. We don't blame her for that."

O'Shay snorted with disdain. "I'm the one tryin' to protect *her.*"

"What?" Will took a slow step forward. "You are a Ribbonman, are you not? Are you telling me that you pulled your sister into this plot?"

"I *was* a Ribbonman. And what I'm tellin' *you* is that I have no bloody idea what this bloody plot is," O'Shay growled. "Bridget wouldn't tell me a goddamned thing or listen to a word I said, no matter how hard I begged her not to get involved with those bastards."

Will started to get a very bad feeling in his gut—one that usually signaled he'd gone off in the wrong direction. "The other men on this list?"

O'Shay nodded then closed his eyes, looking like death. "I'm the one who made her leave Ireland, not the other way around. I wanted to get her away from all that before we got ourselves killed. Get a new start in London. I knew she'd do all right, with her book learnin' and pretty ways, even if I didn't. For a while, I thought she was doin' all right."

The small room was stifling hot, but Will felt a chill pass through his limbs. Alec and Carrington looked equally disturbed.

"So, you're saying that your own sister let you be taken up as guilty for a conspiracy you had no involvement in?" Alec asked slowly.

O'Shay opened his eyes and sucked in a heavy breath, struggling to capture his composure. "Looks that way, don't it?"

Will slowly nodded as the puzzle began to take shape. "That's what you were doing there that night at St. Margaret's. You were trying to convince your sister to walk away, not the other way around."

"Give the man a prize," O'Shay sneered.

"Enough of your shite, man," Alec barked. "We need to know the leader of this little gang, and where we can find him. Things will go better for you if you cooperate."

O'Shay shook his head, almost as if he pitied them. "You bloody fools still don't get it, do you? My sweet sister Bridget is the leader. She's the one with all the answers, not those idiots sniffin' around her skirts."

And then all the puzzle pieces clicked into place in Will's head with hideous clarity. Bridget worked in Sir Gerald Milbank's huge old pile on the Thames—the same Sir Gerald who held weekly dinner parties attended by various members of the government, including the prime minister.

Even, including on occasion, the Duke of York.

He uttered a curse so foul it even startled Alec.

"What?" his cousin asked.

Will shook his head, disgusted that he hadn't thought of it before. "She works in Milbank's house. Who knows what she has access to?"

For a moment, Alec looked dumbstruck, but then shook it off. "Apparently, we are a pack of idiots."

Will grabbed O'Shay by the collar, pulling him half out of the chair. "I need details, man. Tell me where I can find your sister and these other men before it's too late."

O'Shay let out an ugly, bitter laugh. "Figure it out yourselves, you buggerin' bastards. I won't send me own sister to the gallows."

"Your sister is trying to send *you* to the gallows to cover up her crime," Will exclaimed. "How can you keep protecting her?"

O'Shay's expression was a harrowing mix of contempt and despair. "Maybe hangin's what I deserve—what we *all* deserve, including you lot."

Alec grabbed Will by the arm, pulling him off the big Irishman. "Will, you need to tell Aden. I'll go to Milbank's and start the search, but have Aden send reinforcements to help. Carrington and his men can take O'Shay to Bow Street."

Will was already halfway out the door.

"Evie, this is a dreadful idea," Eden said. "Wolf told you to stay close to home until this horrible situation is resolved. I think you should listen to him."

Her twin stood in the middle of Evie's bedroom with her fists propped on her hips and her fair brows pulled into a fierce scowl. It was a typical Eden pose when she was trying to boss Evie about. Most of the time, it worked. But not this time, because there was simply too much at stake.

"Will needs to stop acting like he's already my husband," Evie replied as she finished buttoning up her spencer. "He has no business ordering me about and he knows it."

"And what about when he is your husband?" Eden asked in a sarcastic tone. "Will you let him order you about then?"

Evie let out an impatient sigh. She truly didn't have time for this. "Yes, no . . . oh, I don't know. Honestly, Edie, I don't even know if Will and I *should* be getting married. Not like this, anyway. It's all such a terrible mess."

Her sister hurried to give her a quick hug. "I know, darling, but Wolf's just trying to keep you safe. He likes to put on that stern, soldier's manner, but you know he adores you." She cocked her head and gave Evie a smile. "In fact, I suspect you have him eating out of your hand by now, don't you?"

Evie's stomach dipped at the idea of Will adoring her but knew it wasn't true. Yes, he cared a great deal for her and certainly seemed to enjoy making love to her, but she knew he wouldn't have asked her to marry him unless his hand had been forced. Every time she thought of being hopelessly in love with a man who couldn't return that depth of emotion, a part of her heart seemed to cringe with shame. It was rudely ironic that there was a man who *did* truly adore her and would still probably pledge his life to her. But Evie could no longer envision wedding Michael—or anyone else, for that matter. For her, there would now only and ever be Will, which struck her as a rather perilous situation.

She forced away her gloomy thoughts and stepped around her sister, heading to the wardrobe. "I don't know where you get such an idea, Edie. No one ever tells William Endicott what to do. Well, except for his father, perhaps."

Eden rolled her eyes and flopped down onto the chaise. "Don't think I don't know what's going on between you two."

Evie jerked to a halt and slowly turned. She shared almost everything with her sister, but she had *not* shared the fact that she and Will had been physically intimate. It was something so profoundly life-changing that she was still trying to sort it out in her head. Besides, Eden would want details, and Evie couldn't think of any way to describe what had happened without making it sound sordid or cheap. It had been anything but that, but there was no denying she'd violated all boundaries of decency and decorum. Under the circumstances, she supposed she should count herself lucky that Will wanted to marry her at all.

"I have no idea what you're talking about," she said, sounding stupid and stiff.

Eden's eyebrows distorted into a comical lift. "Really? Well, you certainly made a good start on things the other night in the library. After that episode, I assumed that Will would have taken advantage of any opportunity to engage in, well, a little more exploration."

Evie breathed out a tiny sigh of relief and dredged up a smile. "Well, perhaps just a little bit, but nothing worth talking about. Not that Will isn't a very good kisser," she hastily added when Eden looked more than slightly appalled. "He's a very good kisser, naturally."

"Well, that's good to know. But I was hoping for a little more detail than that. I haven't had very good luck in that particular area."

Eden sounded so disgruntled that Evie was tempted to laugh. Her sister might have a reputation as an outrageous flirt, but it was mostly for show. When it came right down to it—when it came right down to *men*—Eden wasn't much more experienced than Evie in any way that counted.

Except that now Evie was a great deal more experienced than any gently bred spinster had a right to be, thanks to the aptly named Wolf Endicott.

"I'll tell you all about it when I get back from St. Margaret's," Evie said, fetching a plain bonnet and gloves from her wardrobe. "I promise to wait up until you get back from Mrs. Parkminster's musicale. I can't tell you how happy I am that Mamma is allowing me to miss that."

"Yes, I told her you were simply worn out from all the excitement of the last few days, and that you needed a good rest."

"Thank you, dear. It's the truth, you know. And I'm dreading what happens when Mamma finally announces that Will and I are engaged." Suddenly feeling overwhelmed, she sank down onto the padded bench in front of her dressing table. "Even if Michael's name is cleared and no one finds out about this horrid conspiracy, everyone's been expecting us to announce our engagement for ages. The gossips will simply love the fact that I've apparently thrown over Michael for Will."

Eden went down on her knees in front of Evie, taking her hands in a comforting grip. "I hate to be too much of a stickler, old girl, but you *have* thrown Michael over for Wolf."

"Only because I was forced to do it."

"But you do love Wolf, don't you?"

Evie grimaced. "Of course I do, but I'm afraid that isn't enough. It's not like he truly wanted to marry me."

"Have you asked him? I mean, really asked him to be honest with you?"

Evie nodded.

"Well," Eden said a little impatiently, "what did he say?"

"He said he wanted to marry me."

Her twin sat back on her heels. "Then why won't you believe him? He's never lied to you before."

When Evie gaped at her, Eden flapped a hand. "I'm not talking about being a spy or suspecting Michael of trying to kill people. I mean about you and him, and how he feels about you. Wolf's always been honest about that."

Evie couldn't hold back a bitter little laugh. "Yes, and I have the scars to prove it." Then she glanced at the clock on the mantelpiece. "Goodness, it's getting late. I have to go, Edie. Bridget's note said I had to meet her at St. Margaret's at seven o'clock because she could only slip away for a few minutes."

Eden pressed her hands to Evie's knees, holding her in place. "I'm really not sure about this. How do you know you can trust her? And I don't think it's safe to go there without escort, especially at night."

"You've never raised that objection before," she said.

Eden grimaced. "Because no one was using the place to plot murder before."

"And there's no proof that they are now, dear. Besides, Bridget isn't involved in something like that, and I truly don't believe her brother is, either. In fact, her note expressly said that she had proof that could clear both Terence's and Michael's names."

"If that's true, then she should tell Will and Captain Gilbride," Eden said doggedly. "There's no reason for you to get any more involved than you already are."

Evie forced herself to be patient. "Bridget is afraid of them, I already told you. And she has every reason to be, given her experiences in Ireland. Neither she nor her brother has any reason to trust the British military. Bridget trusts me and she trusts Michael, and she only feels safe speaking with me at St. Margaret's. Besides, I won't be alone. Mrs. Rafferty will be there, and I expect Father O'Kelley will be about too."

Eden made a funny growling noise in the back of her throat. "Why don't you at least take a footman or a maid with you?"

"And if I do that, how long will it take for Mamma to find out what I've done? Thank you, but no." She patted her sister's hands and then took her by the shoulders. "I promise I'll be fine. Now, stand up before you wrinkle that pretty dress of yours."

Eden came to her feet and let Evie collect her things, although she didn't look happy about it. "Evie, I still think this is a very bad idea."

"Don't worry. I'll take a hackney and ask the driver to wait until I'm finished. Then I'll come straight home."

She'd almost made it to the door when her sister's voice stopped her again.

"You're angry with Will, aren't you?" Eden said, once more standing with her feet planted and her hands on her hips.

"Well, yes," Evie had to admit. "Wouldn't you be?"

"Maybe, but I wonder if you're doing this to punish Will for trying to tell you what to do."

Her words gave Evie a hard mental jolt, and she had to think about it for a few moments. "No," she finally said. "That's not it. But I can't let him order me about, either, or stop me from doing what I believe is right. Bridget O'Shay needs my help, and I'm going to give it to her."

She opened the door and slipped from the room before her sister could raise any more objections.

Chapter Twenty-Three

"I'll pay you an additional shilling to wait for me. I promise I won't be long," Evie said, digging into her reticule.

The hackney driver weighed her offer, but his fears won out. His animal seemed to agree since he began shaking his shaggy head in an agitated fashion as if to tell his master to be off.

"Sorry, miss," said the grizzled old man. "I'd like to earn the extra blunt, but it's not worth me risk." He rolled a worried eye around the deserted courtyard behind St. Margaret's. "St. Giles at night ain't fit for no one, especially young ladies. You'd best be coming back with me or stay in the church till morning."

Evie sighed as she stuffed her change purse back in her reticule. Perhaps she should have chosen a younger, burlier driver, but she'd been in a hurry and had hailed the first empty vehicle. Bridget's hastily scrawled missive had made it clear she couldn't wait long for Evie.

"Thank you for your concern, but I'll be fine," she said.

The driver shrugged. "Suit yourself."

He muttered a comment that called Evie's sanity into

question, then turned his conveyance and rattled away over the cobblestones. The noise quickly died, leaving an unusual hush over the courtyard. With nightfall rapidly approaching, the deepening dusk seemed as gloomy and threatening as a scene from Mrs. Radcliffe's novels. As she stood there debating the wisdom of her actions, Evie couldn't repress a shiver of premonition.

She impatiently shook her head—just like the driver's horse a few minutes ago, she thought—and strode across the yard to the back door. She blamed her tightly strung nerves for her superstitious response. Though understandable, it would not be helpful in dealing with her upcoming interview with Bridget. The poor girl would no doubt be in a terrible state, and Evie needed to be as calm as possible in order to elicit information that would be of use to Will.

She could only pray that Bridget would provide them with the information needed to bring this dreadful situation to a conclusion.

The door was unlocked, and Evie slipped inside. A quick glance revealed an empty parlor, so she quickly made her way to the back of the building. Bridget would likely be in the kitchen with Mrs. Rafferty and possibly Father O'Kelley. The priest had been in Lincoln for the last few weeks but was expected home at any time. His calming presence would be most welcome.

When she heard the soft murmur of a masculine voice issuing from the kitchen, she smiled. Father O'Kelley had indeed returned, thank goodness, and was already providing Bridget the spiritual support she needed.

Evie pushed open the door and stepped quietly down the short set of stairs to the kitchen, coming up short before she reached the bottom. There *was* a man present, his wide back and hulking shoulders turned to her as he spoke with Bridget, but it certainly wasn't Father O'Kelley. When he whipped around to face her, a startled look on his features, it took a few moments to place him. Then she realized he was one of the men she'd seen the other night at that odd meeting in the kitchen with Bridget and Terence. And just like the other night, neither Mrs. Rafferty nor Father O'Kelley was there.

"Miss Evie," Bridget exclaimed. "We didn't hear you come in."

The girl's color was high, and her eyes glittered feverishly as she rushed forward to greet her. Evie took an involuntary step back then almost lost her balance as she stumbled into the rise behind her heel.

"Watch yourself, miss," Bridget cried as she grabbed her elbow. "You don't want to be fallin' and knockin' your head. Have a seat and I'll make you a nice cup of tea."

Evie allowed Bridget to steady her as she stepped down onto the flagstones of the kitchen floor. But she resisted the girl's concerted effort to tow her to the table, pulling her arm away.

"I'm fine, and I don't need a cup of tea." She glanced at the big man standing against the wall with a kind of tense alertness, as if he expected trouble. "Bridget, please introduce me to your companion. I don't believe I caught his name the other night."

The man's lips curled back in a slow smile. "I'm thinkin' you don't need to know, miss," he responded in a thick Irish brogue.

A chill skated down Evie's spine at the ruthless nature of that smile. The man's look was the kind a cat gave a mouse before it pounced. When she switched her gaze back to Bridget, her stomach plunged with a sickening swoop.

If anything, the ruthlessness in Bridget's gaze exceeded that of her companion's. It was beginning to dawn on Evie that the young Irishwoman was not the innocent she'd always taken her for. In fact, she now had to assume that Bridget was involved in the conspiracy too—if for no other reason than to protect her brother.

Next time I'll listen to my premonitions.

She had to swallow a few times before she could speak. "Bridget, what have you done with Mrs. Rafferty and her son?"

"Ah, are you figurin' things out now, love?" Bridget replied in a voice laden with contempt. "Took you long enough, but I suppose I shouldn't be surprised given how bloody softhearted you are."

Then her expression changed again, transforming in an instant to that of a frightened girl. Lips quivering, she dramatically clutched her hands to her breasts. "Oh, Miss Evie, please help me," she exclaimed. "My brother, he's in trouble, and I don't know what to do!"

When she laughed, Evie thought she would choke on the bile that rose in her throat. The girl looked and sounded demented.

"It was as easy as cake foolin' you and Beaumont," she said. "I did worry a bit about Mrs. Rafferty. She's no lightweight, but we was able to put her off, too."

"Where are Mrs. Rafferty and her son?" Evie repeated, beginning to fear the worst.

Bridget tossed her head. "You've no need to worry about them, you silly twit. We locked them in the vestry of the church. They're Irish, so I won't be harmin' them." She chuckled. "But they won't be gettin' out anytime soon to raise the alert, neither."

The vestry was little more than a windowless closet that only opened onto the chancel. "Bridget, I don't know what you're planning—"

"If you sit down and shut your gob, I'll tell you."

The girl jerked her head at her silent companion and the

man slapped a massive hand on Evie's shoulder. Propelling her toward the kitchen table, he shoved her into one of the chairs. Evie didn't resist. Her legs felt shaky, and she was grateful for the opportunity to sit and regroup.

When Bridget leaned a hip against the table, smirking at her, Evie adopted as calm a manner as she could. "Please tell me what's going on. Maybe I can help you."

The girl let out a hoot of laughter. "Who says I want your help? Although I suppose I should thank you for gettin' me that job at Milbank's house. It made everything so much easier."

Evie gasped. "Then there is a plot to kill someone. Is it Sir Gerald?"

Bridget snorted. "That blockhead is hardly worth the effort, though he won't be survivin' the night. But he's not who we want."

"Who then?" Evie forced herself to ask.

"Orange Peel and Liverpool," Bridget answered. "And anyone else we can bring down with them."

Evie frowned at the first reference, but then she remembered something Michael had told her some months ago. Orange Peel was the nickname some of the Irish had given Robert Peel, the much-loathed Chief Secretary of Ireland, orange being the color of those who supported the rights and interests of the British Crown. It was a bad joke made even worse by the circumstances.

"You're going to kill Peel and the prime minister?" she asked, skeptically. "How in God's name do you intend to do that?"

Bridget crossed her arms as if getting comfortable and leaned closer in a confiding manner, as if she were enjoying the discussion. "Me men and me," she said, nodding at her compatriot, "have been plannin' it since afore we left Ireland. Didn't quite know how we'd pull it off until you got

me that job at Milbank's. He lives in one of those bleedin'
great mansions on the Thames, with all its cellars and even
a deserted undercroft. The cellars are half-fallin' down but
the undercroft was clean enough and dry. So we've been
smugglin' gunpowder into it for three months now, enough
to blow the whole bleedin' mess sky high."

Evie gaped at her, dumbstruck with horror. Sir Gerald's
house was one of the few remaining mansions on the Strand,
an architectural holdover from Jacobean times. It was huge
and sprawling, and she wasn't surprised to hear its cellars
included an undercroft, a vaulted chamber primarily used
for storage. Newer houses lacked the undercrofts that
made Sir Gerald's mansion horribly perfect for nefarious
activities.

It took several hard swallows to find her voice. "It
sounds like the Gunpowder Plot," she said, thinking of the
conspiracy of the previous century to blow up the Parlia-
ment buildings.

Bridget tapped the side of her nose. "Where do you think
we got the idea, especially storin' the gunpowder in
the undercroft? No one ever goes down there anymore, so
it was dead easy." She laughed, as if she'd just made an up-
roarious joke. "Well, 'cept for me and Stanley, the junior
footman. He showed me the undercroft one day, hopin' he
could get me to flip up my skirts for him. As soon as I saw
it, I knew it was perfect."

Evie struggled to make sense of what she was hearing,
because it sounded both unbelievable and insane. "How did
you get the gunpowder and smuggle it in with nobody
seeing you?"

"We stole it off the barges that come down the river with
gunpowder for the London Magazine." She grimaced. "That
was tricky, but we managed to get a full barrel off one night.

Then we used the old landing behind Milbank's house to bring it in."

Evie pressed a hand to her chest, as if she could slow her pounding heart. "How . . . how many are involved in this wicked plot? Who else from St. Margaret's?"

Bridget sneered at her. Her ugly expression was entirely at odds with the sweet, pretty girl Evie thought she'd known. What a naïve fool she'd been.

"Don't worry, dearie, your precious charity is safe. There's just me and the men you saw the other night, and a few others you don't need to know about. 'Course, not that it'll make a difference once it all comes out. Just knowin' I came through here will make trouble for you, I suppose." She shrugged. "I'm actually sorta sorry for that, but it can't be helped."

"What is your brother's role in this?"

Bridget jerked up from the table, a spasm of pain crossing her face. Then the look in her eyes went glacial. "Terry had his chance to support the cause. To support *me*. But ever since we came to this bleedin' place he's gone soft."

Evie blinked. She'd obviously been wrong about Terence, as she had been about so many things. "I'm sure he wanted to keep you safe," she finally managed.

"He ain't a real man," Bridget replied with contempt. "A real Irishman, anyway." She glanced at the mantel clock then reached for the shawl she'd draped over one of the kitchen chairs.

Evie shook her head, sick at heart to hear Bridget's definition of a *real man*. Poor Terence had obviously tried to save his sister, yet even his love hadn't been enough to triumph over hatred. "When is this happening?"

"Tonight." Bridget tossed the shawl over her shoulders. "Milbank's havin' a dinner party with a bunch of government nobs, including Peel and Liverpool. We're all set to blow them to hell and back."

Evie's desperation drove her to her feet, but the thug pushed her back down.

"Now, Miss Evie," Bridget said in a horrible parody of an affectionately scolding voice, "you just sit yourself back down. You won't be goin' nowhere for a while yet."

Evie tried to calm the screeching in her mind. She needed to think and get as much information out of Bridget as she could. "You don't seem all that much in a hurry. Won't you be there when this happens?"

"Just waitin' for all the guests to arrive at the party, love," she answered. "We don't want to be leavin' anyone out."

"But . . . but I thought you said you couldn't stay long. Won't your presence be missed?"

Bridget shrugged. "And what of it? It's not like I'll be gettin' my old job back, now will I?"

Evie closed her eyes and put a hand over her mouth, feeling like her stomach was crawling into her throat. Where was Will? Were he and Gilbride still wasting time looking for Terence in the rookeries?

Her eyes popped open. It was certainly possible that Will had already run Terence to ground. If he had, the Irishman might have revealed at least some of the details of the plot, if he knew them, and that meant Will could be at Sir Gerald's house right now. He'd be in mortal danger, along with everyone else there.

She twisted around in her chair to face Bridget, who was speaking quietly with her confederate. "Bridget, please don't do this. Let me help you. I'll speak with Michael. We'll get you money, and get you and your friends out of the country. You can go to America, with Terence."

Bridget threw her an almost disinterested glance. "Too late for that, Miss Evie."

Evie could only stare at her with horror. "Why, Bridget?" she managed. "Why are you doing this?"

The girl's pretty blue eyes suddenly blazed with such ferocity that Evie cringed. Bridget swooped forward, grabbing the collar of her spencer and half-lifting her out of her chair.

"You really want to know, you silly bitch? It's because I hate you and your kind with every particle of my soul," Bridget hissed. "You destroyed everything I loved. You destroyed my life, grindin' it into shite and piss and death. I was only a wee girl when your bloody bastard soldiers massacred my family during the rebellion. My parents, my little sister . . . everyone but Terry. We were the only two you didn't kill off, although God knows you tried. You drove us out of our home and left us to starve in the hedgerows like rats. Like scum under the heels of your fancy boots."

She flung Evie away, as if she couldn't stand to touch her. Evie's elbow connected with the table and pain lanced up through her arm, but she hardly felt it. She was too stunned by the enormity of what she heard and by the hell she saw in Bridget's rage-filled gaze.

"Do you think a child could ever forget that?" Bridget stormed. "Do you wonder why I've been plannin' for this moment every day of my bloody life? There's nothin' you could offer that would turn me back. Even if I don't survive this night, it'll be worth dyin' if I take those foul, murdering bastards with me."

"Enough jawin', girl," her companion interrupted. "You've got to get goin'."

Bridget flashed him an irate scowl but gave a grudging nod. "Don't you think I know that? I just wanted this one to know what was goin' to happen to her precious, fine gentlemen." She flicked her attention back to Evie. "You don't make no trouble, hear? If you're good, you might get out of this with a whole skin."

That prompted the question Evie should have asked right away. "Why did you bring me down here, Bridget? What *do* you want from me?"

The girl lifted a mocking eyebrow. "Because your damn lover's gettin' too close to the truth. I've got him off searching the stews for Terry, and it's only a matter of time till he finds him."

"And if he does?" Evie challenged. "If he tries to stop you?"

Bridget let out a laugh so rough and ugly it scraped like a rasp over Evie's ears. "We'll use you to get out of London. You're my ace in the hole, darlin'. I'm bettin' your pretty boy will do anything to keep you safe."

After abandoning the hackney in favor of going on foot, Will took the last three blocks through Seven Dials at a fast clip. London's main streets were busy late into the evening, and running was faster than crawling along in a carriage.

As he'd feared, Evie had defied him, and Will had every intention of imposing an appropriate punishment as soon as he held her safe in his arms—like never letting her out of his sight again unless accompanied by two footmen and a very large dog to protect her. He wasn't a man who prayed much, but he'd been running a litany through his head ever since he left Hereford Street.

After dealing with Terence O'Shay, Will had reported to Aden and then followed Alec to Milbank House. Alec had already ordered Sir Gerald to send the dinner guests home— all of them blustering and demanding explanations—after which he'd initiated a search of the house. It hadn't taken long to find a chilling store of gunpowder in the undercroft.

Alec and his men had also surprised two of Bridget O'Shay's coconspirators in the act of laying down the match cords in final preparations for blowing up Milbank's house.

Bridget, however, had not been present, and her men refused to give up her whereabouts. Will had left Alec to try to extract whatever information he could and headed to the Reese town house. If anyone knew where the girl might go to ground, it would be Evie.

To his shock, Evie had already run headfast into danger. Eden, worried about her sister and returning home early from an evening out, had told Will about the note from Bridget. Will had ordered Eden to send a message to Alec before racing out to the street to find yet another hackney.

He rounded the corner into White Lyons Street and slowed as he headed into the laneway behind St. Margaret's. Drifting into the shadow of a house opposite the back entrance, he decided to go in through the front. Bridget would expect him—or anyone, for that matter—to come in through the back building, so he would go through the church and—he hoped—catch her and whoever she had with her by surprise. On short notice, it was the best plan he could come up with to rescue Evie. He'd likely have to forgo capturing Bridget, but he could make his peace with that, under the circumstances.

He swiftly made his way around to the front door of St. Margaret's. He'd never broken into a church before, but he supposed there was a first for everything. Extracting his picklocks, he crouched in the shadows of the narrow porch and went to work.

After a minute, he eased the heavy oak door closed behind him and slipped into the vestibule. The small church had whitewashed walls and pews lining the narrow aisle up to the canopied altar. A sanctuary lamp provided some light, as did high windows reaching up to the vaulted arch of the roof. Still, most of the church was thick with shadows. Will stood as motionless as the statue of St. Michael in the niche beside him, straining to see or hear anyone who might be lurking.

Satisfied that he was alone, he cast an ironic glance at the stone angel looming over him. It *would* be Archangel Michael who stared down at him with an expression on his austerely carved features that issued a challenge to protect the innocent and fight evil. That's what Michael Beaumont had been trying to do, however misguidedly, and now it was up to Will to finish the job.

After tapping the angel's sword for good luck, Will moved swiftly up the aisle, searching for the door to the kitchen and offices. Not for the first time, he wished he'd had a chance to do a thorough exploration of the church complex. Unlike Alec, who rather delighted in the unexpected, Will always wanted to know everything he could about a mission. Given the stakes—which included the life of the woman he loved—he hated even more than usual that he was going in nearly blind.

He'd reached the lectern when muffled voices froze him in place. They came from behind a small door on the right side of the chancel. A dim light filtered out from underneath the doorframe, perhaps from a candle or small lamp. He moved closer, taking his pistol from his coat pocket.

Crouching down, Will stared through the keyhole then breathed a curse. He saw—and heard—enough to realize that a child was huddled on the stone floor, sobbing as he hugged a woman's skirts. As far as he knew, the only child at St. Margaret's belonged to the housekeeper, Mrs. Rafferty. That the boy and his mother were locked away certainly suggested they were not part of any conspiracy.

He tapped lightly on the door, and the child's weeping cut off in mid-sob.

"Mrs. Rafferty, it's Captain Endicott," he murmured, his mouth close to the keyhole. "I'm Miss Evelyn's friend, come to help."

He heard nothing but silence for a few seconds, then a soft scrambling.

"Can you get us out?" Mrs. Rafferty hissed.

"Hang on," Will murmured.

It took less than a minute to pry open the rusted old lock. When he opened the door, a small body startled to hurtle out. Will picked up the boy and stepped into the room, closing it behind him. He set the lad, who looked no more than seven, on his feet. His mother grabbed him by the shoulders and hugged him to her dark skirts.

"Ain't you goin' to let us out, mister?" the boy asked plaintively, staring up at him.

Will hunkered down before him. "Yes, of course, but I want to keep you out of trouble, too. What's your name?"

"Billy," he said with a sniff.

"I'm a William, too, although my friends call me Will. I'm going to get you out of here, but you need to be very quiet. Can you do that?"

The boy rubbed his nose and nodded.

Will stood and cast an assessing glance over the mother. She was a trim, calm-looking woman in her mid-thirties, he guessed, neatly garbed in a dark blue dress with a plain collar. One side of the collar was ripped and hanging off her shoulder, and her hair was coming down from the knot at the back of her head.

"Did they hurt you?" he asked.

"We're fine, sir, just frightened," she replied in a soft Irish brogue. "But I'm worried about Miss Evie and what they'll do to her."

Will clamped down on the rush of fear that tightened his muscles. "Did you see Miss Evie?"

"No, sir. They put us in here before she arrived, but I heard that bi—" She stopped, glancing at her son. "I heard Bridget talking about her to one of those men. She said she'd use Miss Evie as hostage, if she needed to."

Now Will's fear whirled through him like an icy gale before settling into a cold, steady anger. "How many of them were there?"

"Bridget and two men, as far as I know, but they locked us in here sometime ago." Mrs. Rafferty glanced down again at her child, then back up at Will. "I'd like to help in any way I can, sir, but I need to get my boy to safety."

"Of course. I'm going to get you out of here, and then I want you to go directly to Bow Street. Tell them that Captain William Endicott of the First Royal Dragoons sent you, and try to get someone here as quickly as you can. Tell them I'm working with Sir Dominic Hunter. They'll know him. Do you understand?"

Mrs. Rafferty nodded and took her son by the hand.

"One more thing. Where's the door into the other building, and where does it lead?"

After the woman explained the layout, Will swiftly led them through the church to the front door. A fast inspection outside showed him that all seemed quiet, and he sent them on their way. Every muscle in his body urged him to race to the other building to rescue Evie, but he forced himself to watch Mrs. Rafferty and Billy until they disappeared around a corner.

A minute later, Will was easing open the door between the church and the back building. It led into an anteroom— a small space filled with shelves that clearly served as a pantry. The pantry had no door and opened directly onto the kitchen. That was a lucky break, since it meant he wouldn't have to fumble with locks and creaking hinges while trying to maintain the element of surprise.

He moved silently to the opening, hunkering down by a set of shelves. He craned out just a bit, catching sight of Evie in a chair on the other side of a long, oak table, just in front of the hearth. She leveled a fierce glare in the direction of the opposite door, her scowl clearly directed at someone over there. Not a hair appeared out of place, and her neat bonnet and tidily buttoned spencer gave evidence to the fact that she hadn't been manhandled.

Relief rushed through him, so encompassing that he had to pull back for a few seconds to catch his breath. He clamped down on his emotions, gave a quick shake of his head, and leaned out again.

Hell and damnation.

From his angle, he couldn't see how many of her captors were at the other end of the room since a large dresser—he remembered it held a great deal of crockery—blocked his view. Of course, that meant that they couldn't see him, which he could use to his advantage.

He thought about it for a few seconds, then slowly rose to his feet without making a sound. That clearly put him in Evie's line of sight. It was a risky move, but he needed to get her attention. He could only hope she had the discipline not to react when she saw him.

The seconds crawled by. Finally, Evie sighed and rolled her shoulders, trying to stretch on the uncomfortable-looking cane chair. Her gaze drifted in Will's direction and then she suddenly sat bolt upright, staring at him with round eyes. He grimaced in warning and jerked his head in the direction of whoever was watching her.

To his immense relief, she let out another tedium-filled sigh and slumped down again. She let a good minute pass before she twisted in her chair, as if trying to get comfortable. She'd turned enough so she could see him quite naturally, maintaining her slumped back posture as if she'd given up any hope of rescue.

He rewarded her with a smile and held up one finger, then two, again jerking his head toward the door. She casually lifted her hands—which were tied together at the wrists—making a show of scratching her nose, then lifted her index finger in a fleeting movement.

One.

Good girl, he mouthed.

A tiny, self-satisfied smile quirked up the corner of her lush mouth. God, how he loved her. And he would spend the rest of his life proving that to her once he got them out of this blasted mess.

He faced a hard decision. Act now, or wait for Alec to show or for Mrs. Rafferty to fetch help from Bow Street. The problem with waiting was that he couldn't be certain when help would arrive or how it would manifest itself. If rescuers came storming into the place, it was entirely possible that the man who stood guard over Evie—at gunpoint, he had to presume—would either shoot her or use her as a shield to get away. That wasn't a risk he was prepared to take.

He went down in a crouch. Evie watched him out of the corner of her eye as he pointed in the direction of the dresser. He pantomimed reaching up, grabbing something, and then throwing it. No doubt he looked like an idiot, but figured she would understand what he was trying to communicate.

Evie looked vaguely puzzled for a moment or two before switching her gaze forward with a tiny nod. It made Will's stomach clench that he had to use her as a distraction, but it was their only chance.

"Excuse me," she said after clearing her throat, "but I need to use the necessary."

Will had to repress a snort of laughter as he began to inch forward into the room. It was a simple, entirely believable request that somehow mocked their dire circumstances.

"Did you hear me?" she asked, letting asperity color her voice. "I have to visit the necessary."

Will hugged the wall as he crawled toward the dresser. The room was dimly lit, with only a small fire on the hearth and one branch of candles on the mantel. Deep shadows reached into the corners, but he could now see Evie's captor, a tall, brawny man holding a pistol. He sat on the stairs that led to the corridor and Beaumont's office. All the man had to do was look down and to the right and he would see Will, too.

Fortunately, his attention remained on Evie.

"Shut your gob," he growled. "You'll not be distractin' me with that nonsense."

"Good God," she exclaimed. "Do you really think I would ask a complete stranger—one holding me hostage—such an indelicate request if it wasn't essential? And I distinctly remember Bridget telling you not to mistreat me. Not letting me use the necessary certainly counts as mistreatment in my book."

Her outraged, loud tone provided good cover, and Will made it the six feet or so along the wall to the dresser without attracting notice. It was a massive piece of furniture, wide and high, and he was able to pull up into a crouch against it, out of the guard's line of sight. Now, he just needed to reach up and grab something suitably heavy, and do it without being seen.

That would take some doing.

He glanced over at Evie just as she slid him a quick,

sideways look. As if she'd read his mind, she took a deep breath and redoubled her efforts.

"I suppose I shouldn't truly be surprised, though," she said in a haughty voice. "A dirty Irish lout like you wouldn't have the first idea how to treat a lady. No wonder you couldn't hold down a decent day's work. I've seen dogs rooting through garbage with better manners than yours."

Will sucked in a breath at the outraged snarl that came from the other end of the room. He knew he had only a few seconds to act.

As Evie's guard came to his feet in a lumbering rush, murder in his gaze, Will whipped up from his crouch to the front of the dresser. He grabbed a heavy milk pitcher and spun on his heel. As the guard jerked toward him in surprise, Will flung the pitcher across the table, directly at the man's face.

The pitcher hit the man square in the chin and shattered to pieces, dropping to the floor. Evie rolled from her chair and disappeared beneath the table. Once she was clear, Will threw himself across the slab of wood, sliding his full weight forward and crashing into the guard's midsection, cutting off his outraged bellow of surprise and pain. They both went down hard with Will on top.

The guard thrashed beneath him, but the blow to the chin had clearly thrown him off. There was a short, brutal struggle, but Will soon got a knee on the man's chest to hold him down. He grabbed his blooded head and smashed it once, then again on the flagstone floor. The guard let out a harsh groan as his eyes rolled back in his head. Then he went limp.

Will sat up, still straddling the man, and sucked in a huge, slow breath to steady his racing heart. Then he did a quick search, finding a nasty looking blade and a pistol. He shoved the pistol into the back of his waistband and came to his feet.

"Is he dead?" Evie croaked from under the table. She peered up at him, her bonnet tipped comically down over one eye and her spectacles precariously perched on the tip of her nose.

Will righted her chair, then reached down and grabbed her by the elbows, pulling her up and depositing her on the rush seat.

"I don't think so," he said, as he used the knife to saw the rope binding her wrists. "But in any case, he won't be getting up anytime soon."

He freed her hands, but when he raised her to her feet, she stumbled against him.

"They tied my feet, too," she said. "I'd forgotten that for a moment."

Will snorted. "You forgot?" He eased her back into the chair and then knelt to carefully cut through the knots around her ankles.

"I was so worried that beastly man was going to kill you," she said, sounding a little teary. "I would die if anything happened to you."

He looked up into her beautiful, anxious face and smiled. "No chance of that, my love," he said as he gently pushed her spectacles back in place.

"I'm glad to hear it," she said. "And I'm *very* glad to see you." She threw herself at him, almost knocking him to the floor.

Will put down the knife and wrapped his arms around her. Her bonnet was mashed under his chin and they crouched uncomfortably on the cold flagstones, but he didn't give a damn. She was safe and with him, and that's all he bloody well cared about.

"Good God, Evie, you're going to be the death of me,"

he said, struggling with a bizarre combination of immense gratitude and equally immense irritation, now that the crisis was over. "I told you to stay clear of St. Margaret's. Why don't you ever listen to me?"

She hugged him so fiercely he thought his ribs might crack. "I'm sorry. I promise I'll do everything you tell me from now on."

That forced a grudging laugh from his throat. "I'll believe that when I see it."

"Will," she said, pulling back, "we've got to get to Sir Gerald Milbank's house right now because Bridget told me that they're going to blow it up. She's already there." She tugged at his shoulders, as if to yank him to his feet.

"Don't worry, we stopped it in time," he soothed. He untied her crumpled bonnet and tossed it onto the table. "Alec and his men are clearing away the gunpowder as we speak."

She blinked, so adorably startled he had to give her a quick kiss.

"Oh, thank God," she said. "How did you find out about the plot?"

"We dragged it out of Terence." He pulled her up to her feet. "He didn't give us the specifics, but we knew something was afoot at Milbank House. Alec organized a search, starting with the cellars. We found the gunpowder—and Bridget's men—almost immediately. No Bridget, though."

She sagged against him in relief. "I was terrified it would be too late."

He gave her a brief hug. "Everything's fine, but we've got to get moving." He let her go and checked on the guard, who was indeed still alive. "He's out cold, but we need to tie him up until he can be taken to Bow Street."

Evie let out a gasp. "Mrs. Rafferty and Billy! They're locked in the vestry. I've got to let them out."

Will snaked out a hand and grabbed her sleeve. "I did that already. They're fetching reinforcements from Bow Street."

"Thank you," she said, pressing a hand to her chest. "I was so frightened for them."

"Then perhaps you understand how I felt about *you*," he said dryly.

Evie winced. "I'm sorry, Will. I truly am. I had no idea Bridget was involved in this horrible plot, and I thought meeting her at St. Margaret's would be perfectly safe."

"Not just involved. She's the ringleader."

"Yes, I understand that now. It's horrible," she said in a somber tone. Then she cocked an eyebrow. "By the way, how did you know I came here?"

"Eden told me. She'd come home early because she said she had a *premonition* that something was wrong."

Evie smiled. "I suppose I shouldn't be surprised," she said rather cryptically. "But it was a good bit of luck for me that you stopped by the house."

"I thought you would have the best idea about where to find Bridget in that damned rookery. Do you?"

She looked doubtful. "Well, she and Terence are listed in the church records, but I doubt that address will be of much use."

He shrugged. "We'd have to search her room in any event, so at least it's a place to start. Now, help me find some more rope so we can tie this fellow up and be on our way."

Evie nodded and headed for the pantry. "Then what do we do?"

"*I* will get you home, and then carry on with the search for Bridget O'Shay."

"No need for that, you bastard." The soft snarl came from behind them. "I'm right here."

Christ.

The bloody woman had stolen a march on them. Slowly, Will pivoted on his heel. Bridget was standing at the top of the steps, and her pistol was pointed right at his chest.

"I know ye're carrying, Endicott," she snarled. "So, put the gun on the table. And you, Miss Evie, get over by your man where's I can keep an eye on you."

Without a word, Evie came over while Will removed the pistol from his coat and carefully placed it on the kitchen table. He still had the guard's pistol, but it would take him a few seconds to reach behind and pull it out. Bridget's hand was as steady as a rock, so he had little doubt she'd get off a shot before he got to the gun.

Given the hatred etching her features, he had no doubt she'd do it, too, and gladly. And she was close enough that she likely wouldn't miss.

When Evie came alongside him, Will stepped in front of her, shielding her with his body. She expelled an impatient breath, as if annoyed with his instinct to protect her, but then stood quietly, with her hands settling at his waist.

"Aren't you the gent," sneered Bridget. "For all the good it will do you, since your fine lady is comin' with me."

"Over my dead body," Will replied.

The girl's ruthless laugh sent a chill coursing through his veins.

"That's the plan, dearie," she said. "You may have stopped us for now from killing Orange Peel and the rest of those murderers, but I'll still see justice done."

"Whatever it is you're planning," he said, "you won't get away with it. I'll hunt you down, I promise you. It's over, Bridget."

"Ah, and how will you be huntin' me down when ye're dead, me fine captain?" She smiled, looking almost like the good-natured, attractive young woman they'd all assumed her to be. But that pistol never wavered, and the implacable look in her eye signaled a deadly resolution.

"Bridget, you've got to stop this," Evie said in a choked voice. "Killing won't help anyone."

"It'll help me," the girl spat back. "I demand justice, and I'll have it. Even if I can't kill your bloody prime minister or one of your royals, I can kill a royal's son. How do you think your fine Duke of York will feel when he hears I blew his son's brains all over the floor?"

Evie's hands jerked at his waist, but Will confined his surprise to a lifted brow.

"Now that's interesting," he said, willing Bridget to keep talking. Sooner or later, either Alec or Runners from Bow Street would surely show up. "How did you know I'm York's son?"

Bridget shrugged and took a step down to the flagstones. She didn't come too close, though. She was too smart to come within Will's reach. "I had my suspicions about you from the beginnin', with all your sniffin' around here. You and your mate were too bloody interested in St. Maggie's. So I did a little diggin'. Servants love to gossip, so it didn't take long to find out who you really were."

"Then you know that if you hurt Captain Endicott, the duke won't rest until he sees you hanged," Evie said.

Again, Bridget shrugged. "Maybe, but I'll see justice done, for all that."

"Murder is your idea of justice?" Will asked.

"Yes," Bridget retorted. "I learned it from the likes of you."

"Please, Bridget, don't do this," Evie pleaded. Her hands clutched convulsively at the back of Will's coat.

"Don't waste your breath, love," he said. "She's not listening."

"*She's* sick of listenin' to your palaver," Bridget snapped.

"Now, you'd best come out from behind him, Miss Evie, unless you want to get shot too. We need to be on our way before someone comes lookin' for us here."

"I have no intention of going with you," Evie said in a defiant voice.

"Evie, do what she says." There wasn't a damn thing Will could do until he got Evie out of the line of fire.

"She can't force me," Evie answered.

Will felt her hand slip under his coat, and his mind blanked for a second. By the time he'd recovered, she'd already pulled the pistol from his waistband and stepped up beside him.

"Put the gun down, Bridget," she said, "or I'll shoot you."

Bridget instinctively swung her weapon toward Evie. Will put up an arm to shield Evie, but she sidestepped him.

"Evie, for God's sake," he growled.

"Don't move, Will," she said. "Bridget, this is your last chance."

The girl snorted. "You won't shoot me, miss. You don't have it in you." Then her lips peeled back in a death's-head grin. "But I do."

The instant Bridget started to swing her pistol back to Will, Evie fired. Bridget screamed and her gun went off as Will launched at Evie and took her down to the floor. The roar of the echoing shots bounced off the walls, and an overpowering smell of cordite hung in the air.

"Will!" Evie screamed. Her hands clutched frantically at his shoulders. "Are you hit? Did she hurt you?"

He grimaced, taking a quick stock. "I think your shriek all but destroyed my eardrums, but other than that I seem to be fine." He lifted off of her, inspecting her deathly pale face. "Are you all right, love? I did take you down rather hard."

She sucked in a huge gasp and went flat on her back, closing her eyes. "I'm fine. Just give me a moment."

Will hauled himself to his feet and made his way to Bridget. She was lying in a crumpled, bloody heap at the base of the steps. The girl was still alive, but from the glazed look in her eyes and the blood gushing from a hole in her bodice, she wouldn't be for long. Still, he had to try. He pulled out his handkerchief and wadded it up, pressing it against the wound.

A few moments later, Evie crouched down and shoved some dishrags at him. He bundled them up under the soaked handkerchief but knew it was a losing battle.

"Will she live?" she asked in a strangled voice.

"No," he said quietly.

"Oh, God." She sounded sick. "I was aiming for her arm, but I haven't fired a gun in years. Not since my brother last took me quail hunting."

"It was a hell of a shot, under the circumstances." Will spared her a worried glance. She didn't look any better than she had a few minutes ago. "Evie, sit down. Help will be here soon."

"No, I'm all right," she said in a grim, determined voice. "What can I do?"

"Nothing, my sweet. I'm just sorry you had to do this. I would have spared you, if I could." He shot her a glance through narrowed eyes. "Although we *are* going to discuss your propensity to take unnecessary risks. I don't need you dueling with any more madwomen."

Evie sat back on her heels, scowling at him. "She would have killed you. I had no choice."

"Perhaps, but you endangered yourself. I won't have that."

"Well, we'll just have to agree to disagree," she said, sounding encouragingly snippy. But a moment later, she let out another heavy sigh. "Although I certainly hope I never have to shoot anyone again for as long as I live."

Will removed his hand from Bridget's body. Her eyes had clouded over, and blood had completely soaked the front of her bodice. He took a spare rag Evie offered him and started to scrub the blood off his hand.

"It's not your fault, Evie. I think she wanted this . . . wanted to die."

"No one wants this," she replied in a sad little voice. "Bridget had too much grief and anger for any one person to bear."

"I know." He wanted to hug her, but he was covered with blood, so he settled for using his relatively clean hand to help her to stand.

"Evie, why don't you sit and rest for a moment? I still have to—"

He stopped, cocking his head. "Ah, help is finally at hand. All clear," he called, raising his voice.

"A little late, I'd say," Evie muttered. Will was forced to agree.

A moment later, Alec flung open the door at the top of the stairs, pistol at the ready. His eyes widened at the carnage before him, then he did a quick scan of the room. He stowed his pistol and came down the steps, avoiding Bridget's crumpled form.

"Well," he said, eyeing Will and Evie with a sardonic expression. "It would appear that my help wasn't needed, after all."

Chapter Twenty-Four

One minute, Evie was ready to topple over asleep on the soft silk cushions of the settee. The next, she was ready to pace from one end of the morning room to the other in a desperate attempt to bleed off the fractious energy that rattled her nerves. After the momentous events at St. Margaret's last night, her mind had teemed with questions and worries.

Will had been unable to soothe those worries or answer her questions. He'd stayed at the church, directing the ever-increasing number of Bow Street Runners and spies who'd crowded into the kitchen and offices of St. Margaret's. After an hour or so, he'd finally sent her home with an escort of two Runners, despite her protest that she didn't want to leave him.

"You're practically dead on your feet," Will had said as he escorted her to the carriage waiting in the yard. "I have to be here for some time yet, and there's no point in you waiting. I'll see you tomorrow, as soon as I can get away from this mess."

He'd then planted a swift but intoxicating kiss on her lips, bundled her into the carriage, and sent her on her way.

And, truthfully, as much as she'd wanted to stay with him, he was right. She was so tired she could hardly stand on her own two feet.

Unfortunately, her entire family was waiting up for her when she arrived home, all of them in one state or another. Eden was the calmest of the bunch, instinctively knowing that Evie had survived unscathed, but she'd been so worried earlier that she'd blurted out a garbled version of events to their parents and brother. And hadn't *that* gone over like an exploding artillery shell. By the time Evie got home, Mamma had been in hysterics, Papa had roared that nobody ever told him anything, which Matt had unhelpfully seconded, and she had been forced to spend what little energy she had left explaining the whole blasted thing. Everyone started talking at once—or, in Mamma's case, yelling—and Evie had been required to do some yelling herself in order to be heard. That had been followed by much scandalized moaning and groaning, with Papa expressing his dissatisfaction with Will for putting her in danger.

Mamma had placed most of the blame on poor Michael, of course, which had led to a sharp exchange as to who was most at fault. If Evie hadn't threatened to have her own full-blown case of hysterics, they would probably still be arguing.

Everyone had calmed down a bit after that, especially after Evie explained how Will had rescued not only her but the prime minister and half the Cabinet, too. That was a slight exaggeration, but it certainly helped mollify her parents. Though Mamma professed to be *dreadfully* shocked to learn that Will was a spy, Evie had a sneaking suspicion she also found it rather thrilling and romantic. The fact that he'd been operating under his father's orders helped as well. As Mamma had so trenchantly said to Papa, *when a prince commands, one has no choice but to obey.*

Still, it was all rather messy, and both her parents were greatly annoyed that she hadn't taken them into her confidence earlier. Given their response last night, she knew beyond any doubt that she'd been right not to tell them. But she'd kept that opinion to herself, repeatedly apologizing and answering their questions as best she could until Eden had stamped her foot, told her parents to *stop badgering the poor girl,* and dragged Evie off to bed.

She'd lain awake, though, plagued by questions and wound tighter than her father's pocket watch, not dropping off to sleep until the birds started to twitter and the pale light of dawn seeped under her curtains. Even so, she'd awakened a few hours later, and she knew she wouldn't be able to properly rest until she saw Will again. She desperately needed assurances that Michael and the others at St. Margaret's were safe from criminal charges and that the Duke of York wasn't furious with Will for getting engaged to her. The two things certainly weren't on the same order of magnitude, but her sleep-deprived brain seemed to think such was the case.

So, after choking down a cup of tea and a slice of toast, she'd repaired to the morning room, waiting for Will—for somebody—to arrive with answers and put her out of her misery. She was heartily sick of her own company and had all but vowed to go out and hunt Will down if he didn't have the good manners to appear before lunchtime.

The door opened and Eden poked her head into the room. "Still no Wolf? How dreary of him to be so late."

Evie jumped up from the settee and started pacing. "I swear, Edie, if he doesn't show himself soon, I'm going to murder him when he *does* finally get here."

"I know, darling," Eden said in a sympathetic voice. "But he probably *is* a bit busy this morning, what with mopping up a deadly conspiracy and saving the government from death and destruction. I'm sure he'll be over as soon as he's done with those frippery fellows like Lord Liverpool and the Duke of York."

Evie stopped in the middle of the room and let out a rueful chuckle. "You're right, of course. I'm an absolute witch to even think that way. But I'm going positively demented with so many questions swirling in my head."

Eden waved a magnanimous hand. "And no one could blame you. But—" A rap on the front door cut her off. "I bet that's Wolf now. You wait here and pinch some color into those pasty cheeks of yours while I bring him up."

When she disappeared, Evie hurried to the gilt-framed mirror hanging over the hearth. Her sister was right—she did look whey-faced, but at least her hair and gown were up to trim. She'd made an extra effort this morning, although that seemed rather silly given all the drama of the last few days. Will would no doubt have other things on his mind besides her looks.

There was a quick knock, and then Eden opened the door. "It's not Will, but I think you'll be happy to see your visitor."

She stepped aside to reveal Michael. He gave Evie a hesitant smile, as if unsure of his welcome.

Evie gaped at him for a second then threw off her surprise and rushed forward. "Michael, I'm so happy to see you!"

"You are?" he asked, rather incredulous.

She took his hand and dragged him over to the settee. "Of course I am. Why wouldn't I be?"

He gingerly sat next to her, looking ready to bolt at a moment's notice. "I'm rather persona non grata, I expect, especially with your parents." He let out a deep sigh. "After all, I did let Bridget O'Shay and her men take advantage of me, and I still tried to protect them. I was unforgivably naïve."

"If it's any consolation," Eden piped up from the door, "Papa was more displeased with Will than he was with you."

Michael perked up a bit. "Really? And how did your mother react?"

Eden grimaced and waggled her hand. "Well . . ."

"Never mind," Michael said, looking gloomy again. "I can imagine what Lady Reese thought, and I certainly can't blame her."

"Nonsense," Evie said in a bracing tone. "Neither of my parents attaches blame to you."

Her sister's fair eyebrows shot up, but Evie cut her off before she could say anything else. "Edie, could you leave us alone for a minute? I need to speak with Michael in private."

"Mamma won't like that very much," Eden said. "And I can think of someone else who won't be too keen on it, either."

"Don't worry, Miss Eden," Michael said. "I'll only be staying a few minutes. I simply wanted to assure myself that Evelyn was unharmed."

"Edie, you can come back in a little bit," Evie said in a firm voice.

"All right, I'm going," her twin huffed. "No need to get snippy."

"Talk about snippy," Evie muttered as her sister closed the door with a snap.

"She simply wants to protect you," Michael said. "You can't blame her for that."

She sighed. "I know, but sometimes she does have a tendency to smother me."

"I think we all do that, don't we? None of us gives you enough credit."

Evie took his hand. "Not you, Michael. You have always been the dearest and kindest of friends. I only wish . . ." She trailed off. She'd hurt him in so many ways, and a thousand apologies would never be enough.

He squeezed her hand and then released it. "I know, my dear girl. You don't need to explain."

"But I do," she said doggedly. "That incident with Will . . . I never meant for that to happen. I never meant to be with him."

"But you are, and I expect you don't regret it, do you?"

"I regret . . . you finding out that way," she said with a grimace. "It was positively heartless for me to do that to you."

"Well, I'm sure you didn't plan it," he said with a slight smile, "so I won't hold it against you. And you've already apologized to me, Evelyn. You don't need to keep doing so."

She had apologized to him the morning she'd warned him that he was under suspicion of treason. But the dire circumstances had forced her to rush, and she still felt she owed him a proper explanation.

"Michael, I wanted to marry you, I truly did. It's just that . . ."

Good Lord, she seemed incapable of clearly articulating anything this morning. Perhaps she'd simply run out of explanations—for anything. Her life had been turned on its head, and she was still trying to adjust to the momentous changes.

"It's just that you're in love with Captain Endicott," he finished for her. "Are you not?"

"Well, yes, I am," she admitted, her cheeks turning hot. "I suppose that's rather obvious by now."

"Then given that salient fact, it would of course be wrong for you to marry me. And," he said, after a moment's pause, "Endicott loves *you,* does he not?"

Evie's heart thudded with a painful extra beat. Of course

Will loved her—he always had. But would he have truly wished to spend the rest of his life with her if circumstances had been different?

She would not, however, discuss that unanswered question with Michael. It would only upset him, and he might do something silly about it like pick a fight with Will.

"Yes, of course, he loves me," she said. "He always has."

"Well," he said, with a genuinely sweet smile, "then you must know that you have my blessing, Evelyn. I wish you and the captain nothing but the best. You certainly both deserve it."

Evie's eyes started to prickle, and her throat went tight. "Michael," she whispered, "I never meant to hurt you."

"I know, my dear, and it was a blow, I admit. But I also knew that your affections were never as strong as mine." He held up a hand to stop her protest. "Of course you're fond of me, but part of me always knew that you had never stopped loving Endicott. I have only myself to blame for ignoring that."

"I'm sorry," she said, feeling like a complete worm.

"Nonsense," he said, patting her hand again. "Captain Endicott makes you happy, does he not?"

She didn't even have to think about it, God help her. "He does."

"That is what truly matters. As I said, you have my best wishes for your life together, and you have my friendship. Always."

By the end of that heartfelt speech, Evie felt like curling up in a little ball under the settee. *Worm* couldn't even begin to describe it.

Suddenly, Michael laughed. "My dear, the look on your face! Truly, Evelyn, I'll be fine. Good Lord, I'm a free man this morning, thanks to Captain Endicott. Without him—and you—God knows where I would have ended up. Indeed,

I have no cause to feel anything but gratitude despite the travails of the last several days."

Evie threw her arms around him and gave him a quick, fierce hug. "Michael Beaumont, you are the nicest person I've ever met."

He made a great show of clearing his throat. "Thank you, Evelyn." He hastily rose to his feet, as if eager now to escape her. "If you'll forgive me, I must be on my way. There is a great deal to do at St. Margaret's. Everyone is in a terrible uproar, as you can imagine."

Evie rose with him. "But everything's all right, isn't it? Surely no one else at St. Margaret's is under suspicion?"

He gave her a reassuring smile. "Everything is fine. But Runners and government agents have been in and out of the place all night, as I understand it. I'm sure poor Mrs. Rafferty is ready to hand in her notice by now. Captain Gilbride also sent round a note asking to go over a few remaining details about the men in Bridget's gang." His kind eyes clouded with sorrow. "I don't think I will ever understand how I missed what was going on with that poor woman. I feel somehow that I failed her."

"No more than I or anyone else," Evie replied matter-of-factly, knowing Michael's tendency to take the blame for the failings of others. "She'd charted her course long before she met any of us, and I don't suppose there was any turning back for her."

He nodded. "That's true, I suppose." He made a determined effort to shake off his little spell of melancholy. "Well, there's no point in worrying about it now, not when so many people need help. Some will be afraid to come to St. Margaret's after the news gets out, so Father O'Kelley and I must do what we can to restore their trust."

Evie followed him to the door, mustering up her courage.

"Michael, I do hope you'll allow me to continue working at St. Margaret's. I'd like so much to be able to do that."

His eyes widened. "My dear girl, of course you may! The Hibernian Benevolent Association would not even exist without you. I will depend upon your help as greatly as ever."

She gave him a grateful smile, so touched that she found it hard to speak.

"And," Michael added, "I'm depending on Captain Endicott to use his social connections to increase our donations. Ah, that reminds me. I have no idea if Captain Gilbride's interest was genuine, but I *will* be asking him for a donation."

"Ask for a very large one," Evie said. "And don't be afraid to play upon his guilt. After all, he did trick us in the most disgraceful fashion with that thick-headed-Scot routine."

Michael laughed. "That he did," he said, resting a friendly hand on her shoulder.

The door suddenly opened and, with perfectly dreadful timing, Will walked into the room. When his golden brows snapped together in a suspicious scowl at the sight of them, Evie was tempted to march up and give him a shake.

Not that a tiny part of her wasn't thrilled to see such a proprietorial expression on his handsome features.

"Captain Endicott, how good to see you," Michael said in a friendly voice, stepping forward with his hand extended. "I must thank you again for your help in expediting my release. I'm exceedingly grateful, as is my father."

"Oh, of course," Will said, clearly thrown off by Michael's warm demeanor. "I'm glad that your father is . . . glad." He winced a bit at his awkward reply but forged on. "And, naturally, we're all pleased with the outcome of the affair despite its rather untidy ending."

"That would be the dead body on the kitchen floor at St. Margaret's?" Evie asked dryly.

Will shot her an exasperated look.

"Dear me, Evelyn," Michael said, giving her a gentle frown of reproof. "The less said about that, the better."

She gave him an apologetic smile, remembering that Michael tended to be a tad squeamish about such things. Good thing she wasn't or Bridget O'Shay might have killed Will.

"You must excuse me, sir," Michael said to Will. "I'm off to meet Captain Gilbride to tie up the remaining loose ends."

"Then perhaps I'll see you at St. Margaret's later today."

"I'll look forward to it," Michael replied. "And, Captain, please allow me to extend my best wishes on your forthcoming marriage. I sincerely hope for your great happiness together." With another warm smile, he again extended his hand to Will.

"Thank you," Will said, sounding rather bemused as he shook hands.

"Oh, one more thing," Michael added, pausing at the door. "What will happen to Terence O'Shay? I feel quite bad for the man, and I'd like to help if I can."

Will raised his eyebrows in polite enquiry. "Who?"

Michael and Evie exchanged a puzzled glance.

"Terence O'Shay, Bridget's brother," Michael said again.

"Ah, yes," Will said in a musing tone. "There was a man—perhaps that was his name—but he was released early this morning. I believe he had a ship to catch."

Michael's jaw sagged open for a few moments before a smile of overwhelming relief swept across his features. "I understand, and I'm most grateful for your charity, Captain. Again, please accept my sincere congratulations and best wishes."

When Michael slipped from the room, Will stared after him. "Do you think he really meant that? About us?"

"He did. Every word of it," Evie said with a sigh.

Will studied her with a slight smile. "Then why the long face, love?"

"He's being so blasted noble about the whole thing that I feel like a complete worm." She wrinkled her nose at him. "It's not a very comfortable sensation, I assure you."

He laughed and took one of her hands. "Just think how I feel. Not only did I cut the poor man out, I accused him of treason. If anyone should feel like a worm, it's me."

"It's very nice of you to say so, but my behavior to Michael was positively dreadful, and you know it. Besides," she said, drawing him to the settee, "it sounds like you've been off being noble this morning, too, while I've been doing nothing but worry. What exactly *did* you do with poor Terence?"

Will sat beside her, still holding her hand. He slowly wiggled his fingers between hers, looking thoughtful. "Alec and I told the magistrate at Bow Street that we'd arrested the wrong man. I suspect Liverpool and Peel won't approve, but it's too late for them to do anything about it now. He's already on a ship bound to Jamaica."

"Really? How did you manage that?"

Will smiled. "Alec paid for his passage and shoved a fistful of guineas into his coat pocket. I told you he was a soft touch, didn't I?" Then he sobered. "Not that I can blame him. O'Shay was all but destroyed by the news of his sister's end. Why send him to the gallows for the crime of loving his only remaining family member? The poor bastard was simply trying to protect her."

For perhaps the tenth time that morning, Evie's throat went tight. "I'm so glad you did that, Will. There's been too much ugliness already. I only hope Terence can find a better life for himself over there."

"He has the chance now, if he'll take it."

They sat in silence for a few moments while Will played with her fingers.

"I have to ask you something," Evie finally said.

He looked sideways at her, lifting his brows in silent question.

"I'd still like—" She stopped to correct herself. "I intend to keep working at St. Margaret's, Will. I've been thinking about it, and it's something I need to do. The way the Irish have been treated . . . I have to do my part to atone for that."

Many sad things about the last few days would always be with her, and Evie knew the story of Bridget's horrific childhood would haunt her for an especially long time. She could never condone the young Irishwoman's actions, but she understood them. And she needed to do what she could to make things better.

"I know your father won't like it—or my parents to tell you the truth—but it's something I need to do," she said with a touch of defiance. Though she loved Will with all her heart, she couldn't give up doing the things that were important to her.

He nodded. "Of course, my love. I completely understand. God knows we own this tragedy as much as the Irish do."

"Then you truly won't mind if I spend time with Michael?" she asked, a tad skeptical.

He gave her that sideways look again, but this time his eyes had narrowed with warning. "Do I have anything to worry about?"

"Or course not." She scowled a bit as she tried to tug her hand away. "After all that's happened, how can you even think that?"

He surprised her by picking her up and plopping her onto his lap. She let out a little squeak and grabbed his forearms.

"Because, apparently, I'm the jealous sort," he said.

"You have no reason to be," she said, carefully placing her hands on his wonderfully broad shoulders. "I'm madly in love with you, God help me."

He'd been leaning in to kiss her but pulled back. "*God help me?*"

She stewed for a few seconds, but then decided she was done with keeping secrets from him. Done with half-truths and half-trusts. "Because I'm afraid you don't love me as much as I love you. I know that makes me sound like a ninny, but it's not a very comfortable feeling."

He huffed out an exasperated laugh. "Clearly, I've not done a very good job of demonstrating my affections. Evie, you *are* a ninny if you can't see that I'm madly in love with you, too."

Her fingers involuntarily dug into the fabric of his coat. "Really?" she asked, unable to keep the girlishly hopeful note from her voice.

Will kissed the tip of her nose. "Yes, really. I grant you that I've made a hash of things in the past. I was young and stupid and didn't know my own heart. But I've always loved you, Evie, and I always will."

He captured her face between his hands, knocking her spectacles slightly askew. He didn't seem to notice. "You're my lodestone, Evie, my true north. You've always kept me clear and straight, and showed me where I needed to be. I'm sorry I forgot that, and I'm sorry I didn't trust you enough to tell you the truth about everything—about Beaumont and my intelligence work, about what had gone wrong between us, all of it."

"I wasn't much better," she said with a sniff, trying—again—not to cry. "I should have trusted you, too. I should have listened when you tried to warn me, instead of believing I could fix everything on my own."

He adopted a stern expression only partly offset by the slow drift of his hand down her spine. "In fact, I'd like to talk to you about that, because I want no more running off half-cocked into dangerous situations, Evie. If you have a problem or need help, I would ask that you come to me. Not to Michael Beaumont, for instance, or your troublemaking twin."

"Ha, that's the pot calling the kettle black. After all, you're the spy, not me. I expect you throw yourself into harm's way all the time, and I can't say I approve."

"Don't worry," he said dryly. "My spying days are over. I made that abundantly clear to my . . . commanding officer."

"I expect you mean your father."

He gave her a rather sheepish smile.

"You already spoke to him about all this?" she asked.

"First thing this morning," he said in an absent tone of voice.

Evie had the sense he was now more focused on stroking the swell of her bottom than on their conversation. She resisted the impulse to squirm with pleasure and poked him in the shoulder instead. "And what did his Highness say?"

"Hmm? Oh, he was fine with it. He wants me to pursue a regular career in the military or diplomatic corps instead of intelligence work. I told him that I was happy to oblige."

"And did you tell him about us?"

"I did."

"Oh, for heaven's sake, Will," she burst out impatiently. "Please give me some details. Was he very angry?"

He grinned and tickled her bottom. "Initially, he was a bit put out. But when I told him you'd saved my life, he seemed reconciled to our marriage."

She groaned and dropped her head on his shoulder.

"I certainly hope I don't have to go around shooting people to prove I'm worthy of you."

"One would hope not, but I don't really give a damn about his or anyone else's permission. I'm marrying you because I want to, not because I have to."

She lifted her head and smiled at him. "I'm very happy about that."

"Don't think you're going to distract me, sweetheart. I'm still waiting for your promise that you'll steer clear of dangerous situations from now on. Especially when you're working at St. Margaret's."

"I'll do my best," she said as solemnly as she could.

The twist of his mouth signaled he wasn't satisfied with that response.

"Just think of it this way," she added in an attempt to placate him. "If I hadn't stumbled into the middle of that conspiracy, we might never have ended up together."

"That's a nice bit of sophistry. You also wouldn't have been kidnapped and almost murdered."

She poked him in the chest. "Strictly speaking, you were the one who almost got murdered, not me."

"Evie," he started in a frustrated voice.

"Yes, I understand," she said in a soothing voice. "And I will try to stay out of trouble. But you have to admit, at least in this case, that it worked out."

That pulled a grudging laugh from him. "Very well. In this case, I will admit it was worth it. But no more, Evie. Do you understand?"

She stroked a cross atop her bodice. "Cross my heart and hope to die."

"Good God," he sighed. "You are going to drive me insane, aren't you?"

Before she could answer, he leaned forward and kissed her. She eagerly opened her mouth under the questing surge of his tongue, snuggling deeper into his embrace. In his arms, she felt safe and loved and never more ready to face the future.

Will, however, seemed more focused on the immediate moment. He tipped her back over his arm, deepening the kiss until she shivered with pleasure and her spectacles' lenses fogged. When he slipped his hand on her leg and started to inch up her dress, things truly started to get interesting.

Unfortunately, that was exactly the moment she heard the door to the morning room quietly open.

"William Endicott, what are you doing?" screeched Mamma. "Restrain yourself this instant."

Will was so startled he almost dropped Evie to the floor. Carefully, he shifted her onto the settee.

"Er, Lady Reese," he said, coming to his feet. "I didn't hear you come in."

"Obviously," Mamma said as she swept in, followed by Eden and a footman with a tea tray. "Really, William, this is the second time I've caught you engaged in inappropriate activities with Evelyn. It is *not* becoming behavior in an officer and gentleman. I cannot believe your dear father would approve."

Evie had to bite her tongue. Given the positively licentious conduct of all the princes—including the Duke of York—it was a miracle Will didn't burst into laughter at her mother's asinine remark.

He gave her a polite smile. "No, I expect he wouldn't, your ladyship."

Evie had to give him credit, since she heard only the tiniest hint of laughter in his voice.

Her mother settled into an armchair and nodded at the footman to place the tea service in front of her. Eden gave

Evie a droll wink but held her silence as she sat down next to her on the settee. Will eyed her twin, obviously disgruntled that she'd usurped his seat, but he capitulated with a shrug and went to sit in one of the other armchairs.

"Not that I don't understand, you know," Mamma said in a thoughtful tone once the footman had departed. "I was young once, myself, and quite a diamond of the first water. Your father was *passionately* in love with me and very particular in his attentions. *Very* particular."

They digested that comment in silence, Will looking slightly appalled.

"Oh, and William," their mother added, smiling at him in a gracious manner, "there's no need to call me 'her ladyship' or 'Lady Reese.' I give you permission to call me 'Mamma.'"

"Thank you," Will said faintly. Now he looked completely appalled. When Eden started to choke with suppressed laughter, Evie pinched her.

"That's very kind of you, Mamma. Thank you," Evie said as her mother handed her a cup of tea.

"You're welcome, my dear. Now, I do hope that you and William have put to rest all the dreary business of the last few days, because I have something very important I wish to discuss with you."

"And what is that?" Evie enquired cautiously. She recognized the determined glint in her mother's eyes. It never boded well.

"Why, your wedding, of course. There is a great deal of planning to be done in the next few weeks, so we must get to work immediately."

"Lady R—er, Mamma," Will said, sounding a bit desperate. "Evie and I were planning on something very quiet, by special license. We had hoped to marry by the end of this week."

"Certainly not," Mamma exclaimed loudly, climbing up on her high horse. "No daughter of mine will be married in so slipshod a manner. We will have the banns read, and we will have a proper wedding at Maywood Manor."

"That's right, Wolf," Eden said in a mischievous voice. "We're going to have a wedding fit for royalty. It's going to be *big*."

"Good God," Will muttered.

He looked at Evie, and in his blue gaze she saw laughter and love and the dawning recognition that he was now truly part of her interfering, high-spirited, and often highly annoying family. She grinned at him, happier than she could ever remember.

Will shook his head with wry amusement. "Very well, Mamma. Plan away."

Epilogue

"Your bride seems to be enjoying herself, despite all the damned bother, as you put it."

Will lifted his brows at Dominic, who had materialized at his side without warning. Then again, the man was a former spymaster so he shouldn't be surprised at his silent approach.

"She is," he said. His gaze returned to Evie, chatting in an animated fashion with her mother and one of the guests.

She looked lovelier than he'd ever seen her in a creamy silk gown that clung to her lush curves. But it wasn't the expensive dress, her glorious golden tresses, or her delightful figure that was the true source of her beauty. It was her sweet and loving nature, fully unleashed by her unabashed joy on her wedding day. The fact that Will had been able to make her so happy was the most precious of gifts, one he vowed to cherish always.

"Lady Reese seems pleased as well," Dominic added. "She's obviously welcomed you with open arms."

Will threw him a speaking glance. "We all have our crosses to bear."

Dominic laughed. "True, but consider the alternative."

"I have," he said dryly.

Though Lady Reese had been fawning over him, Will expected things would revert to their natural order soon enough. He'd eventually do something to annoy his new mother-in-law, and she'd no doubt put him in his place. But Will had been very encouraged by the warmer relations between Lady Reese and Evie. Her ladyship was genuinely pleased for her daughter, and the two women had spent many happy hours planning the ridiculously overblown wedding at Maywood Manor. That happiness was the primary reason he'd been willing to wait six weeks to marry Evie. He knew it was the first time in her life she'd been able to bask in her mother's heartfelt approval, and Will wasn't about to spoil it.

He was, however, eager for his wedding night. He'd managed to sneak Evie off a few times for quick bouts of lovemaking, but they weren't nearly enough. Of course, a lifetime of his new bride probably wouldn't be enough, but he intended to give it his best effort.

"Your lady looks very well, Sir Dominic," Will said, nodding to where Chloe Hunter sat in earnest conversation with the Duke of York. She held a finger in the air as if making a point, and the duke nodded solemnly, looking much struck by what she was saying. "My father seems to have taken quite a shine to her."

Dominic gazed at his wife, looking as close to a love-struck fool as such an intimidating man possibly could. He was an extremely protective husband, something completely understandable given that his wife was in the later stages of her pregnancy.

"Yes, the duke has been very kind to Lady Hunter." Then Dominic's smile slowly faded and flattened into a hard line. "Unlike some other members of the family," he said, almost as if he were talking to himself.

Will cocked his head, surprised by the abrupt change. "Sorry, what was that?"

Dominic's shoulders tensed, then he gave a slight shrug. "It's nothing. Just an old memory that no longer matters." He flashed Will a smile. "And speaking of wives, I intend to go spend some time with mine, and I suggest you do the same."

Will recognized the dodge—Dominic had always been the most private of men—but he simply nodded. "An excellent idea. I'm sure I'll speak with you and her ladyship before you return to town."

They exchanged friendly bows, and Will strolled across the expansive drawing room to rescue his wife from Lady Reese. As much as mother and daughter were getting along, Will could tell Evie was due for a respite.

"Ah, William," Lady Reese said as he slipped his arm around Evie's waist. "I was just telling Evelyn how gracious your father has been with his compliments. Why, he told Lord Reese that he can't remember the last time he had such a comfortable stay in the country."

Will could believe it, since Maywood Manor had been turned upside down to accommodate his father's royal presence. Lady Reese obviously considered the duke's participation in the wedding festivities as the social coup of a lifetime. She glowed with triumph.

Evie, however, was beginning to look a little strained around the eyes. Obviously, the weeks of preparation and the frenetic activity of the last few weeks were wearing on her.

"I don't doubt he's enjoyed himself," Will said. "Everything's been splendidly done."

His mother-in-law preened. "Thank you, William. I do think it's all come off rather nicely."

She gazed happily around the formal room with its new and expensive Aubusson carpet and freshly hung draperies.

Huge arrangements of roses and mums overflowed the tabletops, and footmen in new livery passed through the room serving the large gathering from generous trays of champagne. A side buffet loaded with cakes and sweetmeats tempted even the most delicate of appetites, and that was simply to hold them over until dinner.

The party was clearly a success, thanks primarily to Evie's hard work and superior organizational skills.

"I wonder, though, if my father might like something else besides champagne," Will said in a musing tone.

Lady Reese's suddenly anxious gaze whipped back to Will. "Do you think so? What might he prefer instead?"

Evie quivered in Will's arms, as if she had to stifle laughter.

"I think he might enjoy some of his lordship's vintage port—the one he keeps in his library," Will said in bland tone.

"Oh, certainly. Thank you, William. I'll take care of it immediately." Lady Reese fluttered an air kiss in her daughter's direction then marched off across the drawing room.

"Will, you beast," Evie said as she snuggled closer into his arm. "You were just trying to get rid of poor Mamma. Does your father truly prefer port to champagne at this hour?"

"Who knows? But I thought you could use a respite from your mother's attentions."

She gave him a comical look. "You're right, but that makes me sound so awful. I don't want you to think I'm not grateful to her for all her hard work—"

"You mean *your* hard work."

"I suppose, but Mamma means well and she has certainly tried this time. I've very much enjoyed *not* fighting with her all the time."

"I'm glad for your sake, my love. Let's hope it sticks."

She wrinkled her nose at him. "I doubt it will."

He drew her closer and brushed a kiss across her soft lips. "Does it truly matter?"

"No, not anymore, but it's a nice change. And speaking of fighting," she said, nodding in the direction of one of the window alcoves, "it would appear that Edie and Captain Gilbride are having yet another argument."

Will followed her gaze. Sure enough, Eden was clearly lecturing Alec, standing in front of him with her fists on her hips and a scowl on her pretty features. It looked rather one-sided, however, since Alec's attention seemed focused mainly on Eden's ample cleavage, nicely displayed by her daringly low-cut bodice.

Evie sighed. "I do wish they would get along better, especially since they're bound to be thrown together now and again."

Will smiled. "I think they get along just fine."

"Really?" she asked, eyeing the couple dubiously.

Alec now had a sly grin on his face as he responded to Eden's lecture. Will would bet ten guineas that his friend was going out of his way to needle her.

"I wouldn't worry about it, love," he said. "I suspect Alec will be heading north to Scotland in the not-too-distant future. His grandfather is most eager for him to return home, and I don't think Alec can put him off much longer."

"Well, that's probably for the best."

He ran his hand up her spine to rest on the satiny-smooth skin of her neck. "In any event, *that's* not our problem."

Evie looked up at him, her eyes gone soft and sultry behind her spectacles. "Oh? What is the problem then?"

"How quickly I can get you away from this blasted reception."

Her mouth quirked up in an answering smile. "You know, at this moment you do look exactly like a wolf."

"Well, that *is* my name, after all."

She laughed. "So it is."

He leaned down to murmur in her ear. "And this wolf is getting rather hungry."

Her slow, sensual smile turned him hard in an instant, and he actually had to resist the urge to growl in response.

"Then I suppose his wife had better feed him, don't you think?" she murmured.

A moment later, completely ignoring the scandalized glances of their guests, Will's beautiful bride led him from the room.

Books by Bestselling Author
Fern Michaels

Available Wherever Books Are Sold!
Check out our website at **www.kensingtonbooks.com**

Books by Bestselling Author

Victoria Alexander

His Mistress by Christmas	1-4201-1708-4	$7.99US/$9.99CAN
The Importance of Being Wicked	1-4201-1707-6	$7.99US/$9.99CAN
My Wicked Little Lies	1-4201-1706-8	$7.99US/$8.99CAN
The Perfect Mistress	1-4201-1705-X	$7.99US/$9.99CAN
The Scandalous Adventures of the Sister of the Bride	1-4201-3224-5	$7.99US/$9.99CAN
The Shocking Secret of a Guest at the Wedding	1-4201-3226-1	$7.99US/$9.99CAN
What Happens at Christmas	1-4201-1709-2	$7.99US/$9.99CAN

Available Wherever Books Are Sold!

Visit our website at **www.kensingtonbooks.com**

Romantic Suspense from
Lisa Jackson